OUTCAST

BY **KIRKMAN**
& **AZACETA**

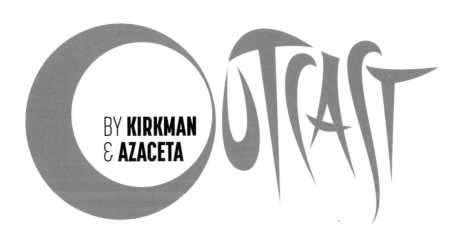

VOLUME **7**: THE DARKNESS GROWS

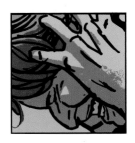

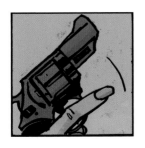

OUTCAST BY KIRKMAN & AZACETA
VOL. 7: THE DARKNESS GROWS
September 2019
First printing

ISBN: 978-1-5343-1239-5

Published by Image Comics, Inc.

Office of publication: 2701 NW Vaughn St., Ste. 780,
Portland, OR 97210.

For information regarding the CPSIA on this printed
material call: 203-595-3636.

Robert Kirkman
Creator, Writer

Paul Azaceta
Artist

Elizabeth Breitweiser
Colorist

Rus Wooton
Letterer

Paul Azaceta
Elizabeth Breitweiser
Cover

Jon Moisan
Editor

Rian Hughes
Logo Design

Carina Taylor
Production

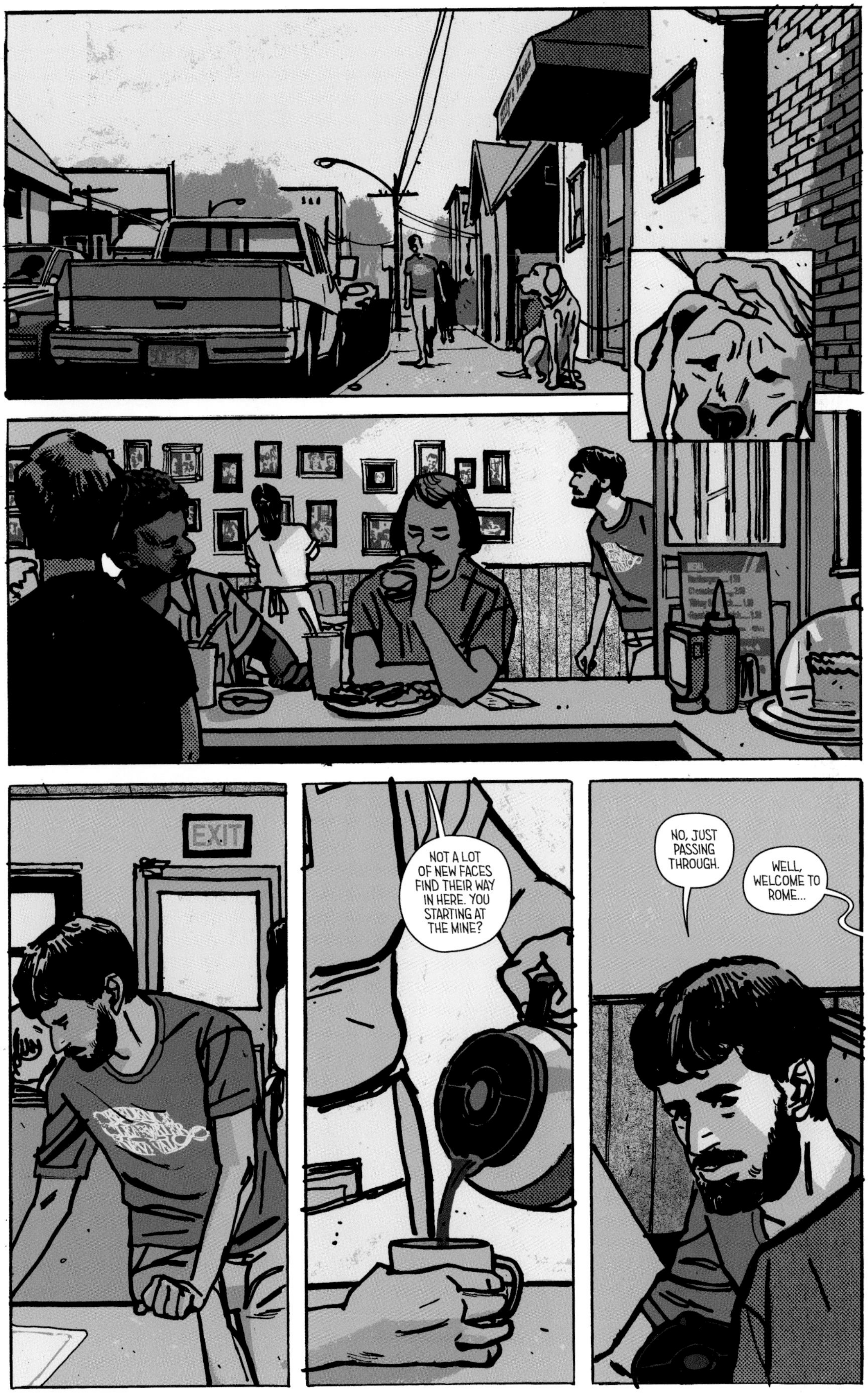
NOT A LOT OF NEW FACES FIND THEIR WAY IN HERE. YOU STARTING AT THE MINE?
NO, JUST PASSING THROUGH.
WELL, WELCOME TO ROME...

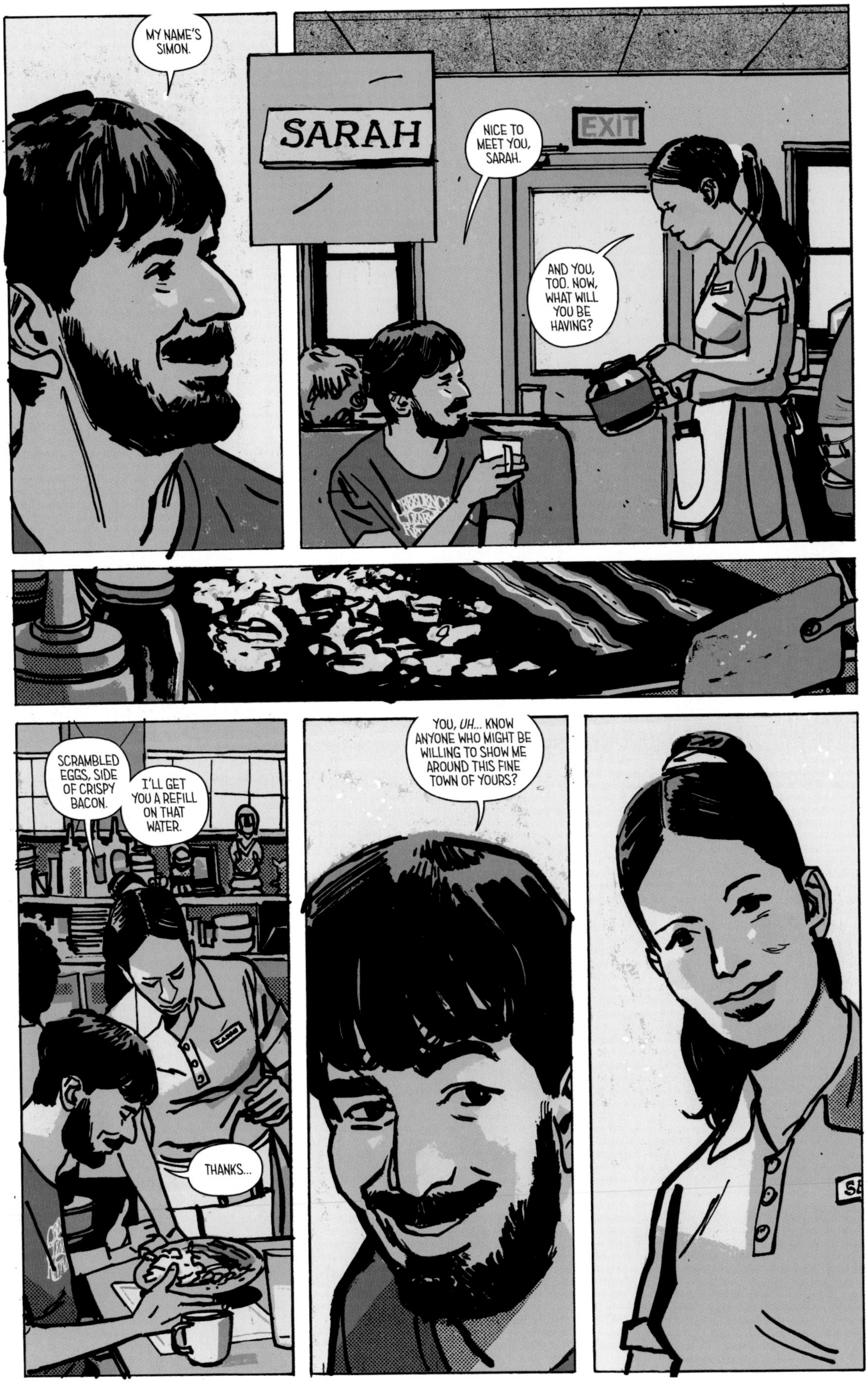
MY NAME'S SIMON.
SARAH
EXIT
NICE TO MEET YOU, SARAH.
AND YOU, TOO. NOW, WHAT WILL YOU BE HAVING?
SCRAMBLED EGGS, SIDE OF CRISPY BACON.
I'LL GET YOU A REFILL ON THAT WATER.
THANKS...
YOU, *UH*... KNOW ANYONE WHO MIGHT BE WILLING TO SHOW ME AROUND THIS FINE TOWN OF YOURS?

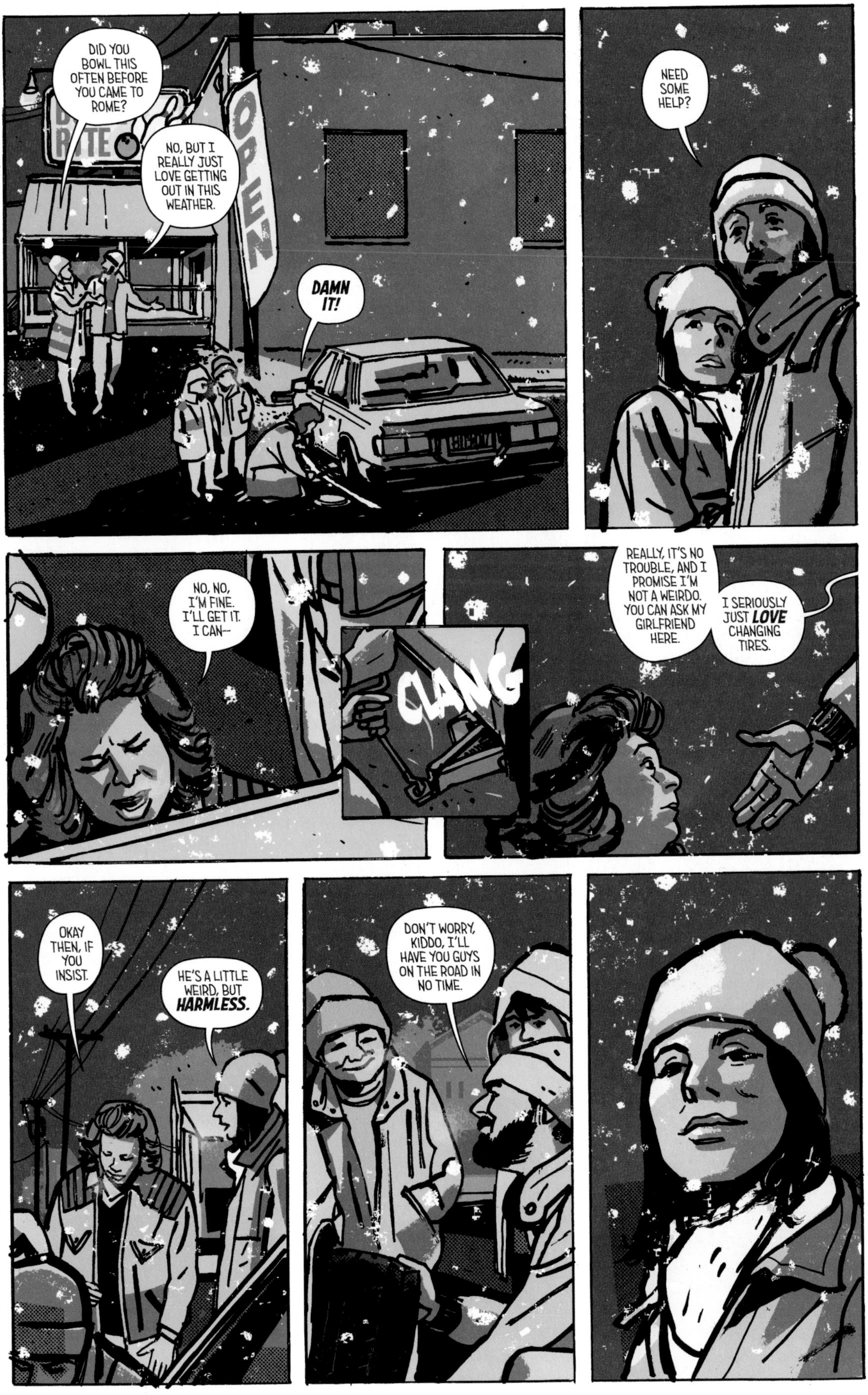
DID YOU BOWL THIS OFTEN BEFORE YOU CAME TO ROME?
NO, BUT I REALLY JUST LOVE GETTING OUT IN THIS WEATHER.
OPEN
DAMN IT!
NEED SOME HELP?
NO, NO, I'M FINE. I'LL GET IT. I CAN--
CLANG
REALLY, IT'S NO TROUBLE, AND I PROMISE I'M NOT A WEIRDO. YOU CAN ASK MY GIRLFRIEND HERE.
I SERIOUSLY JUST LOVE CHANGING TIRES.
OKAY THEN, IF YOU INSIST.
HE'S A LITTLE WEIRD, BUT HARMLESS.
DON'T WORRY, KIDDO, I'LL HAVE YOU GUYS ON THE ROAD IN NO TIME.

OH, GOD!
OH, GOD!
DOING A GREAT JOB, SARAH. JUST KEEP PUSHING!
ALMOST THERE!
HERE IT COMES...
IT'S A BOY.

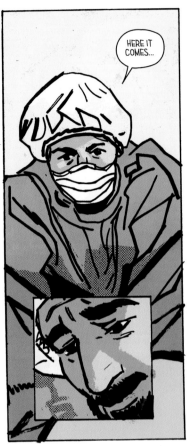

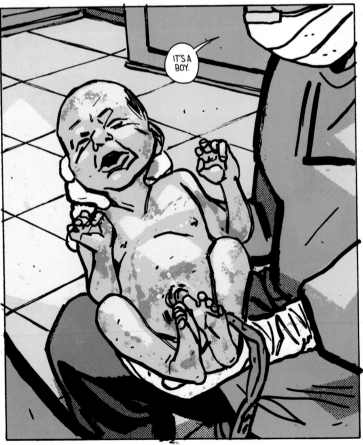

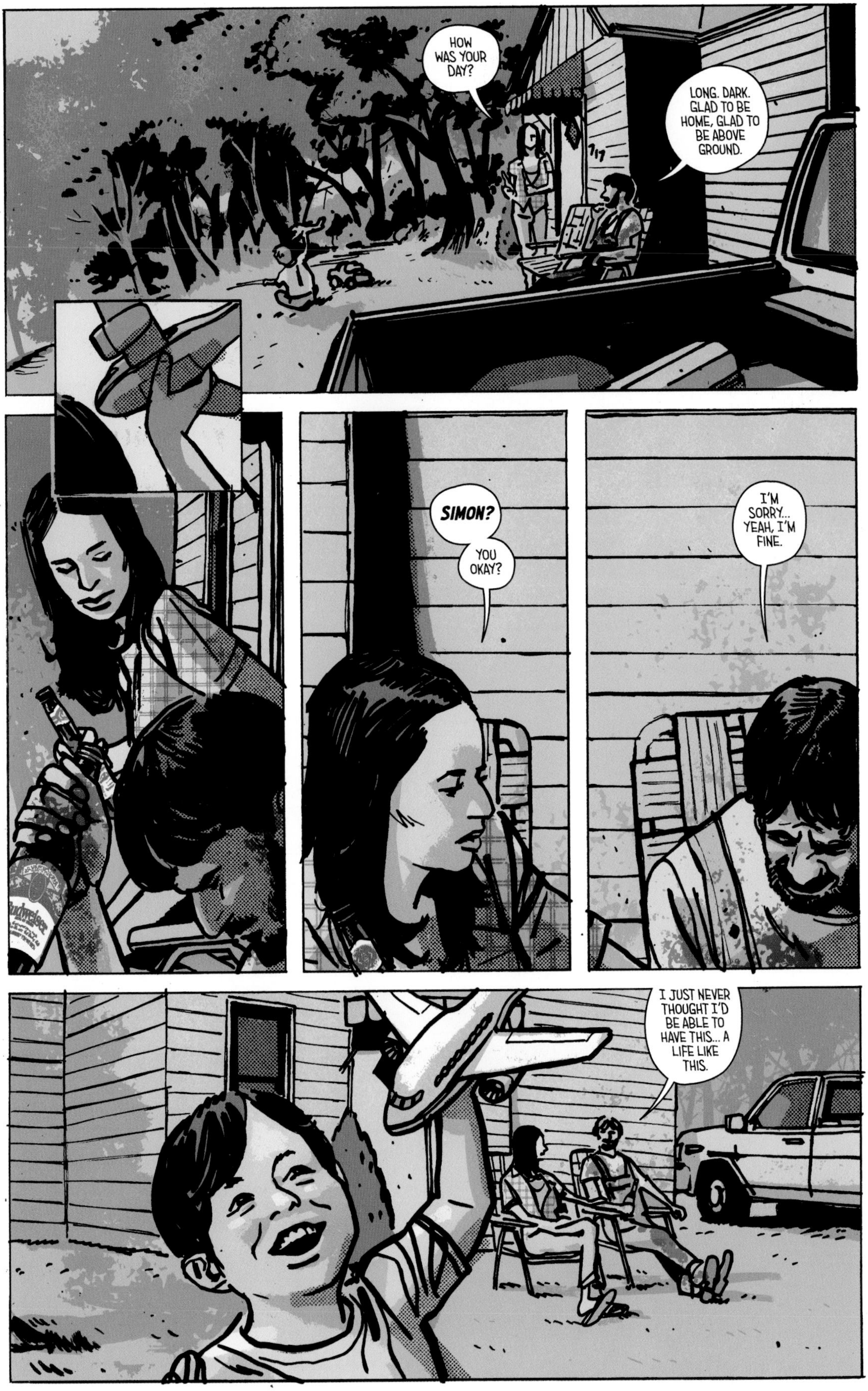
HOW WAS YOUR DAY?
LONG. DARK. GLAD TO BE HOME, GLAD TO BE ABOVE GROUND.
SIMON?
YOU OKAY?
I'M SORRY... YEAH, I'M FINE.
I JUST NEVER THOUGHT I'D BE ABLE TO HAVE THIS... A LIFE LIKE THIS.

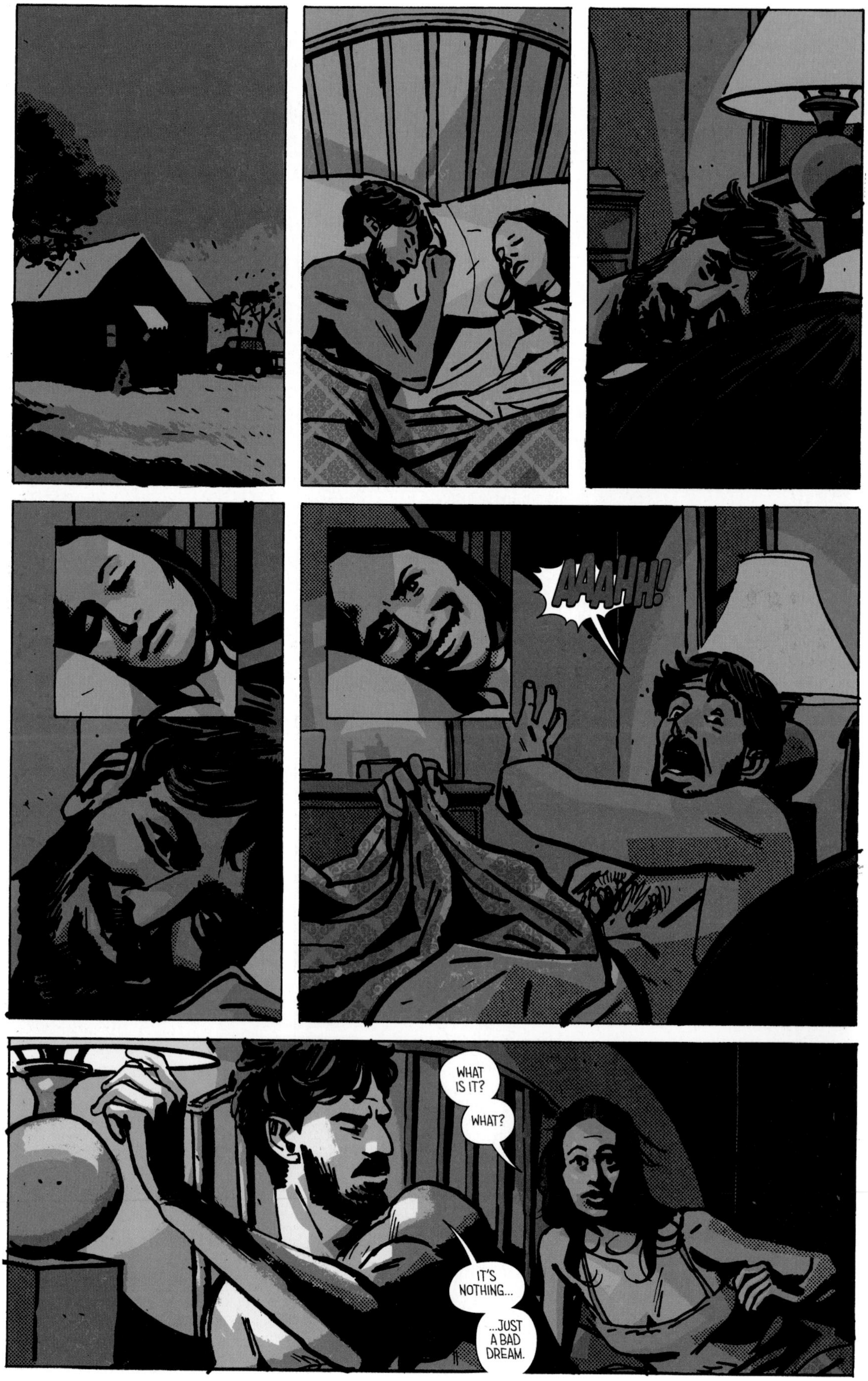

AAAHH!
WHAT IS IT?
WHAT?
IT'S NOTHING...
...JUST A BAD DREAM.

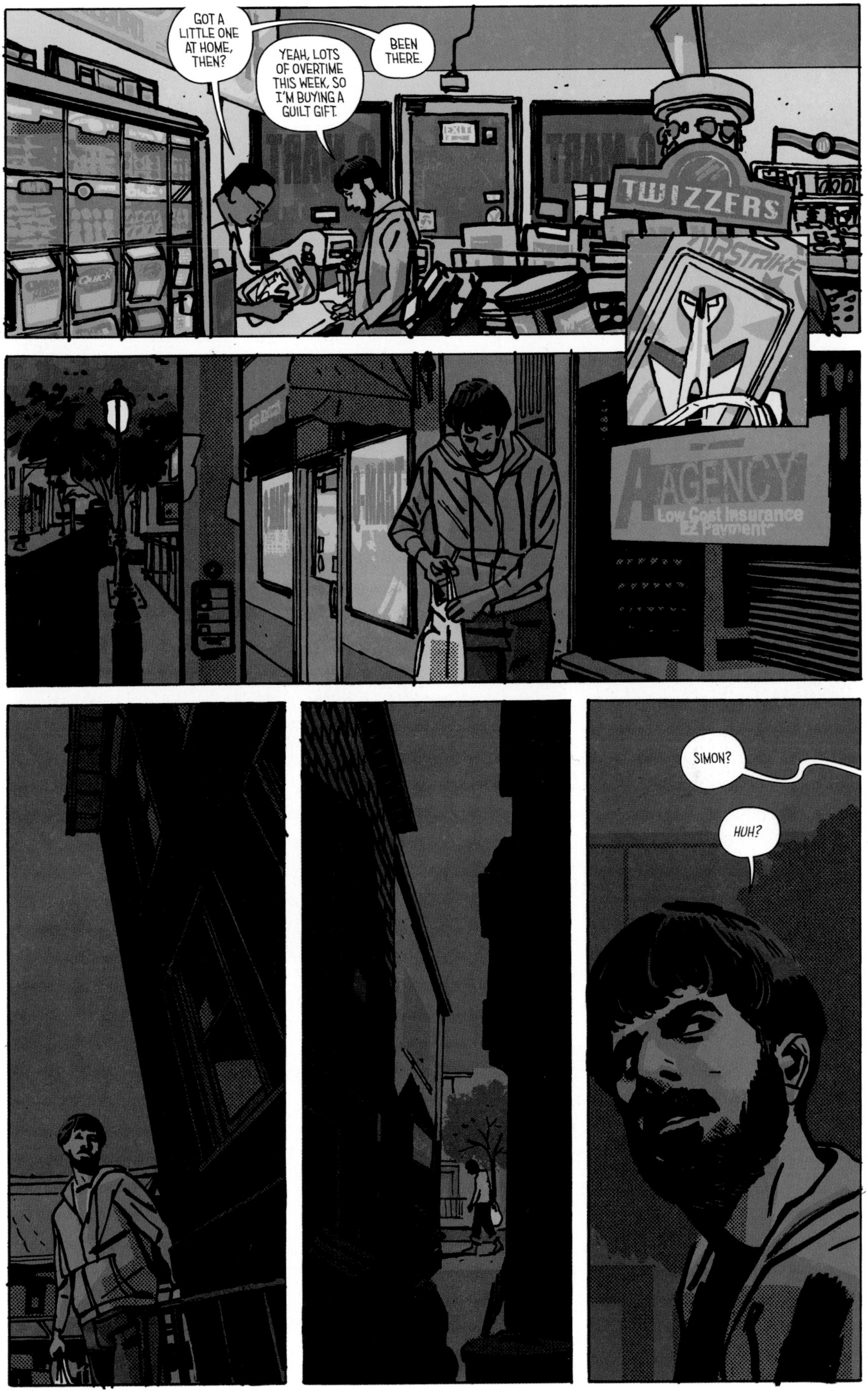
GOT A LITTLE ONE AT HOME, THEN?
YEAH, LOTS OF OVERTIME THIS WEEK, SO I'M BUYING A GUILT GIFT.
BEEN THERE.
TWIZZERS
AIRSTRIKE
AGENCY
Low Cost Insurance
EZ Payment
SIMON?
HUH?

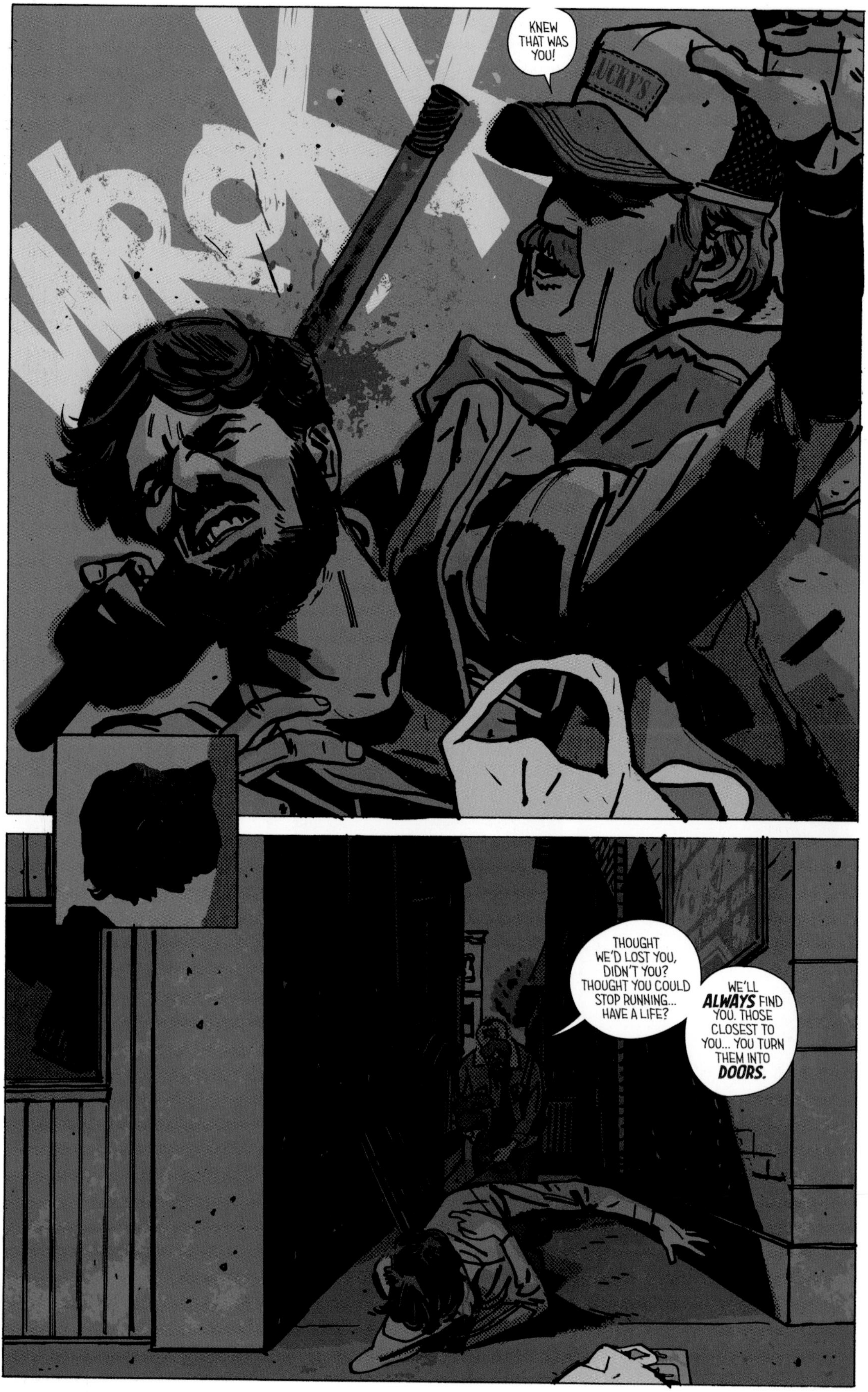
WROK
KNEW THAT WAS YOU!
LUCKY'S
THOUGHT WE'D LOST YOU, DIDN'T YOU? THOUGHT YOU COULD STOP RUNNING... HAVE A LIFE?
WE'LL ALWAYS FIND YOU. THOSE CLOSEST TO YOU... YOU TURN THEM INTO DOORS.

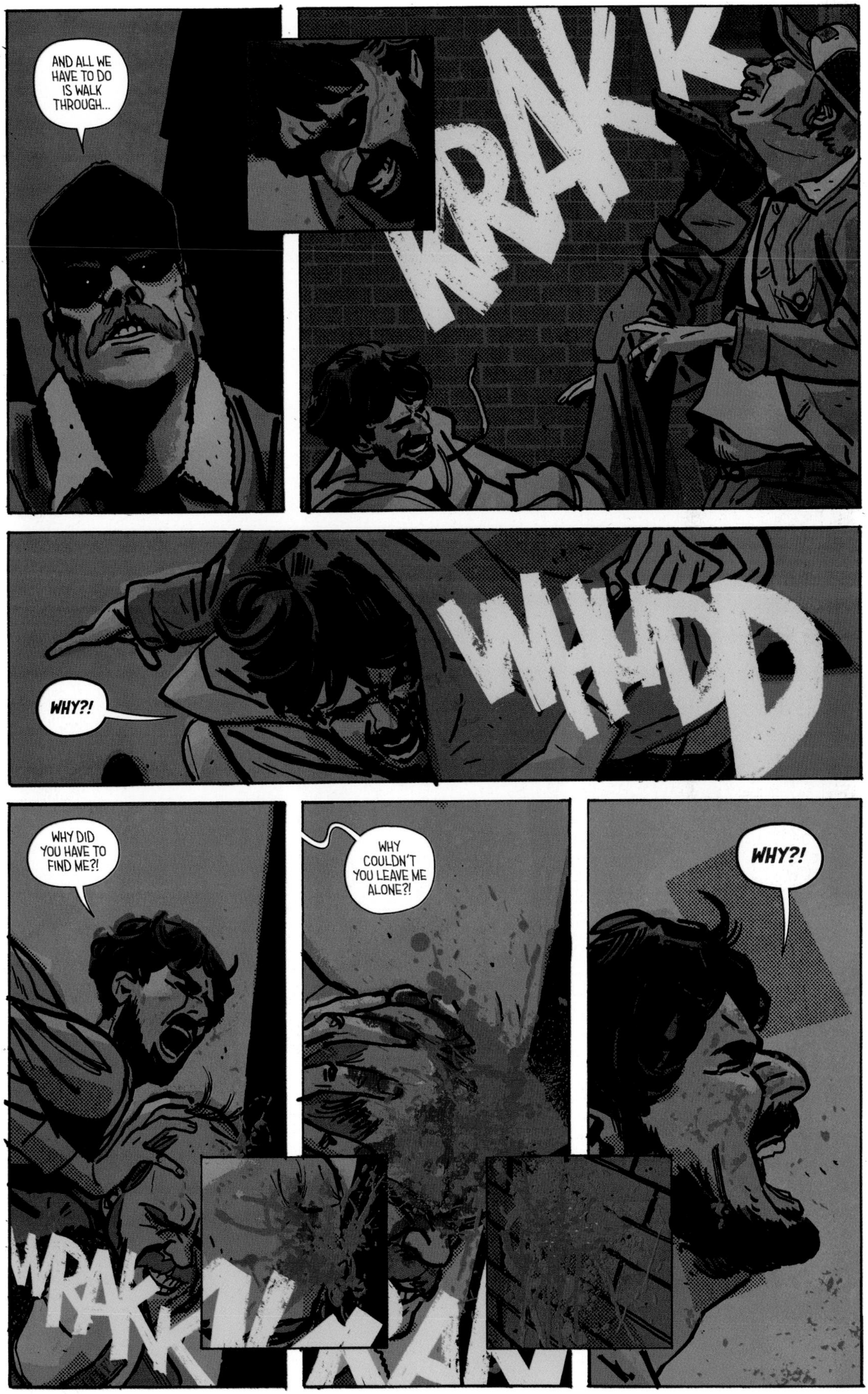
AND ALL WE HAVE TO DO IS WALK THROUGH...
KRAKK
WHUDD
WHY?!
WHY DID YOU HAVE TO FIND ME?!
WHY COULDN'T YOU LEAVE ME ALONE?!
WHY?!
WRAKK

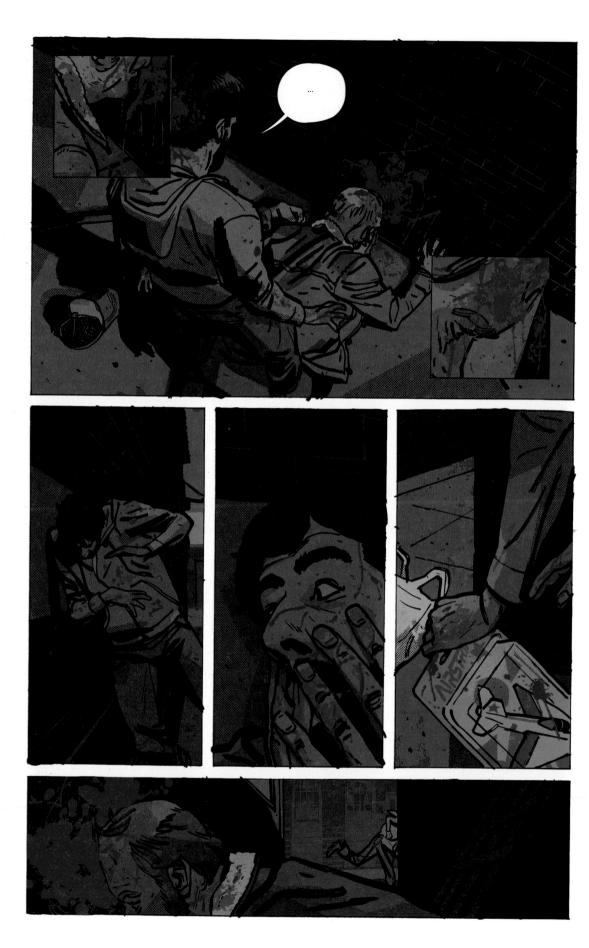

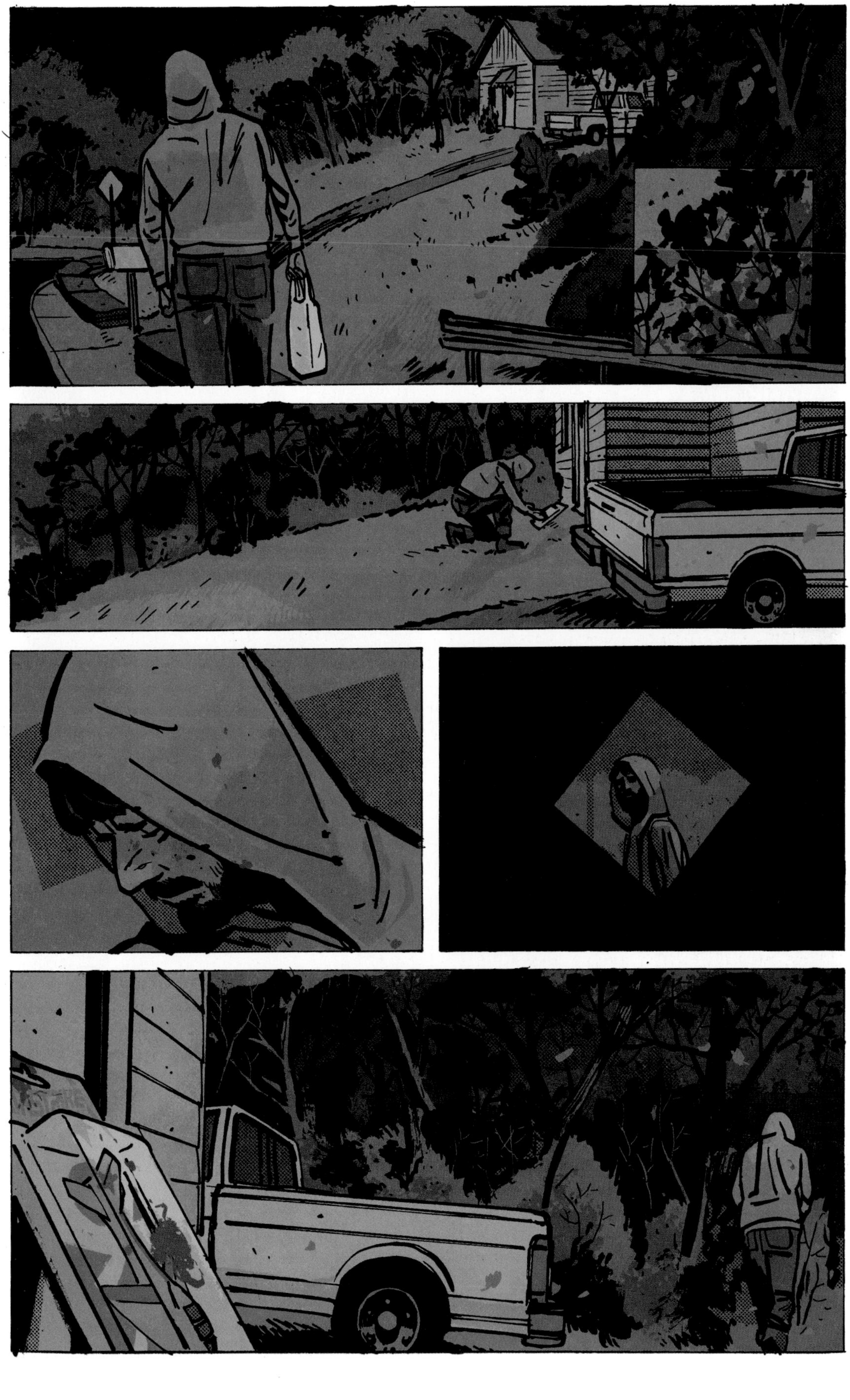

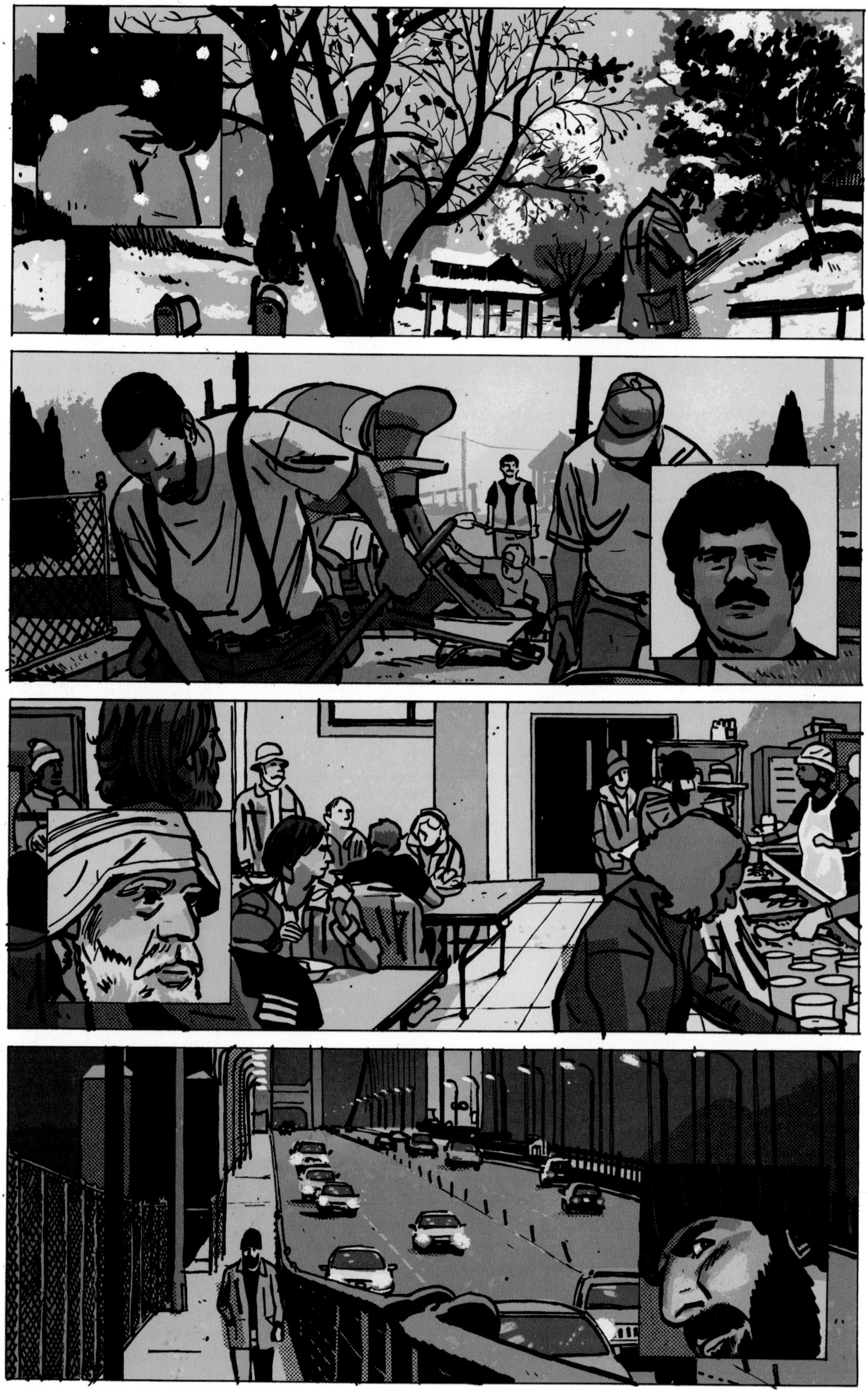

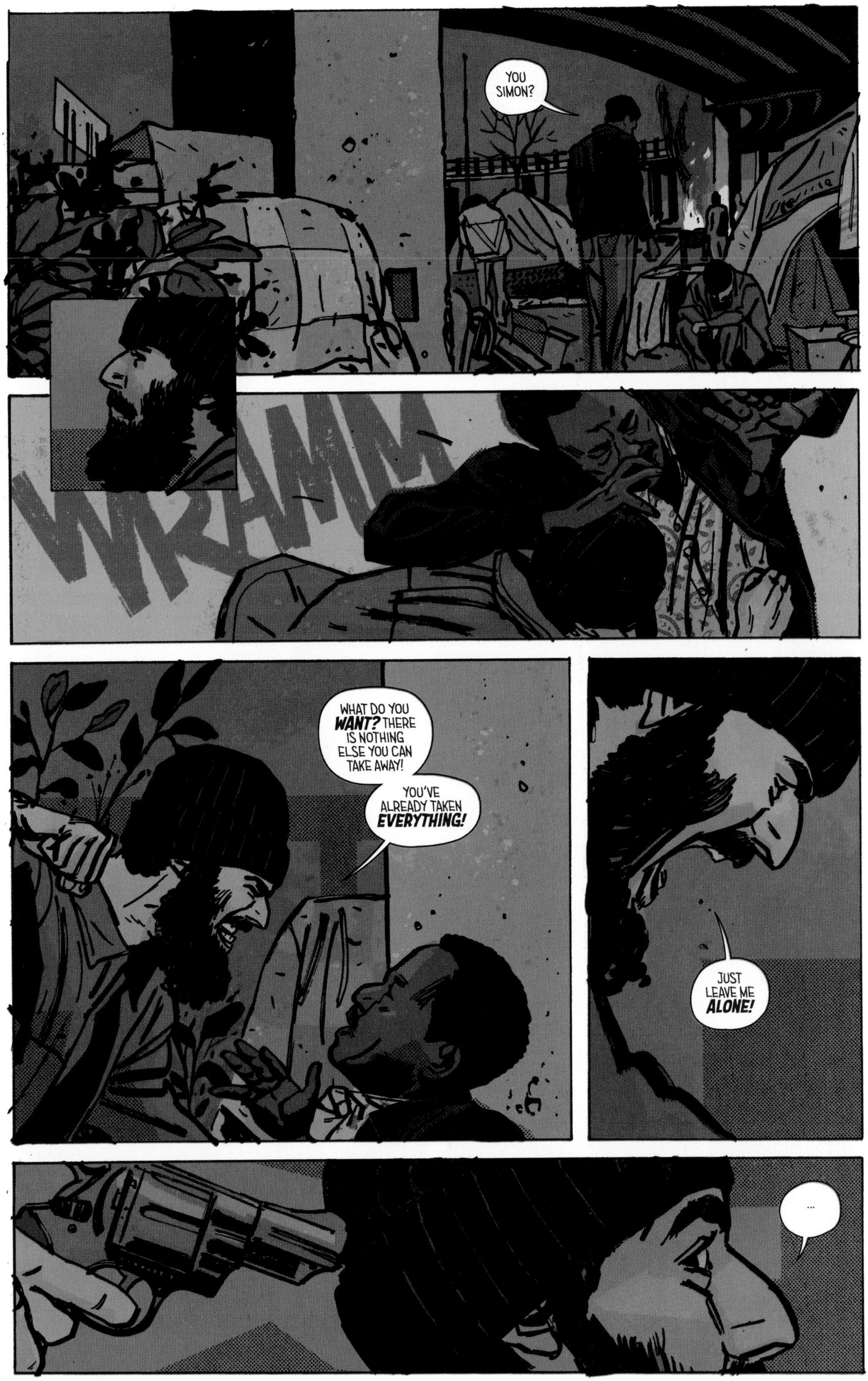
YOU SIMON?
WRAMM
WHAT DO YOU WANT? THERE IS NOTHING ELSE YOU CAN TAKE AWAY!
YOU'VE ALREADY TAKEN EVERYTHING!
JUST LEAVE ME ALONE!
...

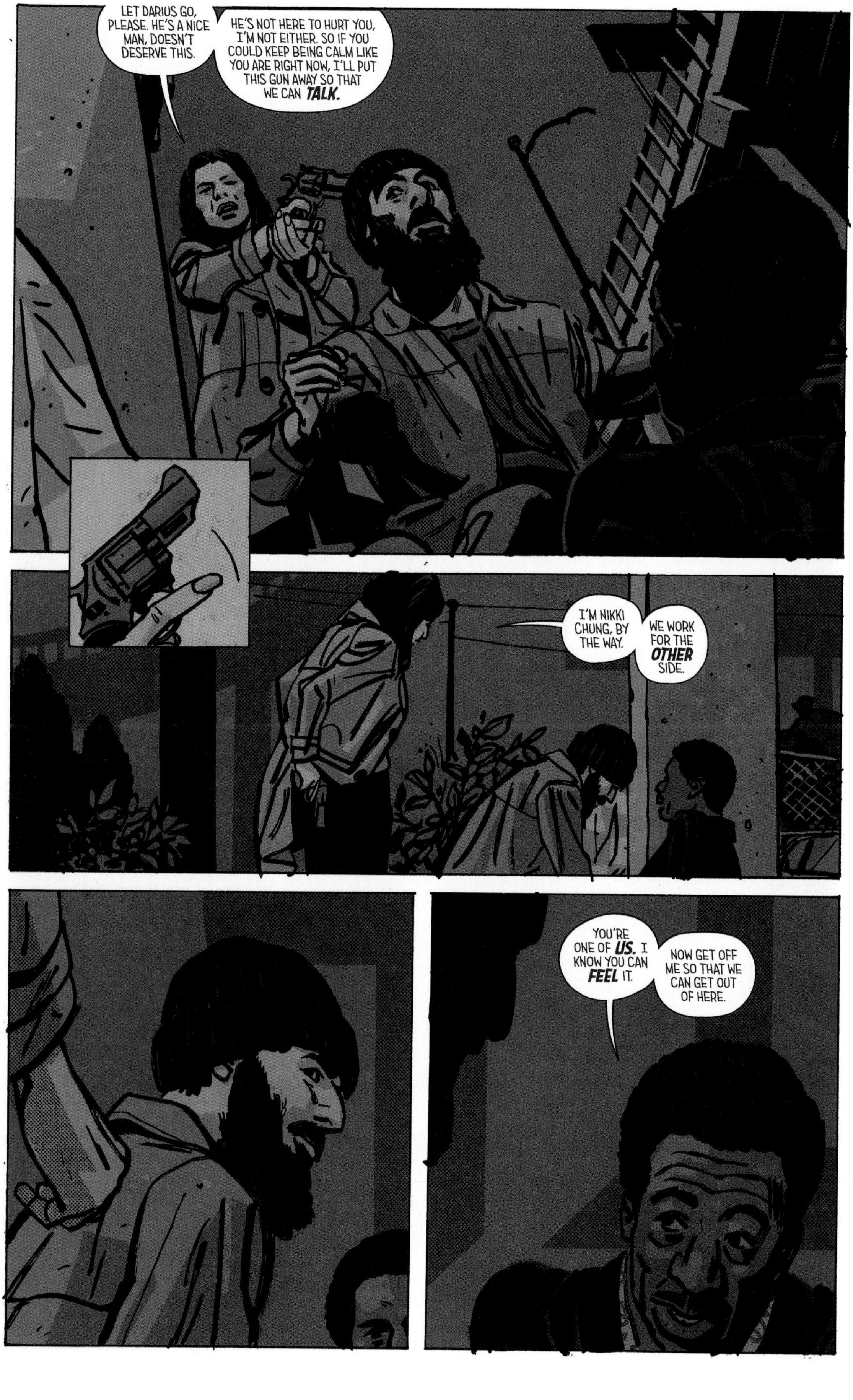
LET DARIUS GO, PLEASE. HE'S A NICE MAN, DOESN'T DESERVE THIS.
HE'S NOT HERE TO HURT YOU, I'M NOT EITHER. SO IF YOU COULD KEEP BEING CALM LIKE YOU ARE RIGHT NOW, I'LL PUT THIS GUN AWAY SO THAT WE CAN **TALK.**
I'M NIKKI CHUNG, BY THE WAY.
WE WORK FOR THE **OTHER** SIDE.
YOU'RE ONE OF **US.** I KNOW YOU CAN **FEEL** IT.
NOW GET OFF ME SO THAT WE CAN GET OUT OF HERE.

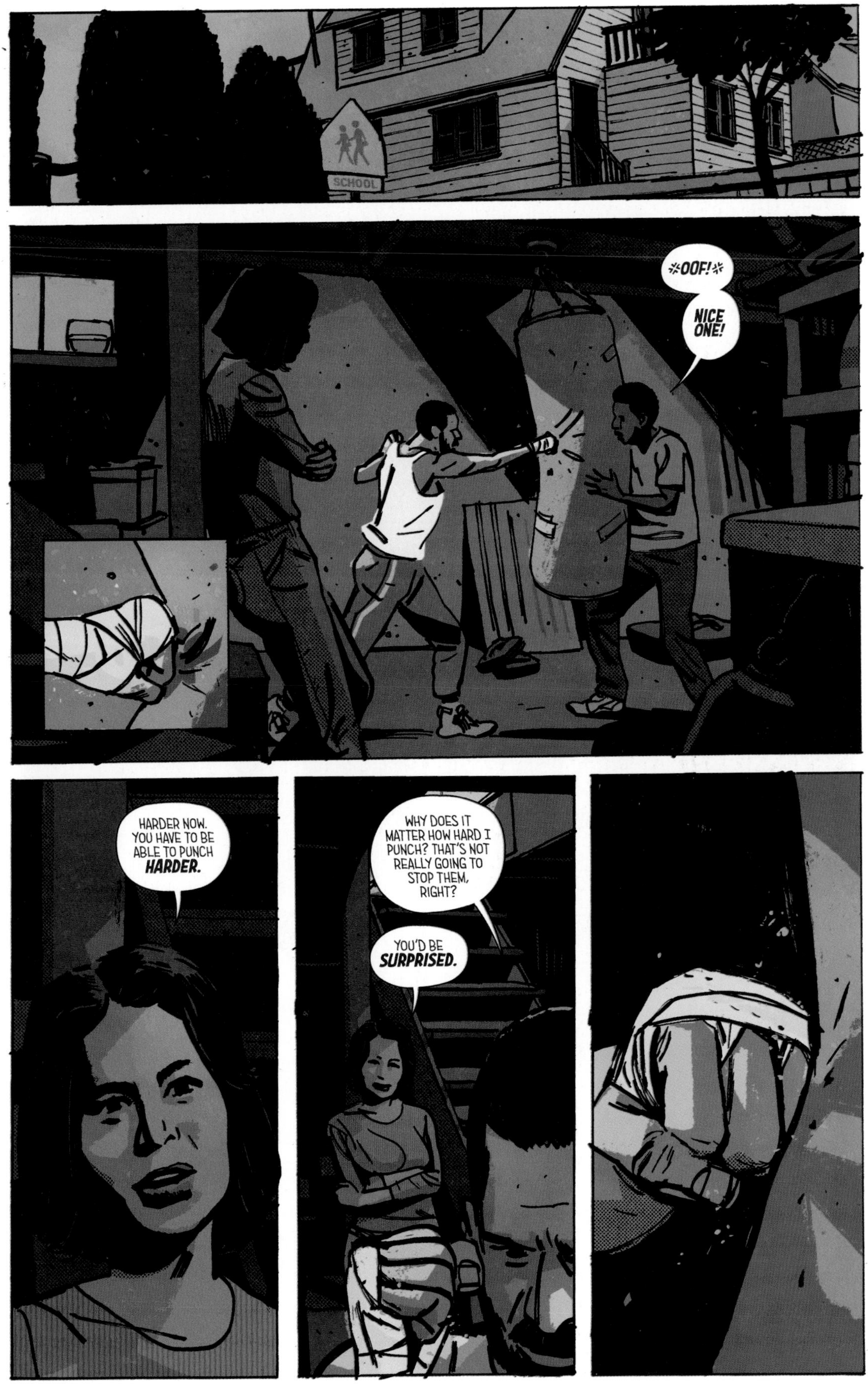
SCHOOL
OOF!
NICE ONE!
HARDER NOW. YOU HAVE TO BE ABLE TO PUNCH HARDER.
WHY DOES IT MATTER HOW HARD I PUNCH? THAT'S NOT REALLY GOING TO STOP THEM, RIGHT?
YOU'D BE SURPRISED.

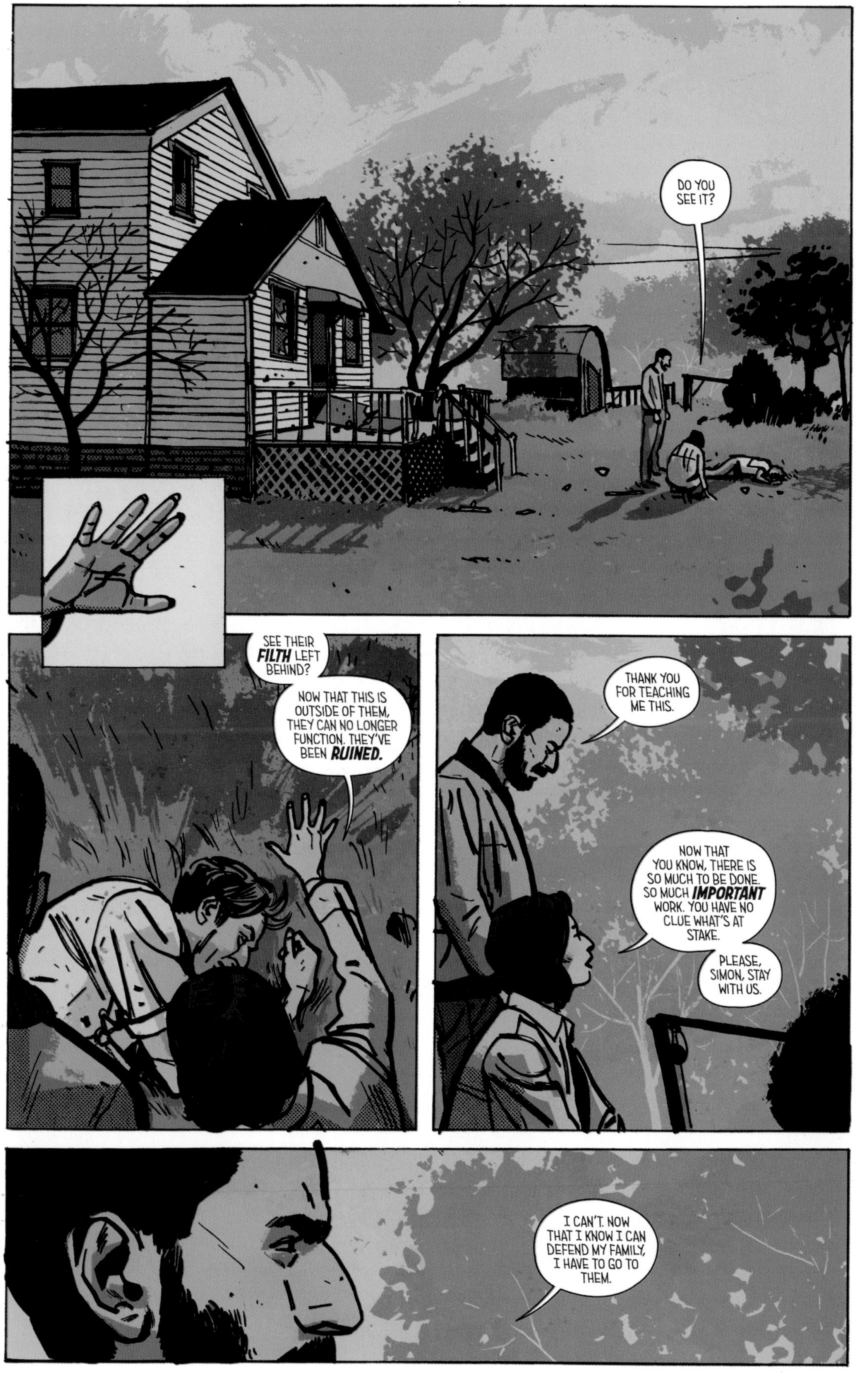
DO YOU SEE IT?
SEE THEIR FILTH LEFT BEHIND?
NOW THAT THIS IS OUTSIDE OF THEM, THEY CAN NO LONGER FUNCTION. THEY'VE BEEN RUINED.
THANK YOU FOR TEACHING ME THIS.
NOW THAT YOU KNOW, THERE IS SO MUCH TO BE DONE. SO MUCH IMPORTANT WORK. YOU HAVE NO CLUE WHAT'S AT STAKE.
PLEASE, SIMON, STAY WITH US.
I CAN'T. NOW THAT I KNOW I CAN DEFEND MY FAMILY, I HAVE TO GO TO THEM.

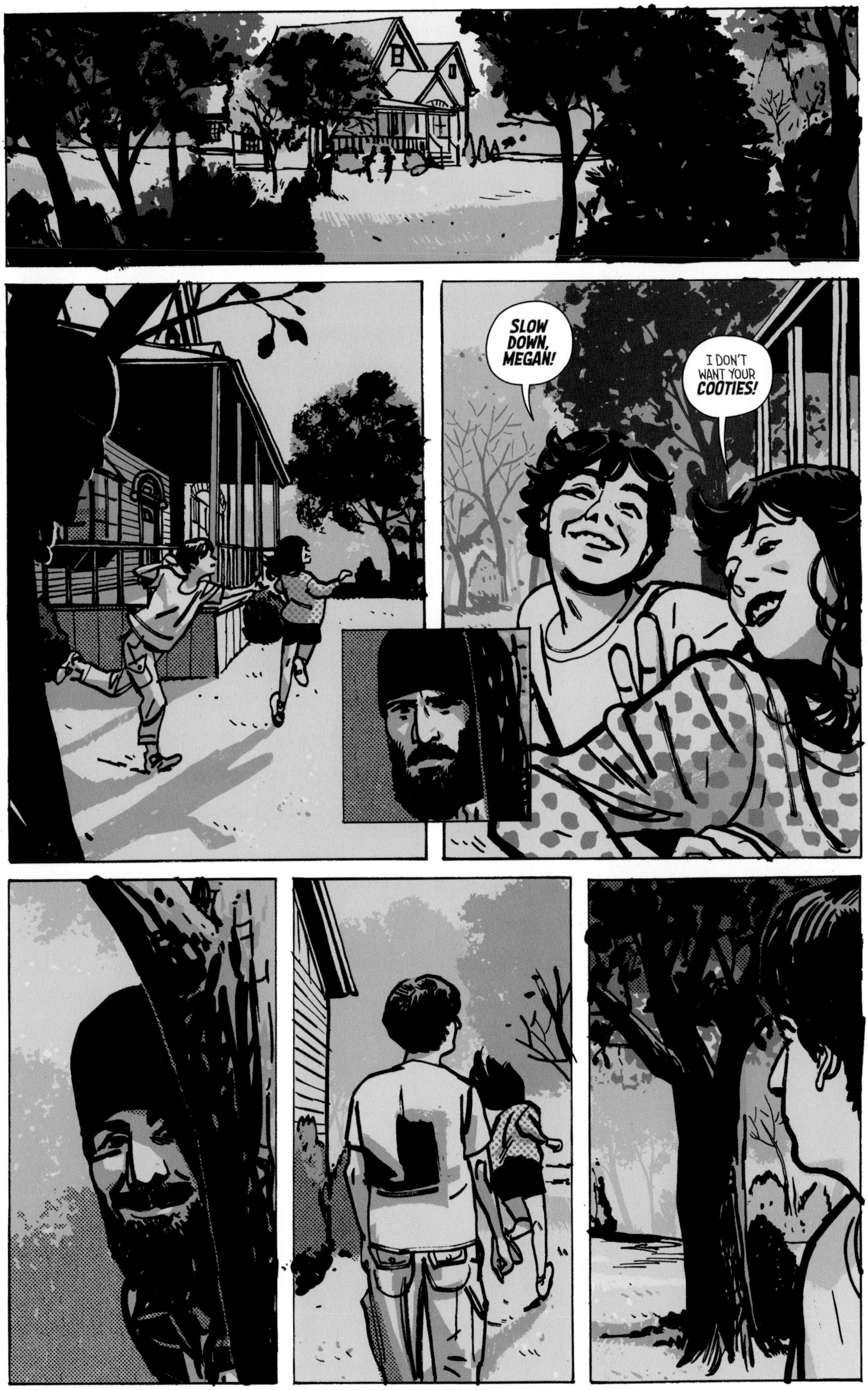
SLOW DOWN, MEGAN!
I DON'T WANT YOUR COOTIES!

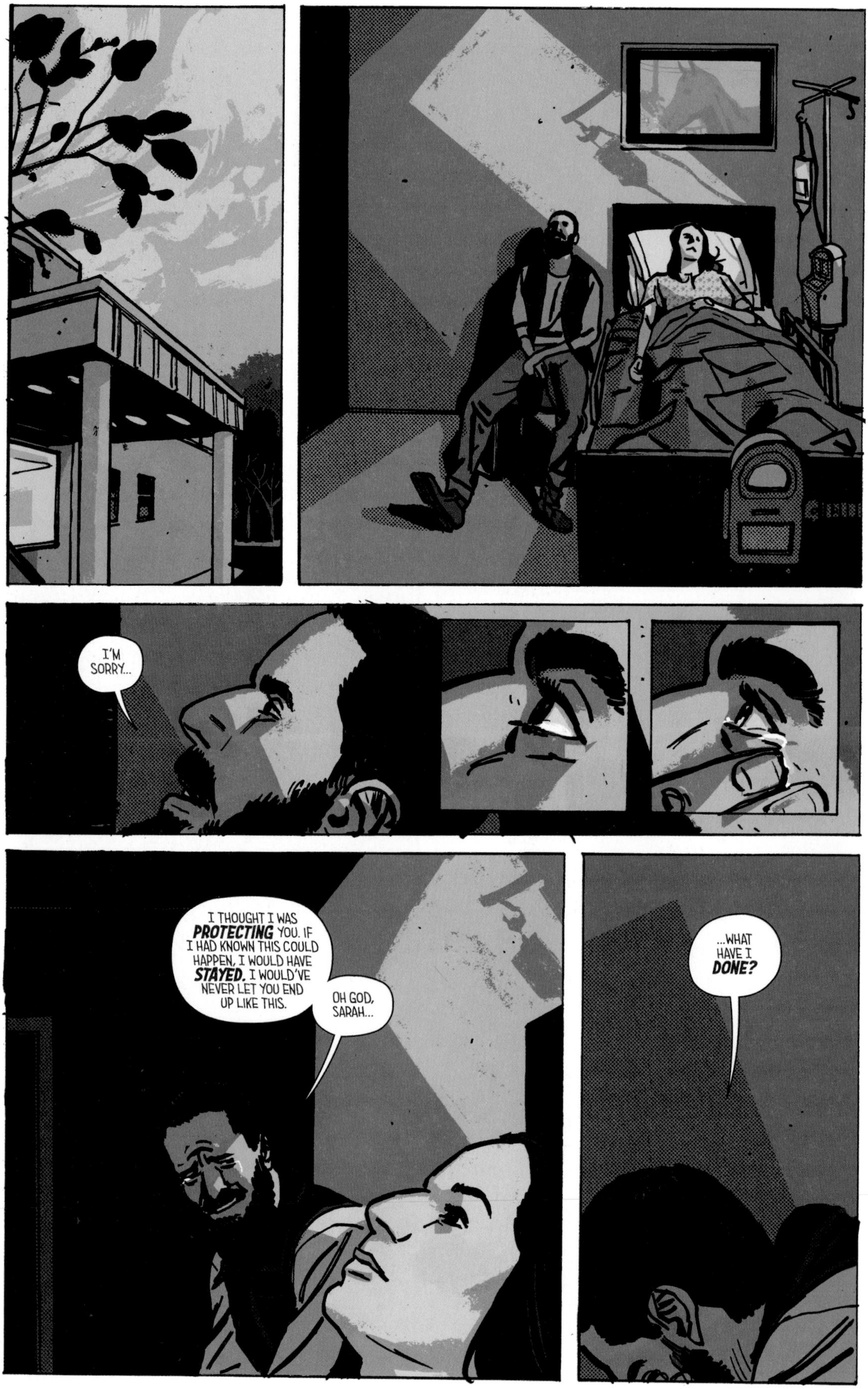
I'M SORRY...
I THOUGHT I WAS PROTECTING YOU. IF I HAD KNOWN THIS COULD HAPPEN, I WOULD HAVE STAYED. I WOULD'VE NEVER LET YOU END UP LIKE THIS.
OH GOD, SARAH...
...WHAT HAVE I DONE?

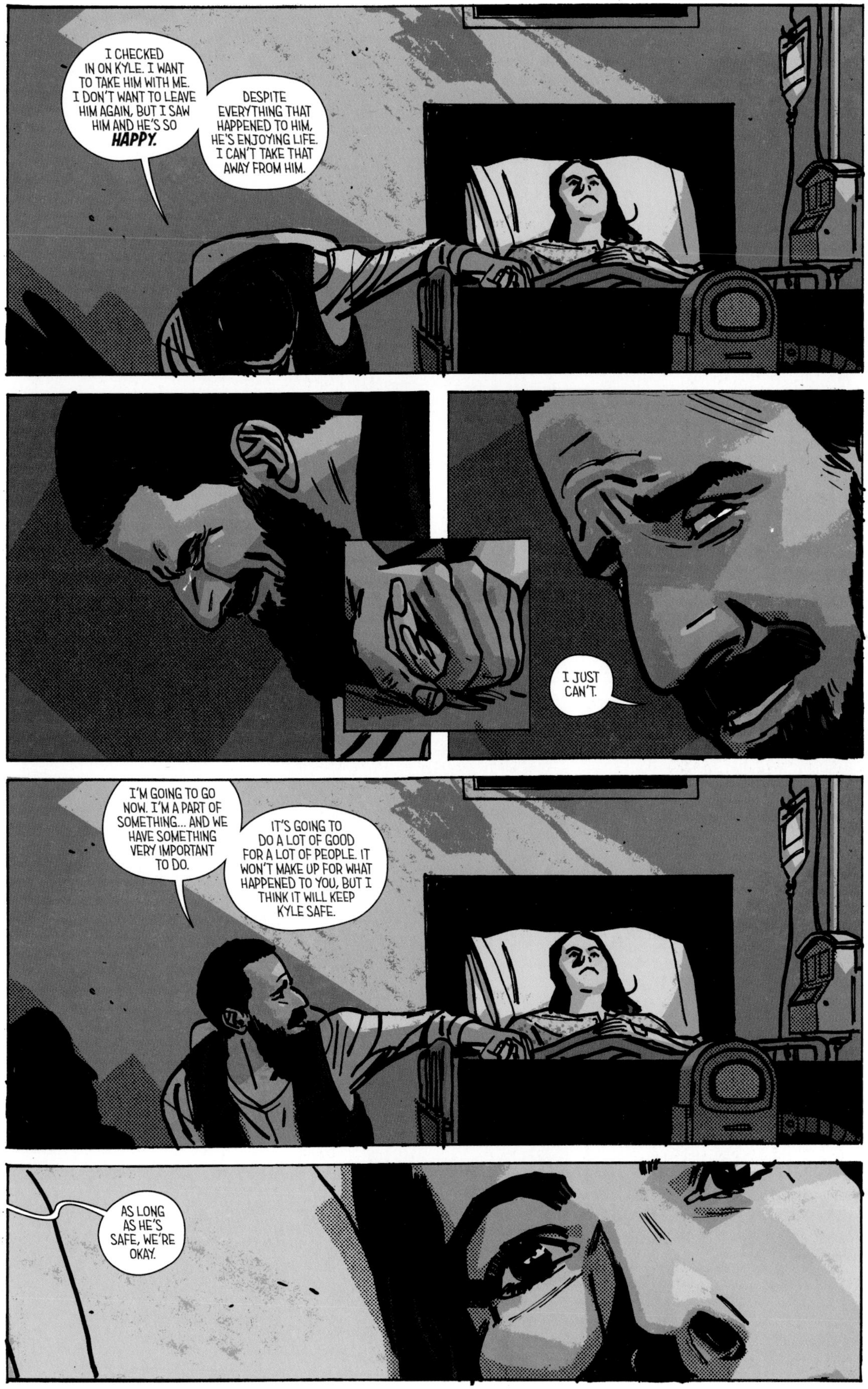
I CHECKED IN ON KYLE. I WANT TO TAKE HIM WITH ME. I DON'T WANT TO LEAVE HIM AGAIN, BUT I SAW HIM AND HE'S SO *HAPPY.*
DESPITE EVERYTHING THAT HAPPENED TO HIM, HE'S ENJOYING LIFE. I CAN'T TAKE THAT AWAY FROM HIM.
I JUST CAN'T.
I'M GOING TO GO NOW. I'M A PART OF SOMETHING... AND WE HAVE SOMETHING VERY IMPORTANT TO DO.
IT'S GOING TO DO A LOT OF GOOD FOR A LOT OF PEOPLE. IT WON'T MAKE UP FOR WHAT HAPPENED TO YOU, BUT I THINK IT WILL KEEP KYLE SAFE.
AS LONG AS HE'S SAFE, WE'RE OKAY.

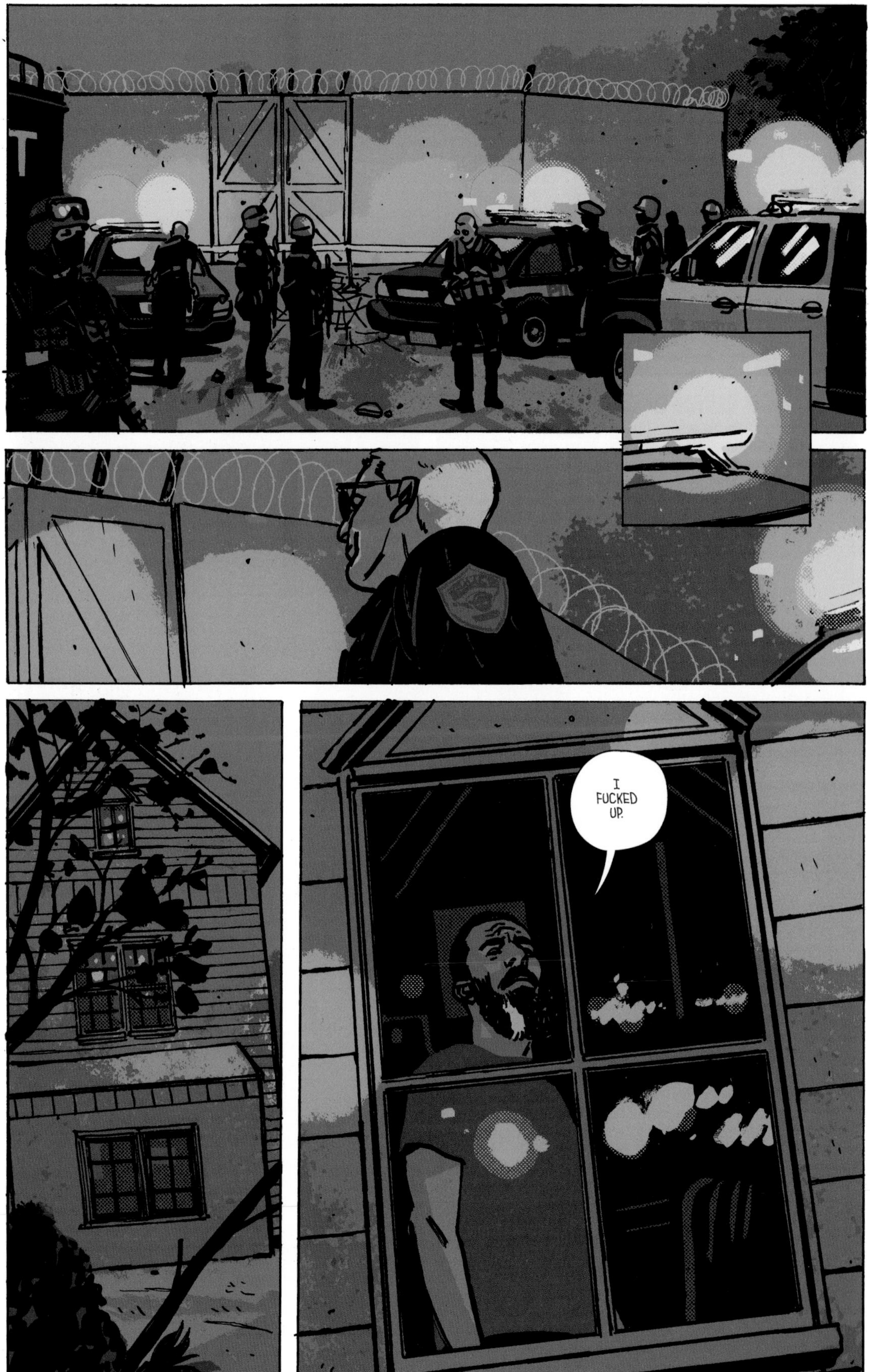
I FUCKED UP.

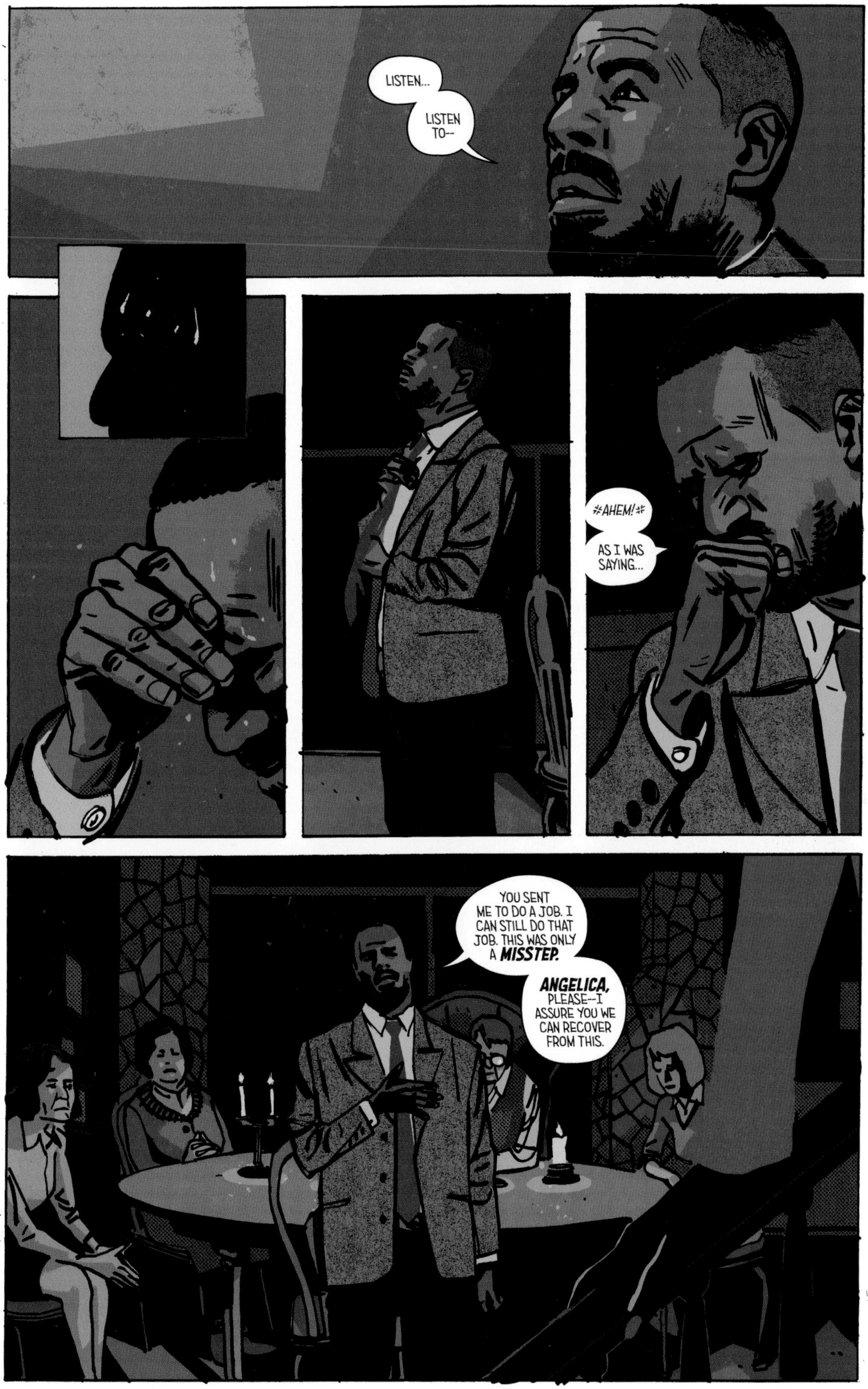
LISTEN...
LISTEN TO--
#AHEM!#
AS I WAS SAYING...
YOU SENT ME TO DO A JOB. I CAN STILL DO THAT JOB. THIS WAS ONLY A MISSTEP.
ANGELICA, PLEASE--I ASSURE YOU WE CAN RECOVER FROM THIS.

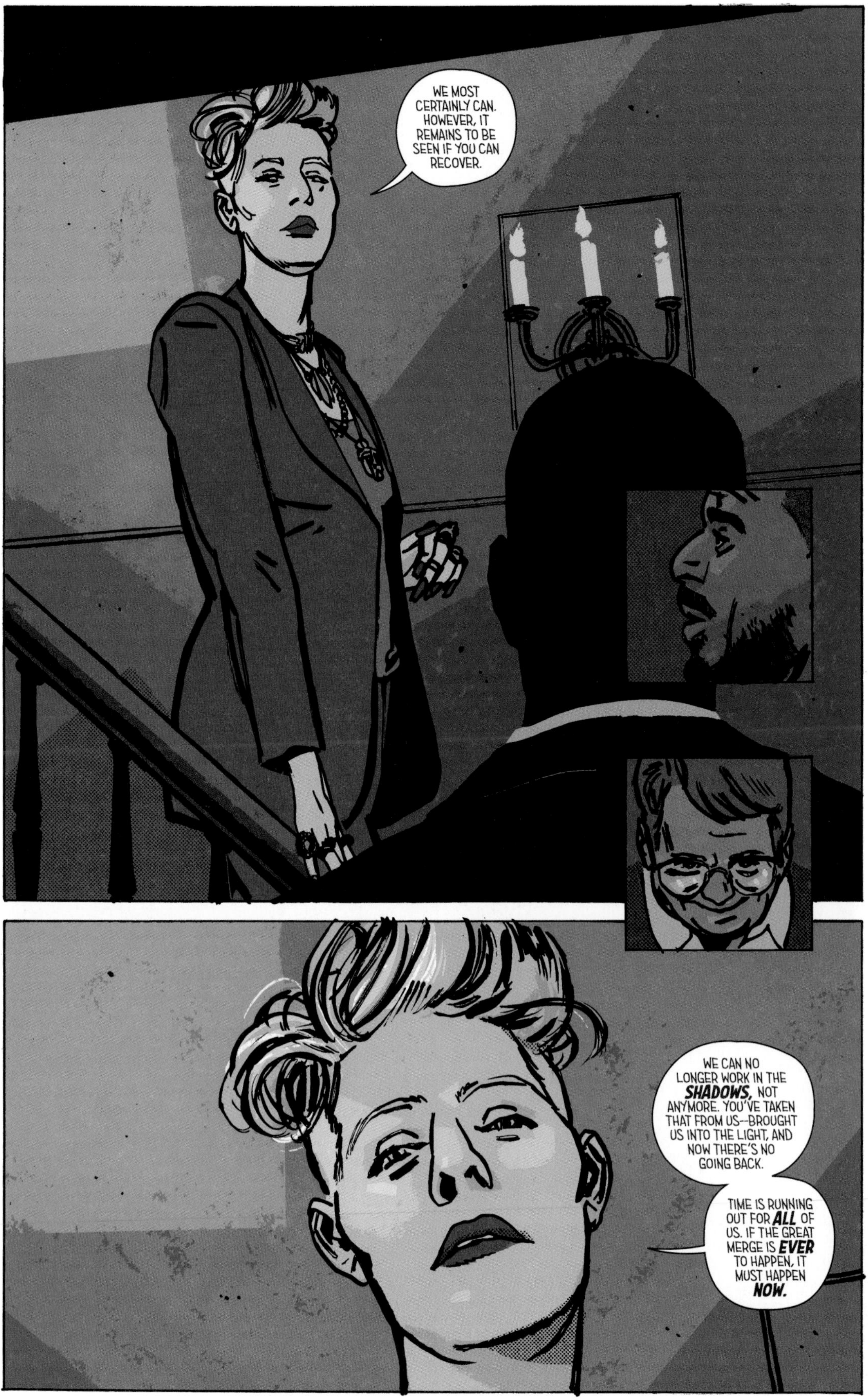
WE MOST CERTAINLY CAN. HOWEVER, IT REMAINS TO BE SEEN IF YOU CAN RECOVER.
WE CAN NO LONGER WORK IN THE SHADOWS, NOT ANYMORE. YOU'VE TAKEN THAT FROM US--BROUGHT US INTO THE LIGHT, AND NOW THERE'S NO GOING BACK.
TIME IS RUNNING OUT FOR ALL OF US. IF THE GREAT MERGE IS EVER TO HAPPEN, IT MUST HAPPEN NOW.

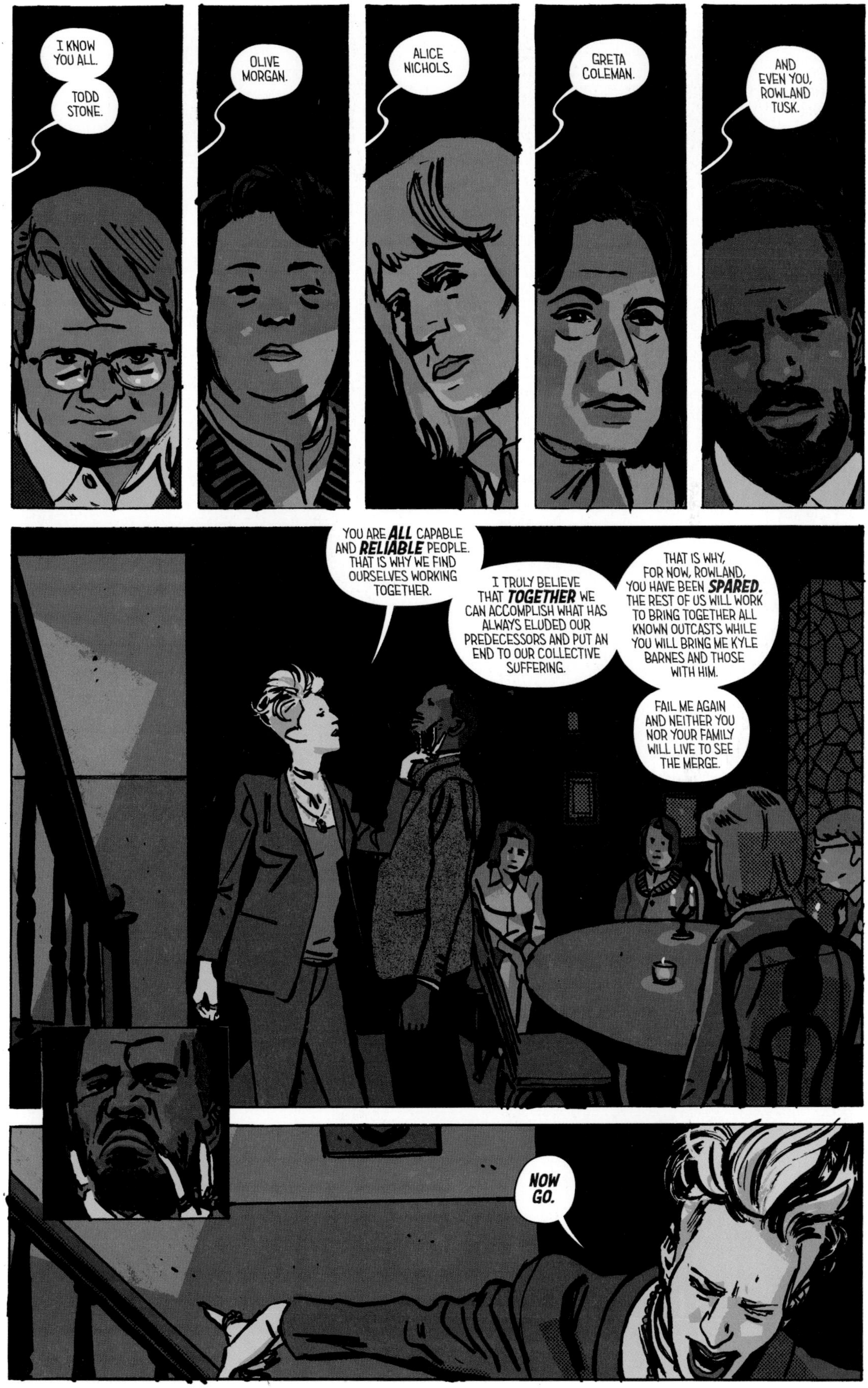
I KNOW YOU ALL.
TODD STONE.
OLIVE MORGAN.
ALICE NICHOLS.
GRETA COLEMAN.
AND EVEN YOU, ROWLAND TUSK.
YOU ARE **ALL** CAPABLE AND **RELIABLE** PEOPLE. THAT IS WHY WE FIND OURSELVES WORKING TOGETHER.
I TRULY BELIEVE THAT **TOGETHER** WE CAN ACCOMPLISH WHAT HAS ALWAYS ELUDED OUR PREDECESSORS AND PUT AN END TO OUR COLLECTIVE SUFFERING.
THAT IS WHY, FOR NOW, ROWLAND, YOU HAVE BEEN **SPARED.** THE REST OF US WILL WORK TO BRING TOGETHER ALL KNOWN OUTCASTS WHILE YOU WILL BRING ME KYLE BARNES AND THOSE WITH HIM.
FAIL ME AGAIN AND NEITHER YOU NOR YOUR FAMILY WILL LIVE TO SEE THE MERGE.
NOW GO.

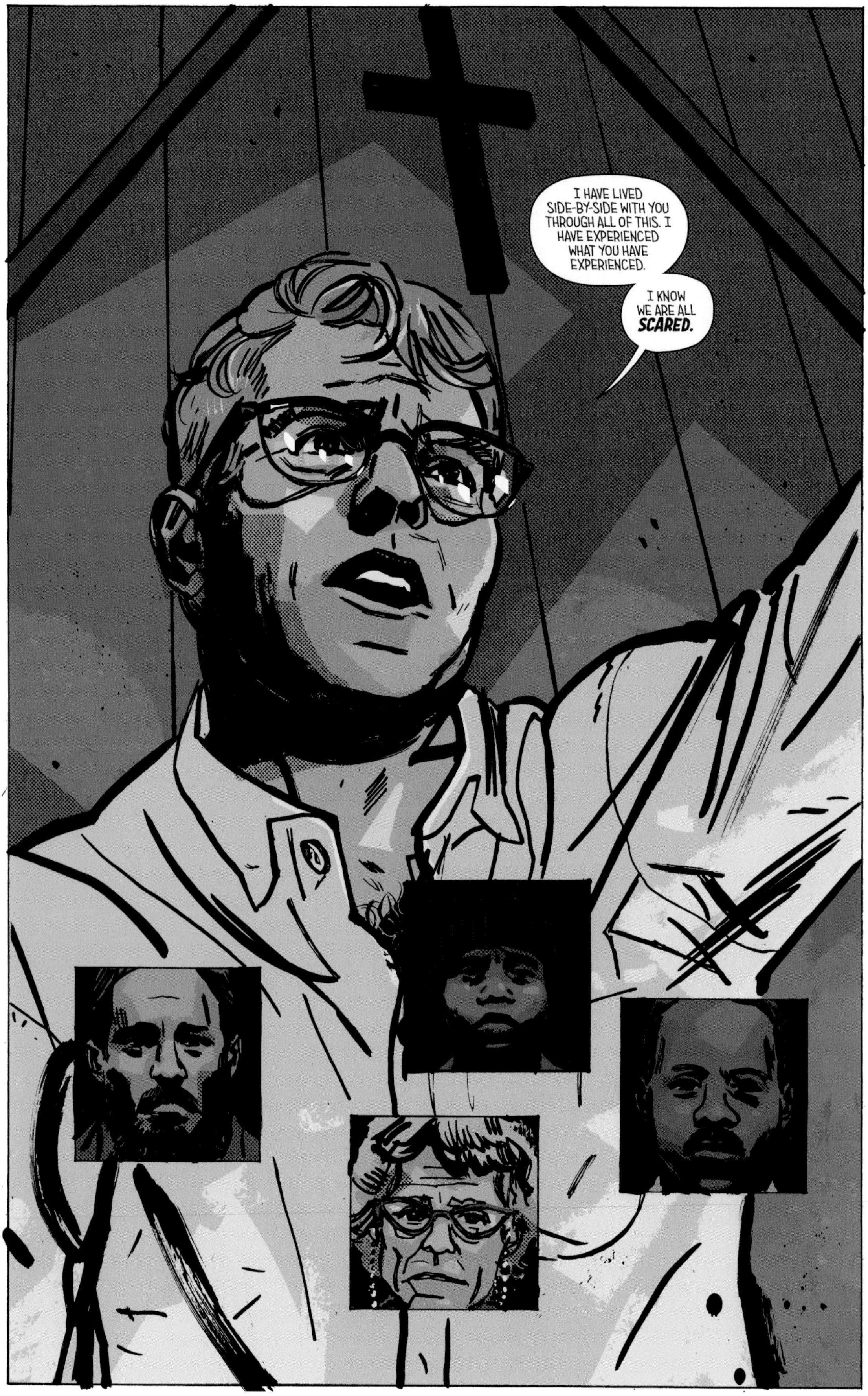

I HAVE LIVED SIDE-BY-SIDE WITH YOU THROUGH ALL OF THIS. I HAVE EXPERIENCED WHAT YOU HAVE EXPERIENCED.
I KNOW WE ARE ALL **SCARED.**

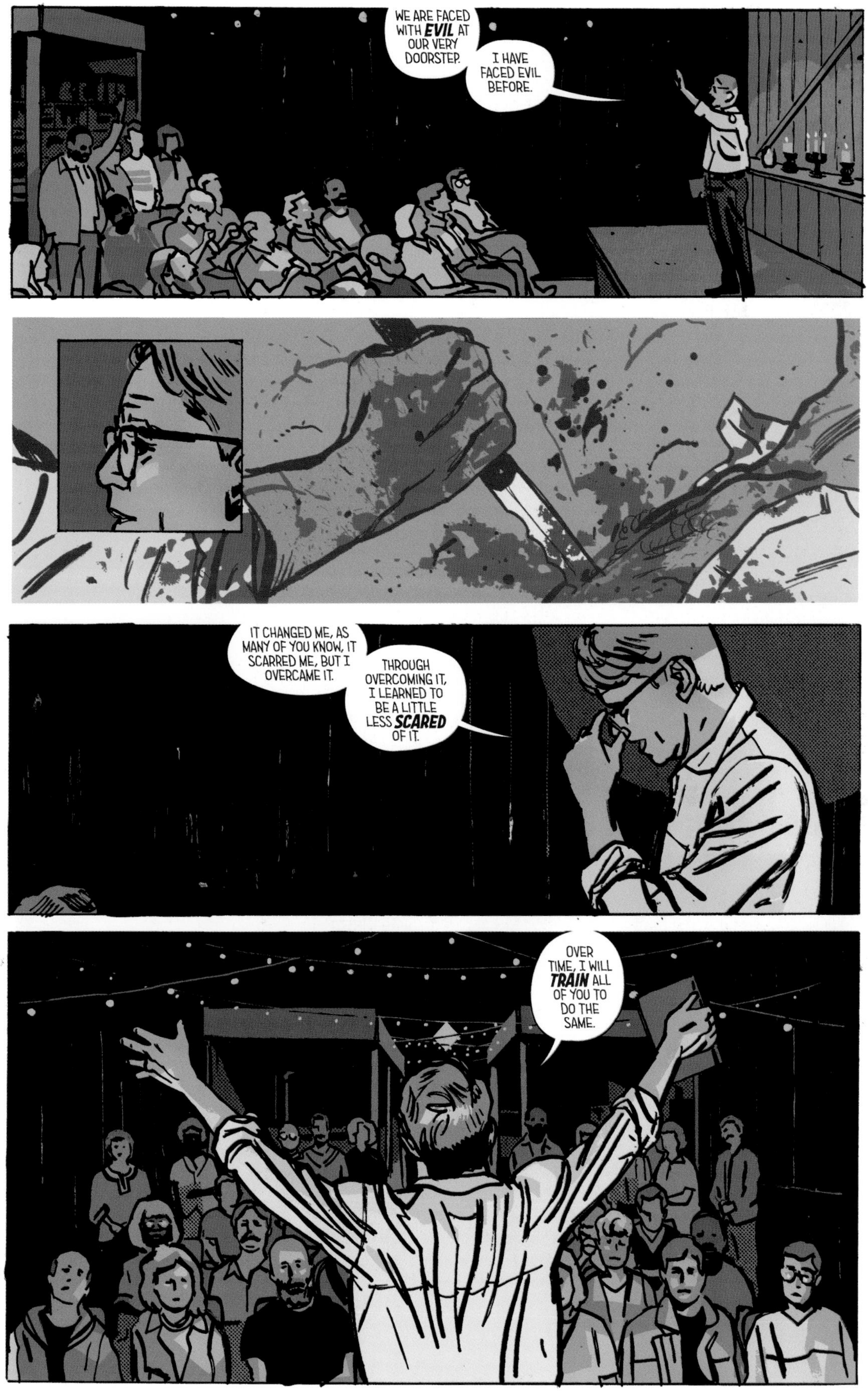
WE ARE FACED WITH EVIL AT OUR VERY DOORSTEP.
I HAVE FACED EVIL BEFORE.
IT CHANGED ME, AS MANY OF YOU KNOW, IT SCARRED ME, BUT I OVERCAME IT.
THROUGH OVERCOMING IT, I LEARNED TO BE A LITTLE LESS SCARED OF IT.
OVER TIME, I WILL TRAIN ALL OF YOU TO DO THE SAME.

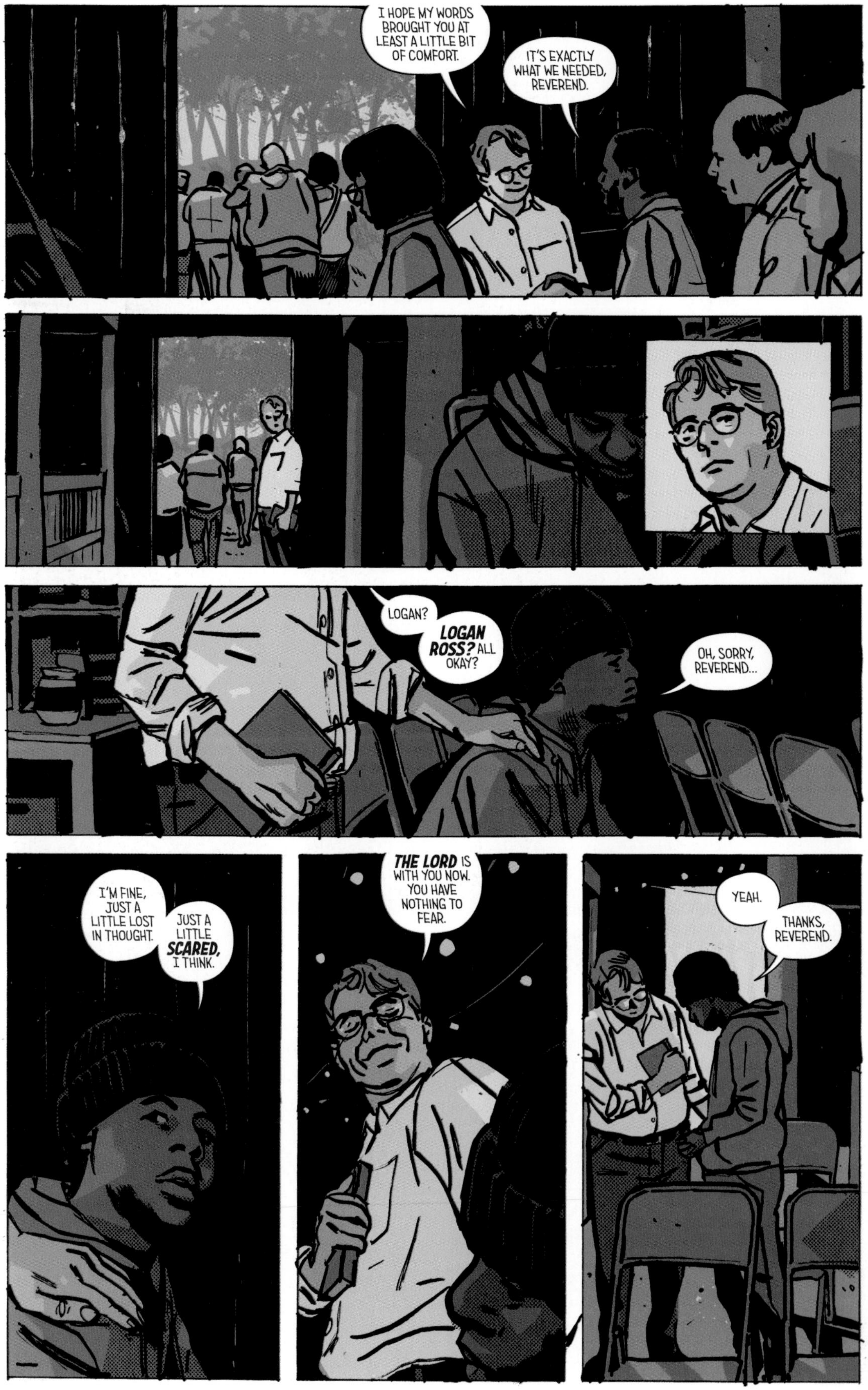
I HOPE MY WORDS BROUGHT YOU AT LEAST A LITTLE BIT OF COMFORT.
IT'S EXACTLY WHAT WE NEEDED, REVEREND.
LOGAN?
LOGAN ROSS? ALL OKAY?
OH, SORRY, REVEREND...
I'M FINE, JUST A LITTLE LOST IN THOUGHT.
JUST A LITTLE SCARED, I THINK.
THE LORD IS WITH YOU NOW. YOU HAVE NOTHING TO FEAR.
YEAH.
THANKS, REVEREND.

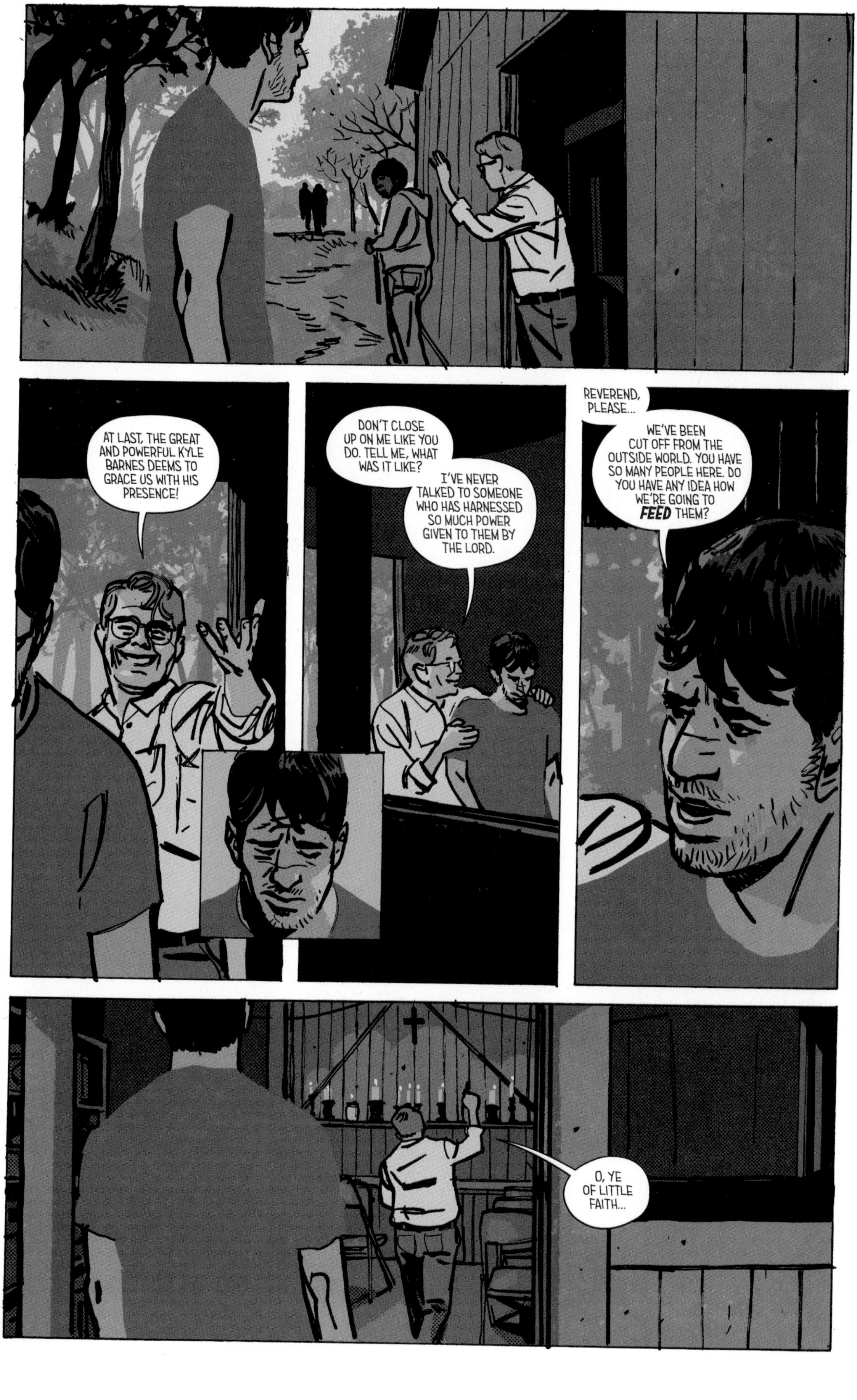
AT LAST, THE GREAT AND POWERFUL KYLE BARNES DEEMS TO GRACE US WITH HIS PRESENCE!
DON'T CLOSE UP ON ME LIKE YOU DO. TELL ME, WHAT WAS IT LIKE?
I'VE NEVER TALKED TO SOMEONE WHO HAS HARNESSED SO MUCH POWER GIVEN TO THEM BY THE LORD.
REVEREND, PLEASE...
WE'VE BEEN CUT OFF FROM THE OUTSIDE WORLD. YOU HAVE SO MANY PEOPLE HERE. DO YOU HAVE ANY IDEA HOW WE'RE GOING TO FEED THEM?
O, YE OF LITTLE FAITH...

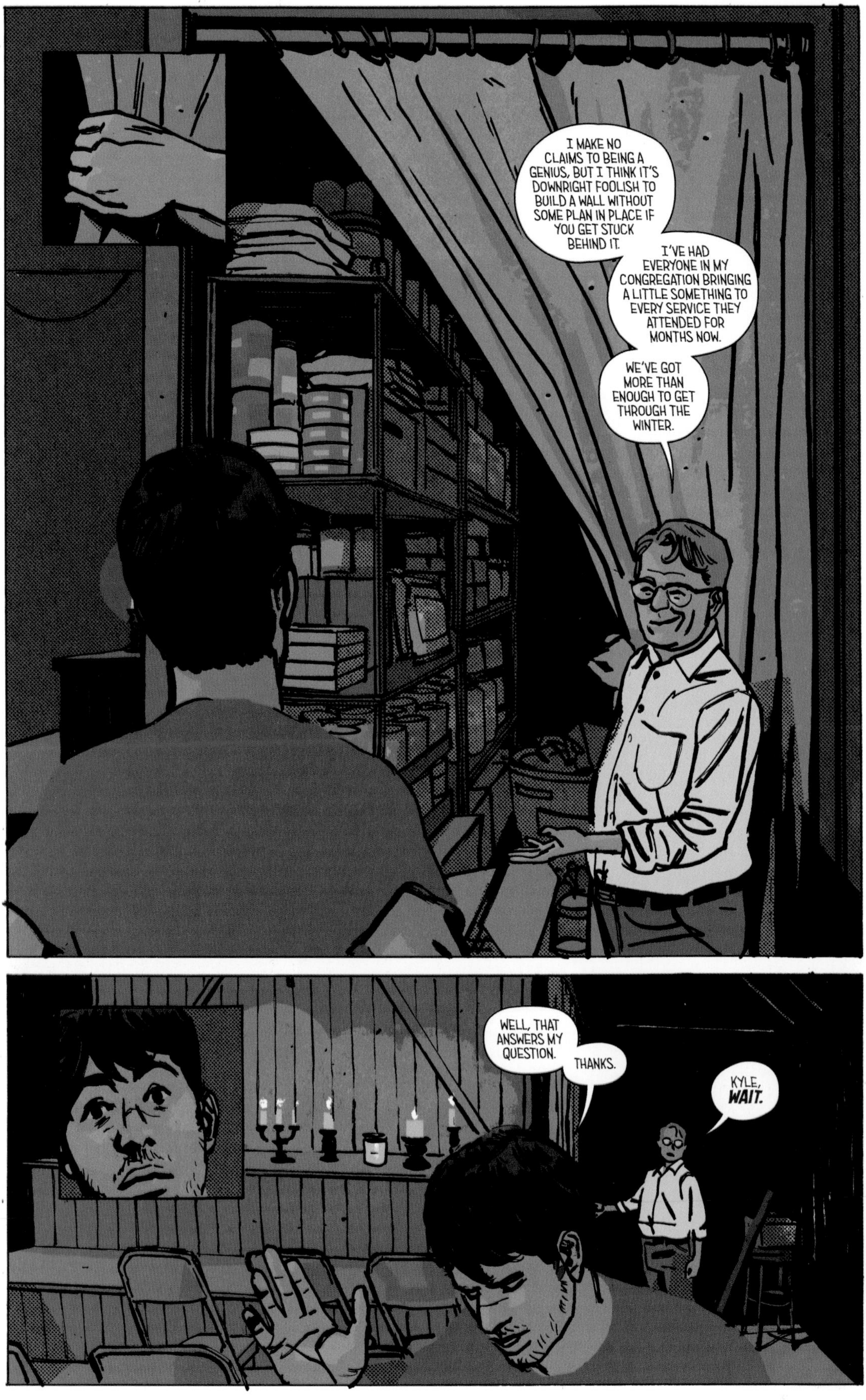
I MAKE NO CLAIMS TO BEING A GENIUS, BUT I THINK IT'S DOWNRIGHT FOOLISH TO BUILD A WALL WITHOUT SOME PLAN IN PLACE IF YOU GET STUCK BEHIND IT.
I'VE HAD EVERYONE IN MY CONGREGATION BRINGING A LITTLE SOMETHING TO EVERY SERVICE THEY ATTENDED FOR MONTHS NOW.
WE'VE GOT MORE THAN ENOUGH TO GET THROUGH THE WINTER.
WELL, THAT ANSWERS MY QUESTION.
THANKS.
KYLE, **WAIT.**

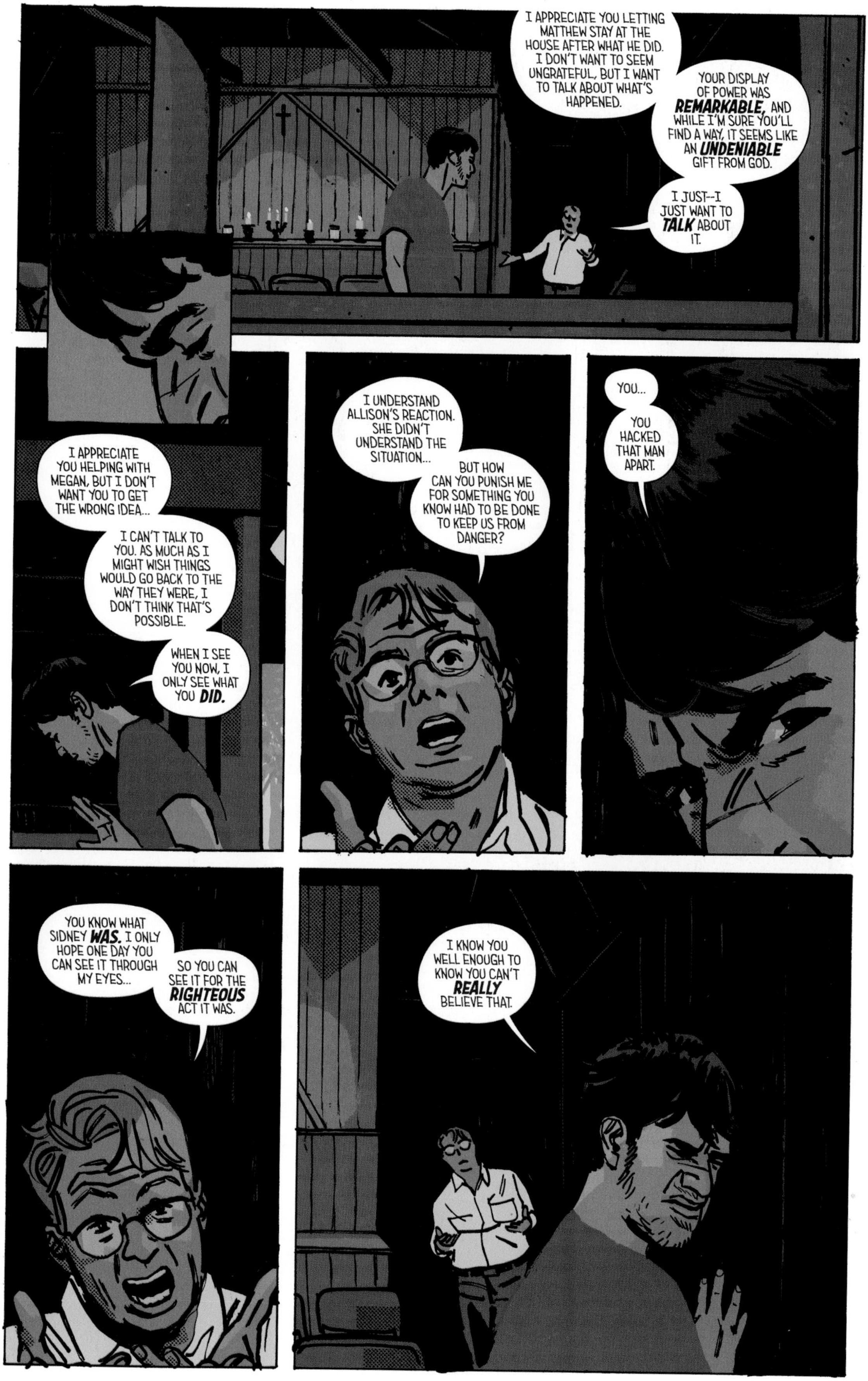
I APPRECIATE YOU LETTING MATTHEW STAY AT THE HOUSE AFTER WHAT HE DID. I DON'T WANT TO SEEM UNGRATEFUL, BUT I WANT TO TALK ABOUT WHAT'S HAPPENED.
YOUR DISPLAY OF POWER WAS REMARKABLE, AND WHILE I'M SURE YOU'LL FIND A WAY, IT SEEMS LIKE AN UNDENIABLE GIFT FROM GOD.
I JUST--I JUST WANT TO TALK ABOUT IT.
I APPRECIATE YOU HELPING WITH MEGAN, BUT I DON'T WANT YOU TO GET THE WRONG IDEA...
I CAN'T TALK TO YOU. AS MUCH AS I MIGHT WISH THINGS WOULD GO BACK TO THE WAY THEY WERE, I DON'T THINK THAT'S POSSIBLE.
WHEN I SEE YOU NOW, I ONLY SEE WHAT YOU DID.
I UNDERSTAND ALLISON'S REACTION. SHE DIDN'T UNDERSTAND THE SITUATION...
BUT HOW CAN YOU PUNISH ME FOR SOMETHING YOU KNOW HAD TO BE DONE TO KEEP US FROM DANGER?
YOU...
YOU HACKED THAT MAN APART.
YOU KNOW WHAT SIDNEY WAS. I ONLY HOPE ONE DAY YOU CAN SEE IT THROUGH MY EYES...
SO YOU CAN SEE IT FOR THE RIGHTEOUS ACT IT WAS.
I KNOW YOU WELL ENOUGH TO KNOW YOU CAN'T REALLY BELIEVE THAT.

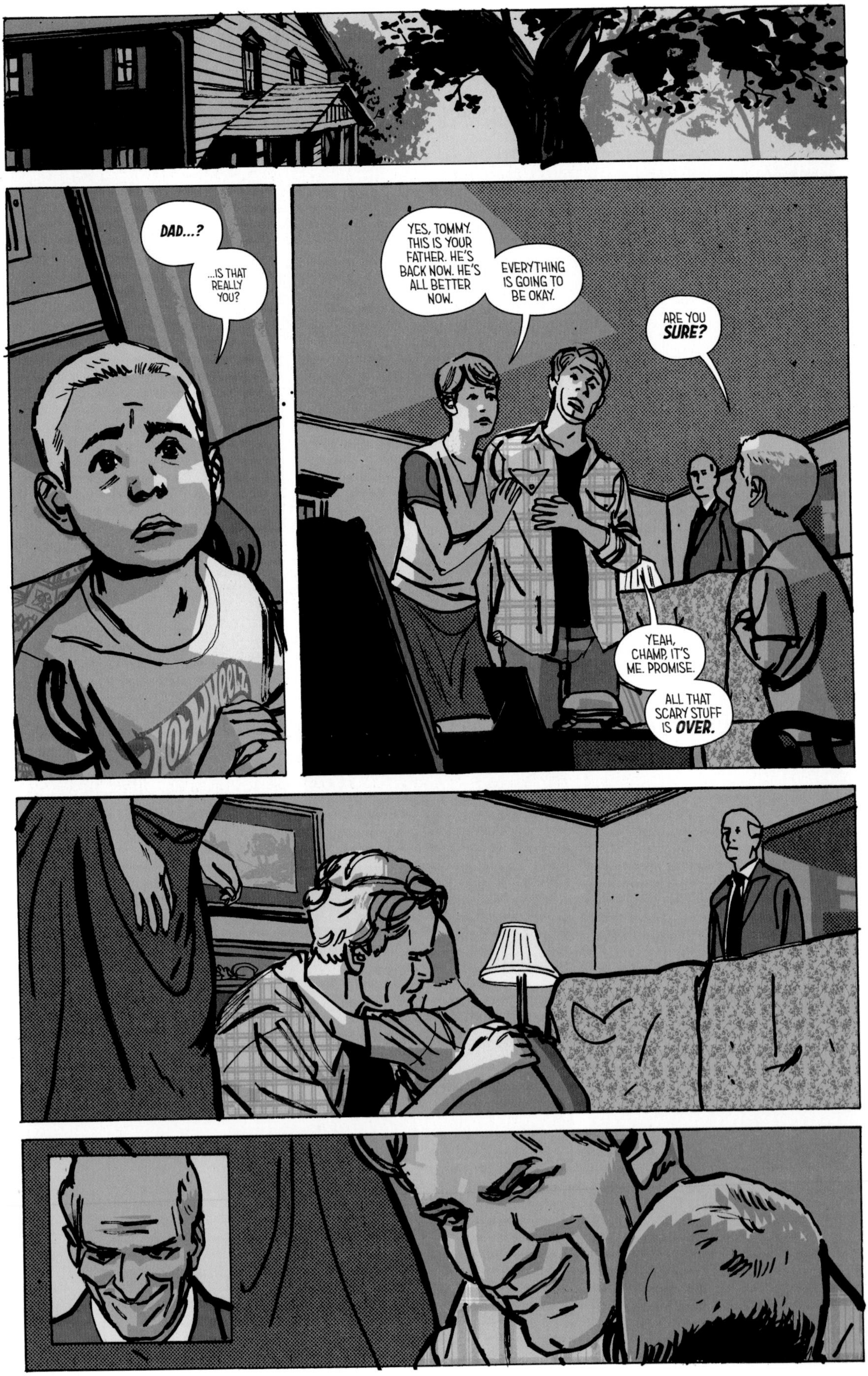
DAD...?
...IS THAT REALLY YOU?
YES, TOMMY. THIS IS YOUR FATHER. HE'S BACK NOW. HE'S ALL BETTER NOW.
EVERYTHING IS GOING TO BE OKAY.
ARE YOU SURE?
YEAH, CHAMP, IT'S ME. PROMISE.
ALL THAT SCARY STUFF IS OVER.

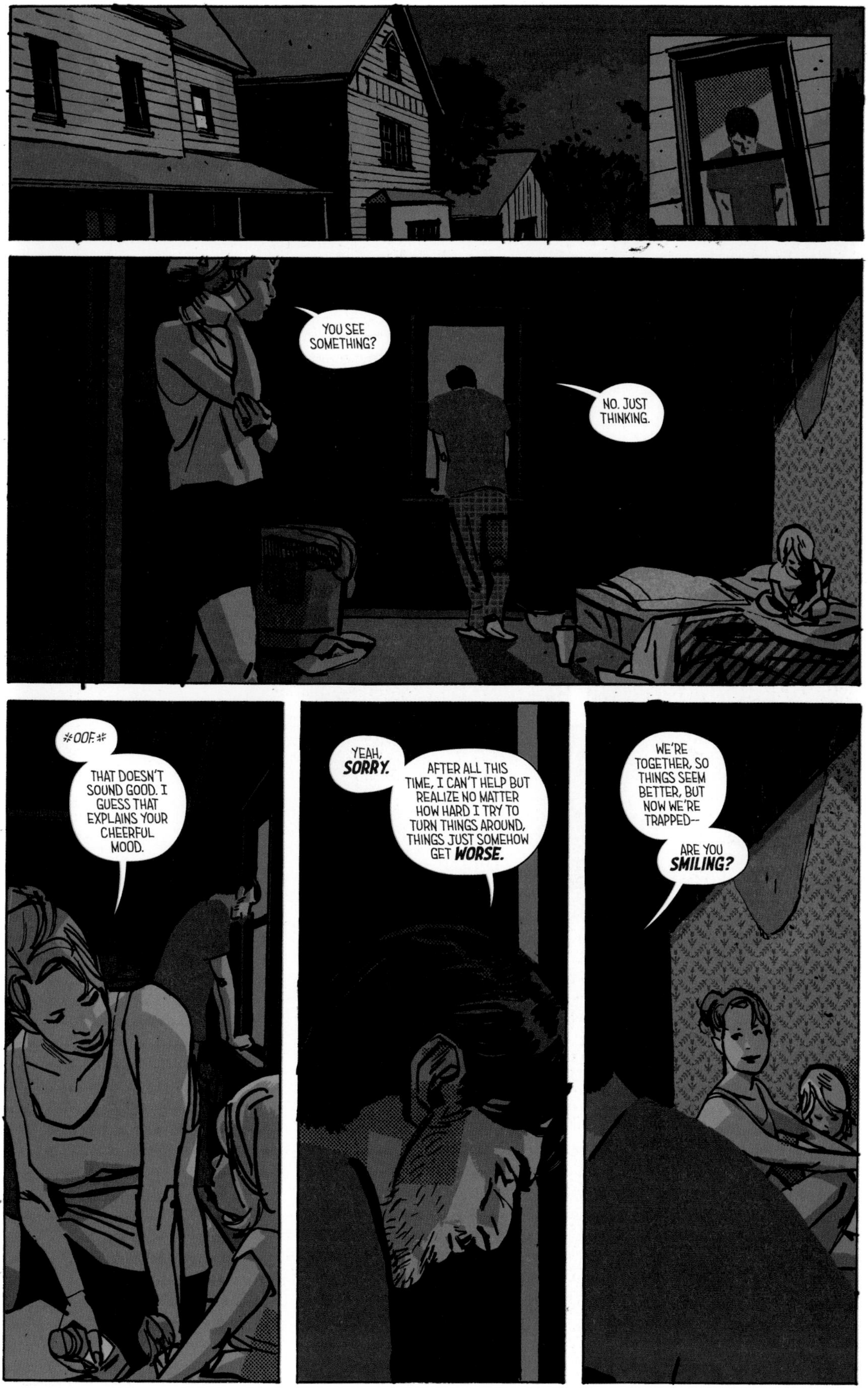
YOU SEE SOMETHING?
NO. JUST THINKING.
#OOF.#
THAT DOESN'T SOUND GOOD. I GUESS THAT EXPLAINS YOUR CHEERFUL MOOD.
YEAH, **SORRY.**
AFTER ALL THIS TIME, I CAN'T HELP BUT REALIZE NO MATTER HOW HARD I TRY TO TURN THINGS AROUND, THINGS JUST SOMEHOW GET **WORSE.**
WE'RE TOGETHER, SO THINGS SEEM BETTER, BUT NOW WE'RE TRAPPED--
ARE YOU **SMILING?**

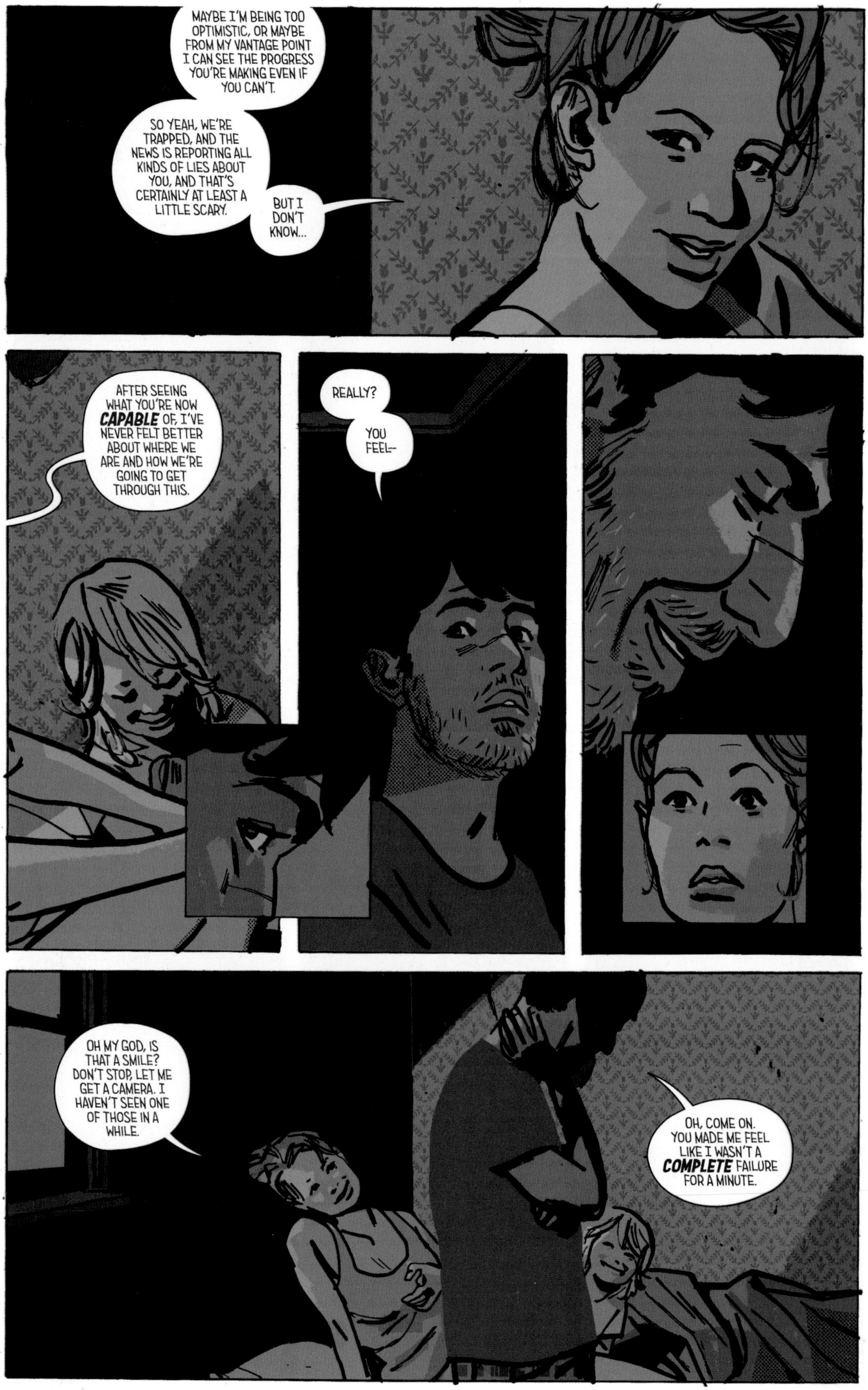
MAYBE I'M BEING TOO OPTIMISTIC, OR MAYBE FROM MY VANTAGE POINT I CAN SEE THE PROGRESS YOU'RE MAKING EVEN IF YOU CAN'T.
SO YEAH, WE'RE TRAPPED, AND THE NEWS IS REPORTING ALL KINDS OF LIES ABOUT YOU, AND THAT'S CERTAINLY AT LEAST A LITTLE SCARY.
BUT I DON'T KNOW...
AFTER SEEING WHAT YOU'RE NOW **CAPABLE** OF, I'VE NEVER FELT BETTER ABOUT WHERE WE ARE AND HOW WE'RE GOING TO GET THROUGH THIS.
REALLY?
YOU FEEL--
OH MY GOD, IS THAT A SMILE? DON'T STOP, LET ME GET A CAMERA. I HAVEN'T SEEN ONE OF THOSE IN A WHILE.
OH, COME ON. YOU MADE ME FEEL LIKE I WASN'T A **COMPLETE** FAILURE FOR A MINUTE.

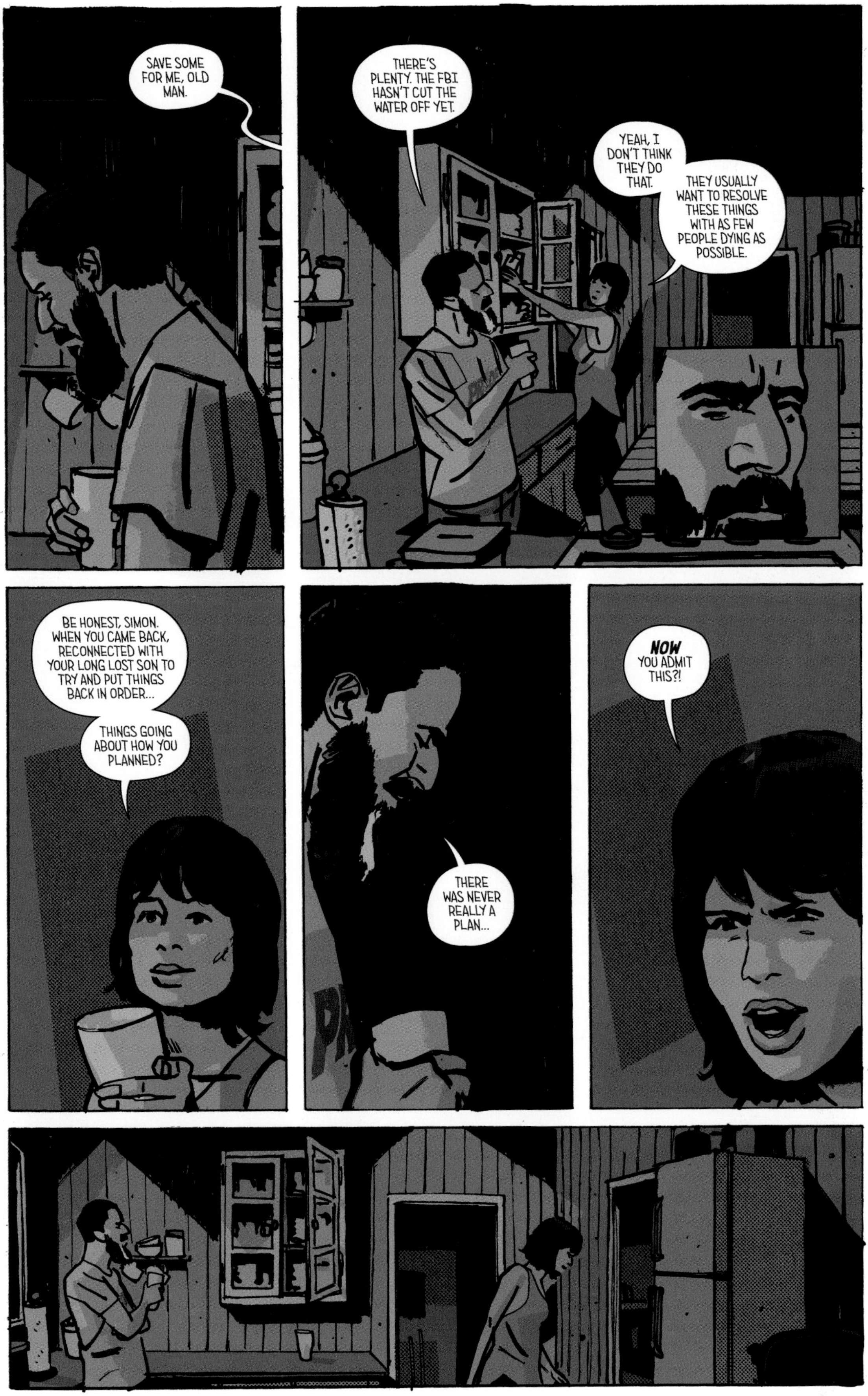

SAVE SOME FOR ME, OLD MAN.
THERE'S PLENTY. THE FBI HASN'T CUT THE WATER OFF YET.
YEAH, I DON'T THINK THEY DO THAT.
THEY USUALLY WANT TO RESOLVE THESE THINGS WITH AS FEW PEOPLE DYING AS POSSIBLE.
BE HONEST, SIMON. WHEN YOU CAME BACK, RECONNECTED WITH YOUR LONG LOST SON TO TRY AND PUT THINGS BACK IN ORDER...
THINGS GOING ABOUT HOW YOU PLANNED?
THERE WAS NEVER REALLY A PLAN...
NOW YOU ADMIT THIS?!

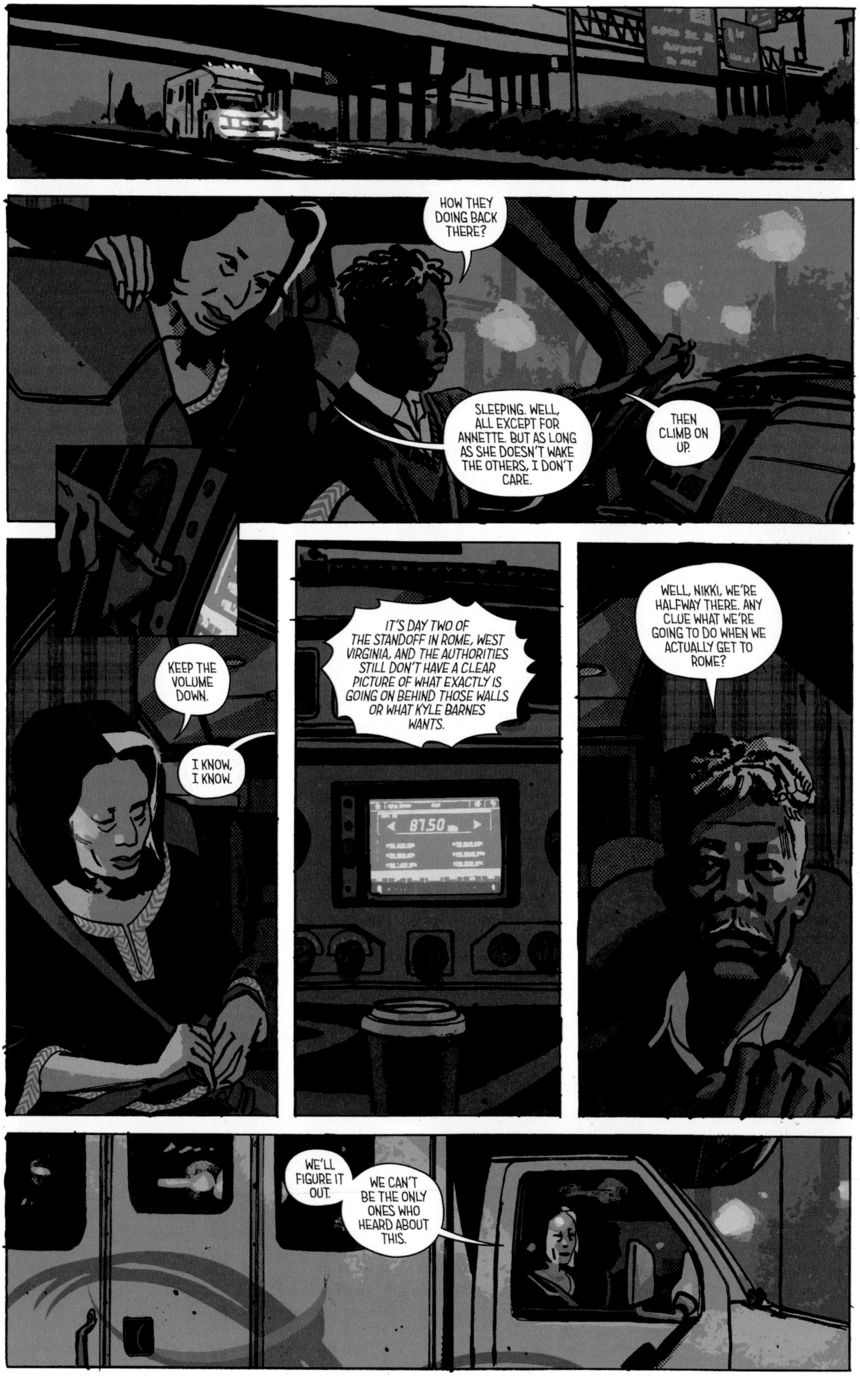
HOW THEY DOING BACK THERE?
SLEEPING. WELL, ALL EXCEPT FOR ANNETTE. BUT AS LONG AS SHE DOESN'T WAKE THE OTHERS, I DON'T CARE.
THEN CLIMB ON UP.
KEEP THE VOLUME DOWN.
I KNOW, I KNOW.
IT'S DAY TWO OF THE STANDOFF IN ROME, WEST VIRGINIA, AND THE AUTHORITIES STILL DON'T HAVE A CLEAR PICTURE OF WHAT EXACTLY IS GOING ON BEHIND THOSE WALLS OR WHAT KYLE BARNES WANTS.
87.50
WELL, NIKKI, WE'RE HALFWAY THERE. ANY CLUE WHAT WE'RE GOING TO DO WHEN WE ACTUALLY GET TO ROME?
WE'LL FIGURE IT OUT.
WE CAN'T BE THE ONLY ONES WHO HEARD ABOUT THIS.

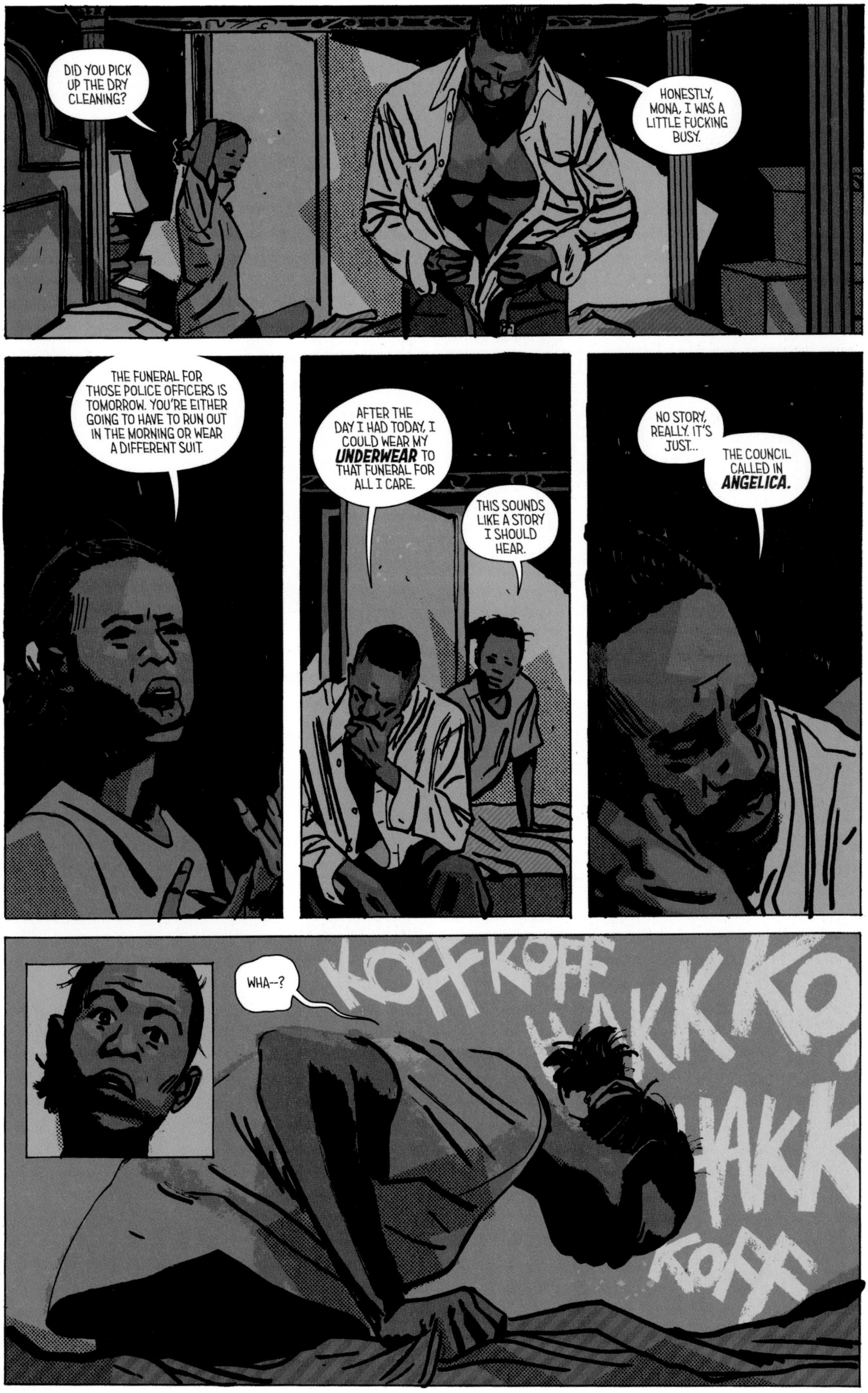
DID YOU PICK UP THE DRY CLEANING?
HONESTLY, MONA, I WAS A LITTLE FUCKING BUSY.
THE FUNERAL FOR THOSE POLICE OFFICERS IS TOMORROW. YOU'RE EITHER GOING TO HAVE TO RUN OUT IN THE MORNING OR WEAR A DIFFERENT SUIT.
AFTER THE DAY I HAD TODAY, I COULD WEAR MY **UNDERWEAR** TO THAT FUNERAL FOR ALL I CARE.
THIS SOUNDS LIKE A STORY I SHOULD HEAR.
NO STORY, REALLY. IT'S JUST...
THE COUNCIL CALLED IN ***ANGELICA.***
WHA--?
KOFF KOFF
HAKK
HAKK
KOFF

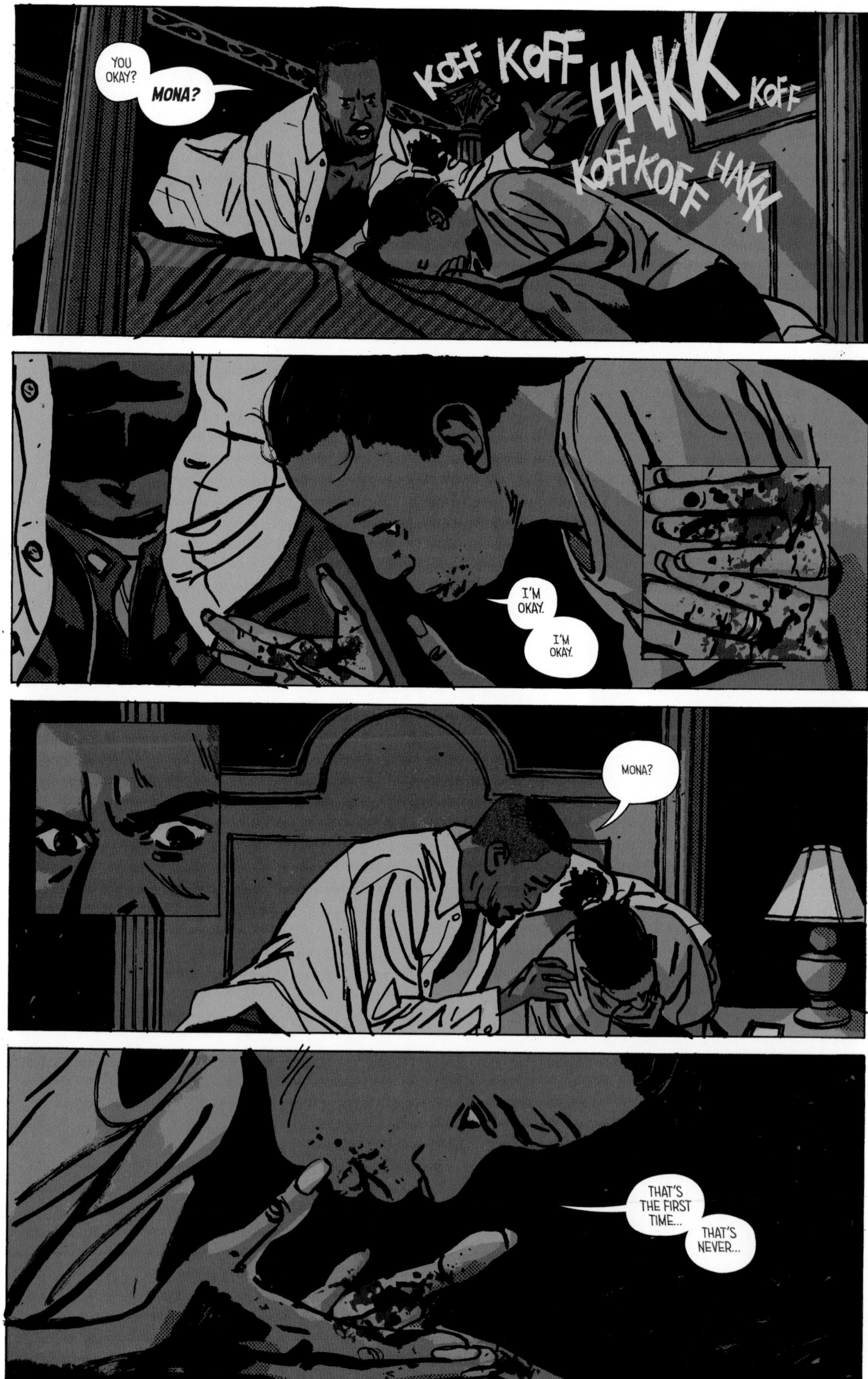
YOU OKAY? MONA?
KOFF KOFF HAKK KOFF
KOFF KOFF HAKK
I'M OKAY.
I'M OKAY.
MONA?
THAT'S THE FIRST TIME...
THAT'S NEVER...

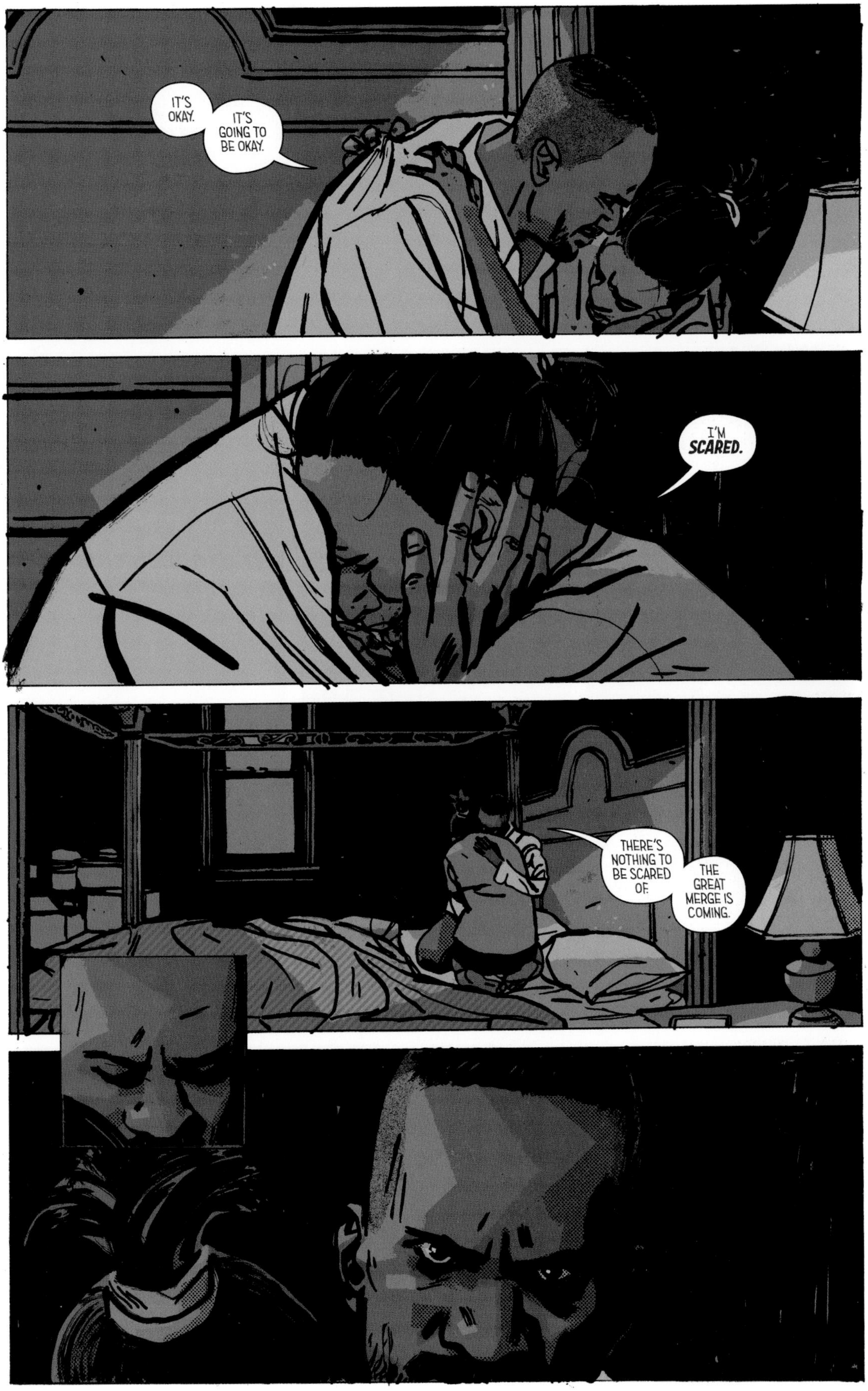
IT'S OKAY.
IT'S GOING TO BE OKAY.
I'M SCARED.
THERE'S NOTHING TO BE SCARED OF.
THE GREAT MERGE IS COMING.

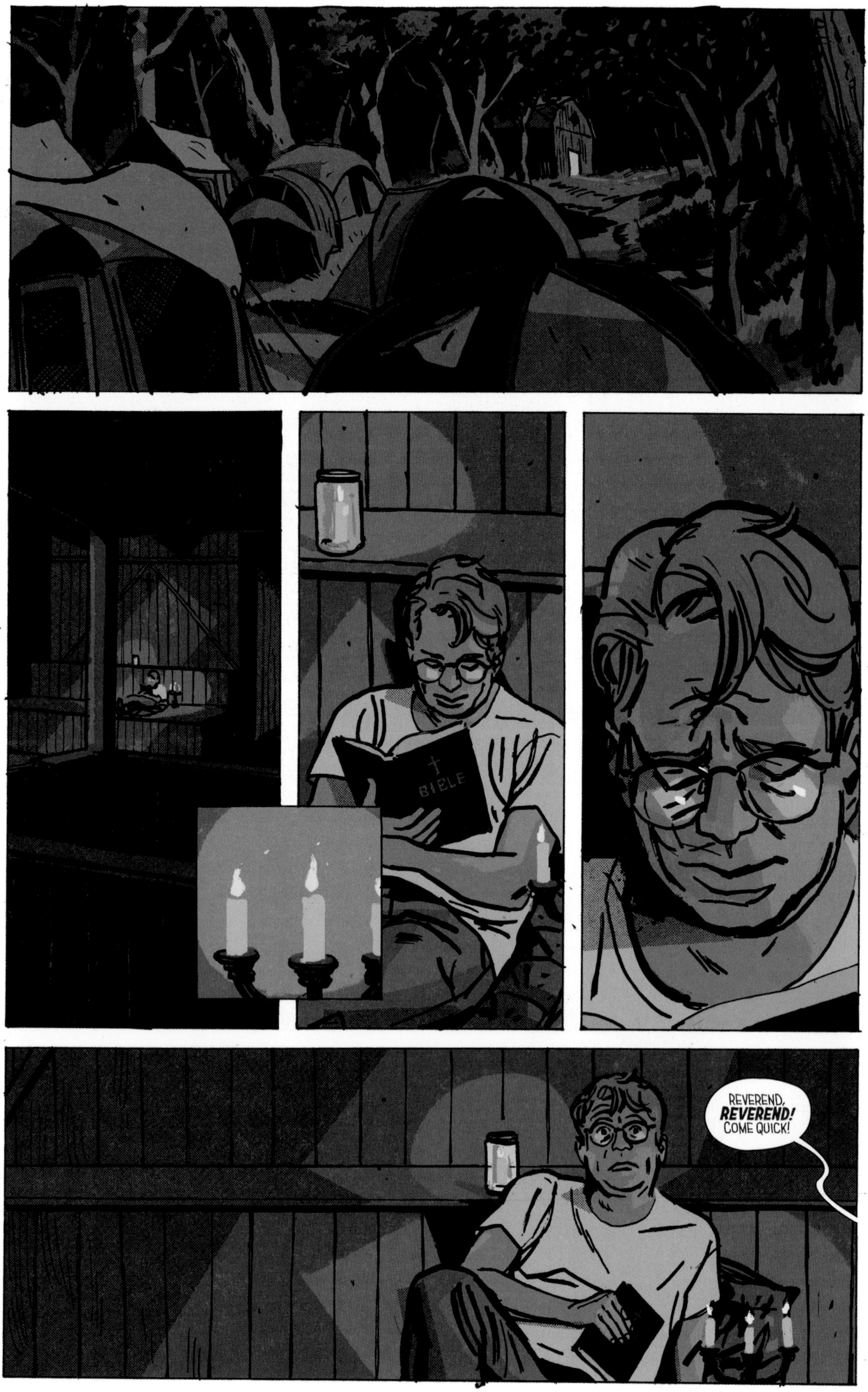
BIBLE
REVEREND, **REVEREND!** COME QUICK!

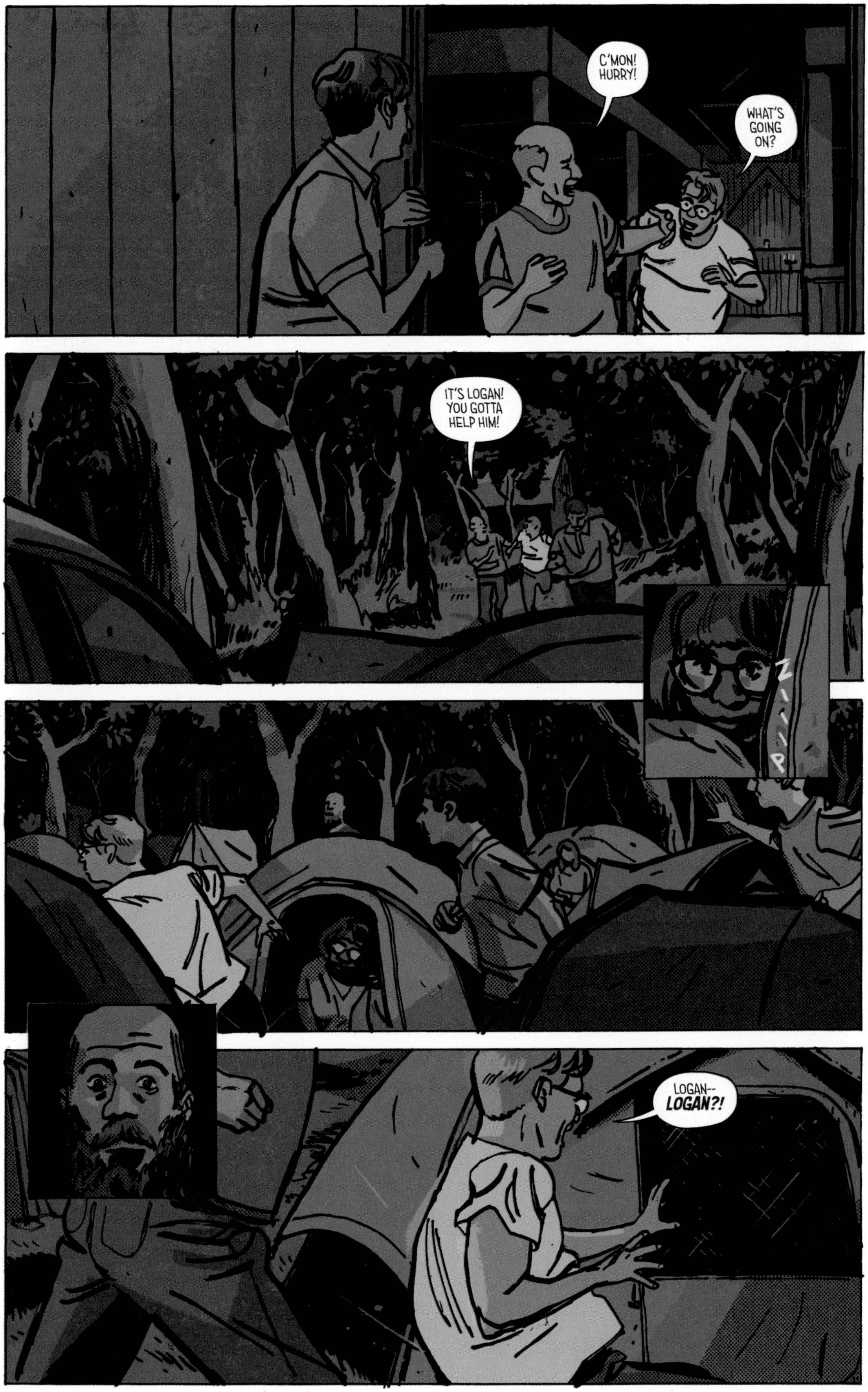
C'MON! HURRY!
WHAT'S GOING ON?
IT'S LOGAN! YOU GOTTA HELP HIM!
ZIIIP
LOGAN--
LOGAN?!

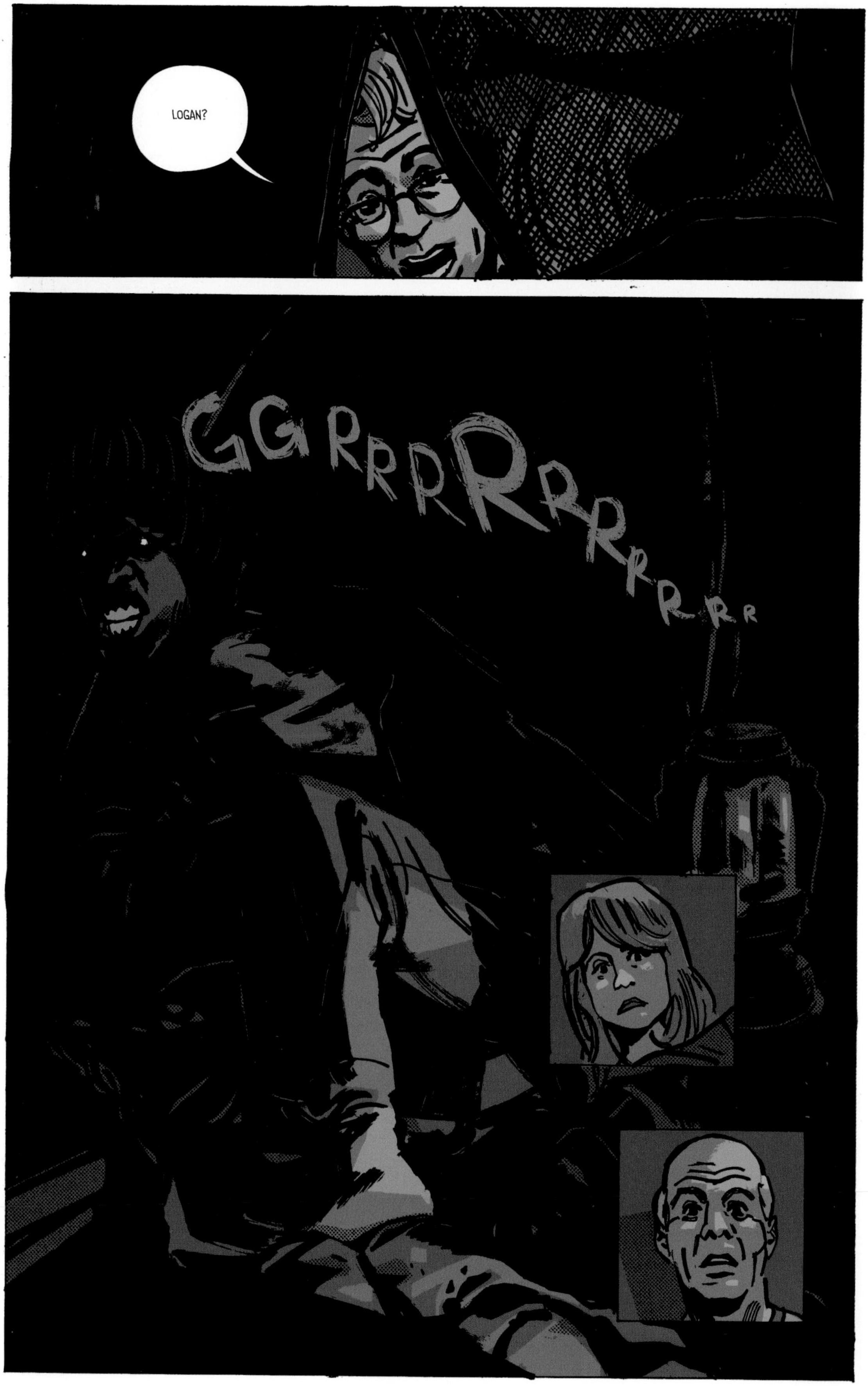

LOGAN?
GGRRRRRRRRRRRR

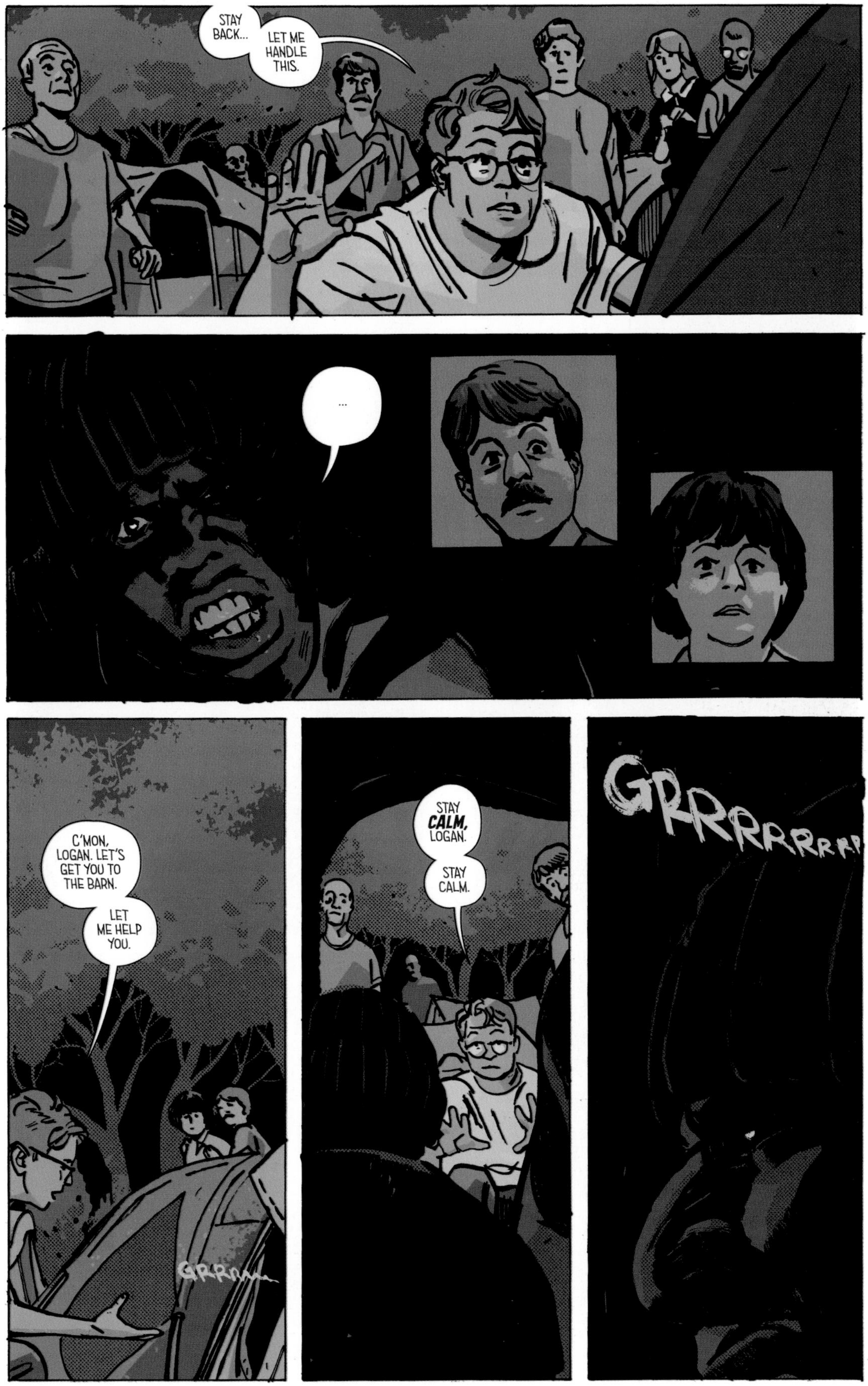
STAY BACK...
LET ME HANDLE THIS.
...
C'MON, LOGAN. LET'S GET YOU TO THE BARN.
LET ME HELP YOU.
GRRRR
STAY CALM, LOGAN.
STAY CALM.
GRRRRRRRRR

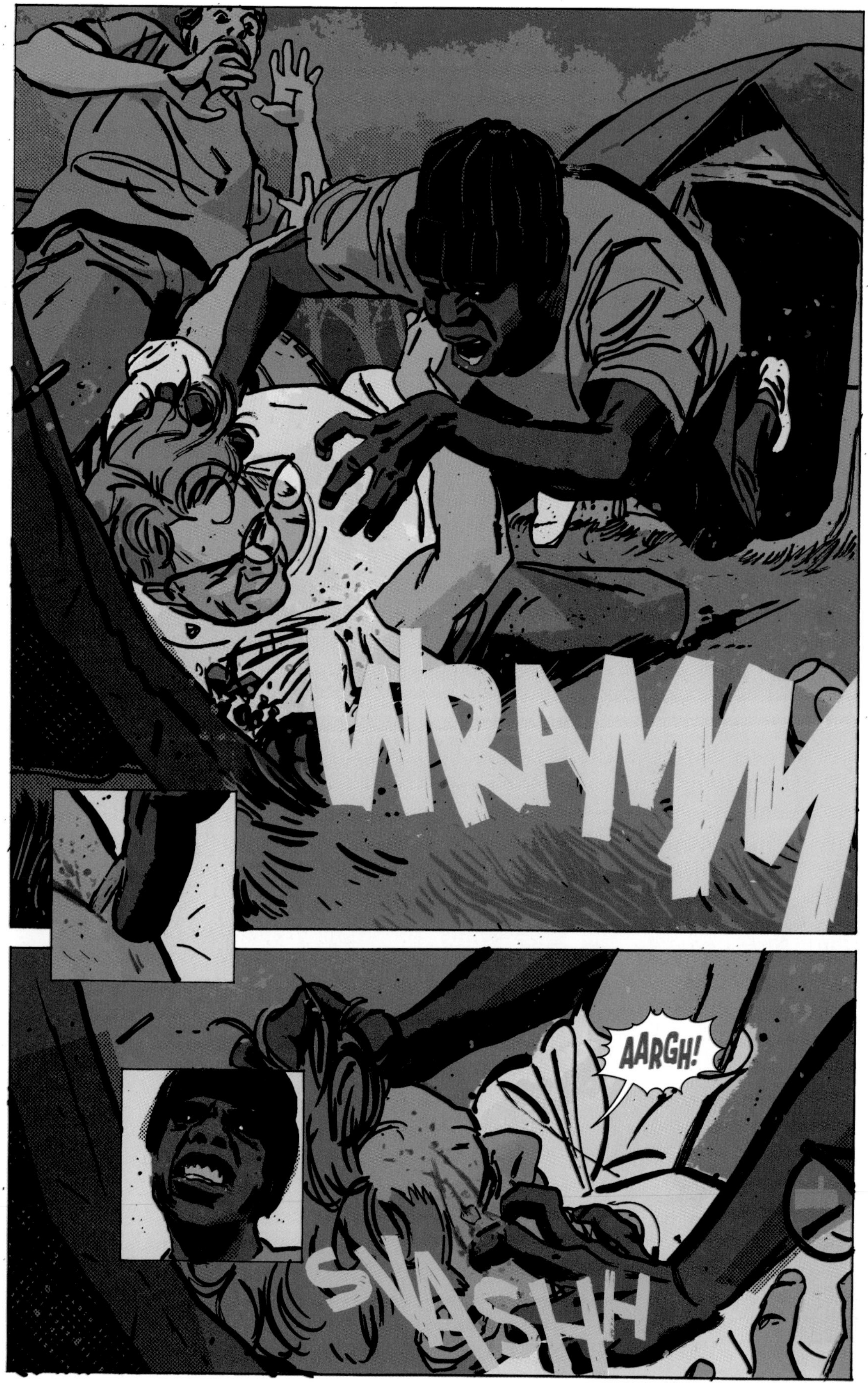
WRAMM
AARGH!
SVASHH

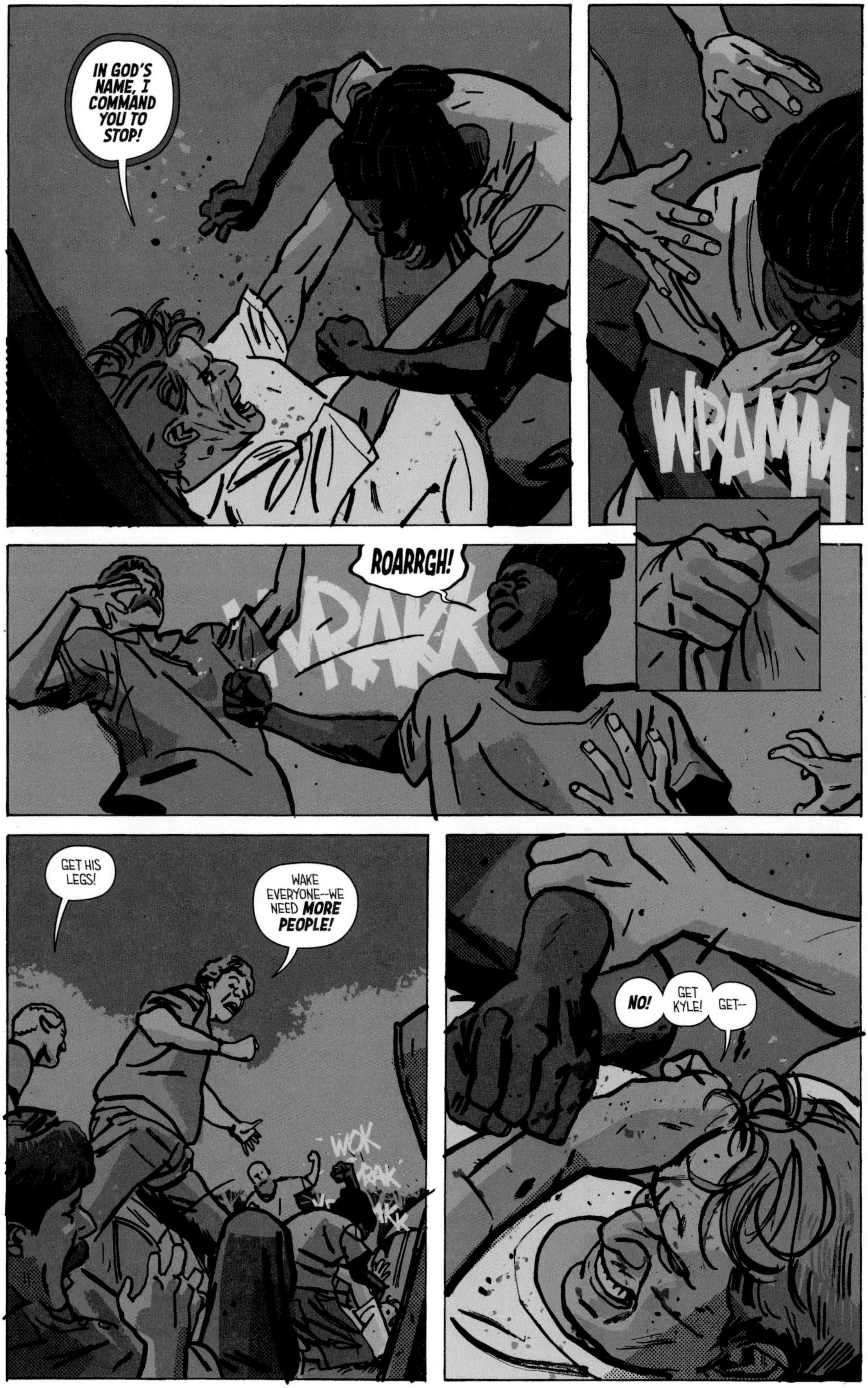
IN GOD'S NAME, I COMMAND YOU TO STOP!
WRAMM
ROARRGH!
WRAKK
GET HIS LEGS!
WAKE EVERYONE--WE NEED MORE PEOPLE!
WOK
WRAK
WAKK
NO!
GET KYLE!
GET--

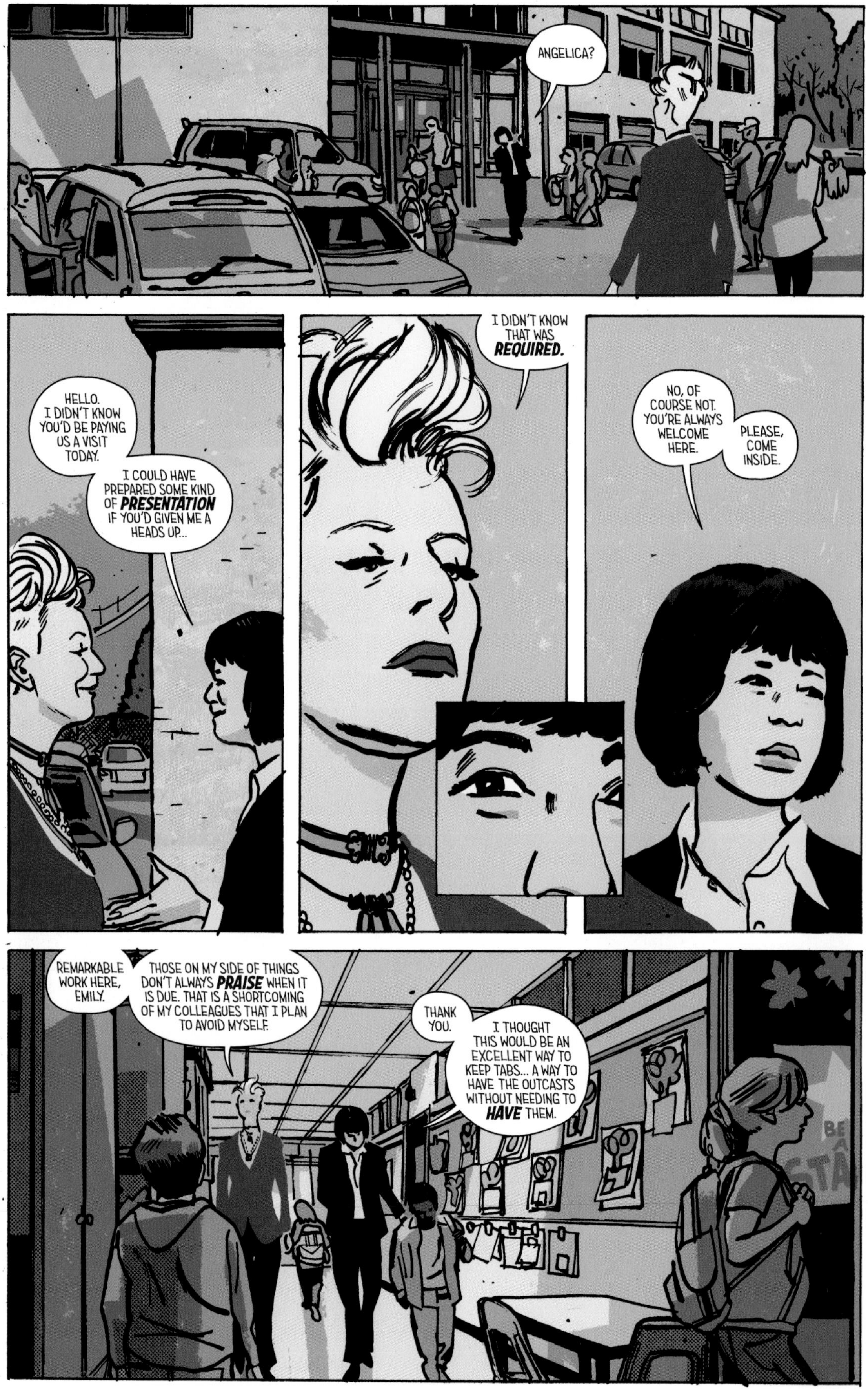

ANGELICA?
HELLO. I DIDN'T KNOW YOU'D BE PAYING US A VISIT TODAY.
I COULD HAVE PREPARED SOME KIND OF **PRESENTATION** IF YOU'D GIVEN ME A HEADS UP...
I DIDN'T KNOW THAT WAS **REQUIRED.**
NO, OF COURSE NOT. YOU'RE ALWAYS WELCOME HERE.
PLEASE, COME INSIDE.
REMARKABLE WORK HERE, EMILY.
THOSE ON MY SIDE OF THINGS DON'T ALWAYS **PRAISE** WHEN IT IS DUE. THAT IS A SHORTCOMING OF MY COLLEAGUES THAT I PLAN TO AVOID MYSELF.
THANK YOU.
I THOUGHT THIS WOULD BE AN EXCELLENT WAY TO KEEP TABS... A WAY TO HAVE THE OUTCASTS WITHOUT NEEDING TO **HAVE** THEM.

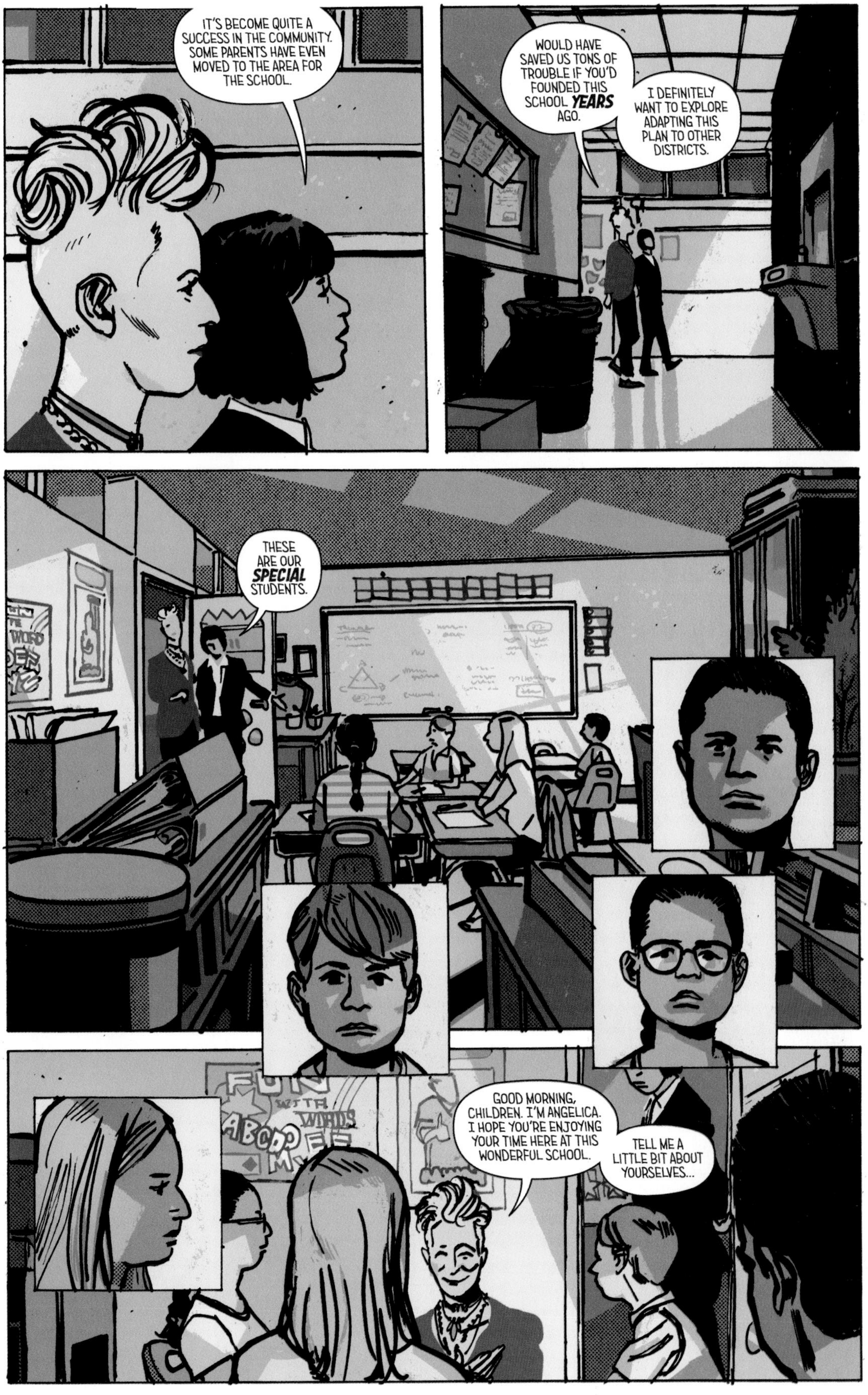
IT'S BECOME QUITE A SUCCESS IN THE COMMUNITY. SOME PARENTS HAVE EVEN MOVED TO THE AREA FOR THE SCHOOL.
WOULD HAVE SAVED US TONS OF TROUBLE IF YOU'D FOUNDED THIS SCHOOL *YEARS* AGO.
I DEFINITELY WANT TO EXPLORE ADAPTING THIS PLAN TO OTHER DISTRICTS.
THESE ARE OUR ***SPECIAL*** STUDENTS.
GOOD MORNING, CHILDREN. I'M ANGELICA. I HOPE YOU'RE ENJOYING YOUR TIME HERE AT THIS WONDERFUL SCHOOL.
TELL ME A LITTLE BIT ABOUT YOURSELVES...

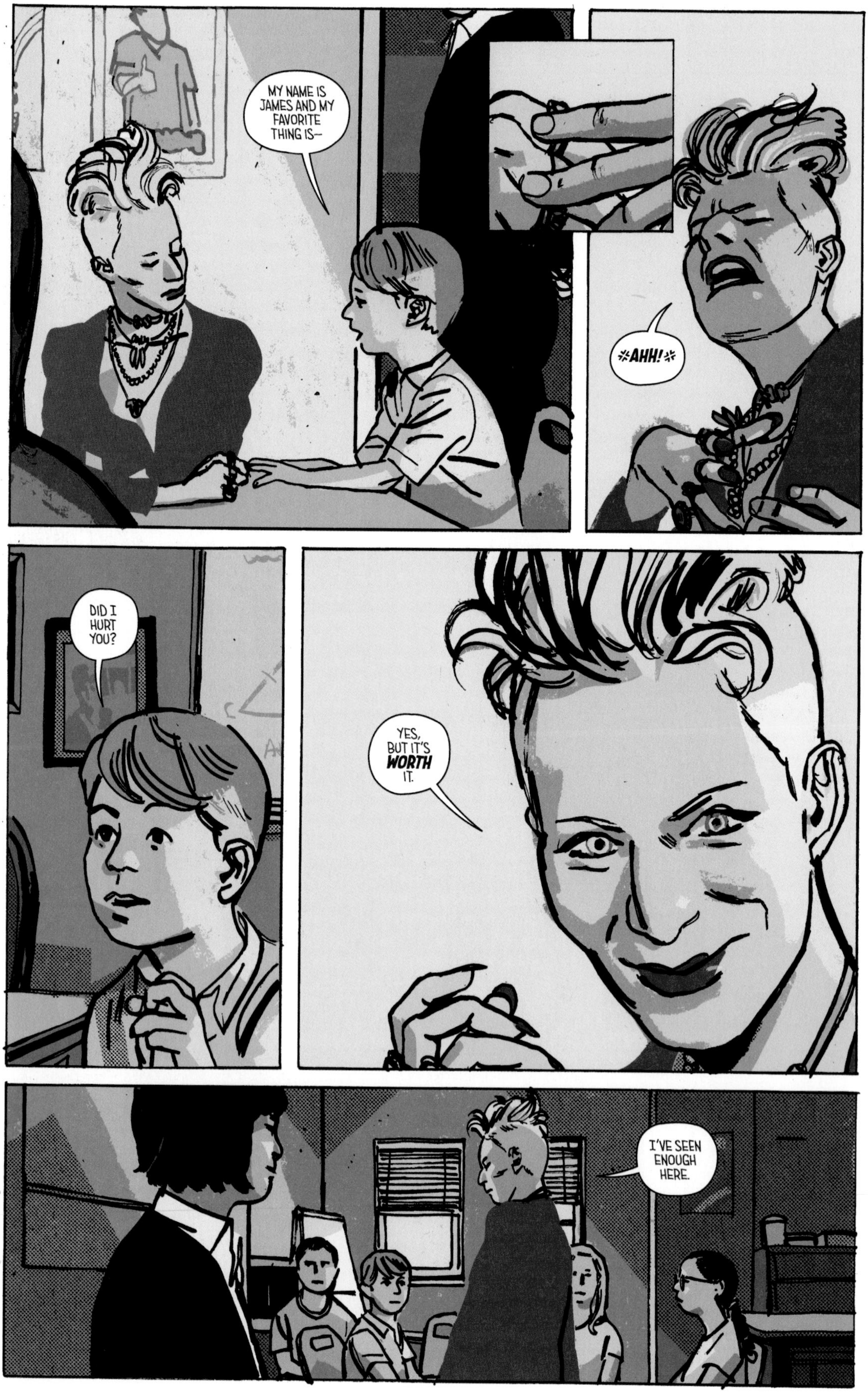
MY NAME IS JAMES AND MY FAVORITE THING IS--
AHH!
DID I HURT YOU?
YES, BUT IT'S **WORTH** IT.
I'VE SEEN ENOUGH HERE.

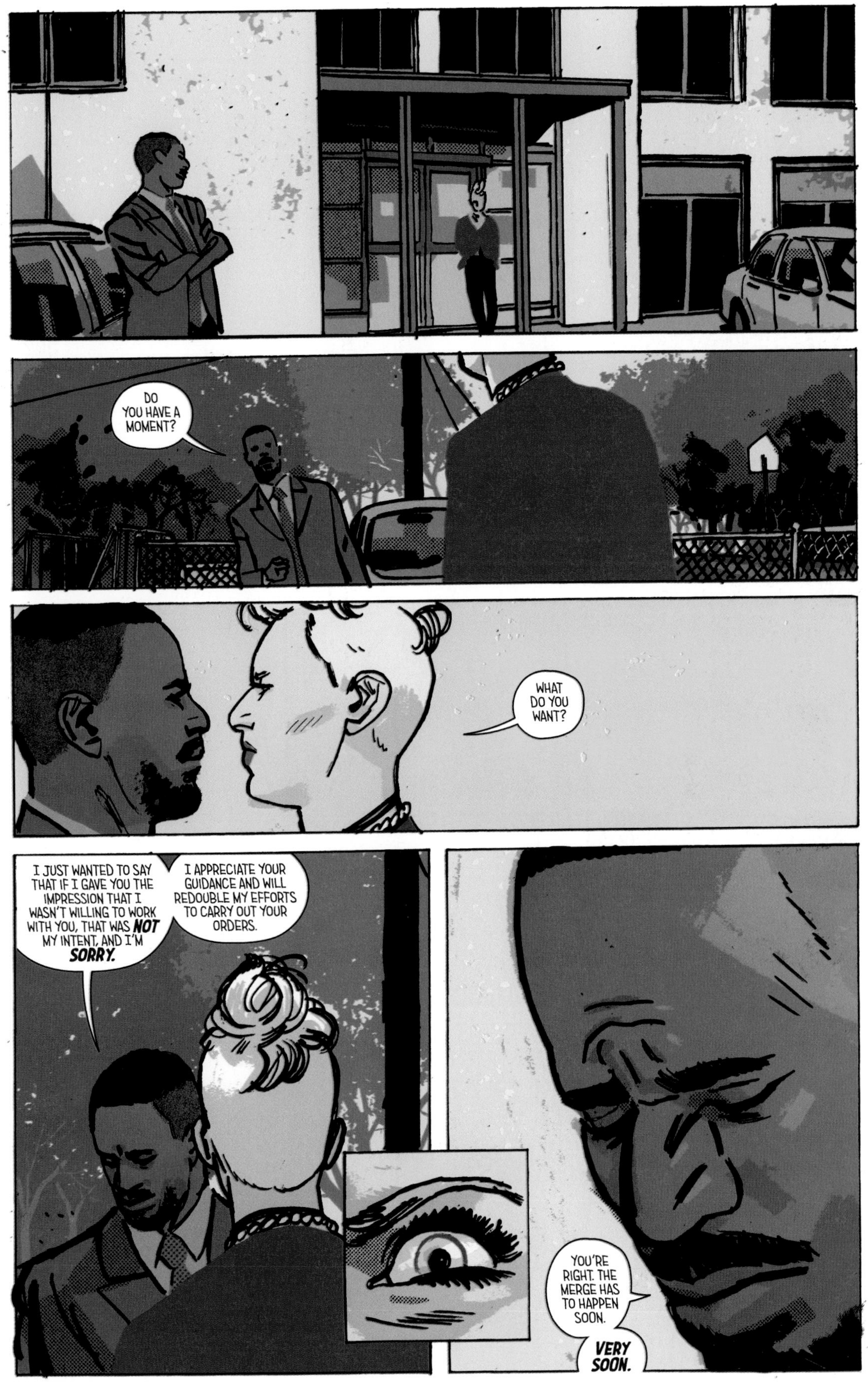
DO YOU HAVE A MOMENT?
WHAT DO YOU WANT?
I JUST WANTED TO SAY THAT IF I GAVE YOU THE IMPRESSION THAT I WASN'T WILLING TO WORK WITH YOU, THAT WAS **NOT** MY INTENT, AND I'M ***SORRY.***
I APPRECIATE YOUR GUIDANCE AND WILL REDOUBLE MY EFFORTS TO CARRY OUT YOUR ORDERS.
YOU'RE RIGHT. THE MERGE HAS TO HAPPEN SOON.
VERY SOON.

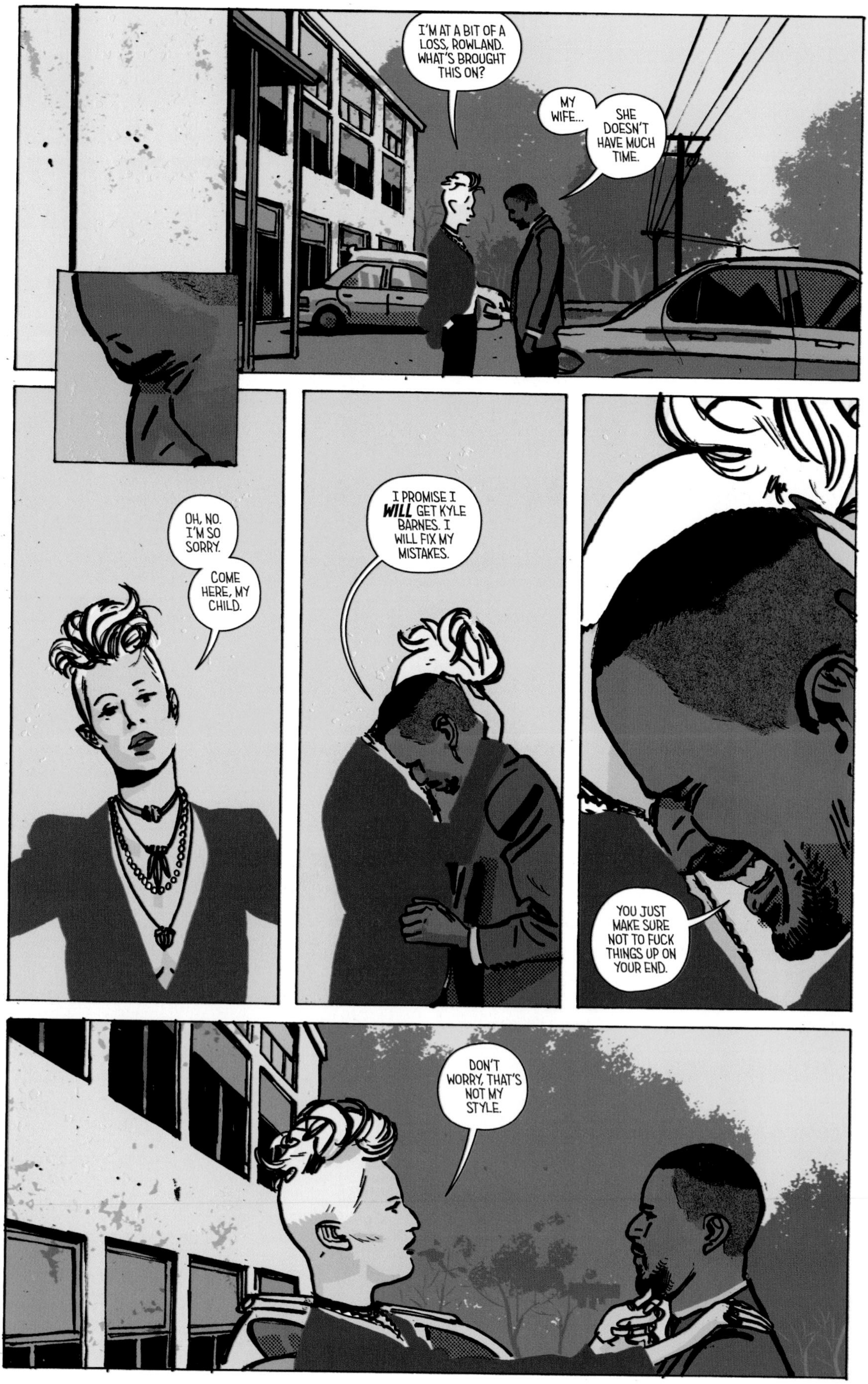
I'M AT A BIT OF A LOSS, ROWLAND. WHAT'S BROUGHT THIS ON?
MY WIFE...
SHE DOESN'T HAVE MUCH TIME.
OH, NO. I'M SO SORRY.
COME HERE, MY CHILD.
I PROMISE I *WILL* GET KYLE BARNES. I WILL FIX MY MISTAKES.
YOU JUST MAKE SURE NOT TO FUCK THINGS UP ON YOUR END.
DON'T WORRY, THAT'S NOT MY STYLE.

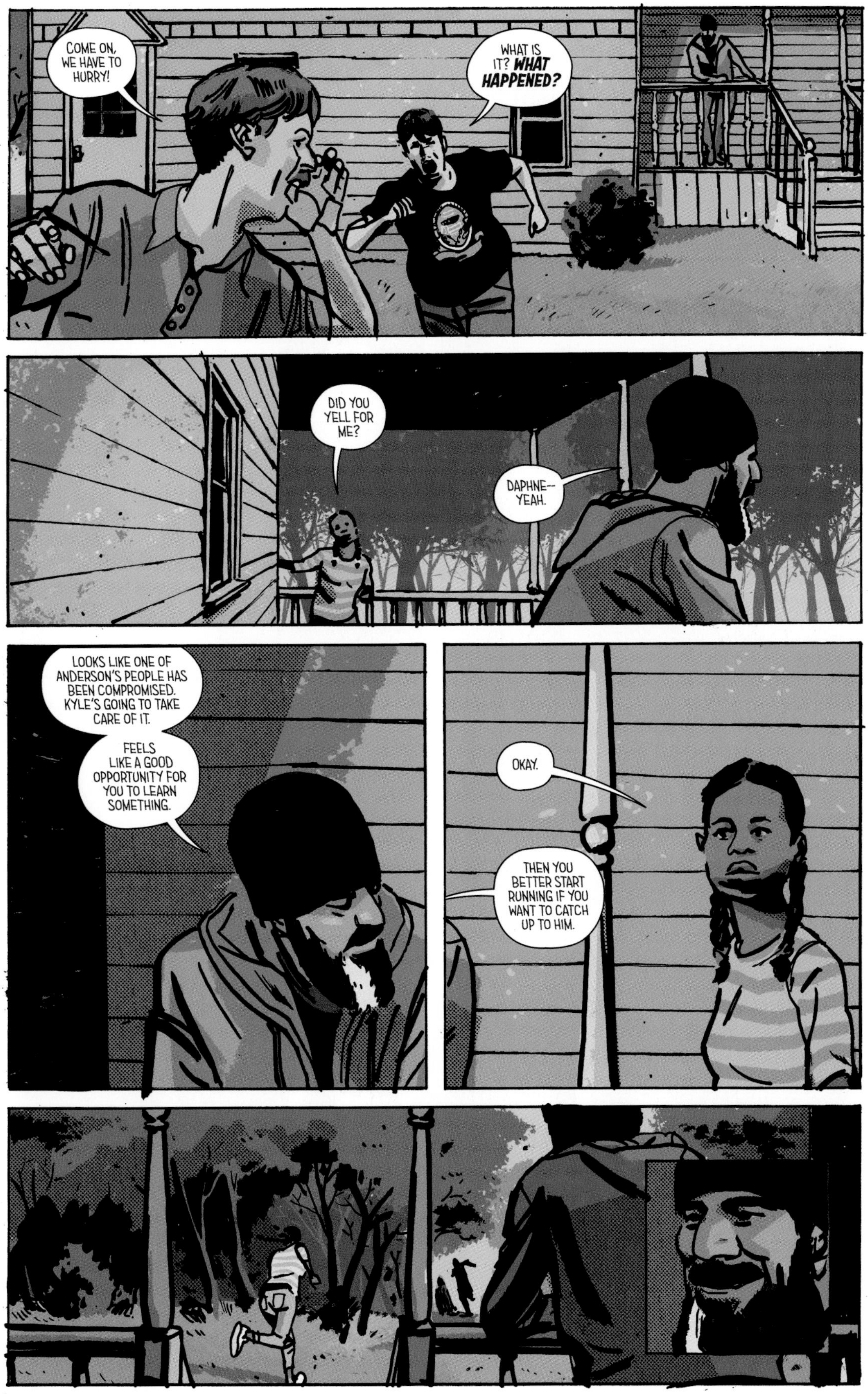
COME ON, WE HAVE TO HURRY!
WHAT IS IT? **WHAT HAPPENED?**
DID YOU YELL FOR ME?
DAPHNE-- YEAH.
LOOKS LIKE ONE OF ANDERSON'S PEOPLE HAS BEEN COMPROMISED. KYLE'S GOING TO TAKE CARE OF IT.
FEELS LIKE A GOOD OPPORTUNITY FOR YOU TO LEARN SOMETHING.
OKAY.
THEN YOU BETTER START RUNNING IF YOU WANT TO CATCH UP TO HIM.

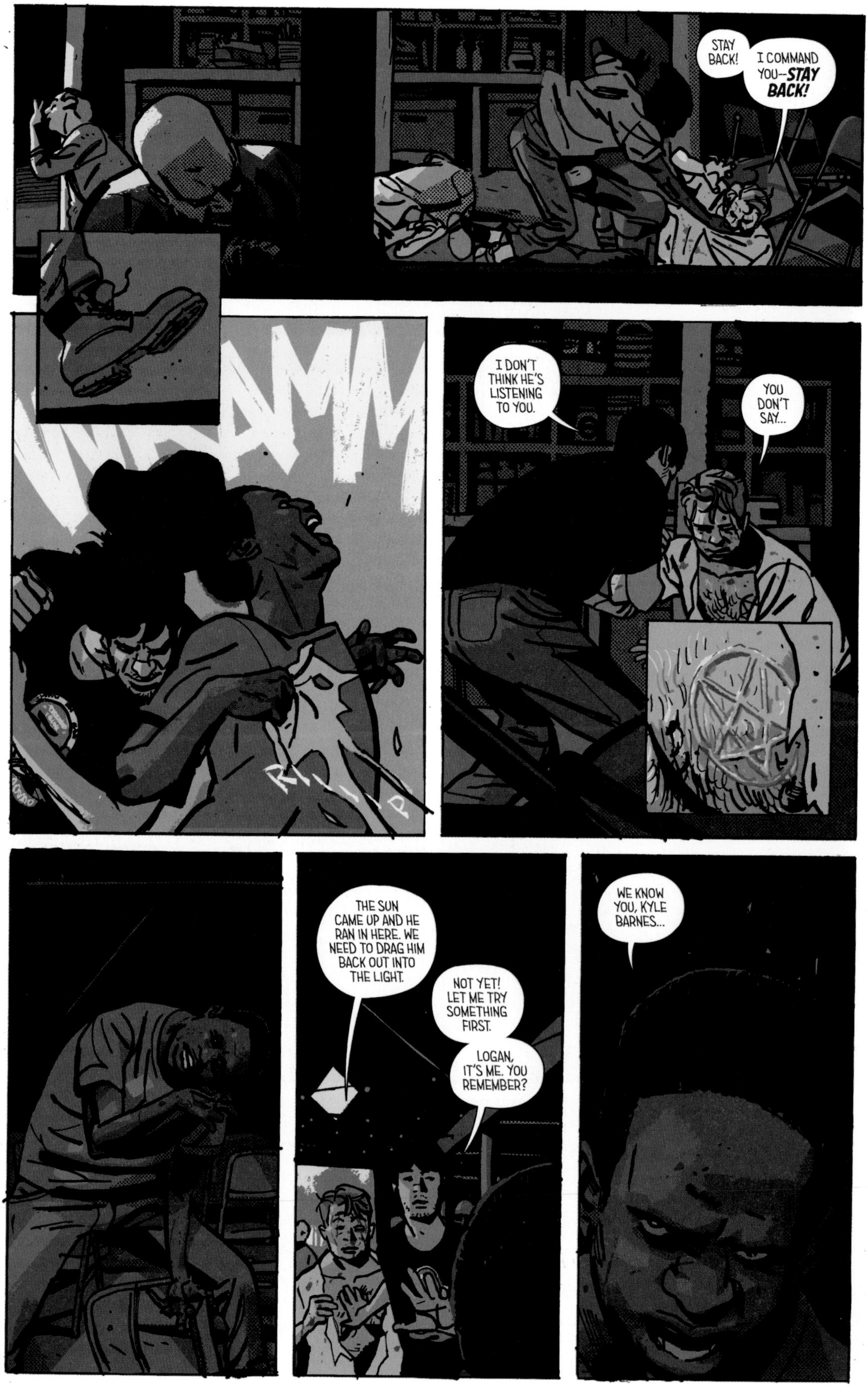
STAY BACK!
I COMMAND YOU--STAY BACK!
WHAMM
RIIIP
I DON'T THINK HE'S LISTENING TO YOU.
YOU DON'T SAY...
THE SUN CAME UP AND HE RAN IN HERE. WE NEED TO DRAG HIM BACK OUT INTO THE LIGHT.
NOT YET! LET ME TRY SOMETHING FIRST.
LOGAN, IT'S ME. YOU REMEMBER?
WE KNOW YOU, KYLE BARNES...

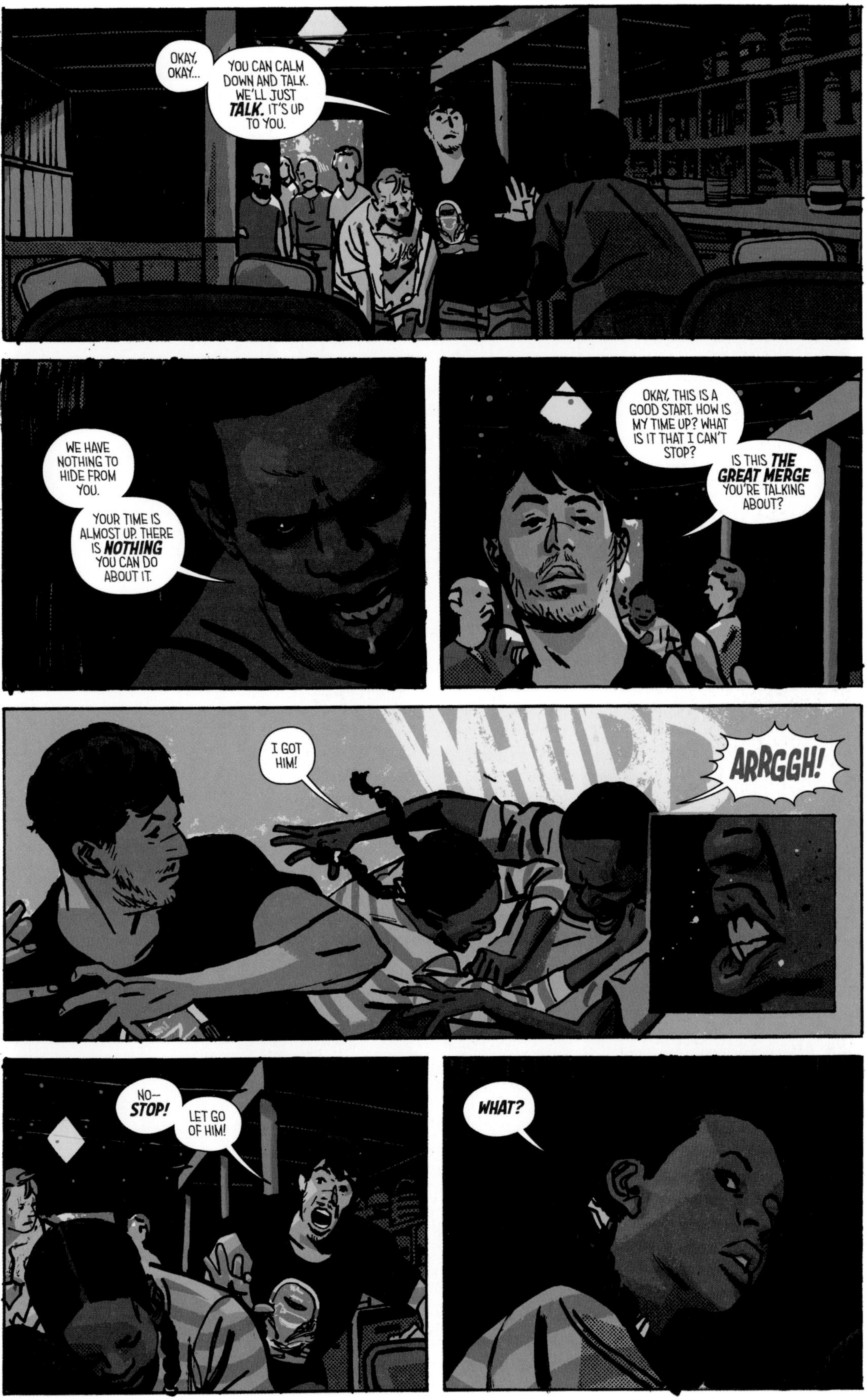

OKAY, OKAY...
YOU CAN CALM DOWN AND TALK. WE'LL JUST **TALK.** IT'S UP TO YOU.
WE HAVE NOTHING TO HIDE FROM YOU.
YOUR TIME IS ALMOST UP. THERE IS **NOTHING** YOU CAN DO ABOUT IT.
OKAY, THIS IS A GOOD START. HOW IS MY TIME UP? WHAT IS IT THAT I CAN'T STOP?
IS THIS **THE GREAT MERGE** YOU'RE TALKING ABOUT?
WHUD
I GOT HIM!
ARRGGH!
NO-- **STOP!**
LET GO OF HIM!
WHAT?

OUR PRESENCE... IT HELPS GIVE THEM CLARITY. THEY'RE NOT A DANGER TO US OR THE PEOPLE HERE. SO IF THEY'RE WILLING TO TALK, I WANT THEM TO TALK.

OKAY.

SORRY.

REVEREND, CAN YOU HELP HIM UP?

THIS MUST BE *TORTURE* FOR LOGAN.

WE CAN'T LEAVE HIM LIKE THIS FOR LONG.

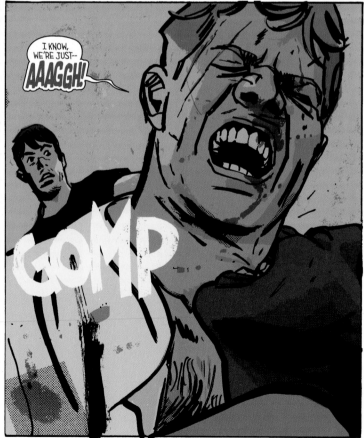

I KNOW, WE'RE JUST--

AAAGGH!

GOMP

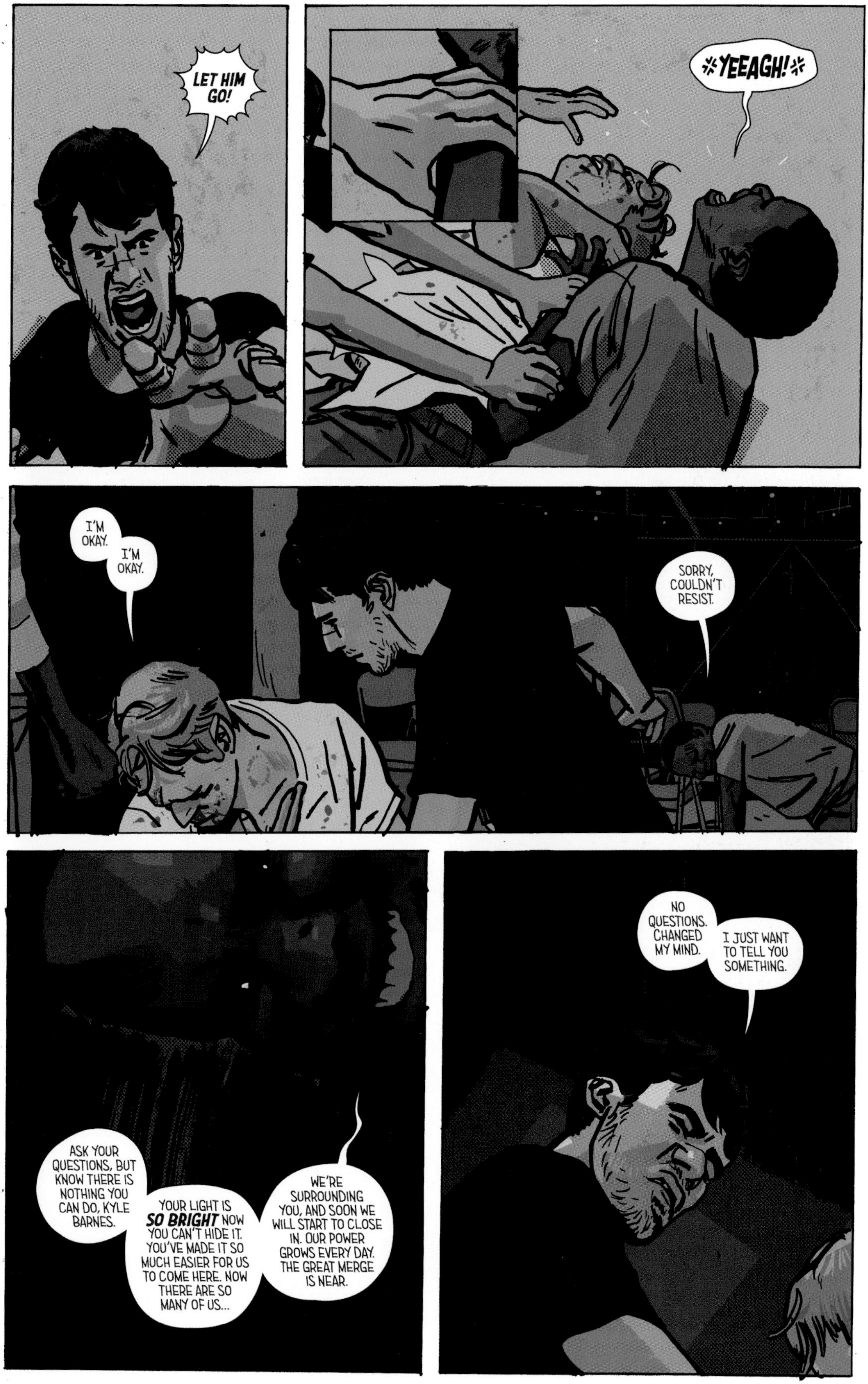
LET HIM GO!
YEEAGH!
I'M OKAY.
I'M OKAY.
SORRY, COULDN'T RESIST.
ASK YOUR QUESTIONS, BUT KNOW THERE IS NOTHING YOU CAN DO, KYLE BARNES.
YOUR LIGHT IS SO BRIGHT NOW YOU CAN'T HIDE IT. YOU'VE MADE IT SO MUCH EASIER FOR US TO COME HERE. NOW THERE ARE SO MANY OF US...
WE'RE SURROUNDING YOU, AND SOON WE WILL START TO CLOSE IN. OUR POWER GROWS EVERY DAY. THE GREAT MERGE IS NEAR.
NO QUESTIONS. CHANGED MY MIND.
I JUST WANT TO TELL YOU SOMETHING.

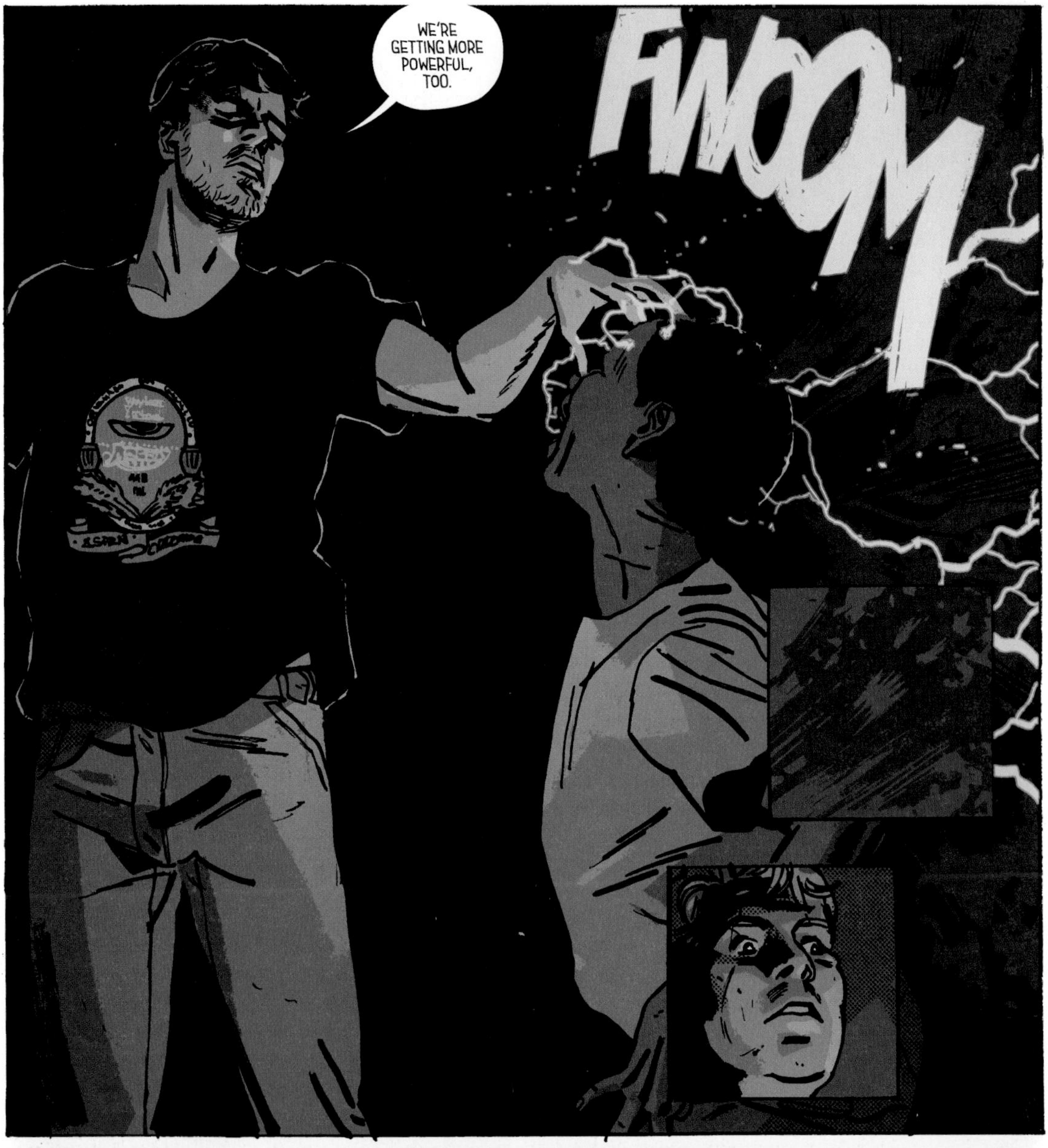
WE'RE GETTING MORE POWERFUL, TOO.
FWOOM

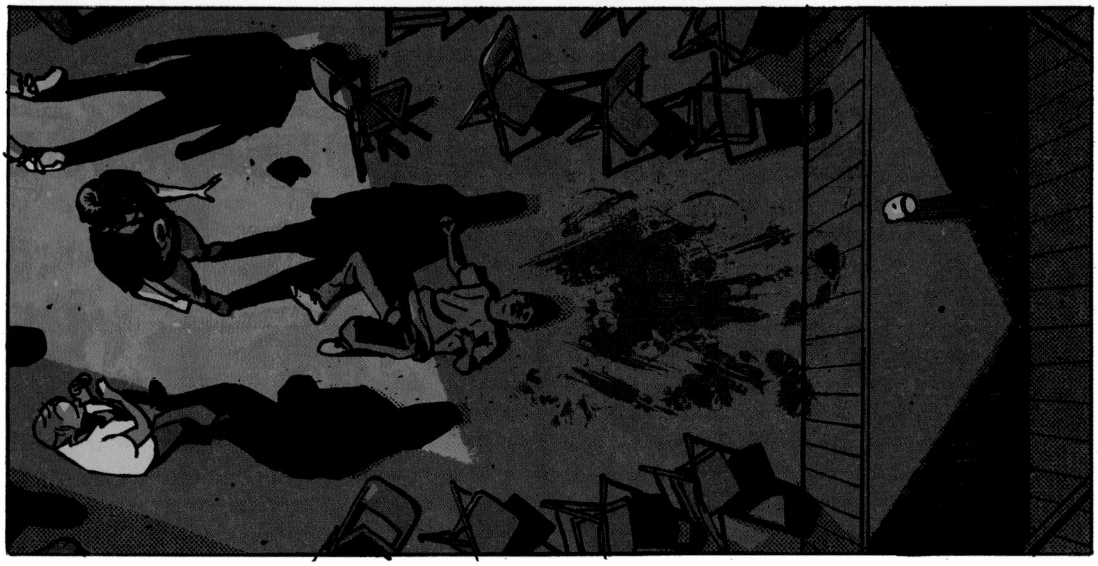

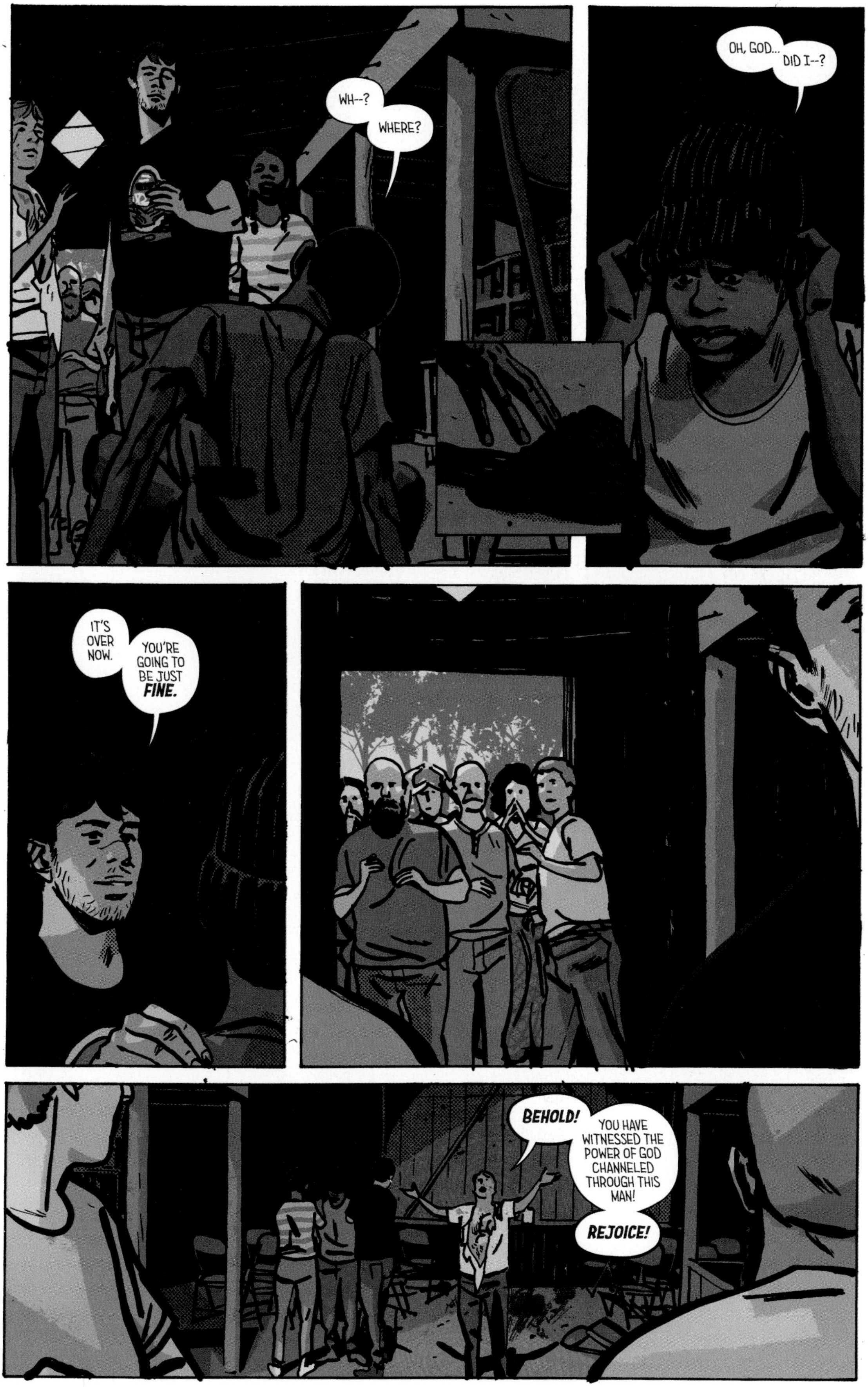
WH--?
WHERE?
OH, GOD... DID I--?
IT'S OVER NOW.
YOU'RE GOING TO BE JUST **FINE.**
BEHOLD!
YOU HAVE WITNESSED THE POWER OF GOD CHANNELED THROUGH THIS MAN!
REJOICE!

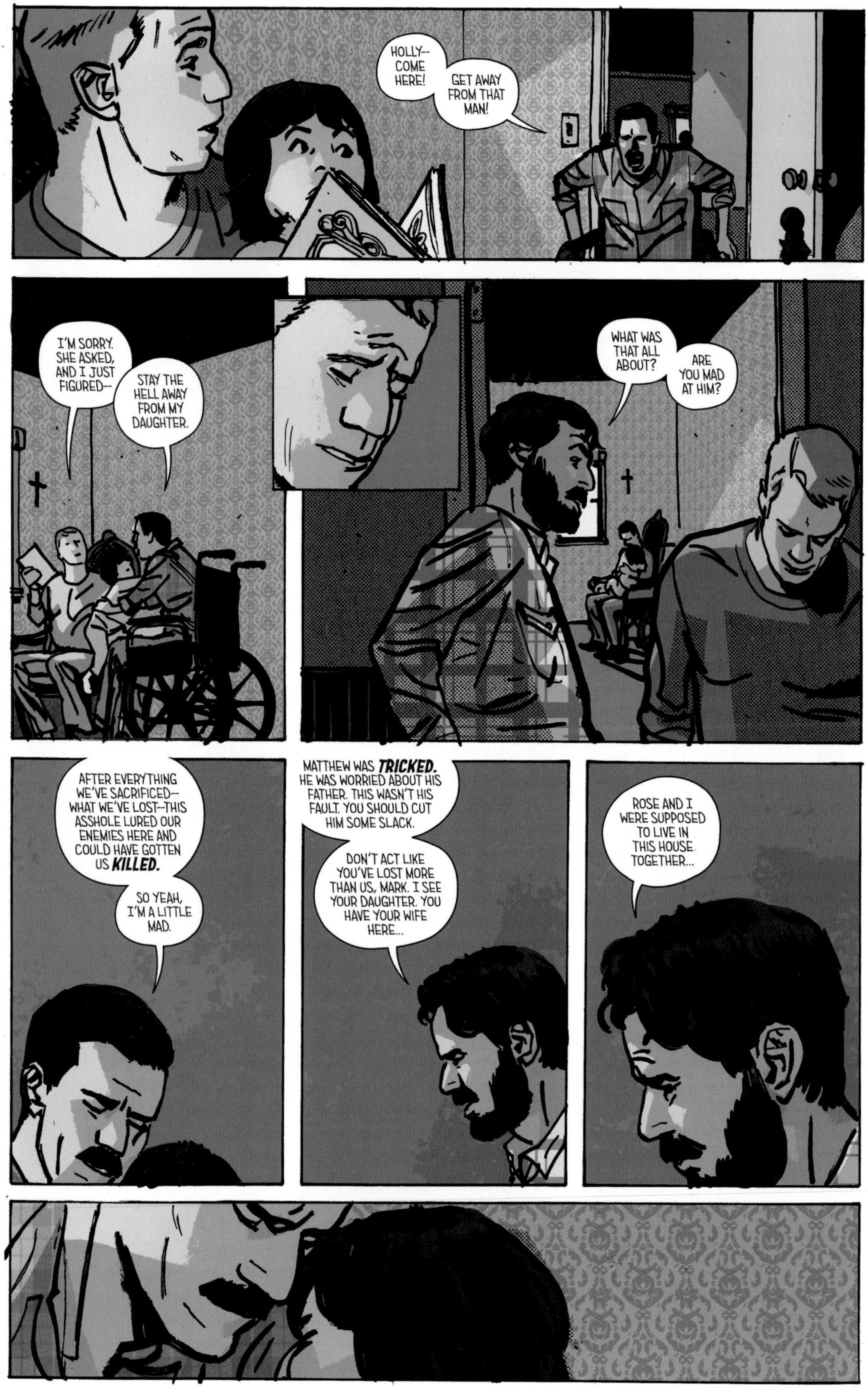
HOLLY-- COME HERE!
GET AWAY FROM THAT MAN!
I'M SORRY. SHE ASKED, AND I JUST FIGURED--
STAY THE HELL AWAY FROM MY DAUGHTER.
WHAT WAS THAT ALL ABOUT?
ARE YOU MAD AT HIM?
AFTER EVERYTHING WE'VE SACRIFICED-- WHAT WE'VE LOST--THIS ASSHOLE LURED OUR ENEMIES HERE AND COULD HAVE GOTTEN US KILLED.
SO YEAH, I'M A LITTLE MAD.
MATTHEW WAS TRICKED. HE WAS WORRIED ABOUT HIS FATHER. THIS WASN'T HIS FAULT. YOU SHOULD CUT HIM SOME SLACK.
DON'T ACT LIKE YOU'VE LOST MORE THAN US, MARK. I SEE YOUR DAUGHTER. YOU HAVE YOUR WIFE HERE...
ROSE AND I WERE SUPPOSED TO LIVE IN THIS HOUSE TOGETHER...

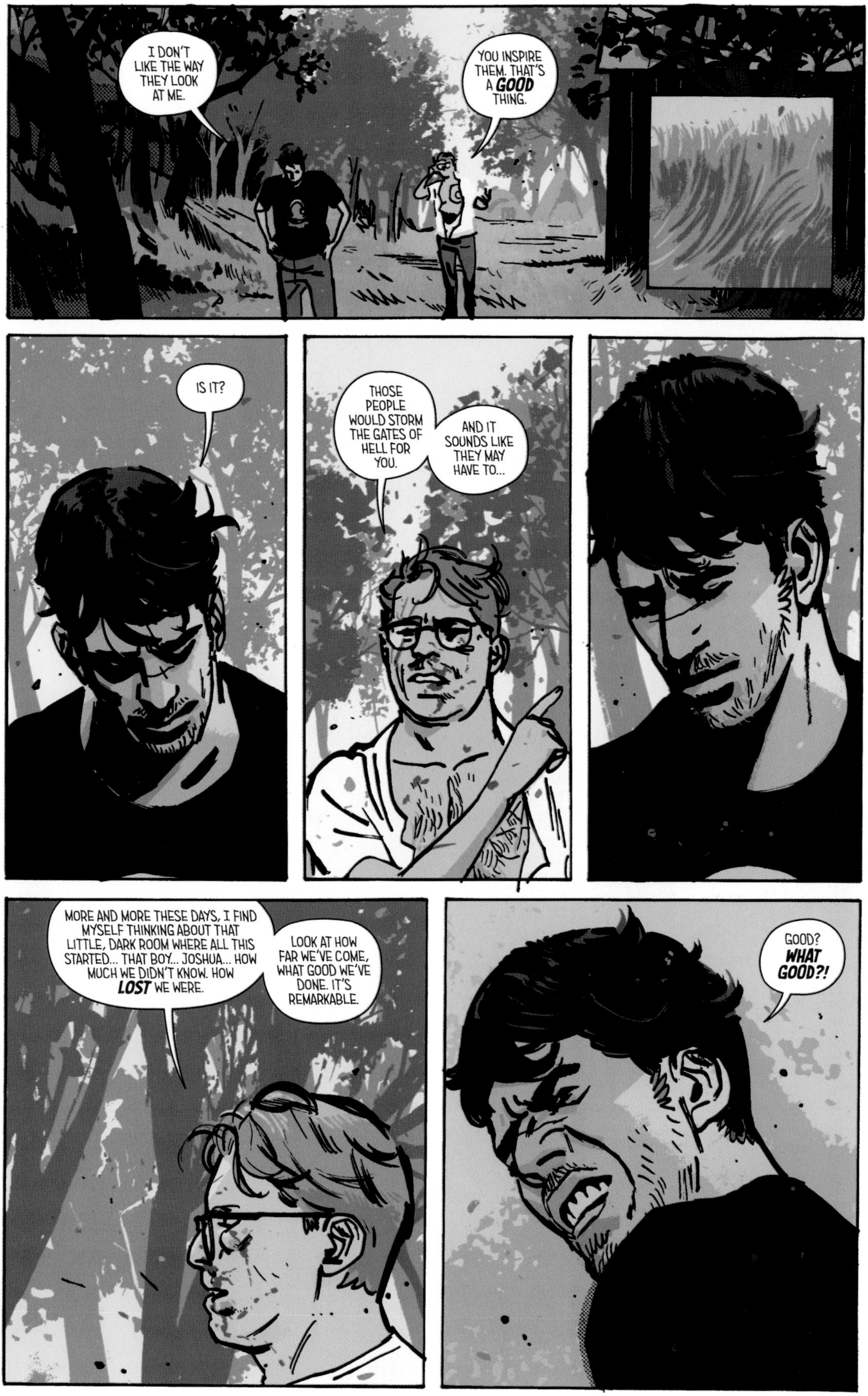
I DON'T LIKE THE WAY THEY LOOK AT ME.
YOU INSPIRE THEM. THAT'S A **GOOD** THING.
IS IT?
THOSE PEOPLE WOULD STORM THE GATES OF HELL FOR YOU.
AND IT SOUNDS LIKE THEY MAY HAVE TO...
MORE AND MORE THESE DAYS, I FIND MYSELF THINKING ABOUT THAT LITTLE, DARK ROOM WHERE ALL THIS STARTED... THAT BOY... JOSHUA... HOW MUCH WE DIDN'T KNOW. HOW **LOST** WE WERE.
LOOK AT HOW FAR WE'VE COME, WHAT GOOD WE'VE DONE. IT'S REMARKABLE.
GOOD? **WHAT GOOD?!**

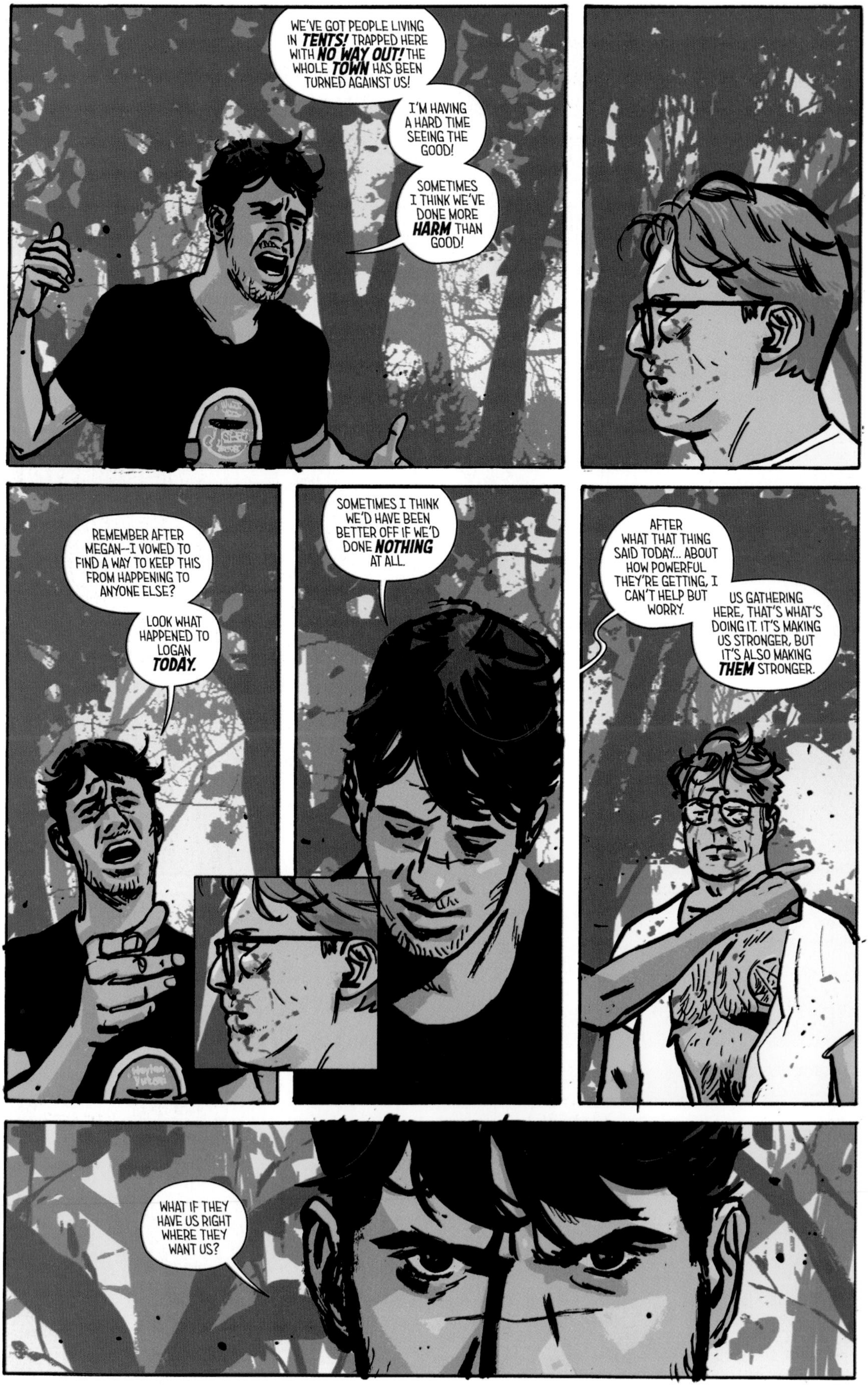
WE'VE GOT PEOPLE LIVING IN TENTS! TRAPPED HERE WITH NO WAY OUT! THE WHOLE TOWN HAS BEEN TURNED AGAINST US!
I'M HAVING A HARD TIME SEEING THE GOOD!
SOMETIMES I THINK WE'VE DONE MORE HARM THAN GOOD!
REMEMBER AFTER MEGAN--I VOWED TO FIND A WAY TO KEEP THIS FROM HAPPENING TO ANYONE ELSE?
LOOK WHAT HAPPENED TO LOGAN TODAY.
SOMETIMES I THINK WE'D HAVE BEEN BETTER OFF IF WE'D DONE NOTHING AT ALL.
AFTER WHAT THAT THING SAID TODAY... ABOUT HOW POWERFUL THEY'RE GETTING, I CAN'T HELP BUT WORRY.
US GATHERING HERE, THAT'S WHAT'S DOING IT. IT'S MAKING US STRONGER, BUT IT'S ALSO MAKING THEM STRONGER.
WHAT IF THEY HAVE US RIGHT WHERE THEY WANT US?

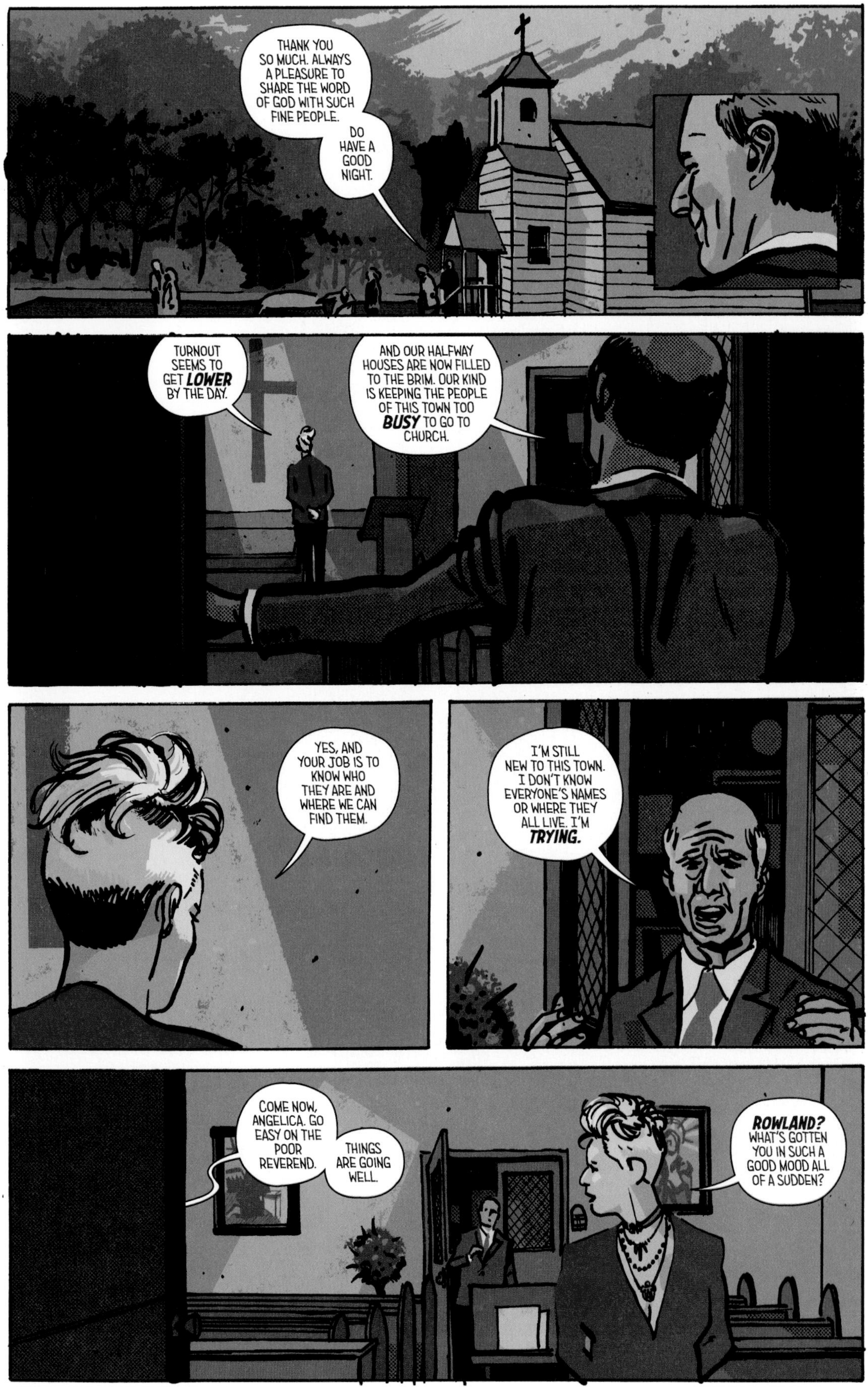
THANK YOU SO MUCH. ALWAYS A PLEASURE TO SHARE THE WORD OF GOD WITH SUCH FINE PEOPLE.
DO HAVE A GOOD NIGHT.
TURNOUT SEEMS TO GET LOWER BY THE DAY.
AND OUR HALFWAY HOUSES ARE NOW FILLED TO THE BRIM. OUR KIND IS KEEPING THE PEOPLE OF THIS TOWN TOO BUSY TO GO TO CHURCH.
YES, AND YOUR JOB IS TO KNOW WHO THEY ARE AND WHERE WE CAN FIND THEM.
I'M STILL NEW TO THIS TOWN. I DON'T KNOW EVERYONE'S NAMES OR WHERE THEY ALL LIVE. I'M TRYING.
COME NOW, ANGELICA. GO EASY ON THE POOR REVEREND.
THINGS ARE GOING WELL.
ROWLAND? WHAT'S GOTTEN YOU IN SUCH A GOOD MOOD ALL OF A SUDDEN?

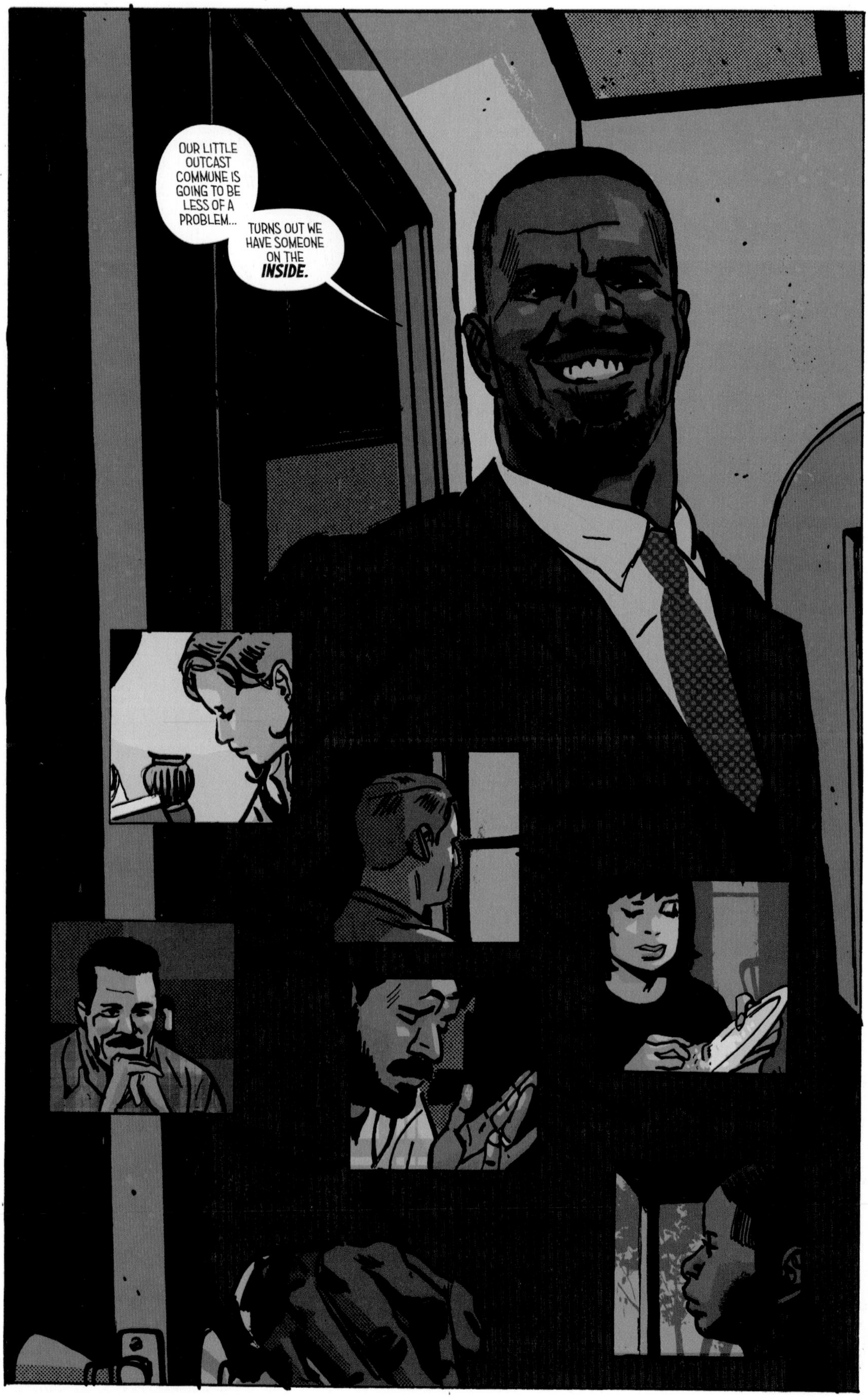
OUR LITTLE OUTCAST COMMUNE IS GOING TO BE LESS OF A PROBLEM...
TURNS OUT WE HAVE SOMEONE ON THE *INSIDE.*

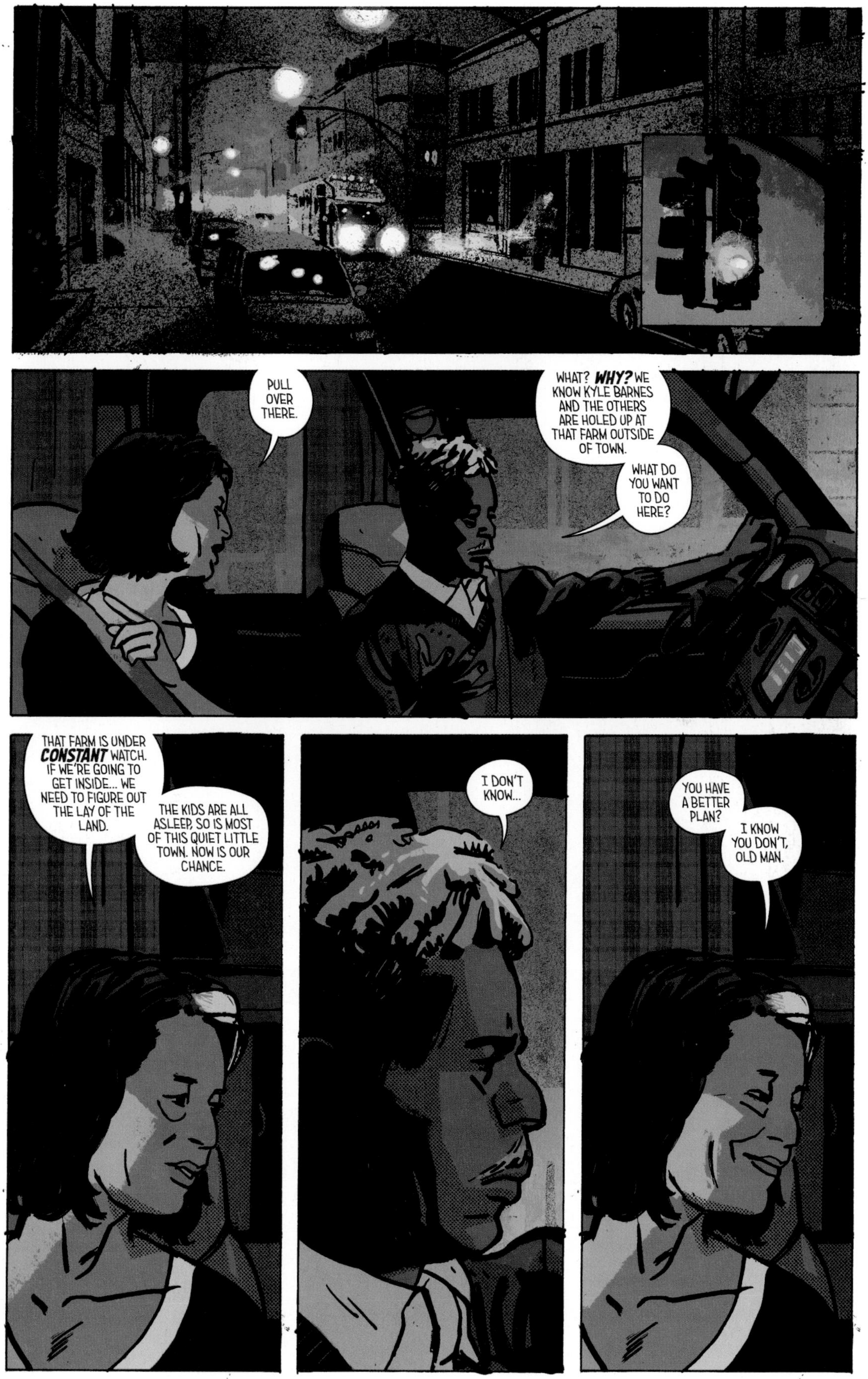
PULL OVER THERE.
WHAT? WHY? WE KNOW KYLE BARNES AND THE OTHERS ARE HOLED UP AT THAT FARM OUTSIDE OF TOWN.
WHAT DO YOU WANT TO DO HERE?
THAT FARM IS UNDER CONSTANT WATCH. IF WE'RE GOING TO GET INSIDE... WE NEED TO FIGURE OUT THE LAY OF THE LAND.
THE KIDS ARE ALL ASLEEP, SO IS MOST OF THIS QUIET LITTLE TOWN. NOW IS OUR CHANCE.
I DON'T KNOW...
YOU HAVE A BETTER PLAN?
I KNOW YOU DON'T, OLD MAN.

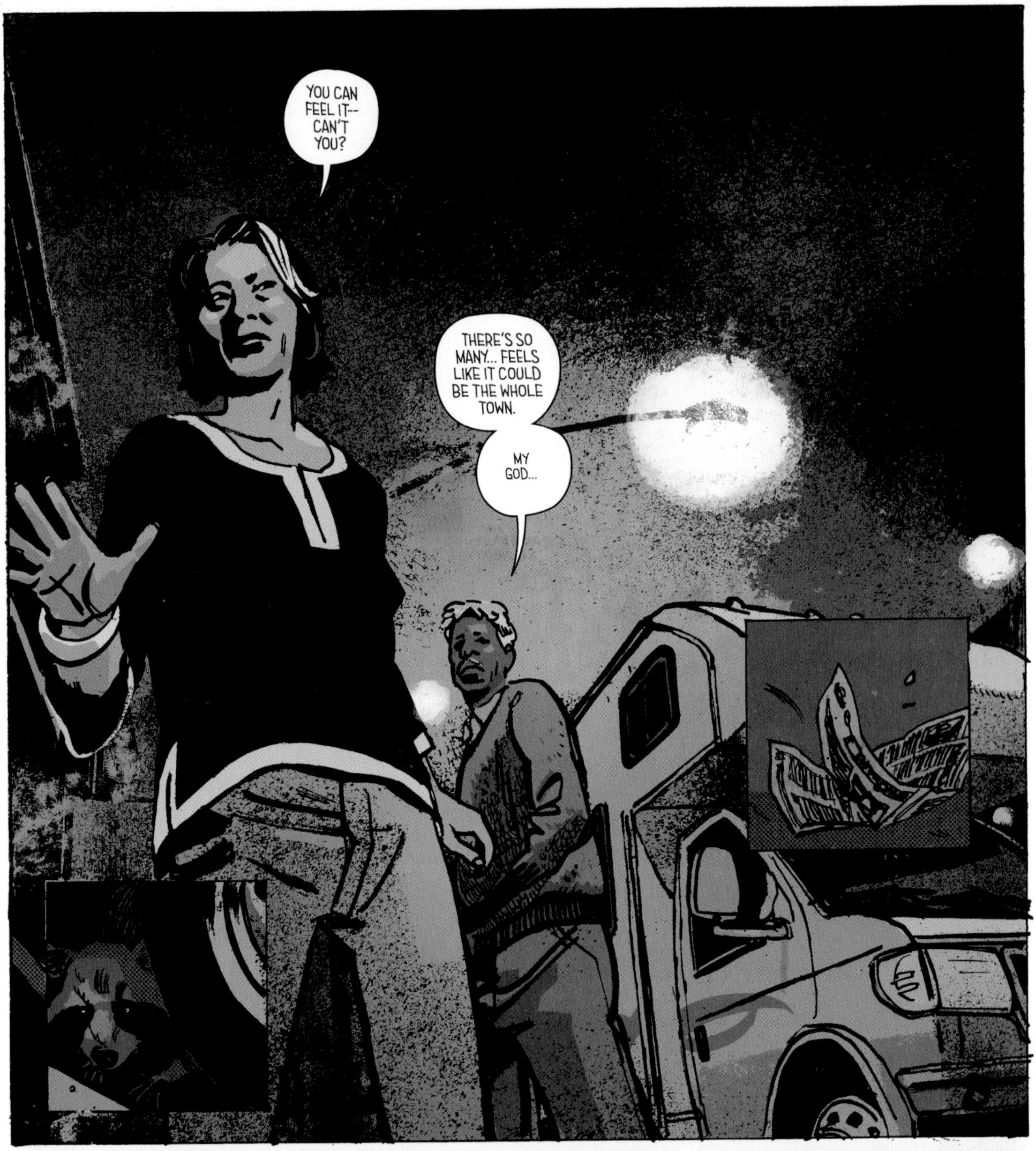
YOU CAN FEEL IT-- CAN'T YOU?
THERE'S SO MANY... FEELS LIKE IT COULD BE THE WHOLE TOWN.
MY GOD...

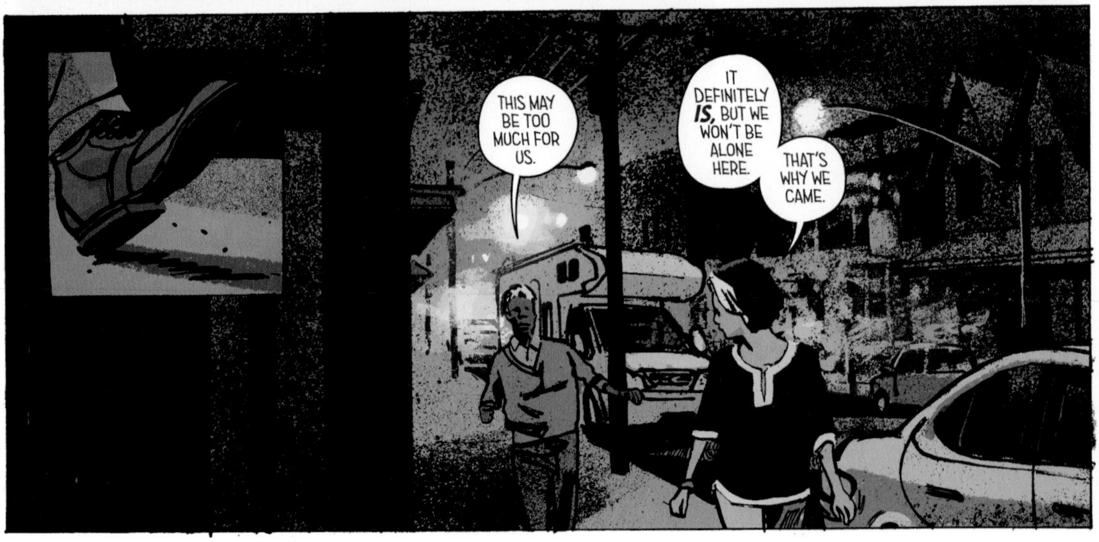
THIS MAY BE TOO MUCH FOR US.
IT DEFINITELY ***IS,*** BUT WE WON'T BE ALONE HERE.
THAT'S WHY WE CAME.

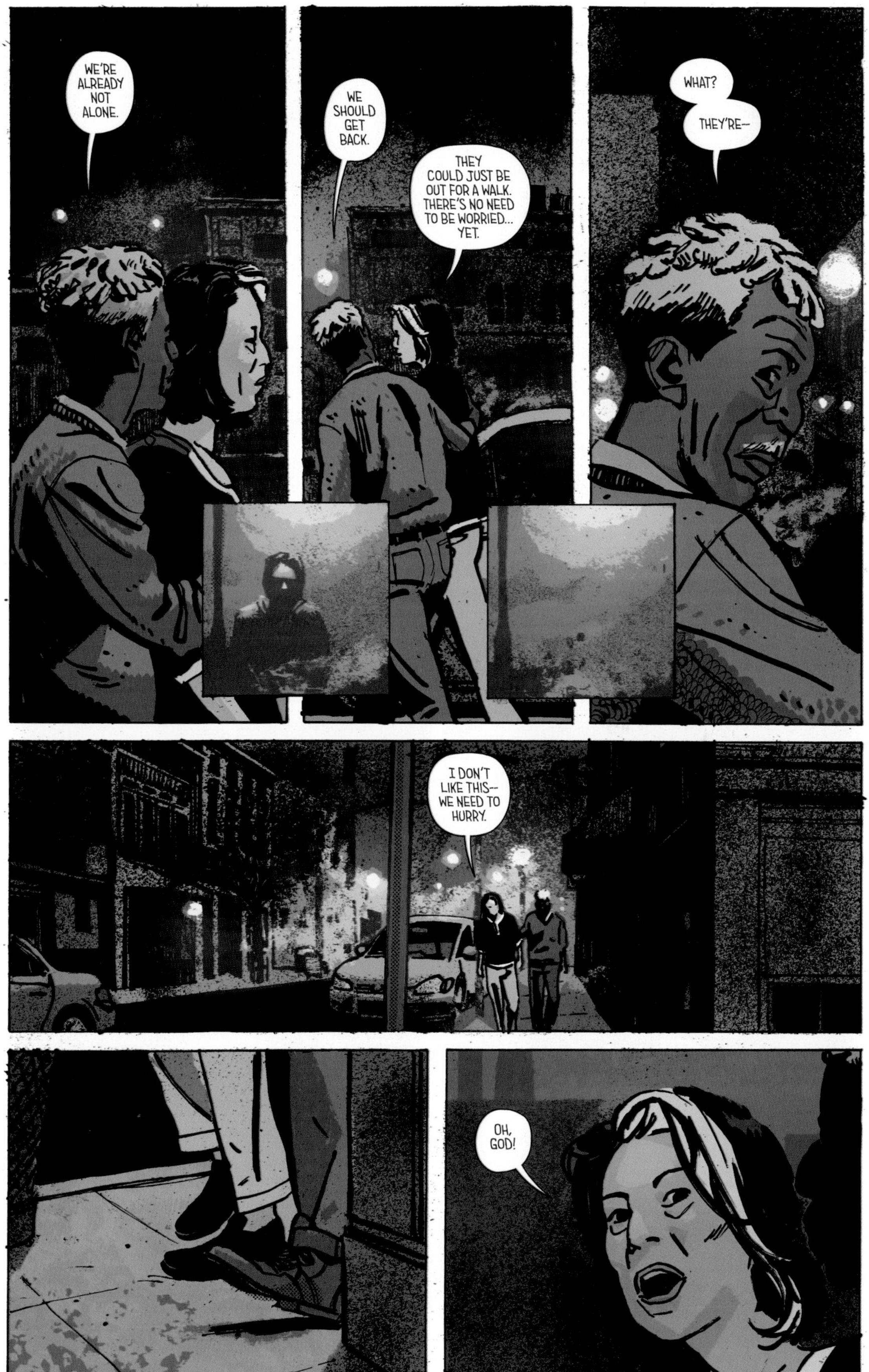
WE'RE ALREADY NOT ALONE.
WE SHOULD GET BACK.
THEY COULD JUST BE OUT FOR A WALK. THERE'S NO NEED TO BE WORRIED... YET.
WHAT?
THEY'RE--
I DON'T LIKE THIS-- WE NEED TO HURRY.
OH, GOD!

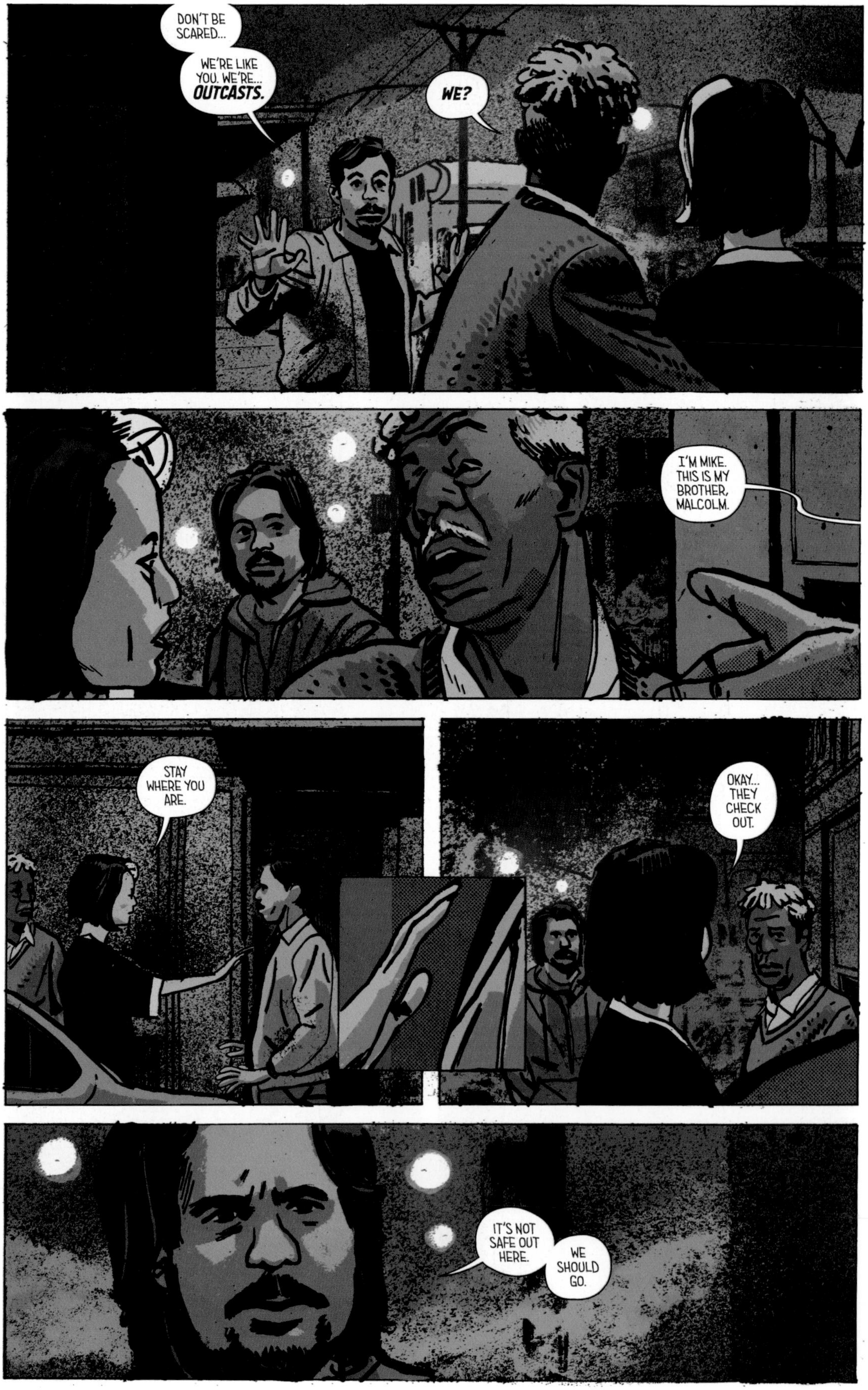
DON'T BE SCARED...
WE'RE LIKE YOU. WE'RE... OUTCASTS.
WE?
I'M MIKE. THIS IS MY BROTHER, MALCOLM.
STAY WHERE YOU ARE.
OKAY... THEY CHECK OUT.
IT'S NOT SAFE OUT HERE.
WE SHOULD GO.

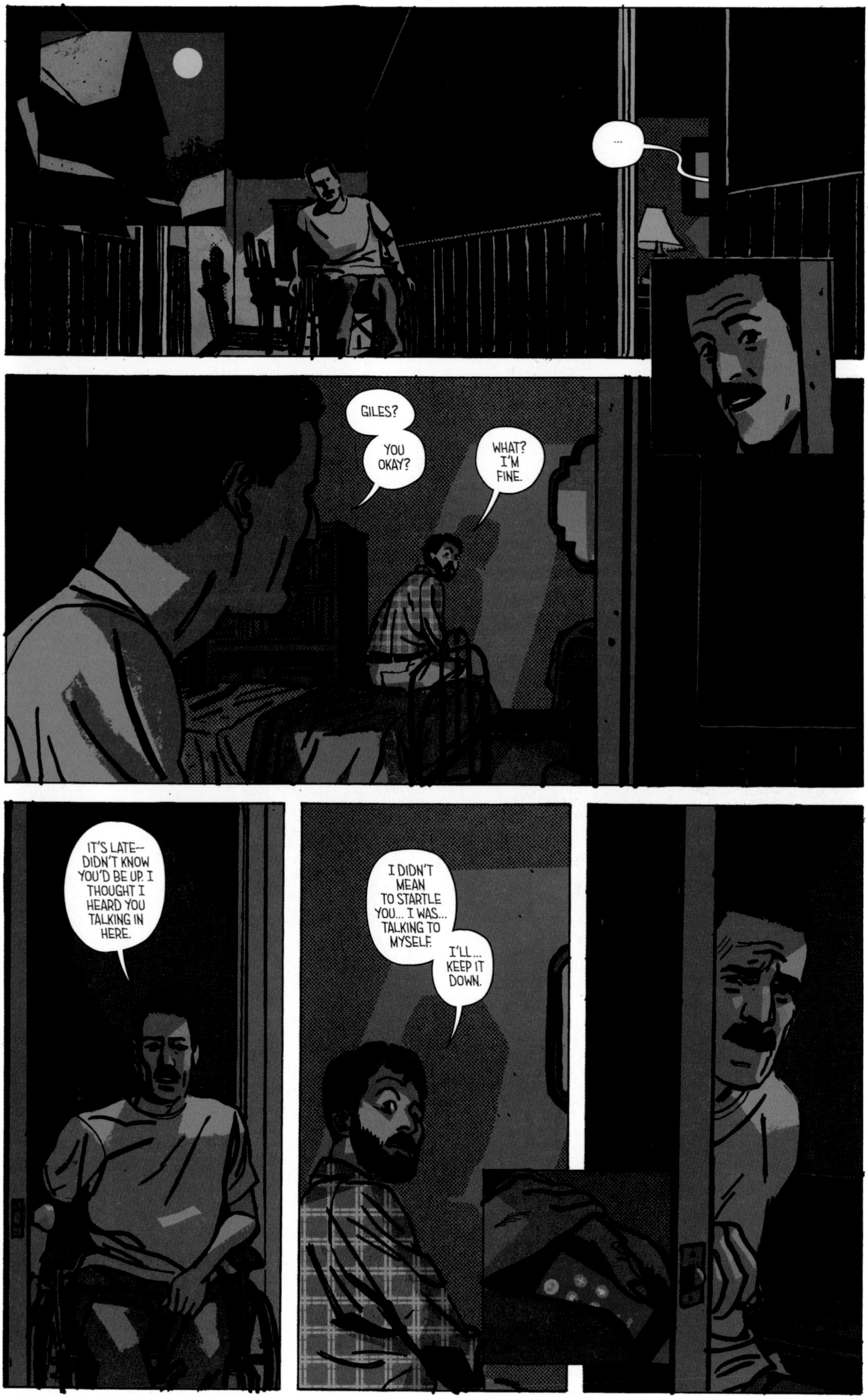
...
GILES?
YOU OKAY?
WHAT? I'M FINE.
IT'S LATE-- DIDN'T KNOW YOU'D BE UP. I THOUGHT I HEARD YOU TALKING IN HERE.
I DIDN'T MEAN TO STARTLE YOU... I WAS... TALKING TO MYSELF.
I'LL... KEEP IT DOWN.

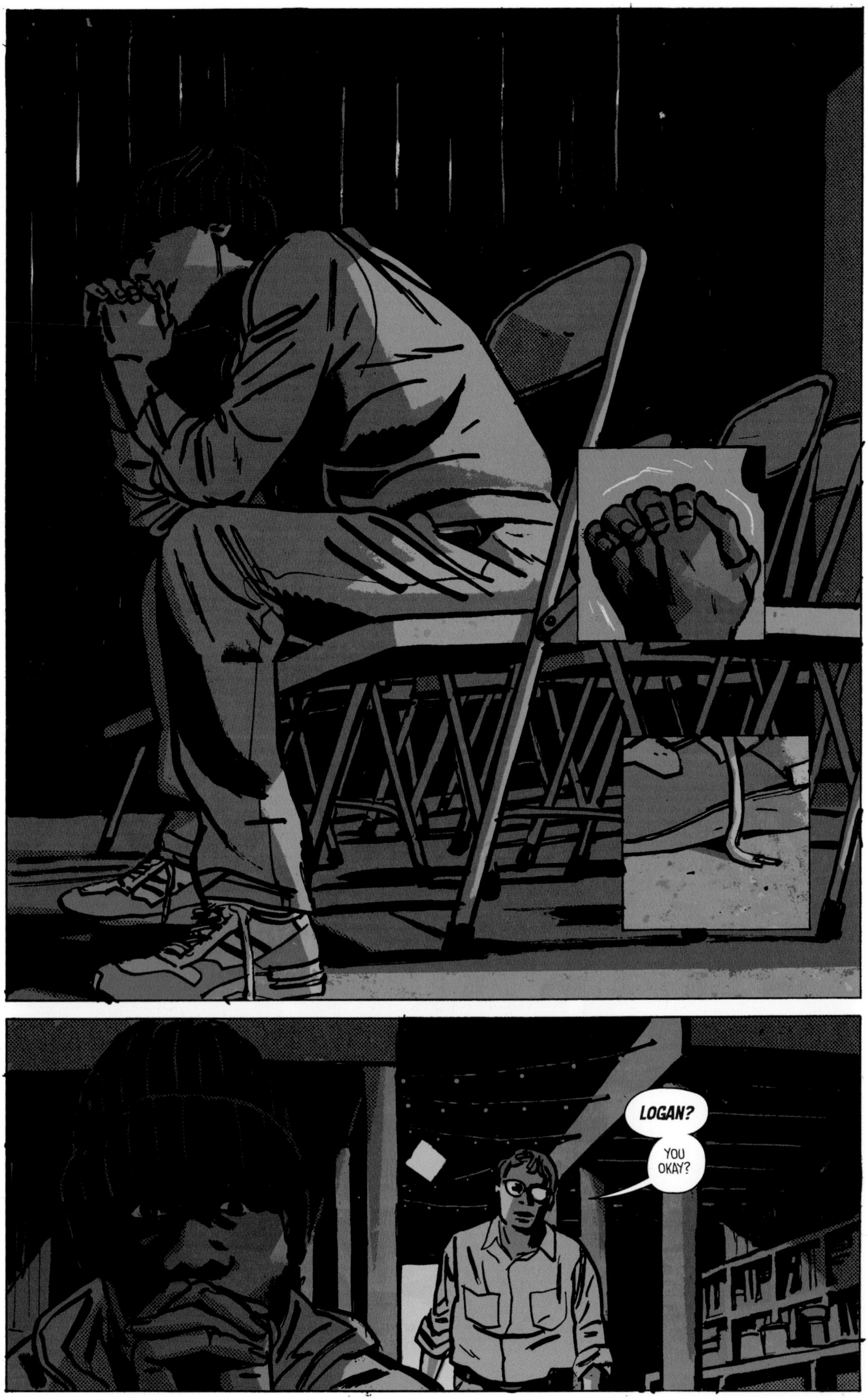
LOGAN?
YOU OKAY?

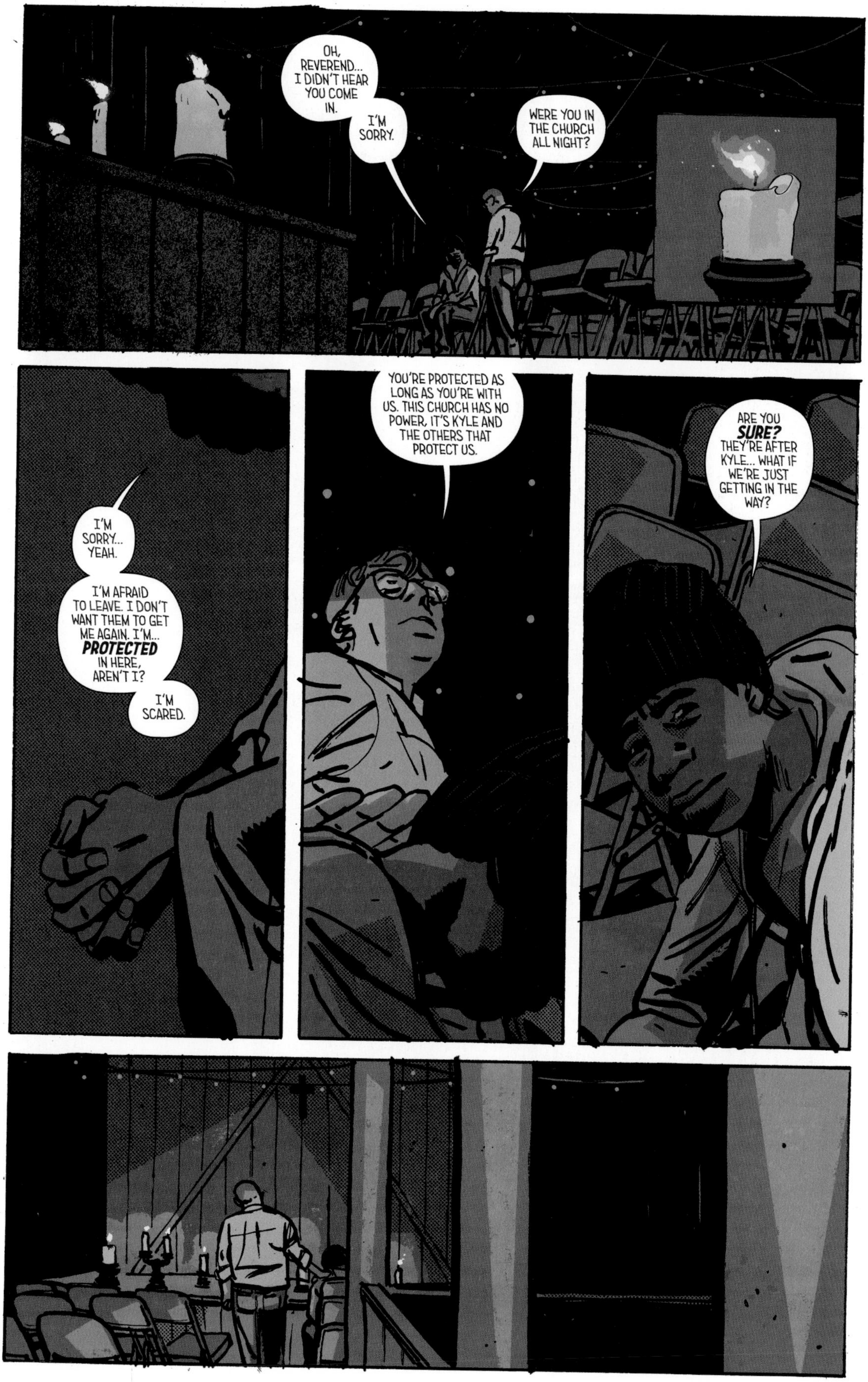
OH, REVEREND... I DIDN'T HEAR YOU COME IN.
I'M SORRY.
WERE YOU IN THE CHURCH ALL NIGHT?
I'M SORRY... YEAH.
I'M AFRAID TO LEAVE. I DON'T WANT THEM TO GET ME AGAIN. I'M... **PROTECTED** IN HERE, AREN'T I?
I'M SCARED.
YOU'RE PROTECTED AS LONG AS YOU'RE WITH US. THIS CHURCH HAS NO POWER, IT'S KYLE AND THE OTHERS THAT PROTECT US.
ARE YOU **SURE?** THEY'RE AFTER KYLE... WHAT IF WE'RE JUST GETTING IN THE WAY?

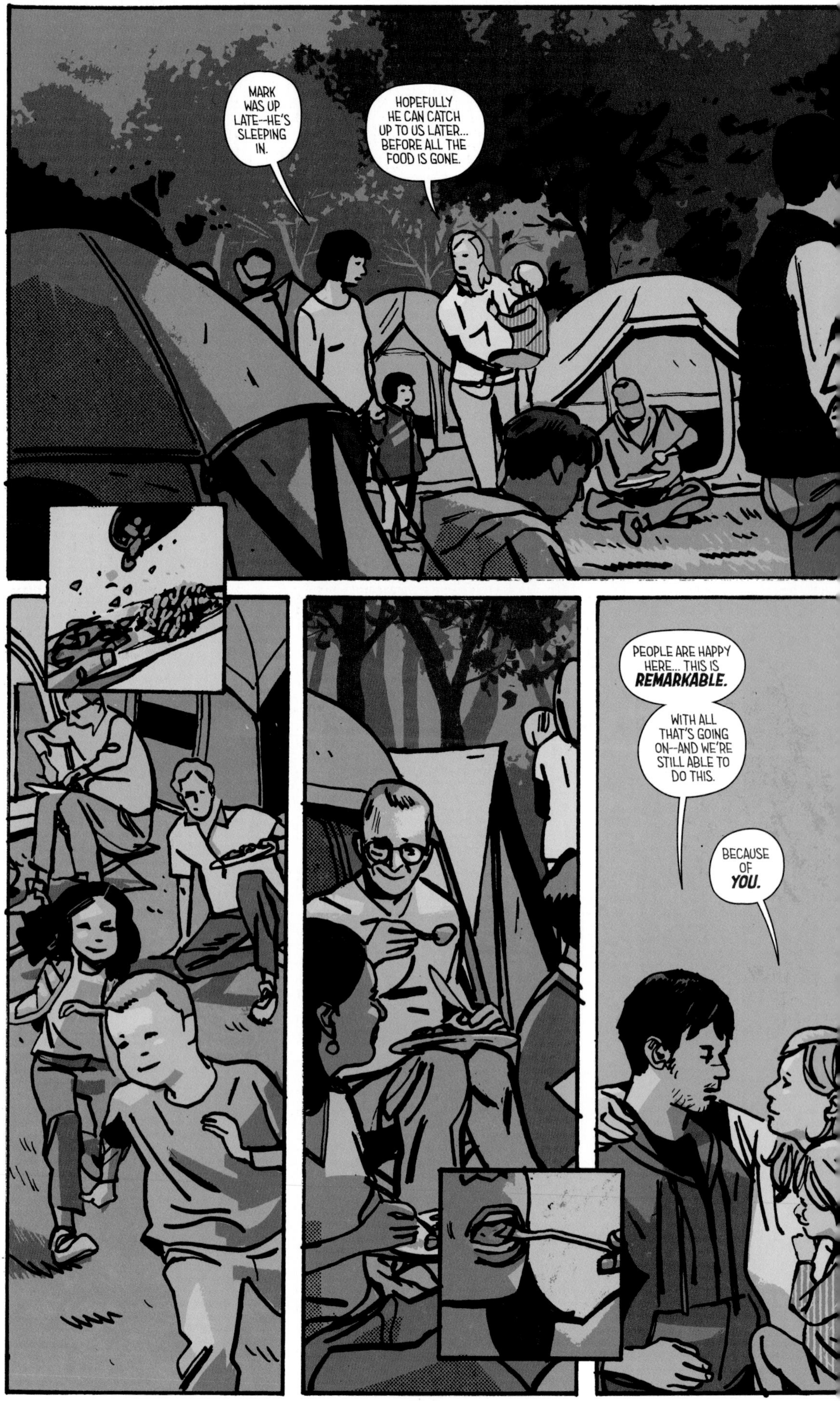
MARK WAS UP LATE--HE'S SLEEPING IN.
HOPEFULLY HE CAN CATCH UP TO US LATER... BEFORE ALL THE FOOD IS GONE.
PEOPLE ARE HAPPY HERE... THIS IS **REMARKABLE.**
WITH ALL THAT'S GOING ON--AND WE'RE STILL ABLE TO DO THIS.
BECAUSE OF ***YOU.***

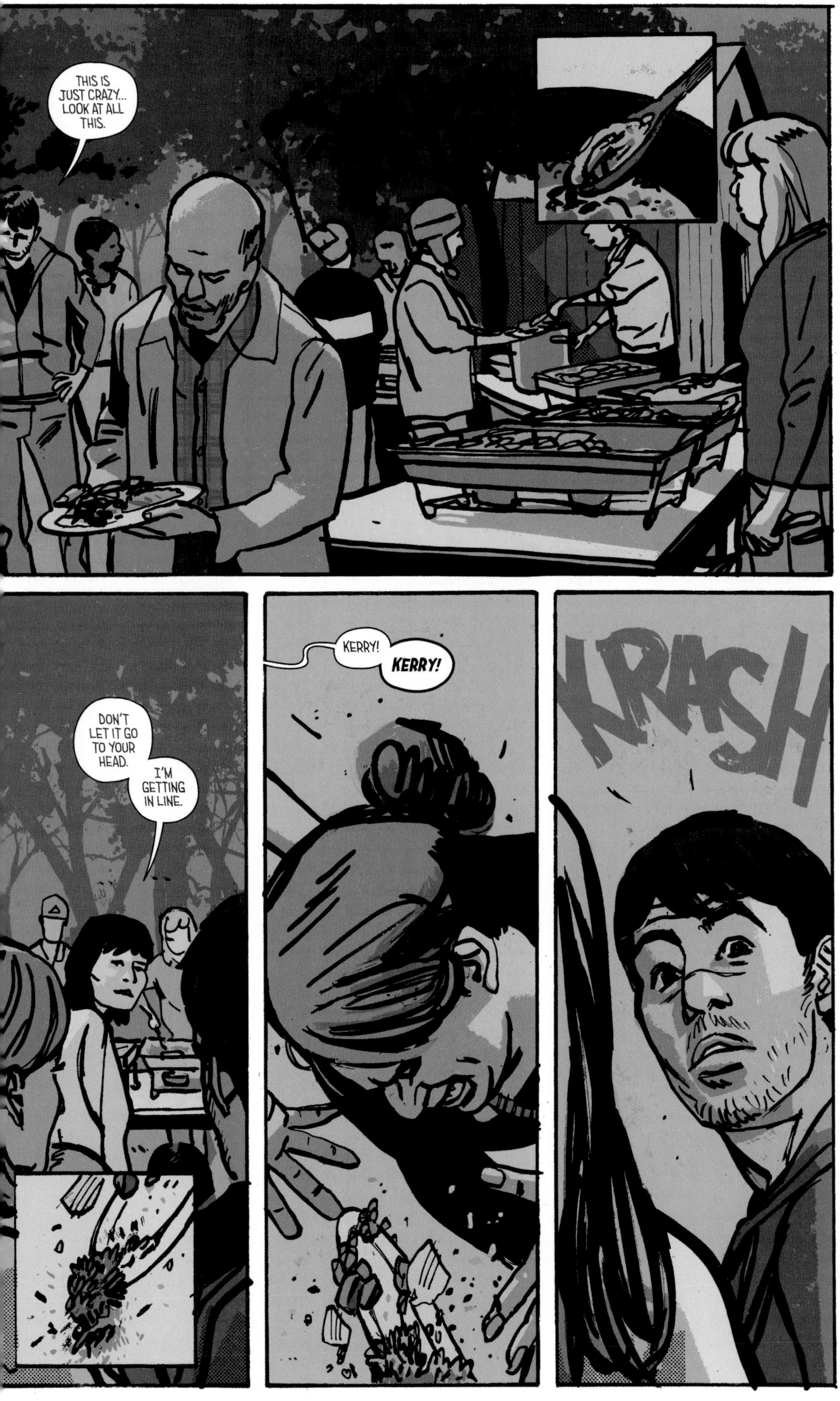
THIS IS JUST CRAZY... LOOK AT ALL THIS.
DON'T LET IT GO TO YOUR HEAD.
I'M GETTING IN LINE.
KERRY!
KERRY!
KRASH

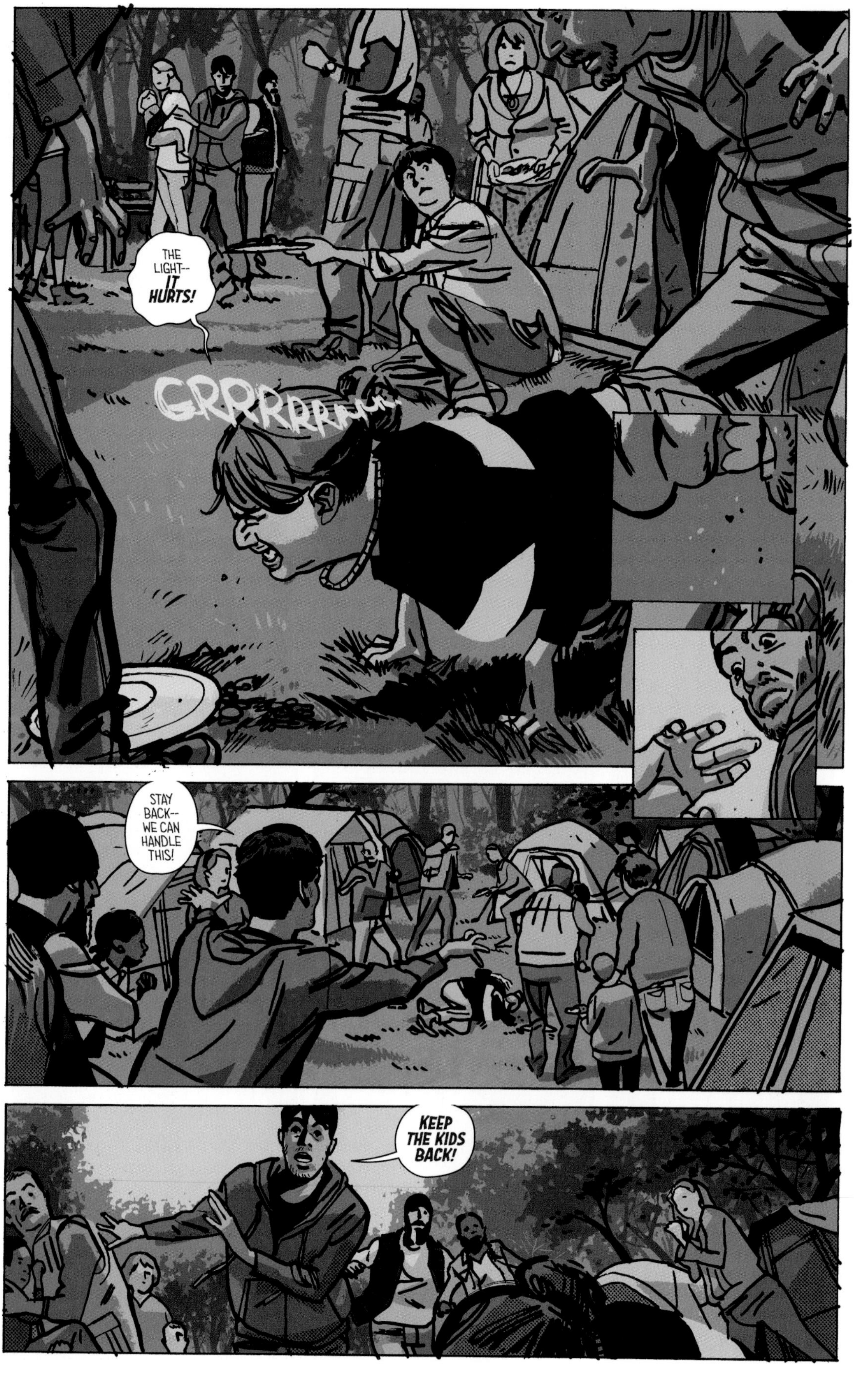
THE LIGHT-- IT HURTS!
GRRRRRR...
STAY BACK-- WE CAN HANDLE THIS!
KEEP THE KIDS BACK!

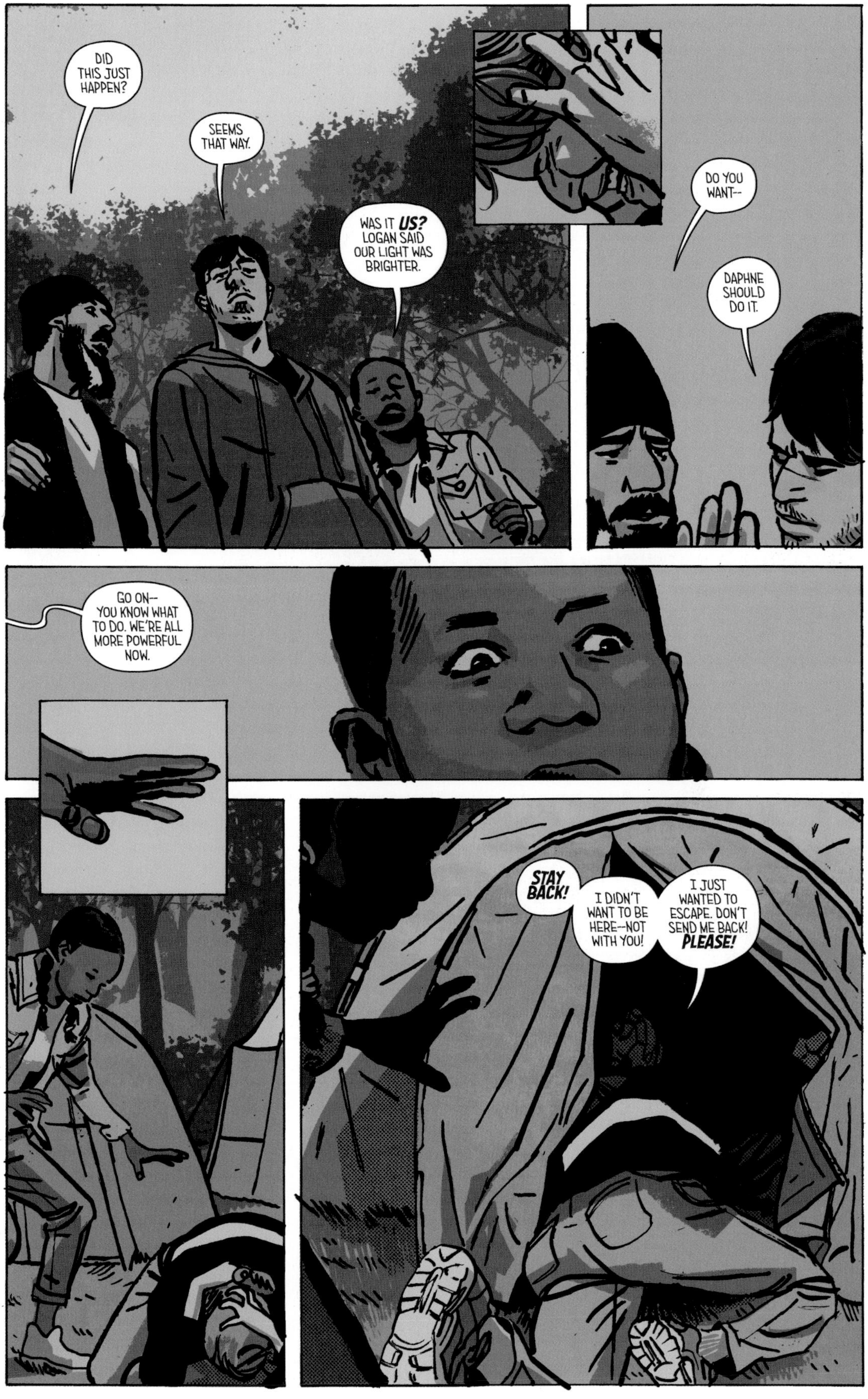

DID THIS JUST HAPPEN?
SEEMS THAT WAY.
WAS IT ***US?*** LOGAN SAID OUR LIGHT WAS BRIGHTER.
DO YOU WANT--
DAPHNE SHOULD DO IT.
GO ON-- YOU KNOW WHAT TO DO. WE'RE ALL MORE POWERFUL NOW.
STAY BACK!
I DIDN'T WANT TO BE HERE--NOT WITH YOU!
I JUST WANTED TO ESCAPE. DON'T SEND ME BACK! ***PLEASE!***

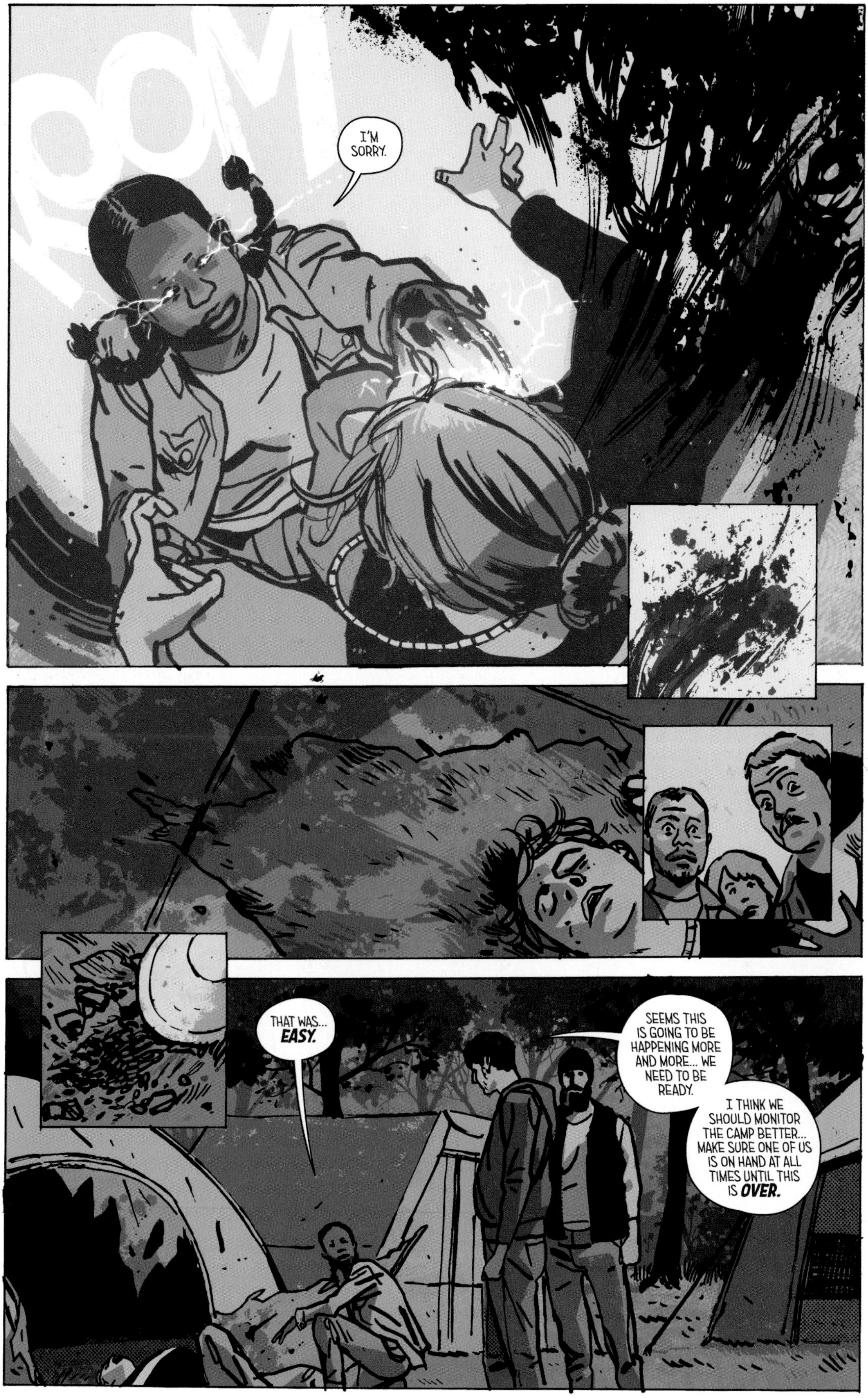

BOOM
I'M SORRY.
THAT WAS... **EASY.**
SEEMS THIS IS GOING TO BE HAPPENING MORE AND MORE... WE NEED TO BE READY.
I THINK WE SHOULD MONITOR THE CAMP BETTER... MAKE SURE ONE OF US IS ON HAND AT ALL TIMES UNTIL THIS IS **OVER.**

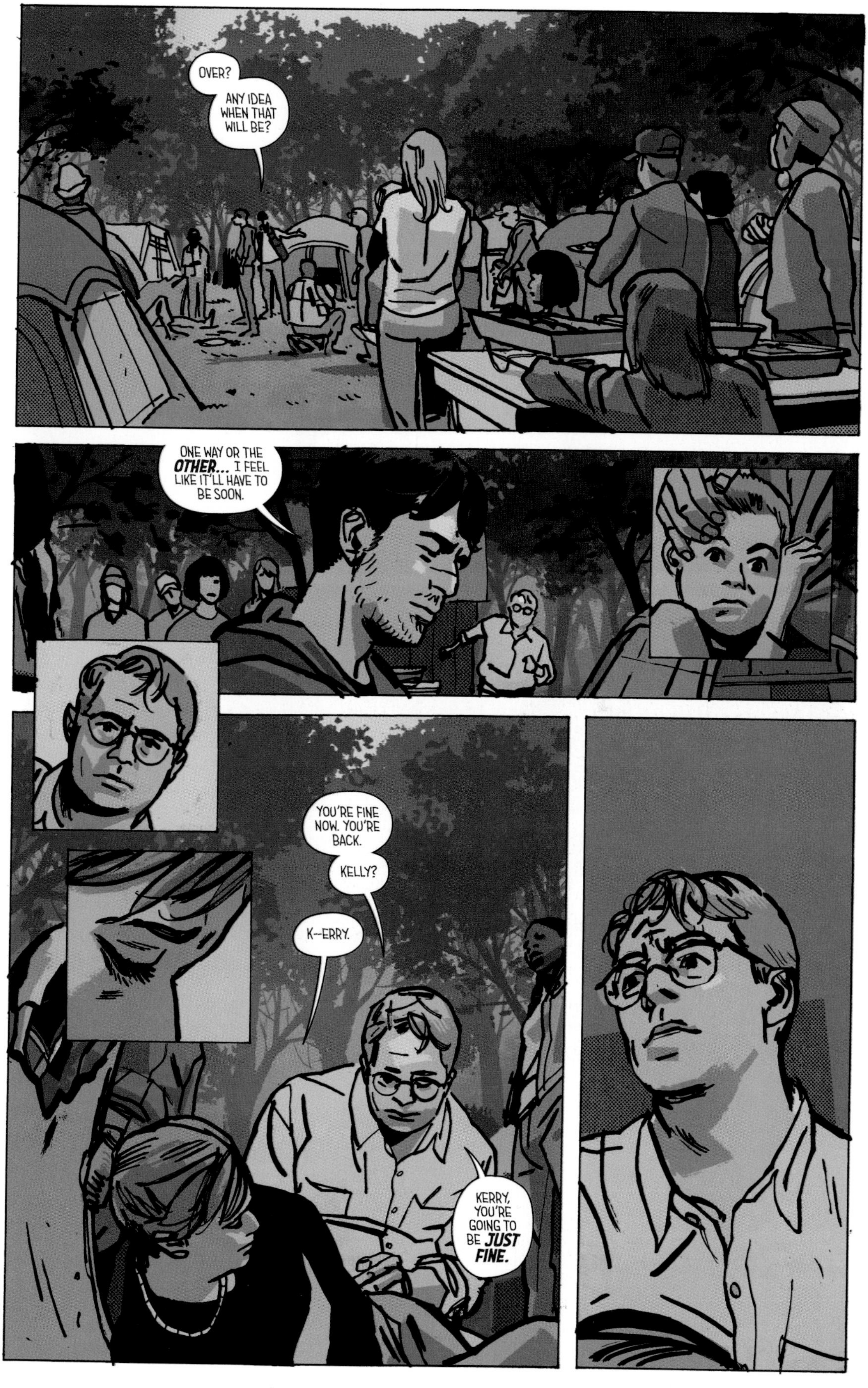
OVER?
ANY IDEA WHEN THAT WILL BE?
ONE WAY OR THE **OTHER...** I FEEL LIKE IT'LL HAVE TO BE SOON.
YOU'RE FINE NOW. YOU'RE BACK.
KELLY?
K--ERRY.
KERRY, YOU'RE GOING TO BE **JUST FINE.**

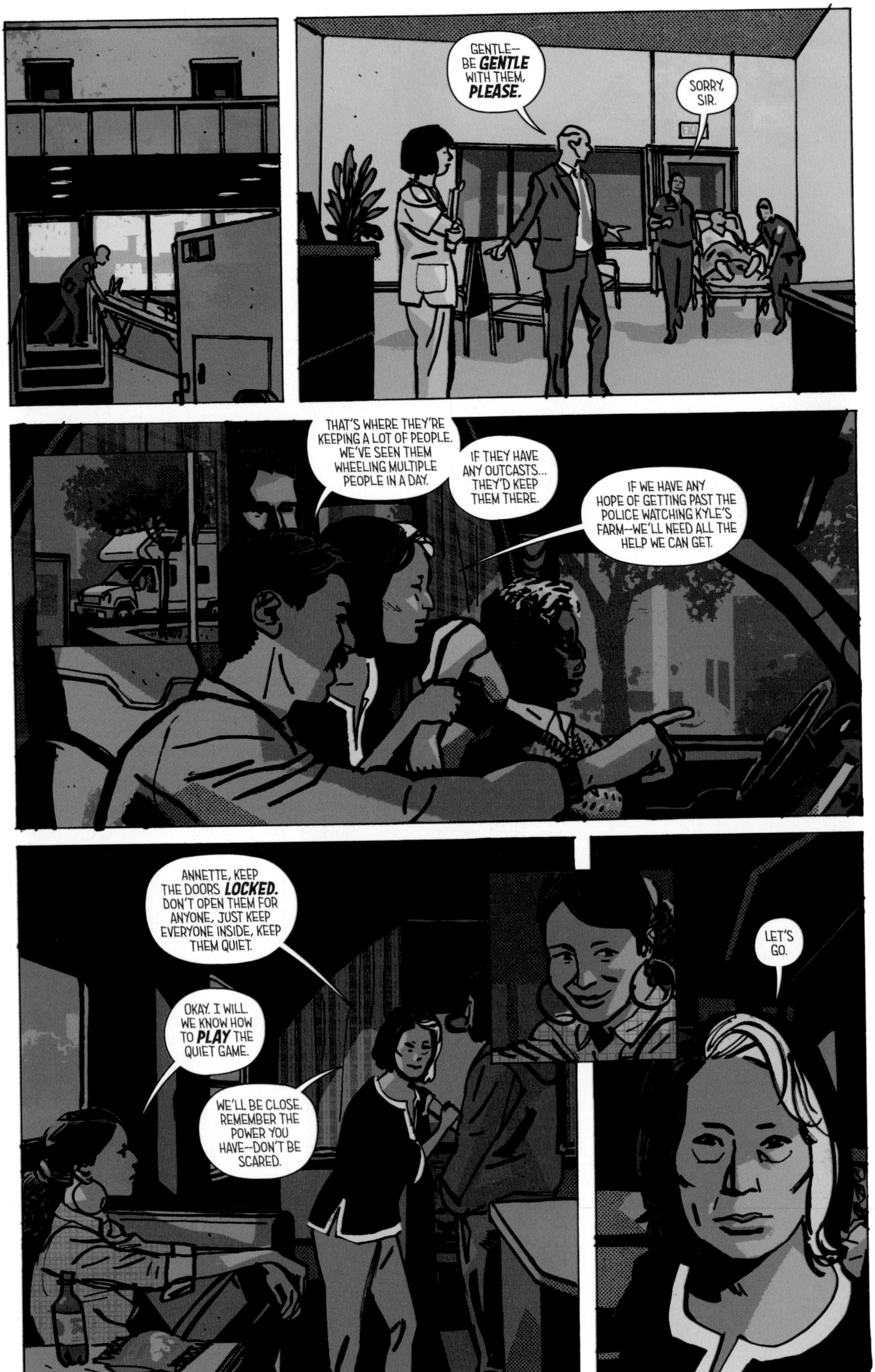
GENTLE--
BE **GENTLE** WITH THEM, **PLEASE.**
SORRY, SIR.
THAT'S WHERE THEY'RE KEEPING A LOT OF PEOPLE. WE'VE SEEN THEM WHEELING MULTIPLE PEOPLE IN A DAY.
IF THEY HAVE ANY OUTCASTS... THEY'D KEEP THEM THERE.
IF WE HAVE ANY HOPE OF GETTING PAST THE POLICE WATCHING KYLE'S FARM--WE'LL NEED ALL THE HELP WE CAN GET.
ANNETTE, KEEP THE DOORS **LOCKED.** DON'T OPEN THEM FOR ANYONE, JUST KEEP EVERYONE INSIDE, KEEP THEM QUIET.
OKAY. I WILL. WE KNOW HOW TO **PLAY** THE QUIET GAME.
WE'LL BE CLOSE. REMEMBER THE POWER YOU HAVE--DON'T BE SCARED.
LET'S GO.

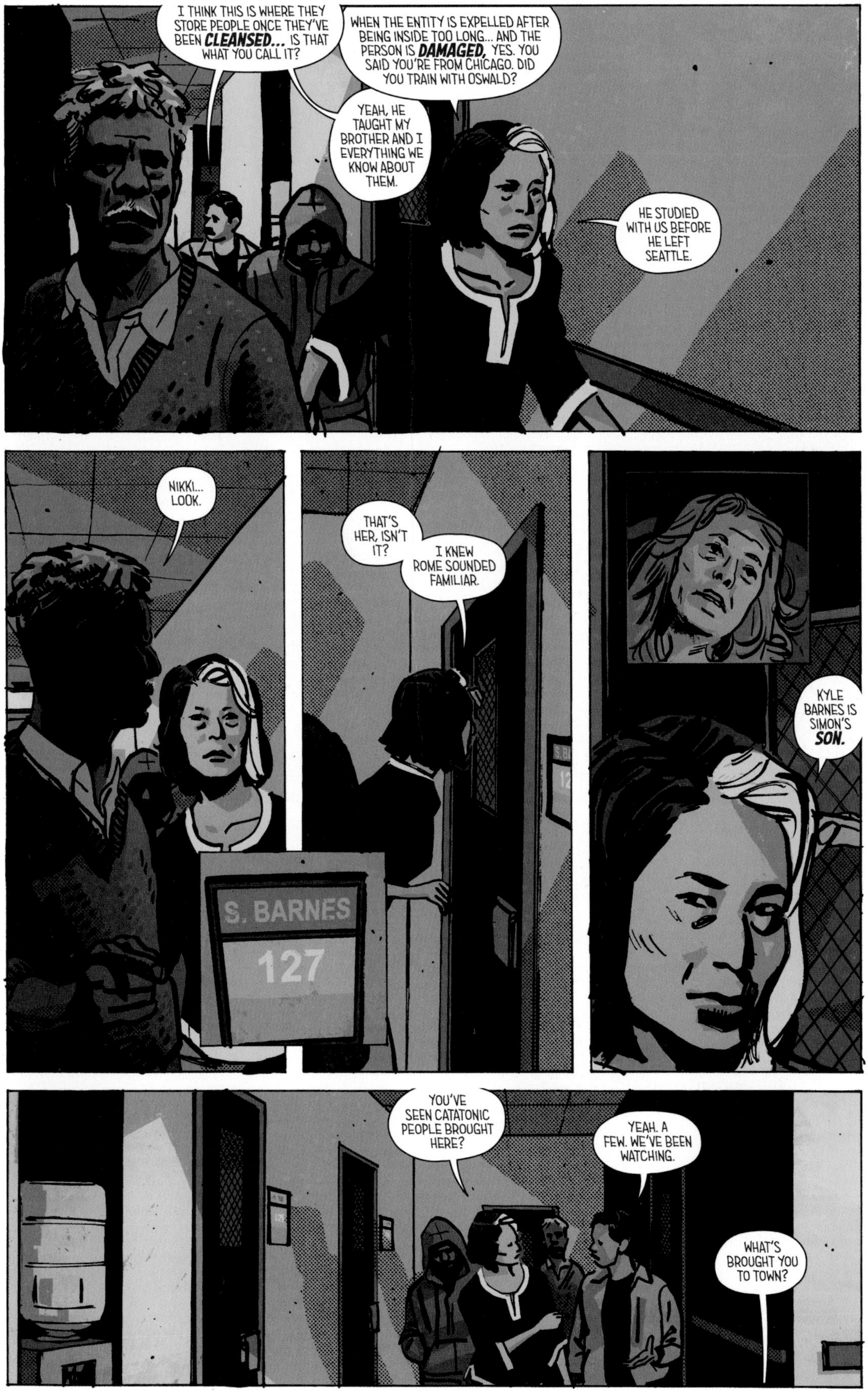
I THINK THIS IS WHERE THEY STORE PEOPLE ONCE THEY'VE BEEN CLEANSED... IS THAT WHAT YOU CALL IT?
WHEN THE ENTITY IS EXPELLED AFTER BEING INSIDE TOO LONG... AND THE PERSON IS DAMAGED, YES. YOU SAID YOU'RE FROM CHICAGO. DID YOU TRAIN WITH OSWALD?
YEAH, HE TAUGHT MY BROTHER AND I EVERYTHING WE KNOW ABOUT THEM.
HE STUDIED WITH US BEFORE HE LEFT SEATTLE.
NIKKI... LOOK.
S. BARNES
127
THAT'S HER, ISN'T IT?
I KNEW ROME SOUNDED FAMILIAR.
KYLE BARNES IS SIMON'S SON.
YOU'VE SEEN CATATONIC PEOPLE BROUGHT HERE?
YEAH. A FEW. WE'VE BEEN WATCHING.
WHAT'S BROUGHT YOU TO TOWN?

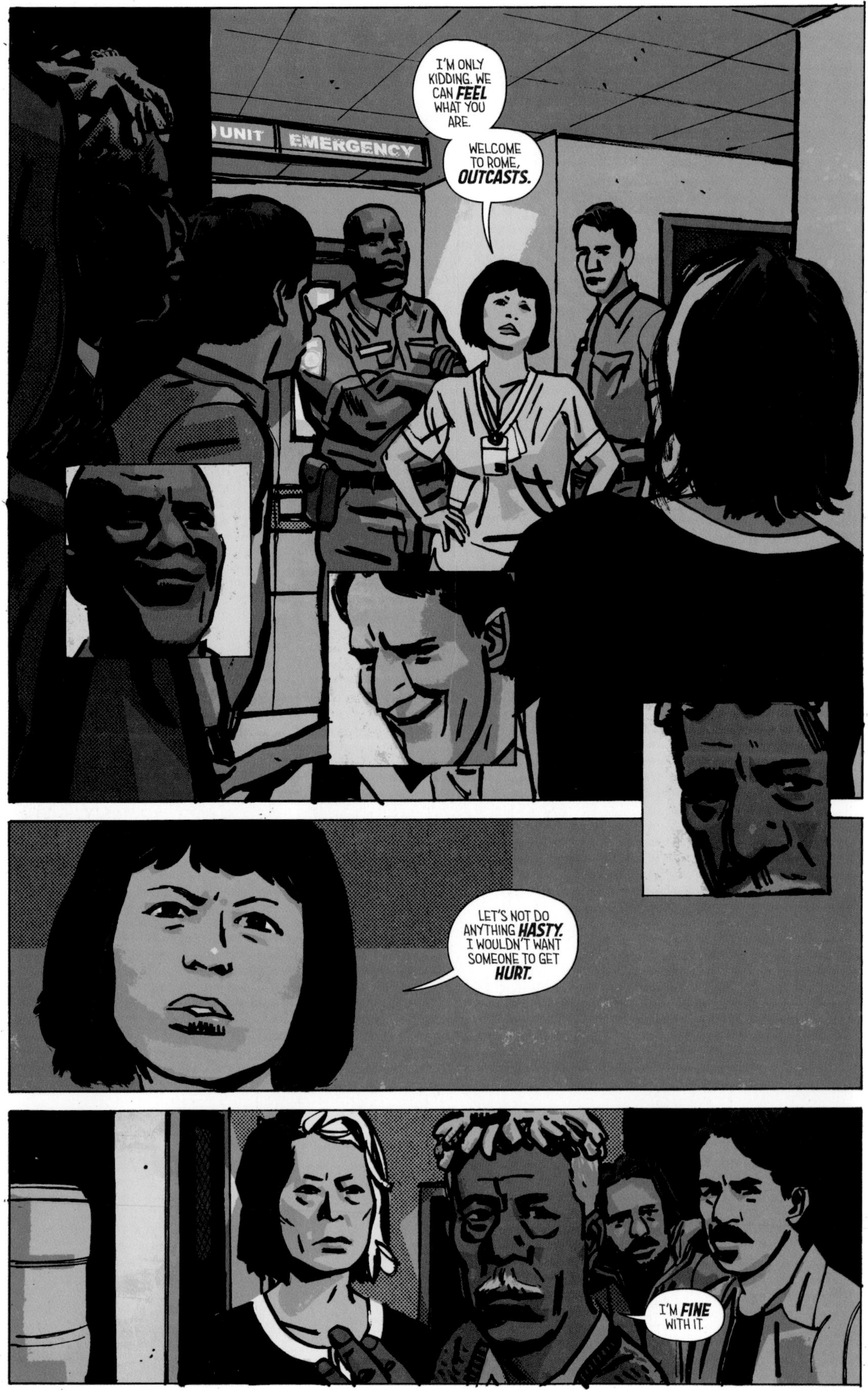

I'M ONLY KIDDING. WE CAN FEEL WHAT YOU ARE.
WELCOME TO ROME, OUTCASTS.
UNIT
EMERGENCY
LET'S NOT DO ANYTHING HASTY. I WOULDN'T WANT SOMEONE TO GET HURT.
I'M FINE WITH IT.

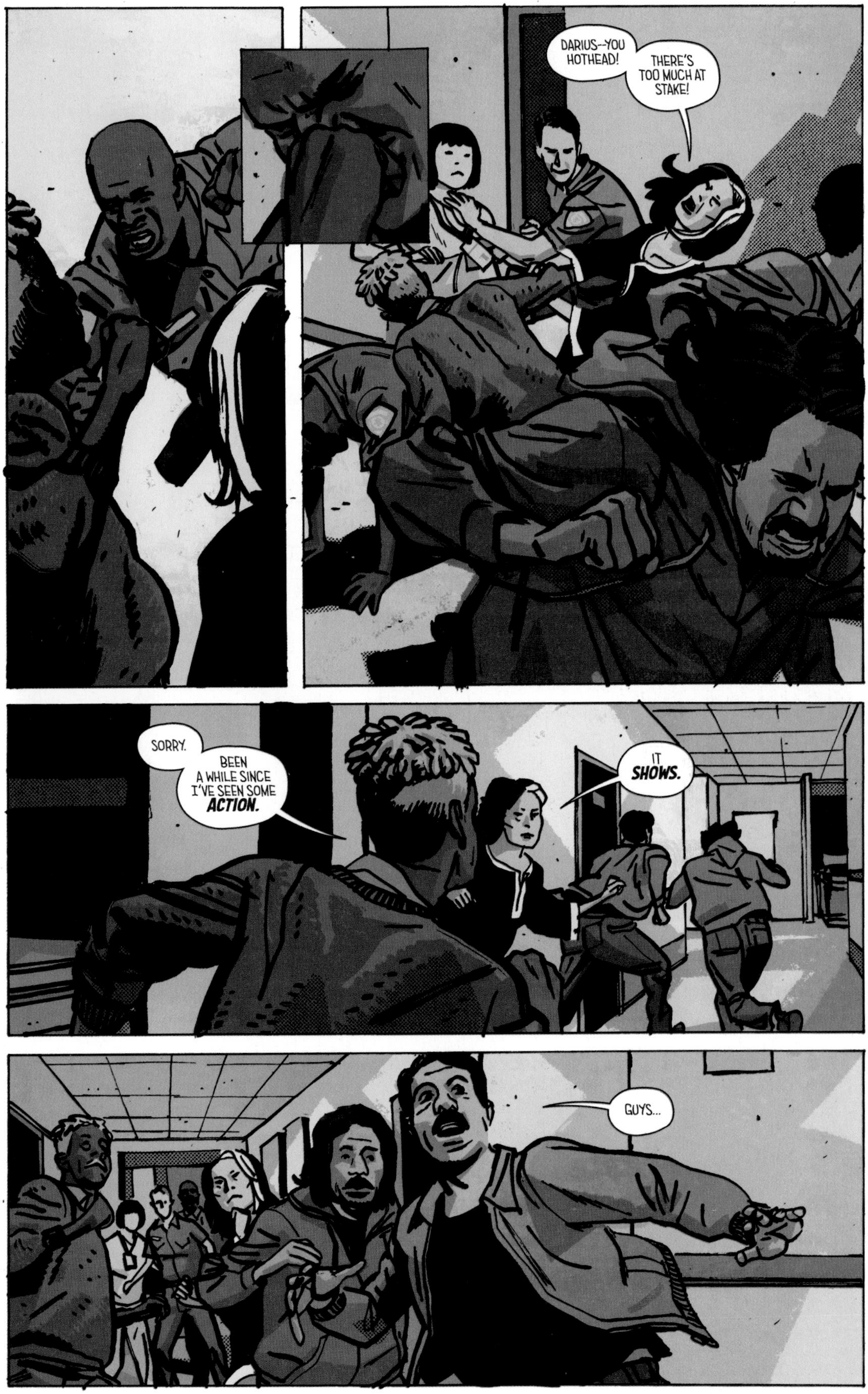
DARIUS--YOU HOTHEAD!
THERE'S TOO MUCH AT STAKE!
SORRY.
BEEN A WHILE SINCE I'VE SEEN SOME ACTION.
IT SHOWS.
GUYS...

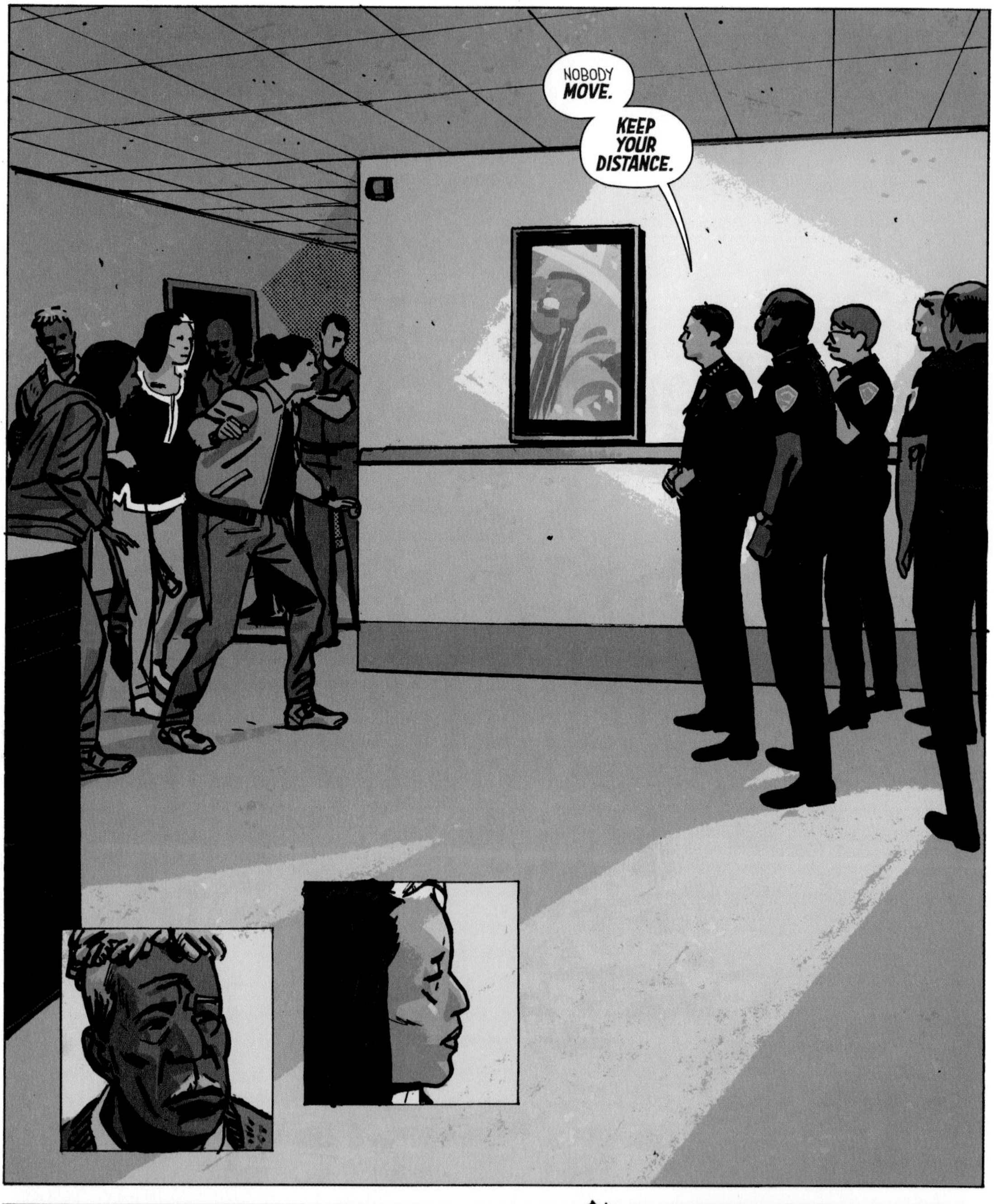
NOBODY MOVE.
KEEP YOUR DISTANCE.
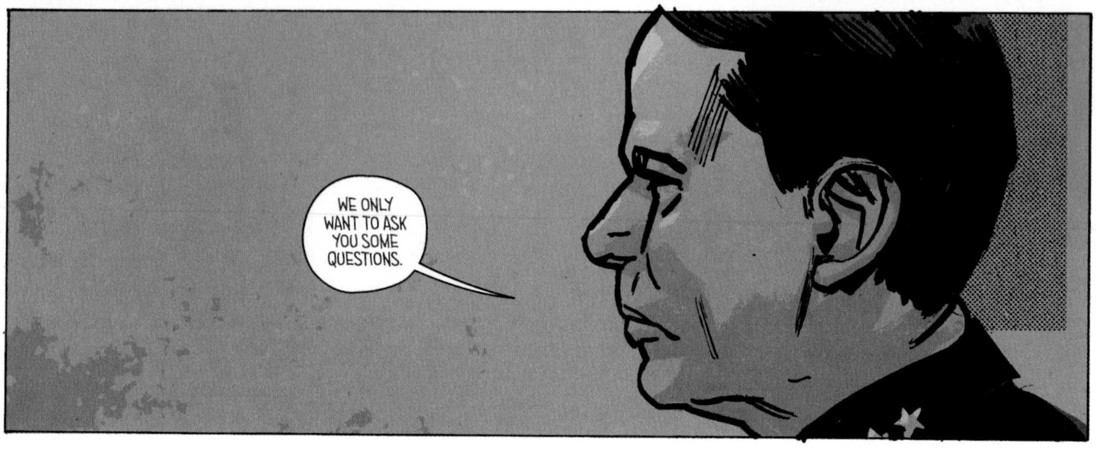
WE ONLY WANT TO ASK YOU SOME QUESTIONS.

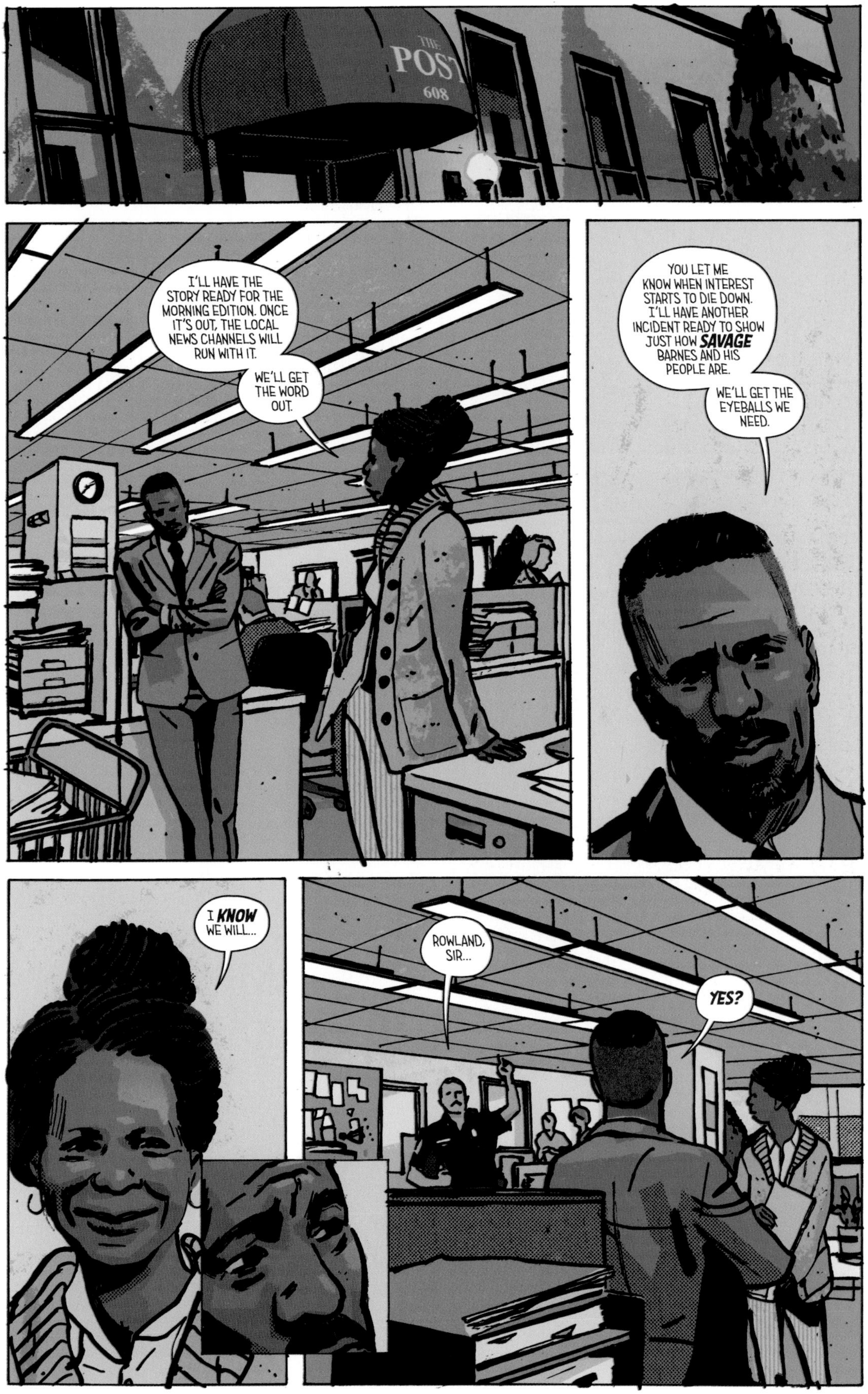
THE POST
608
I'LL HAVE THE STORY READY FOR THE MORNING EDITION. ONCE IT'S OUT, THE LOCAL NEWS CHANNELS WILL RUN WITH IT.
WE'LL GET THE WORD OUT.
YOU LET ME KNOW WHEN INTEREST STARTS TO DIE DOWN. I'LL HAVE ANOTHER INCIDENT READY TO SHOW JUST HOW SAVAGE BARNES AND HIS PEOPLE ARE.
WE'LL GET THE EYEBALLS WE NEED.
I KNOW WE WILL...
ROWLAND, SIR...
YES?

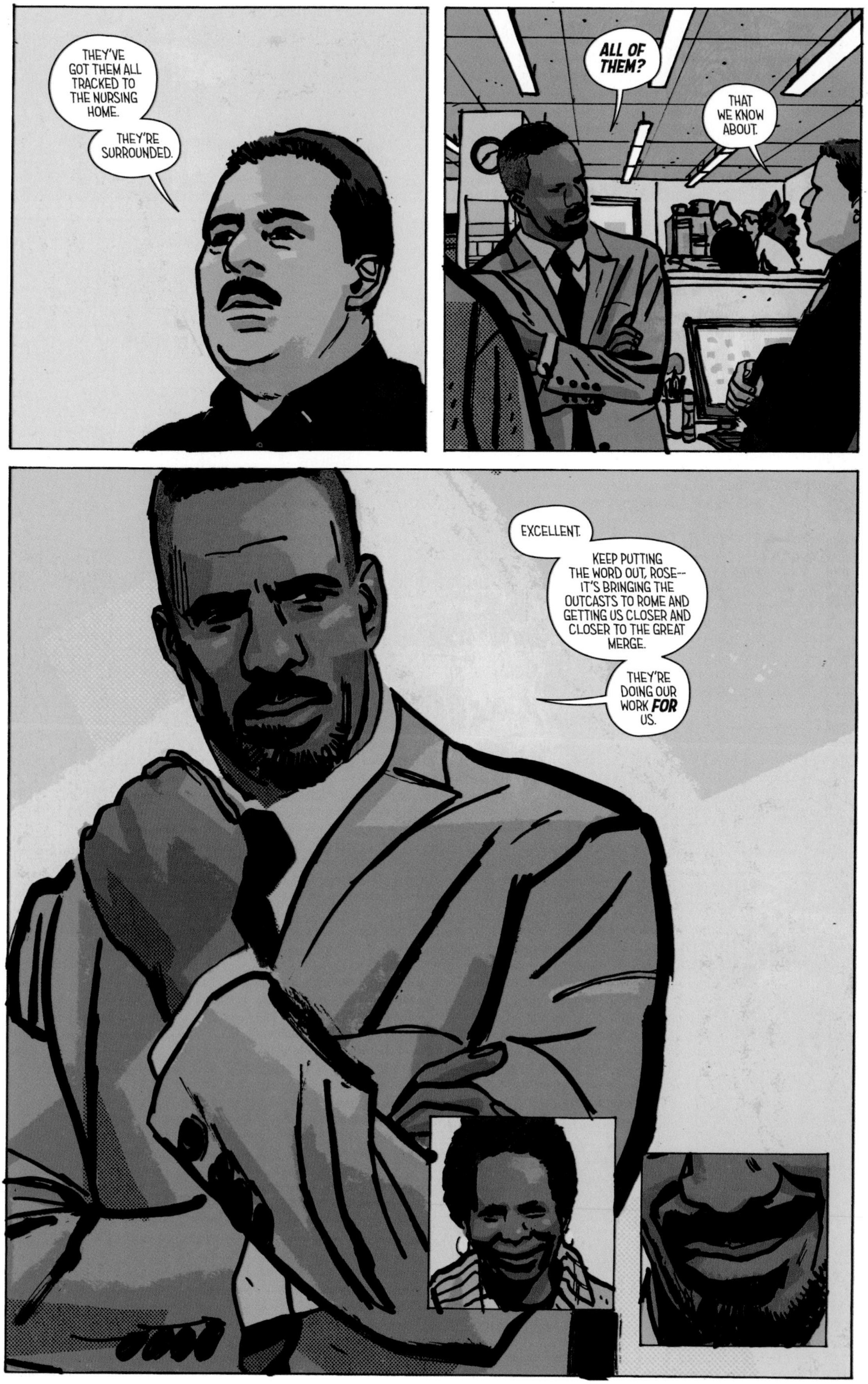

THEY'VE GOT THEM ALL TRACKED TO THE NURSING HOME.
THEY'RE SURROUNDED.
ALL OF THEM?
THAT WE KNOW ABOUT.
EXCELLENT.
KEEP PUTTING THE WORD OUT, ROSE-- IT'S BRINGING THE OUTCASTS TO ROME AND GETTING US CLOSER AND CLOSER TO THE GREAT MERGE.
THEY'RE DOING OUR WORK FOR US.

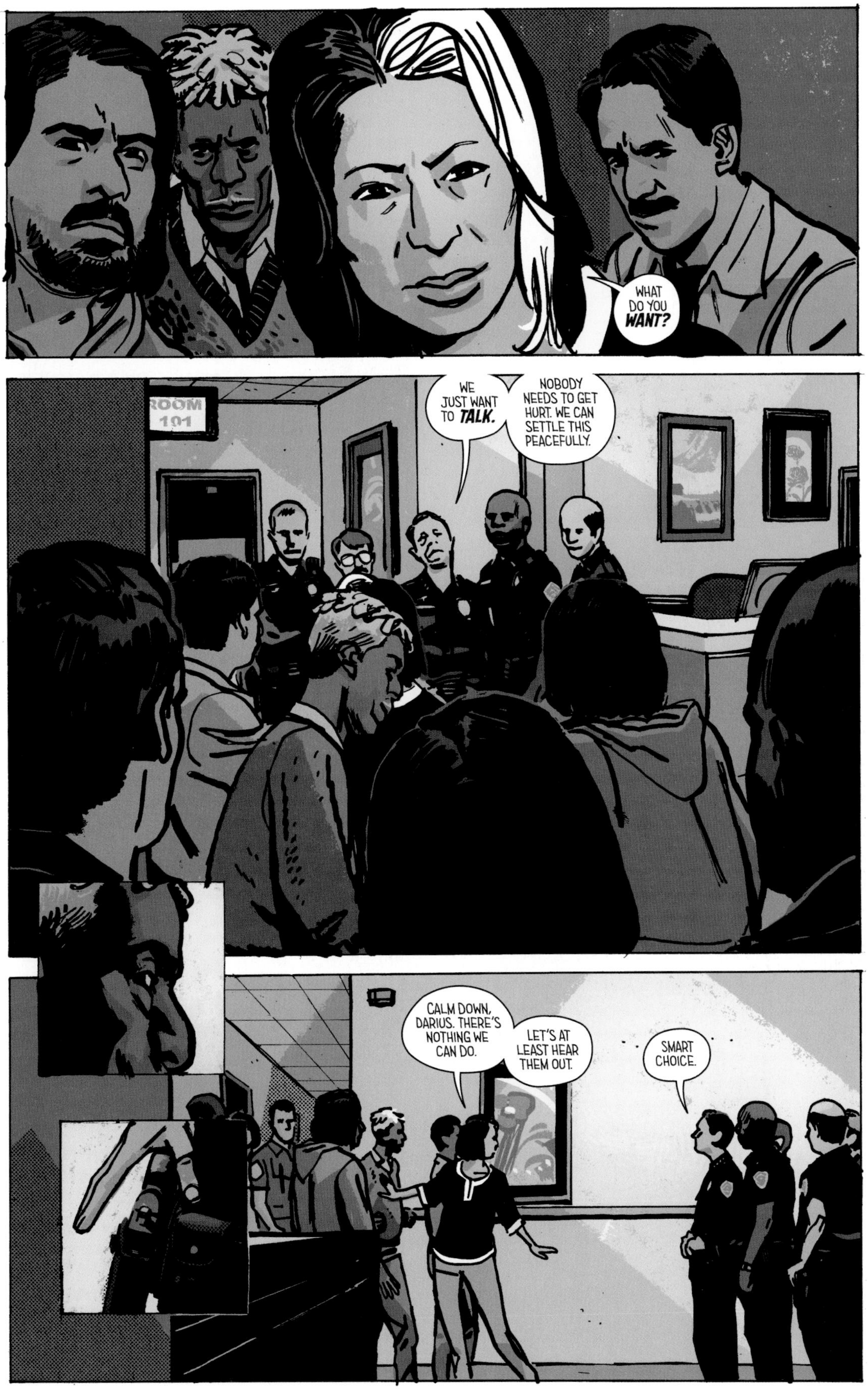
WHAT DO YOU *WANT?*
ROOM 101
WE JUST WANT TO *TALK.*
NOBODY NEEDS TO GET HURT. WE CAN SETTLE THIS PEACEFULLY.
CALM DOWN, DARIUS. THERE'S NOTHING WE CAN DO.
LET'S AT LEAST HEAR THEM OUT.
SMART CHOICE.

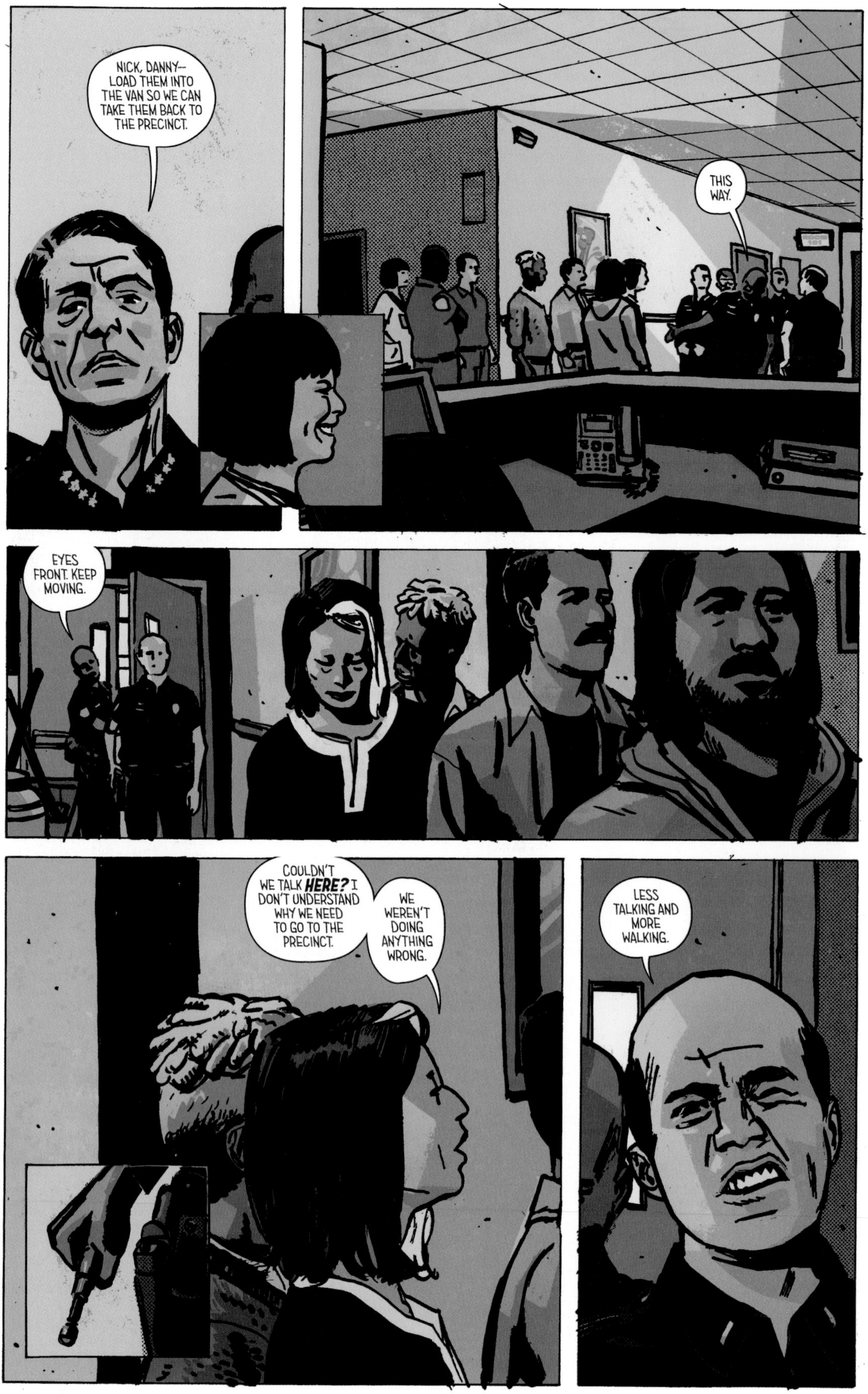
NICK, DANNY—
LOAD THEM INTO THE VAN SO WE CAN TAKE THEM BACK TO THE PRECINCT.
THIS WAY.
EYES FRONT. KEEP MOVING.
COULDN'T WE TALK **HERE?** I DON'T UNDERSTAND WHY WE NEED TO GO TO THE PRECINCT.
WE WEREN'T DOING ANYTHING WRONG.
LESS TALKING AND MORE WALKING.

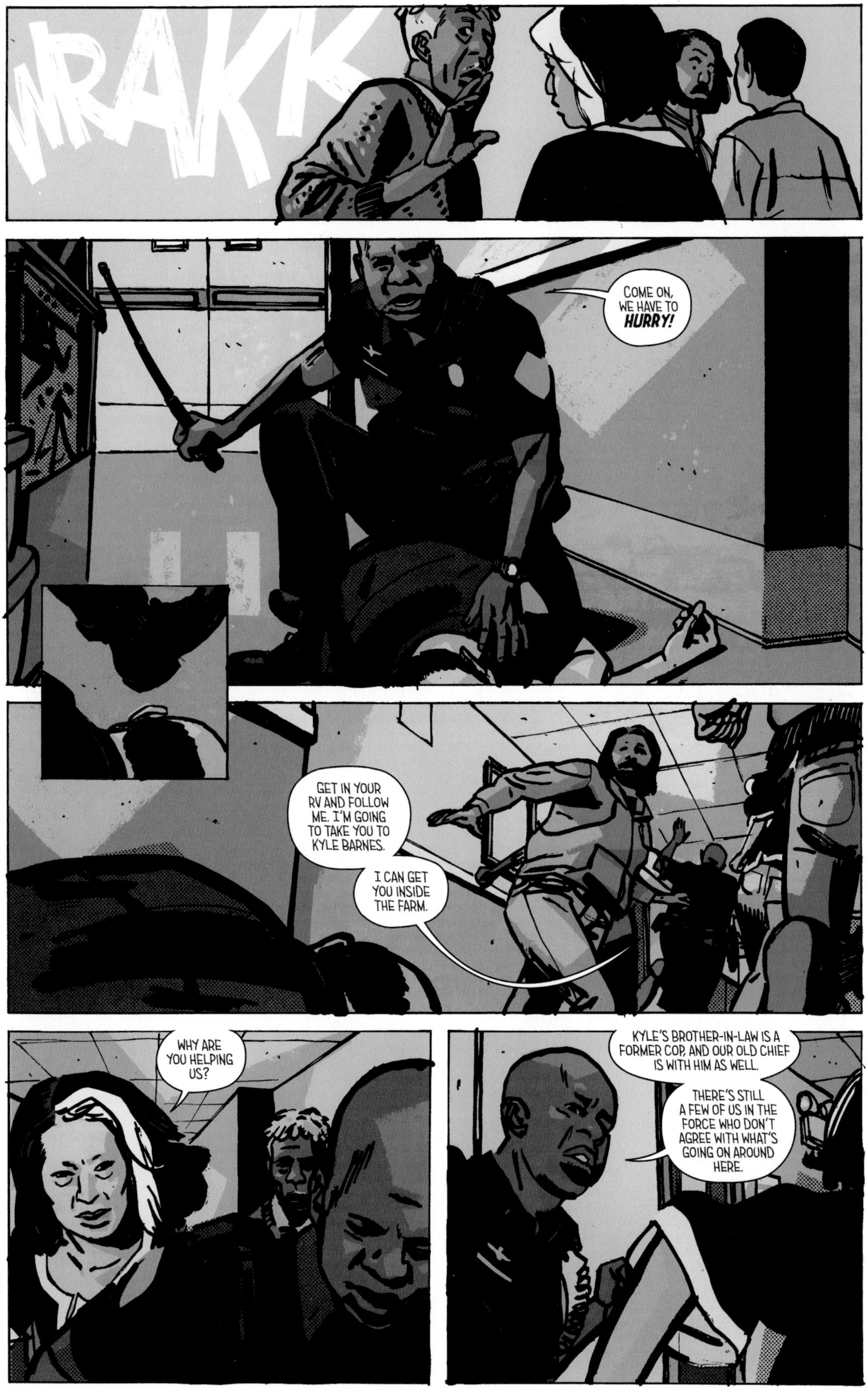
WRAKK
COME ON, WE HAVE TO *HURRY!*
GET IN YOUR RV AND FOLLOW ME. I'M GOING TO TAKE YOU TO KYLE BARNES.
I CAN GET YOU INSIDE THE FARM.
WHY ARE YOU HELPING US?
KYLE'S BROTHER-IN-LAW IS A FORMER COP, AND OUR OLD CHIEF IS WITH HIM AS WELL.
THERE'S STILL A FEW OF US IN THE FORCE WHO DON'T AGREE WITH WHAT'S GOING ON AROUND HERE.

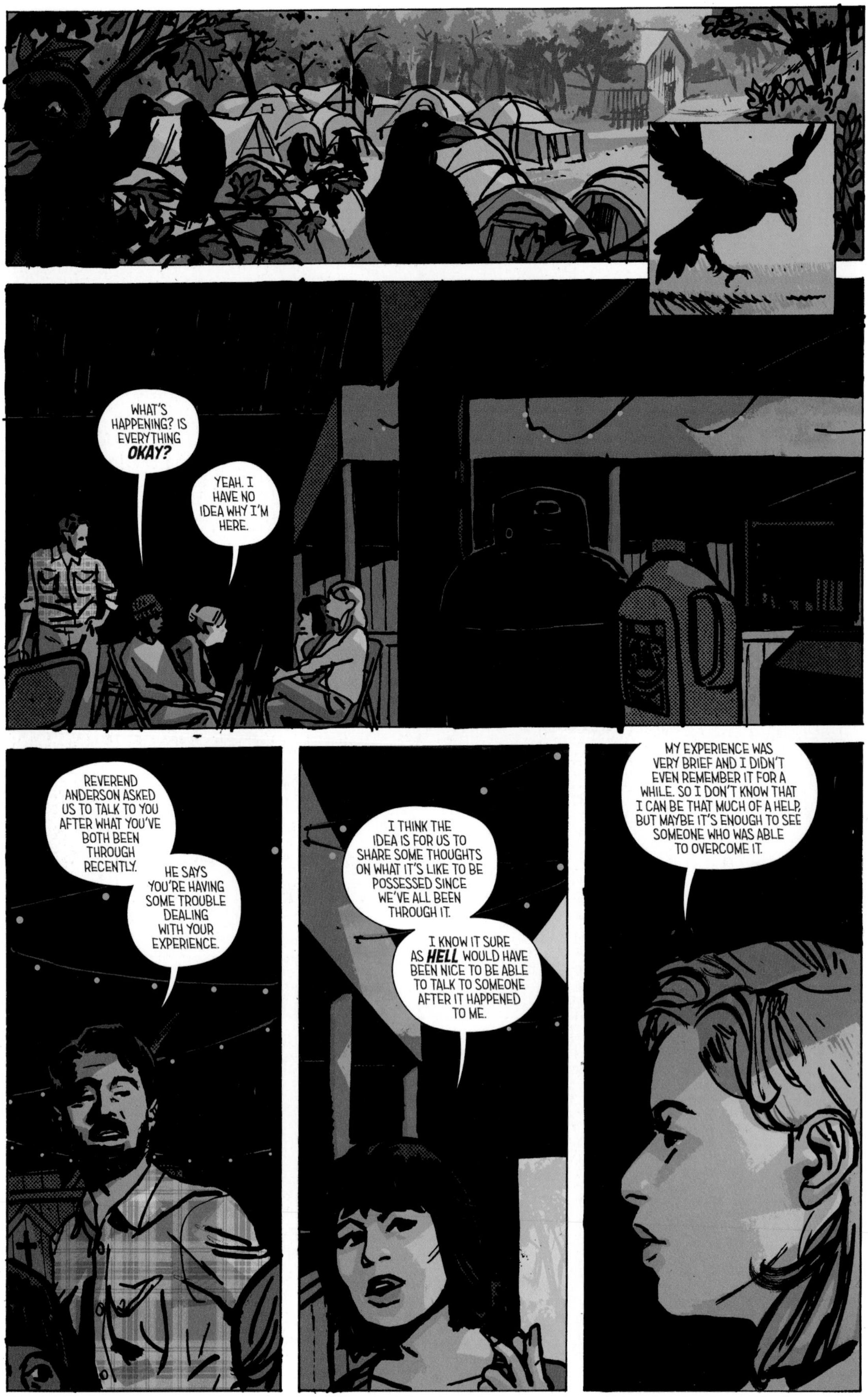
WHAT'S HAPPENING? IS EVERYTHING OKAY?
YEAH. I HAVE NO IDEA WHY I'M HERE.
REVEREND ANDERSON ASKED US TO TALK TO YOU AFTER WHAT YOU'VE BOTH BEEN THROUGH RECENTLY.
HE SAYS YOU'RE HAVING SOME TROUBLE DEALING WITH YOUR EXPERIENCE.
I THINK THE IDEA IS FOR US TO SHARE SOME THOUGHTS ON WHAT IT'S LIKE TO BE POSSESSED SINCE WE'VE ALL BEEN THROUGH IT.
I KNOW IT SURE AS HELL WOULD HAVE BEEN NICE TO BE ABLE TO TALK TO SOMEONE AFTER IT HAPPENED TO ME.
MY EXPERIENCE WAS VERY BRIEF AND I DIDN'T EVEN REMEMBER IT FOR A WHILE. SO I DON'T KNOW THAT I CAN BE THAT MUCH OF A HELP, BUT MAYBE IT'S ENOUGH TO SEE SOMEONE WHO WAS ABLE TO OVERCOME IT.

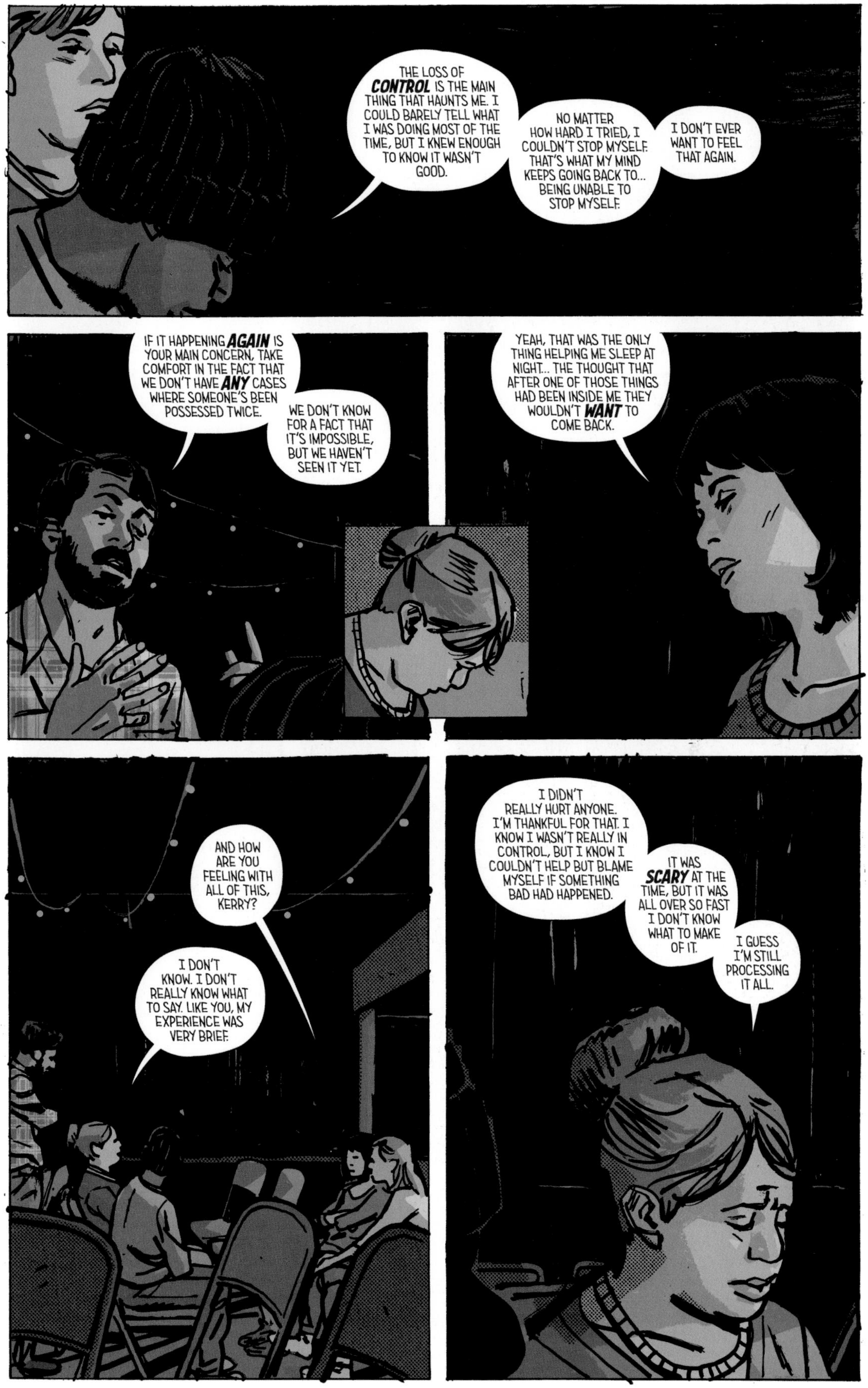
THE LOSS OF **CONTROL** IS THE MAIN THING THAT HAUNTS ME. I COULD BARELY TELL WHAT I WAS DOING MOST OF THE TIME, BUT I KNEW ENOUGH TO KNOW IT WASN'T GOOD.
NO MATTER HOW HARD I TRIED, I COULDN'T STOP MYSELF. THAT'S WHAT MY MIND KEEPS GOING BACK TO... BEING UNABLE TO STOP MYSELF.
I DON'T EVER WANT TO FEEL THAT AGAIN.
IF IT HAPPENING **AGAIN** IS YOUR MAIN CONCERN, TAKE COMFORT IN THE FACT THAT WE DON'T HAVE **ANY** CASES WHERE SOMEONE'S BEEN POSSESSED TWICE.
WE DON'T KNOW FOR A FACT THAT IT'S IMPOSSIBLE, BUT WE HAVEN'T SEEN IT YET.
YEAH, THAT WAS THE ONLY THING HELPING ME SLEEP AT NIGHT... THE THOUGHT THAT AFTER ONE OF THOSE THINGS HAD BEEN INSIDE ME THEY WOULDN'T **WANT** TO COME BACK.
AND HOW ARE YOU FEELING WITH ALL OF THIS, KERRY?
I DON'T KNOW. I DON'T REALLY KNOW WHAT TO SAY. LIKE YOU, MY EXPERIENCE WAS VERY BRIEF.
I DIDN'T REALLY HURT ANYONE. I'M THANKFUL FOR THAT. I KNOW I WASN'T REALLY IN CONTROL, BUT I KNOW I COULDN'T HELP BUT BLAME MYSELF IF SOMETHING BAD HAD HAPPENED.
IT WAS **SCARY** AT THE TIME, BUT IT WAS ALL OVER SO FAST I DON'T KNOW WHAT TO MAKE OF IT.
I GUESS I'M STILL PROCESSING IT ALL.

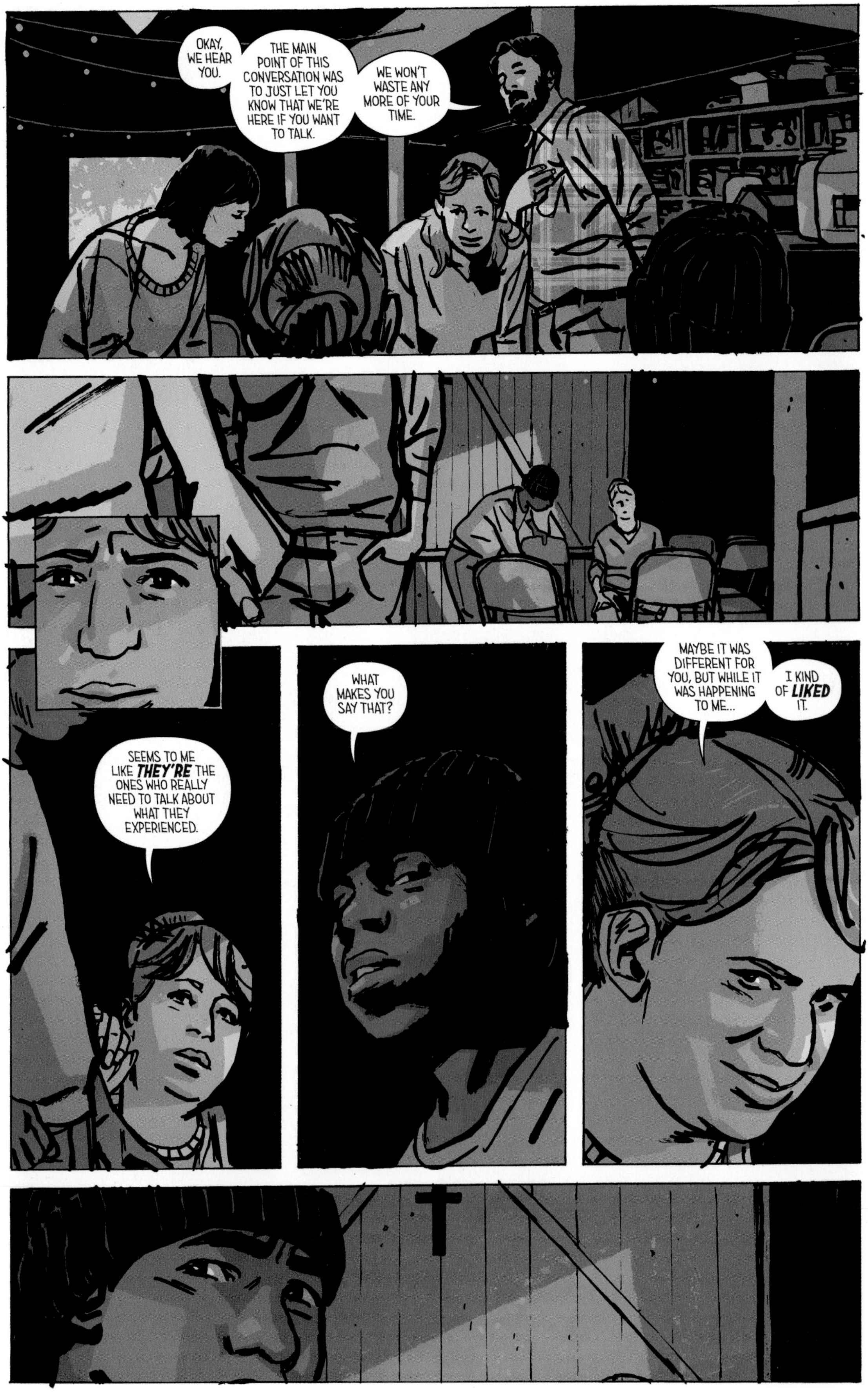
OKAY, WE HEAR YOU.
THE MAIN POINT OF THIS CONVERSATION WAS TO JUST LET YOU KNOW THAT WE'RE HERE IF YOU WANT TO TALK.
WE WON'T WASTE ANY MORE OF YOUR TIME.
SEEMS TO ME LIKE THEY'RE THE ONES WHO REALLY NEED TO TALK ABOUT WHAT THEY EXPERIENCED.
WHAT MAKES YOU SAY THAT?
MAYBE IT WAS DIFFERENT FOR YOU, BUT WHILE IT WAS HAPPENING TO ME...
I KIND OF LIKED IT.

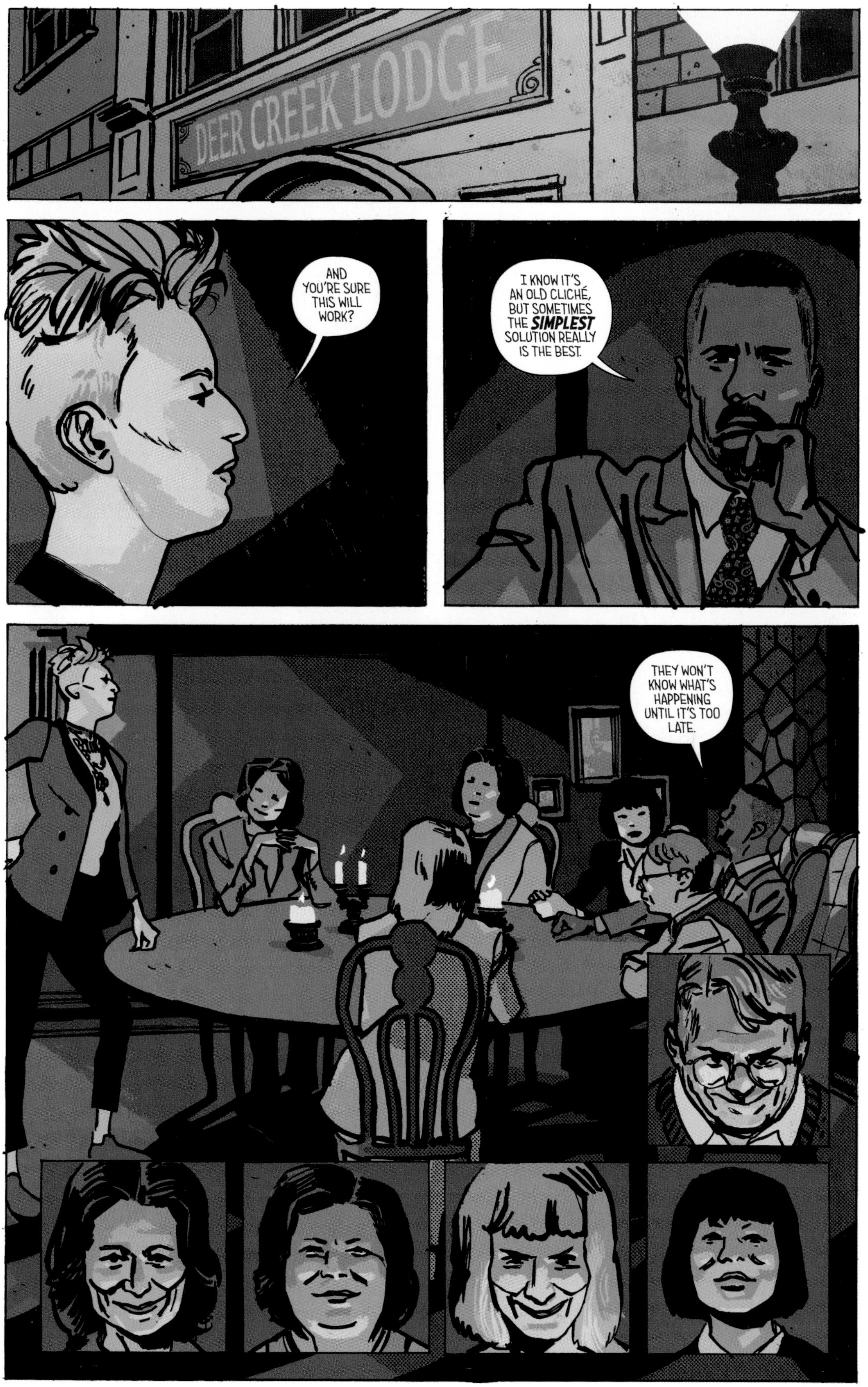
DEER CREEK LODGE
AND YOU'RE SURE THIS WILL WORK?
I KNOW IT'S AN OLD CLICHÉ, BUT SOMETIMES THE ***SIMPLEST*** SOLUTION REALLY IS THE BEST.
THEY WON'T KNOW WHAT'S HAPPENING UNTIL IT'S TOO LATE.

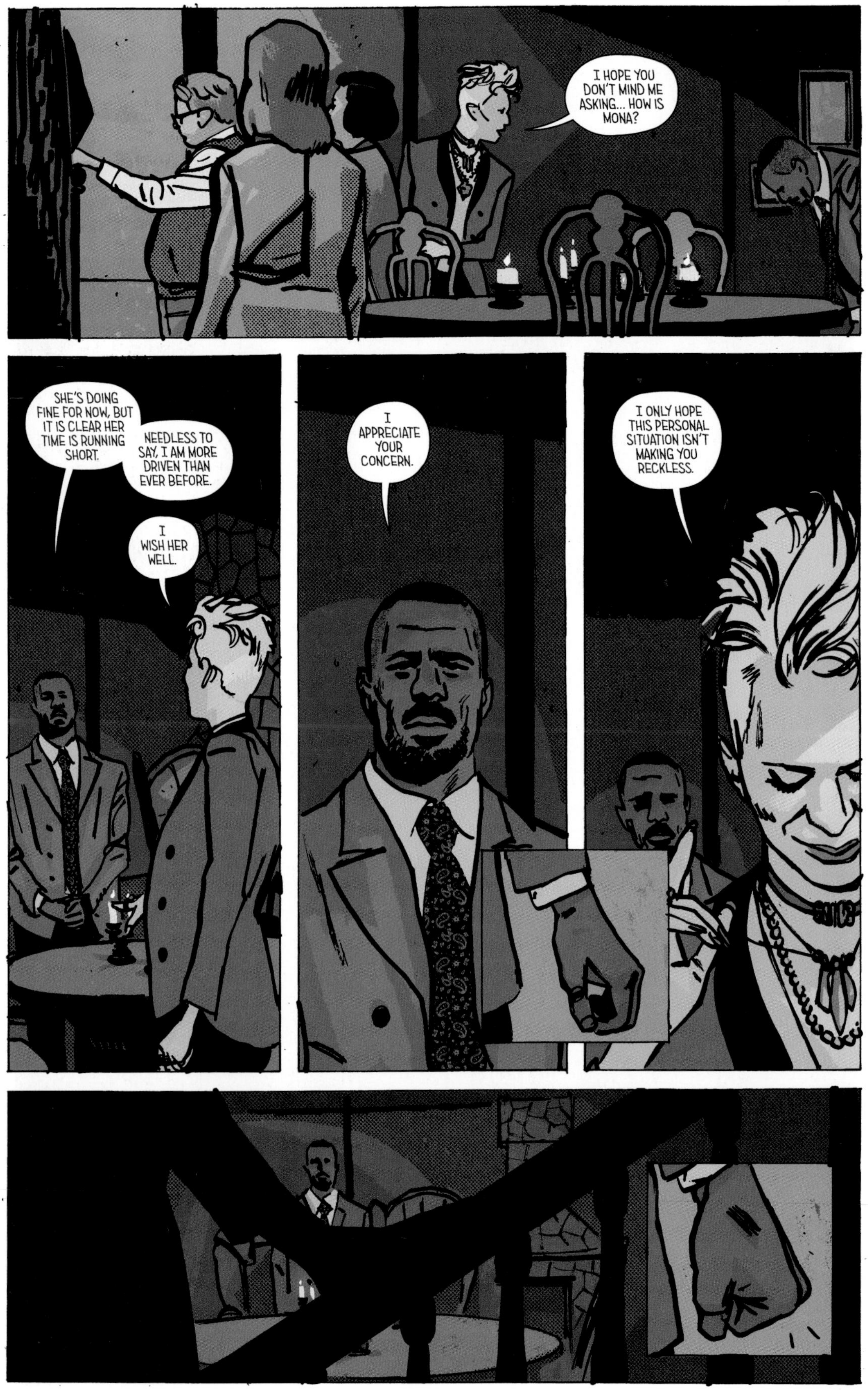
I HOPE YOU DON'T MIND ME ASKING... HOW IS MONA?
SHE'S DOING FINE FOR NOW, BUT IT IS CLEAR HER TIME IS RUNNING SHORT.
NEEDLESS TO SAY, I AM MORE DRIVEN THAN EVER BEFORE.
I WISH HER WELL.
I APPRECIATE YOUR CONCERN.
I ONLY HOPE THIS PERSONAL SITUATION ISN'T MAKING YOU RECKLESS.

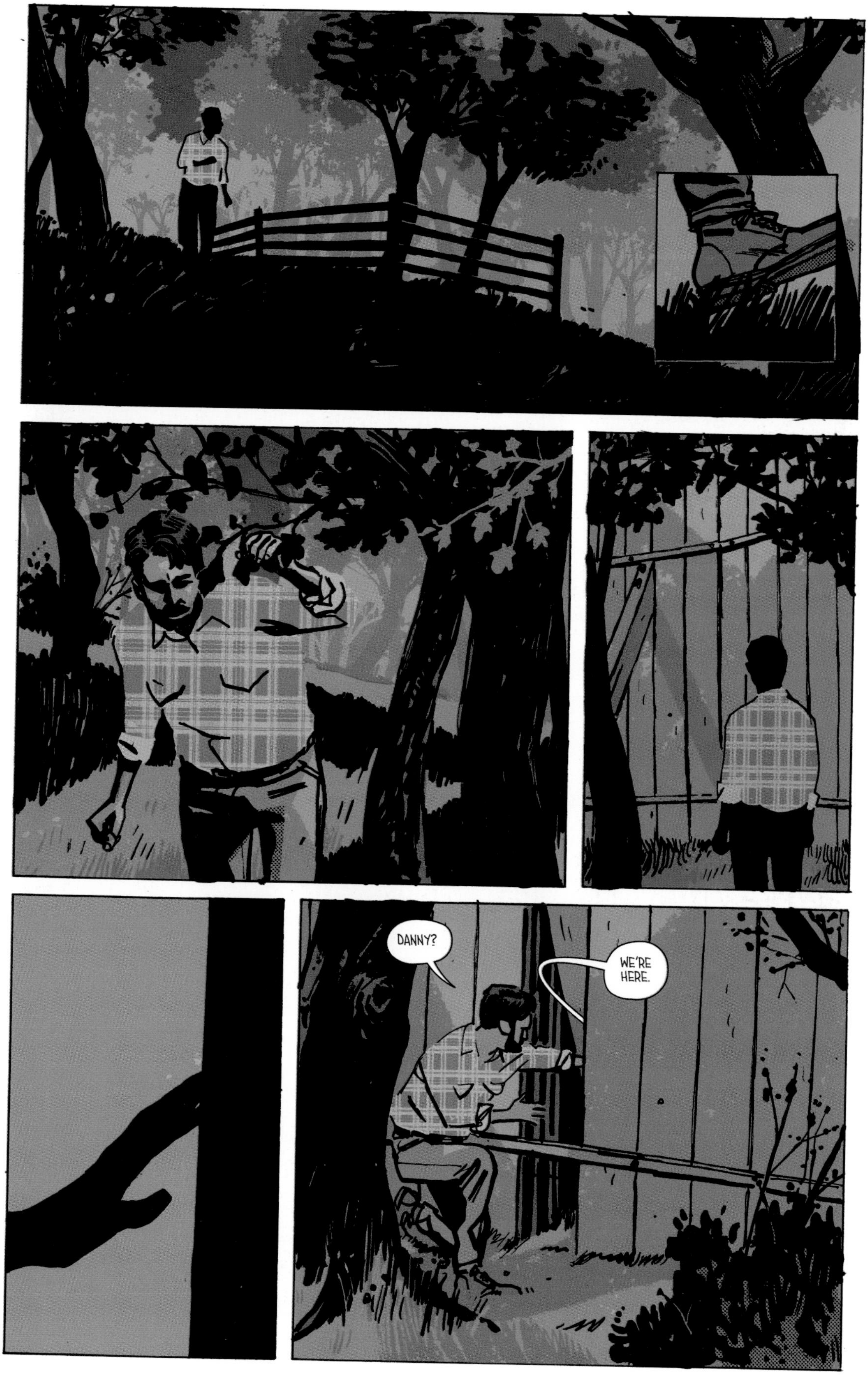
DANNY?
WE'RE HERE.

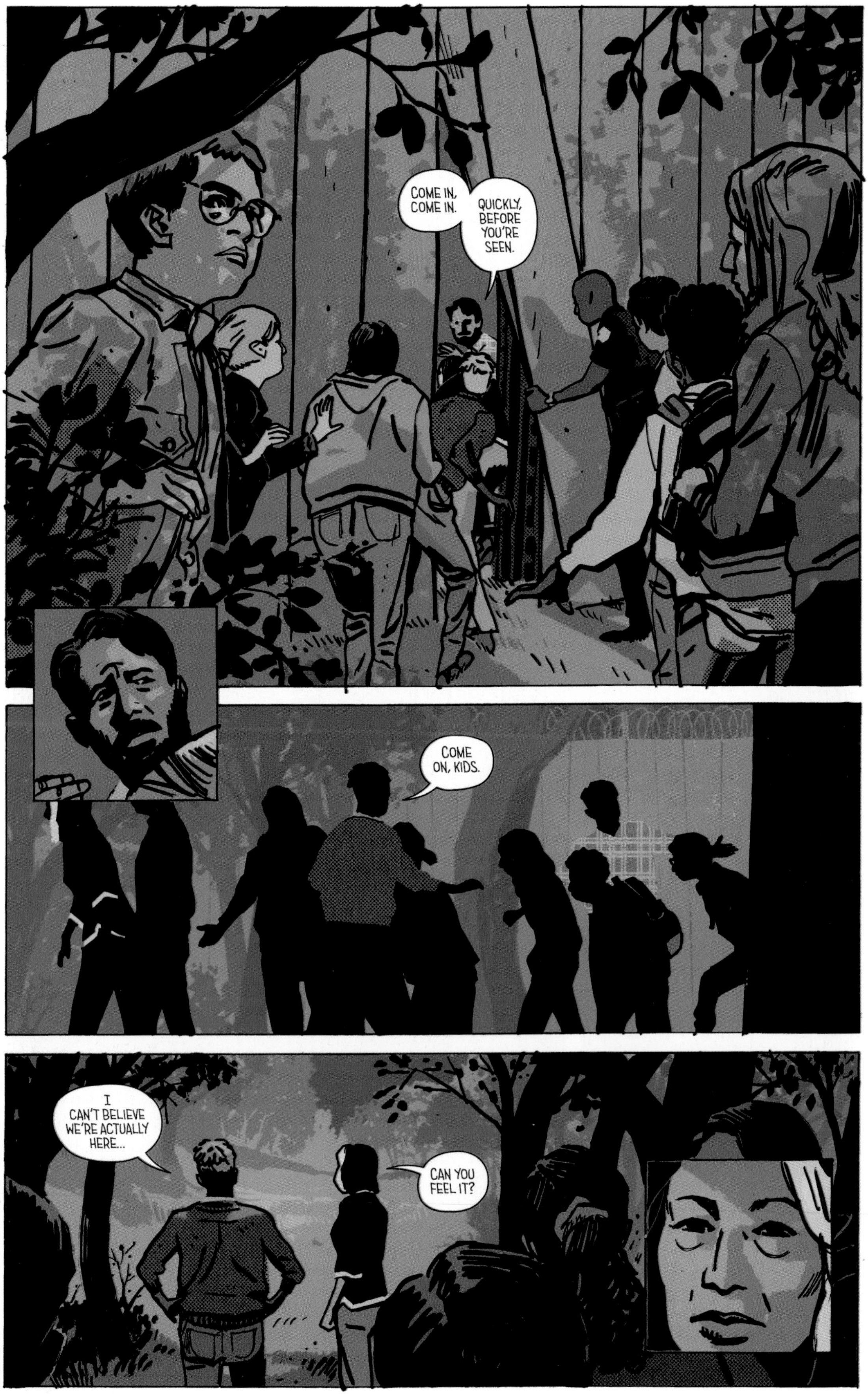
COME IN, COME IN.
QUICKLY, BEFORE YOU'RE SEEN.
COME ON, KIDS.
I CAN'T BELIEVE WE'RE ACTUALLY HERE...
CAN YOU FEEL IT?

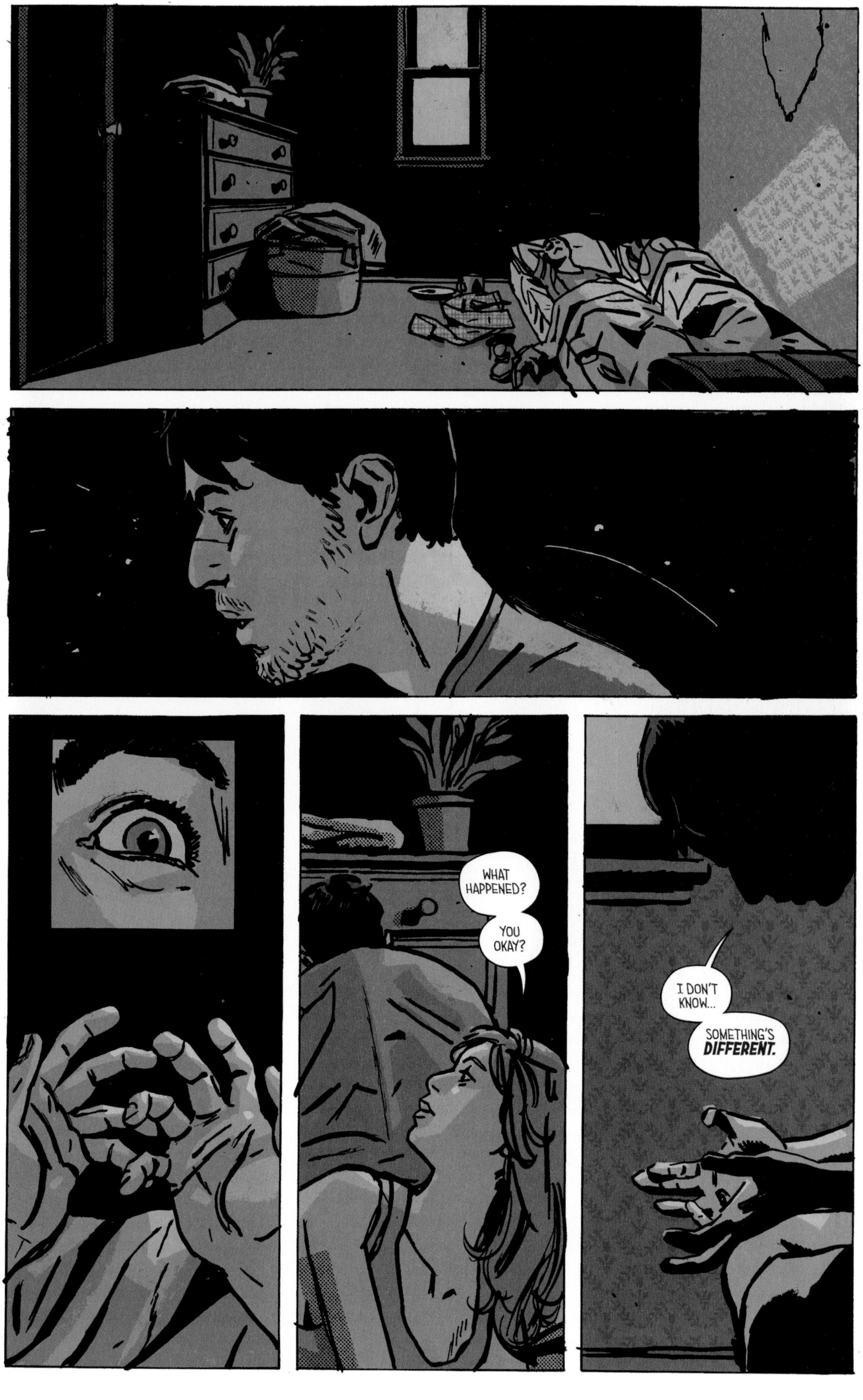
WHAT HAPPENED?
YOU OKAY?
I DON'T KNOW...
SOMETHING'S **DIFFERENT.**

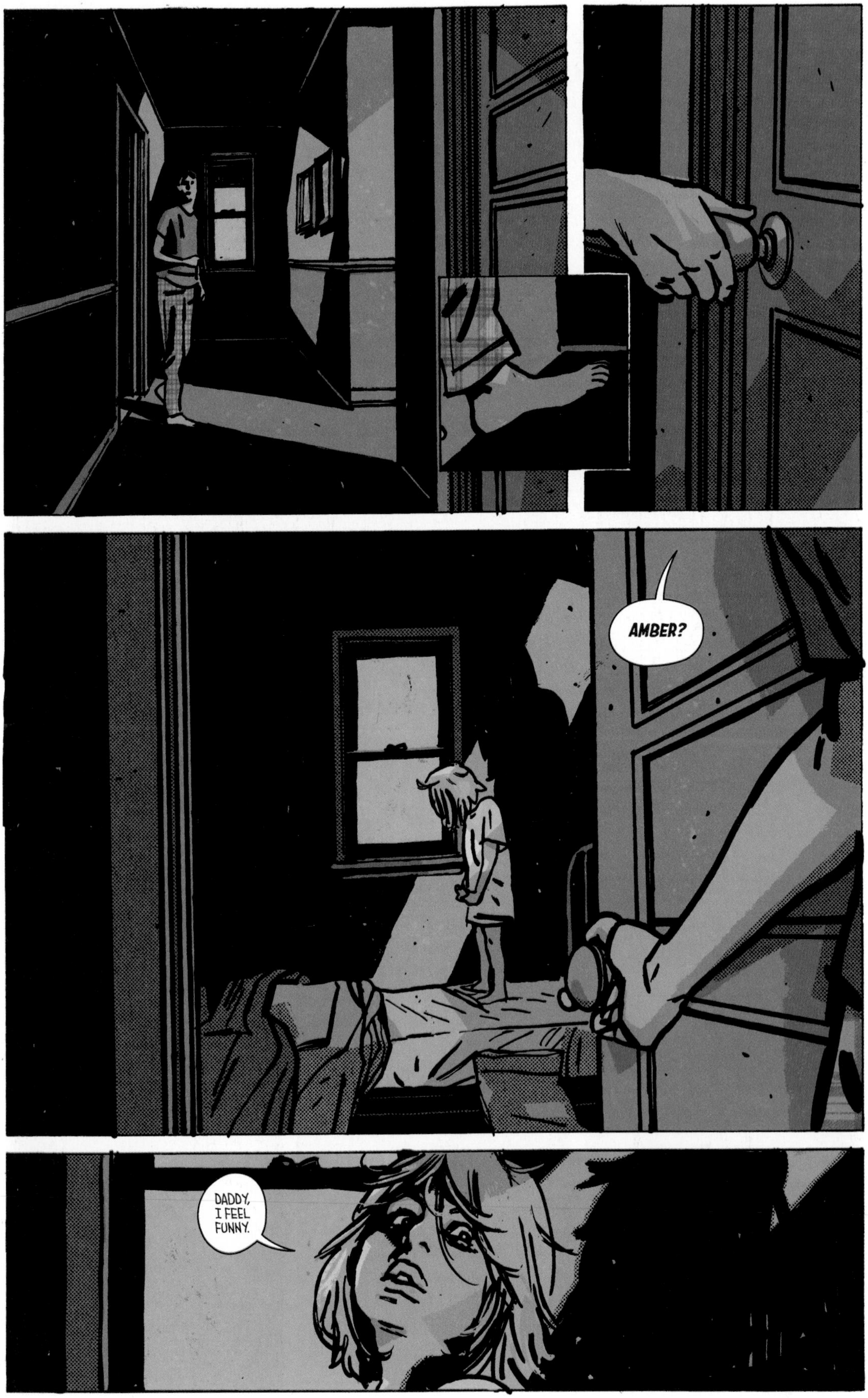
AMBER?
DADDY, I FEEL FUNNY.

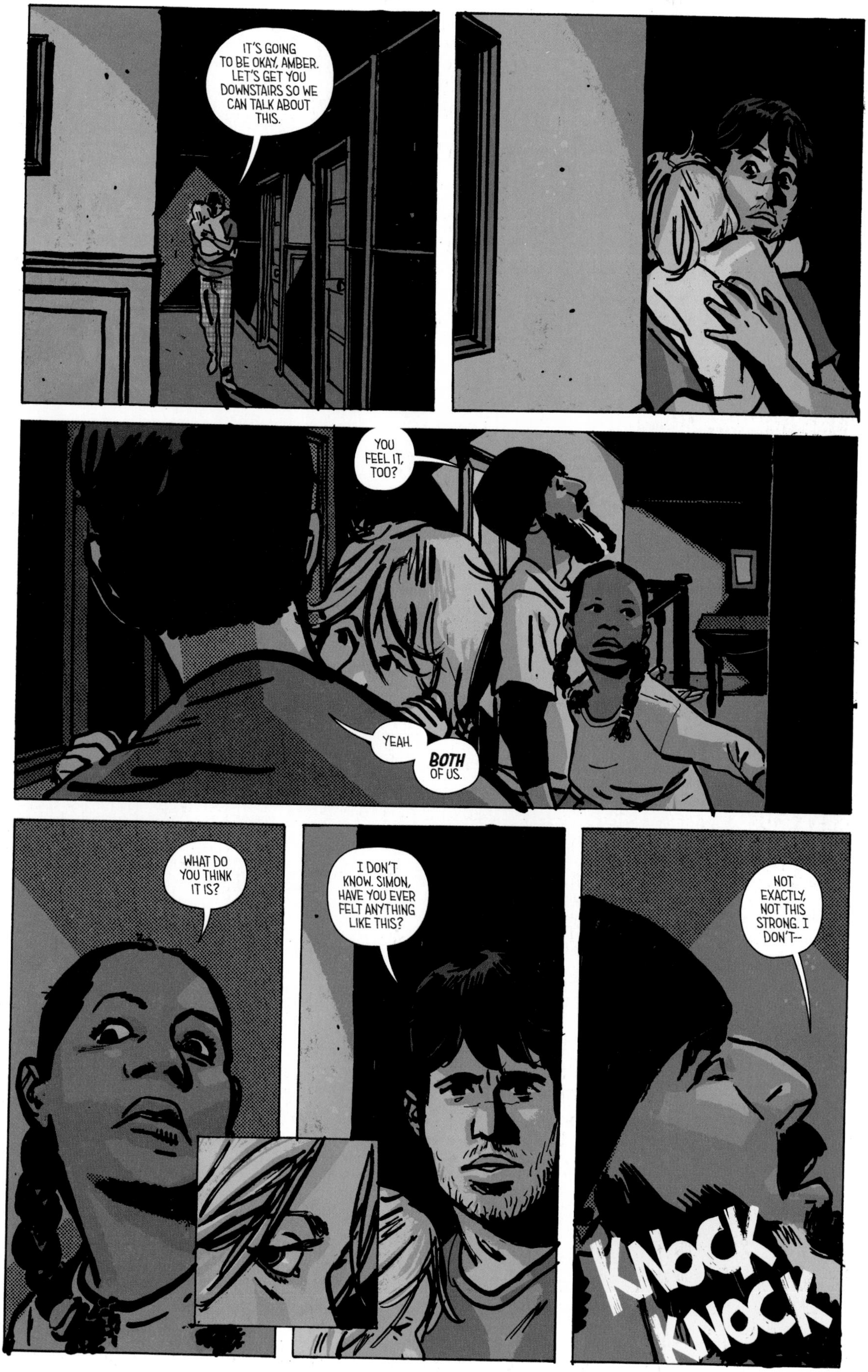

IT'S GOING TO BE OKAY, AMBER. LET'S GET YOU DOWNSTAIRS SO WE CAN TALK ABOUT THIS.
YOU FEEL IT, TOO?
YEAH. BOTH OF US.
WHAT DO YOU THINK IT IS?
I DON'T KNOW. SIMON, HAVE YOU EVER FELT ANYTHING LIKE THIS?
NOT EXACTLY, NOT THIS STRONG. I DON'T--
KNOCK KNOCK

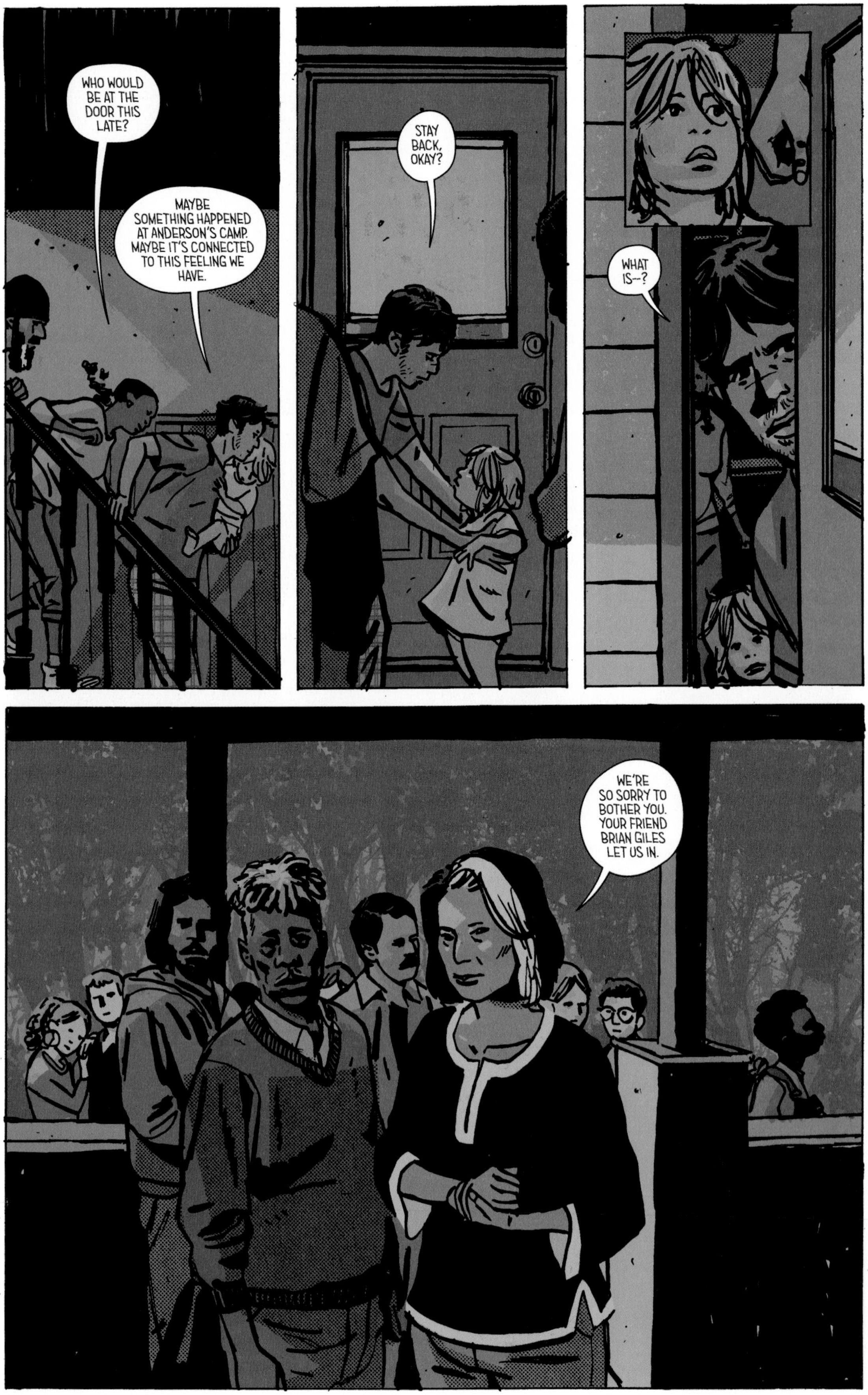
WHO WOULD BE AT THE DOOR THIS LATE?
MAYBE SOMETHING HAPPENED AT ANDERSON'S CAMP. MAYBE IT'S CONNECTED TO THIS FEELING WE HAVE.
STAY BACK, OKAY?
WHAT IS--?
WE'RE SO SORRY TO BOTHER YOU. YOUR FRIEND BRIAN GILES LET US IN.

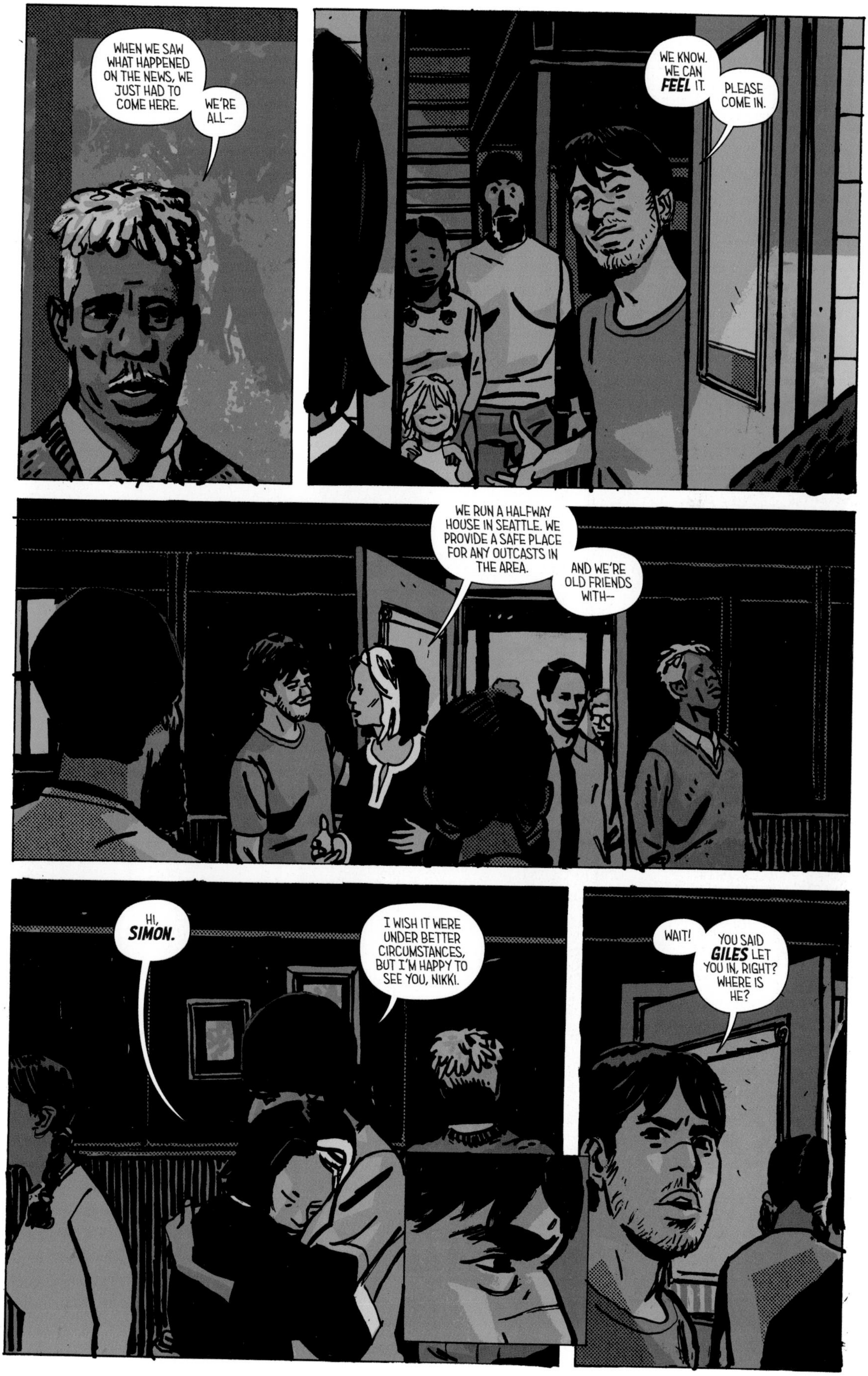
WHEN WE SAW WHAT HAPPENED ON THE NEWS, WE JUST HAD TO COME HERE.
WE'RE ALL--
WE KNOW. WE CAN FEEL IT.
PLEASE COME IN.
WE RUN A HALFWAY HOUSE IN SEATTLE. WE PROVIDE A SAFE PLACE FOR ANY OUTCASTS IN THE AREA.
AND WE'RE OLD FRIENDS WITH--
HI, SIMON.
I WISH IT WERE UNDER BETTER CIRCUMSTANCES, BUT I'M HAPPY TO SEE YOU, NIKKI.
WAIT!
YOU SAID GILES LET YOU IN, RIGHT? WHERE IS HE?

WHAT ARE YOU DOING?

MAKING SURE THIS SPOT ISN'T OBVIOUS.

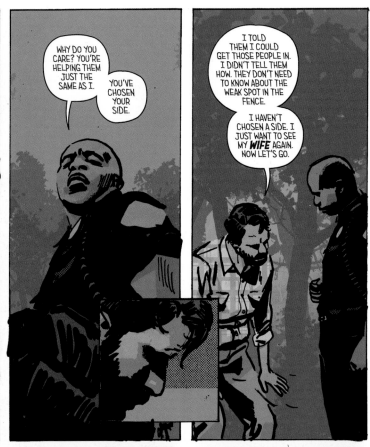

WHY DO YOU CARE? YOU'RE HELPING THEM JUST THE SAME AS I.

YOU'VE CHOSEN YOUR SIDE.

I TOLD THEM I COULD GET THOSE PEOPLE IN. I DIDN'T TELL THEM HOW. THEY DON'T NEED TO KNOW ABOUT THE WEAK SPOT IN THE FENCE.

I HAVEN'T CHOSEN A SIDE. I JUST WANT TO SEE MY *WIFE* AGAIN. NOW LET'S GO.

WHATEVER YOU GOTTA TELL YOURSELF, MAN.

YOU GOT ANY CLUE WHAT'S GOING TO HAPPEN TO THOSE PEOPLE IN THERE NOW? TRUST ME, MAN, THEY'RE *FUCKED.*

A WEAK SPOT IN THE FENCE IS THE *LEAST* OF THEIR WORRIES.

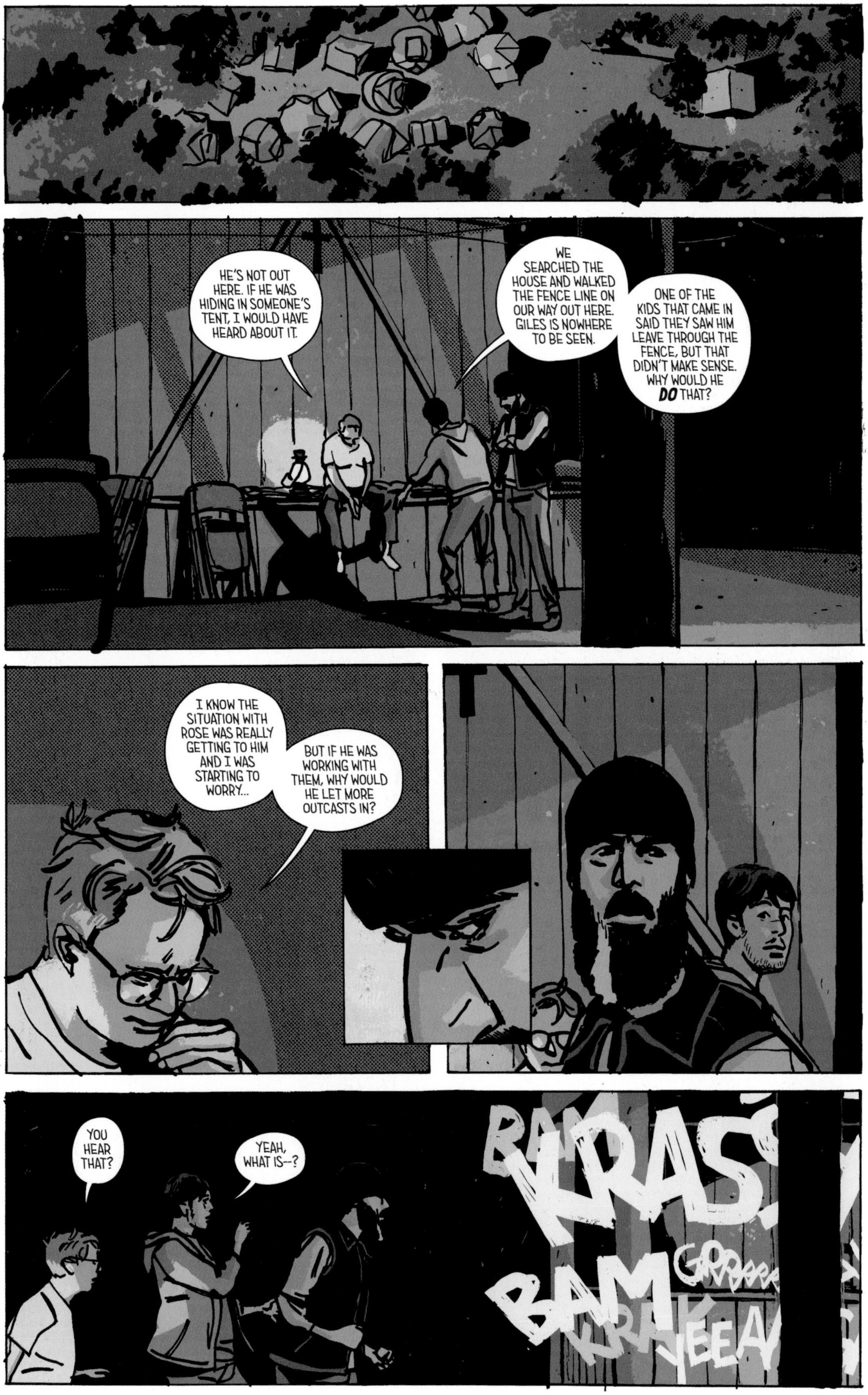
HE'S NOT OUT HERE. IF HE WAS HIDING IN SOMEONE'S TENT, I WOULD HAVE HEARD ABOUT IT.
WE SEARCHED THE HOUSE AND WALKED THE FENCE LINE ON OUR WAY OUT HERE. GILES IS NOWHERE TO BE SEEN.
ONE OF THE KIDS THAT CAME IN SAID THEY SAW HIM LEAVE THROUGH THE FENCE, BUT THAT DIDN'T MAKE SENSE. WHY WOULD HE **DO** THAT?
I KNOW THE SITUATION WITH ROSE WAS REALLY GETTING TO HIM AND I WAS STARTING TO WORRY...
BUT IF HE WAS WORKING WITH THEM, WHY WOULD HE LET MORE OUTCASTS IN?
YOU HEAR THAT?
YEAH, WHAT IS--?
KRAS
BAM
YEEA

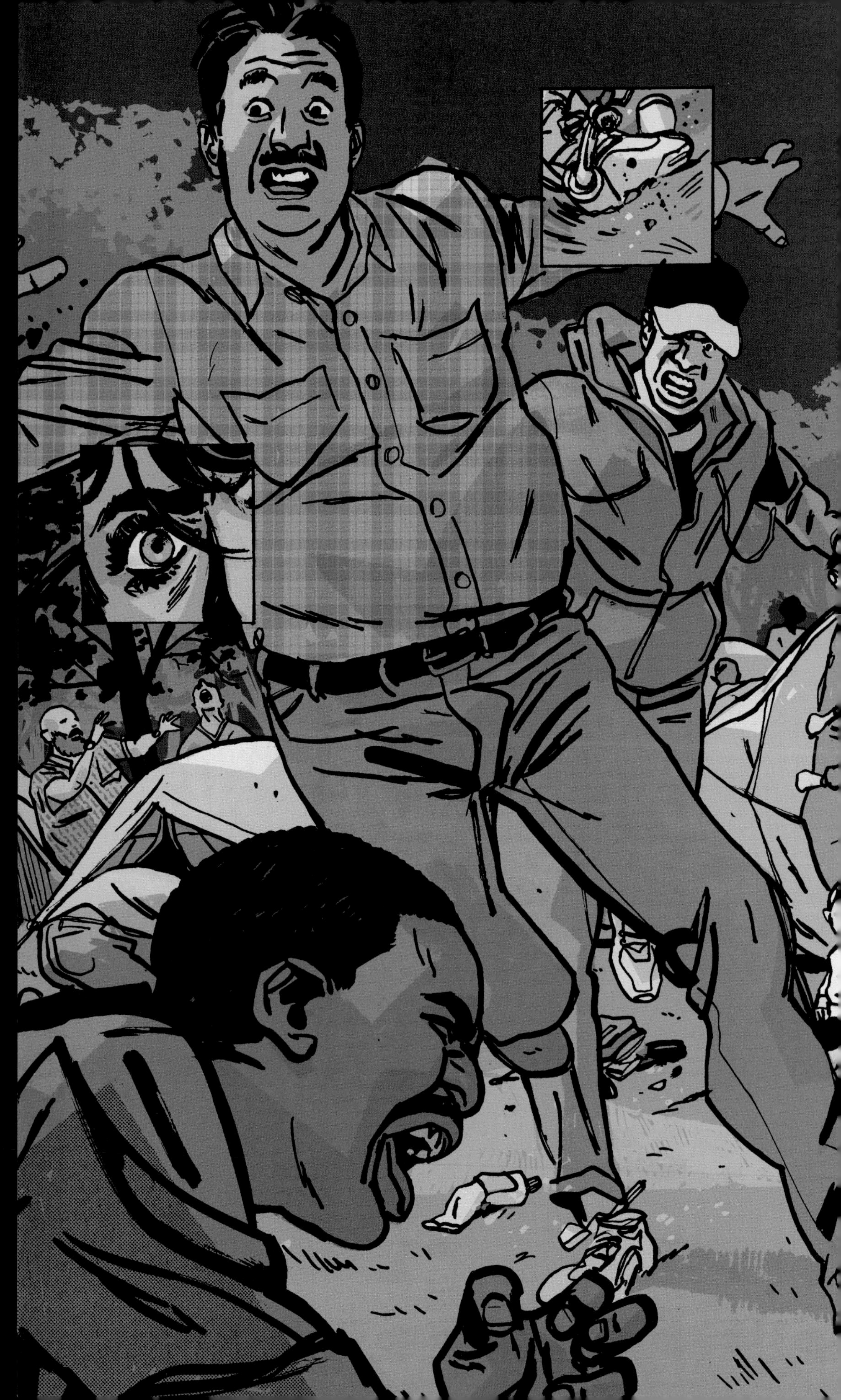

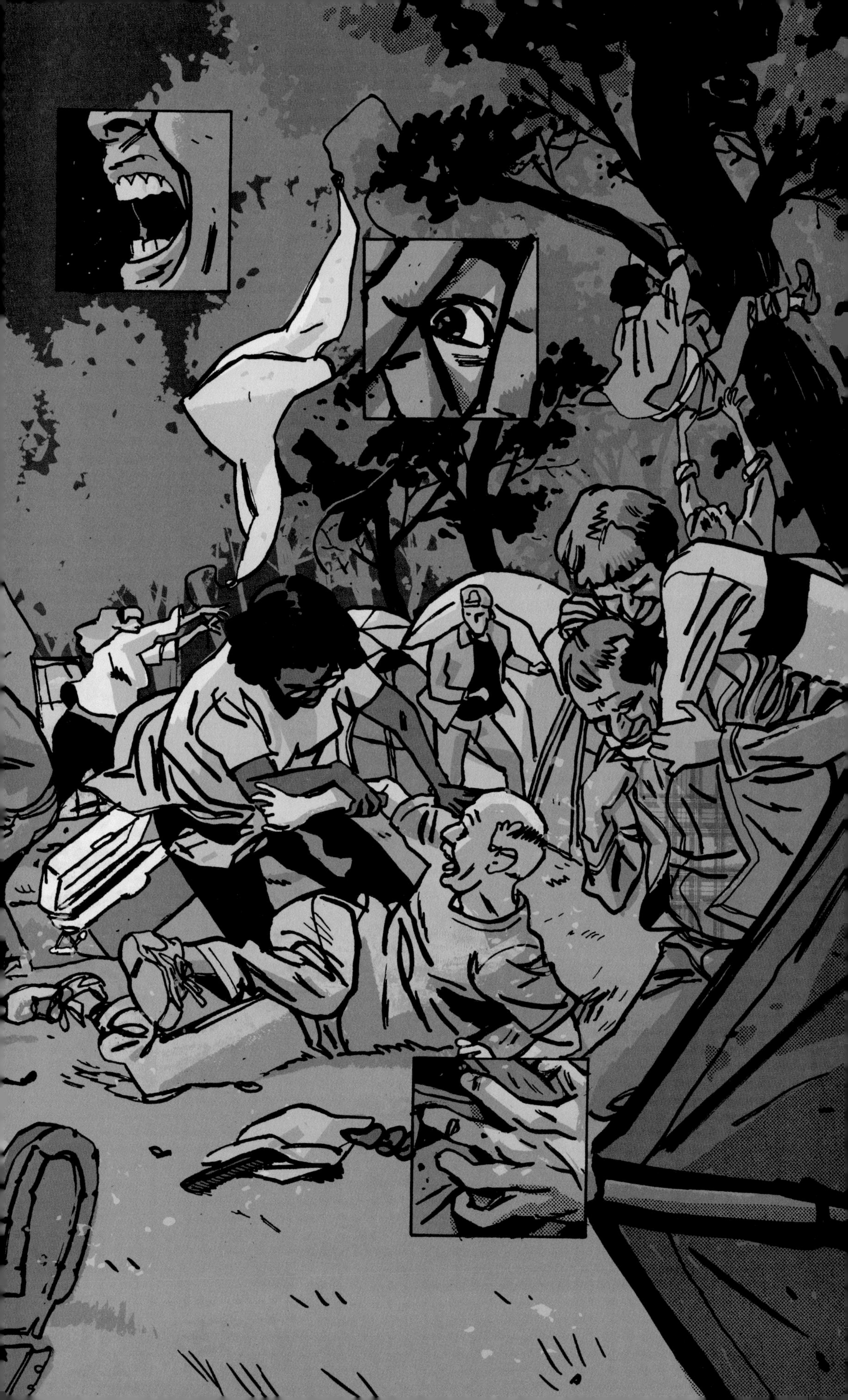

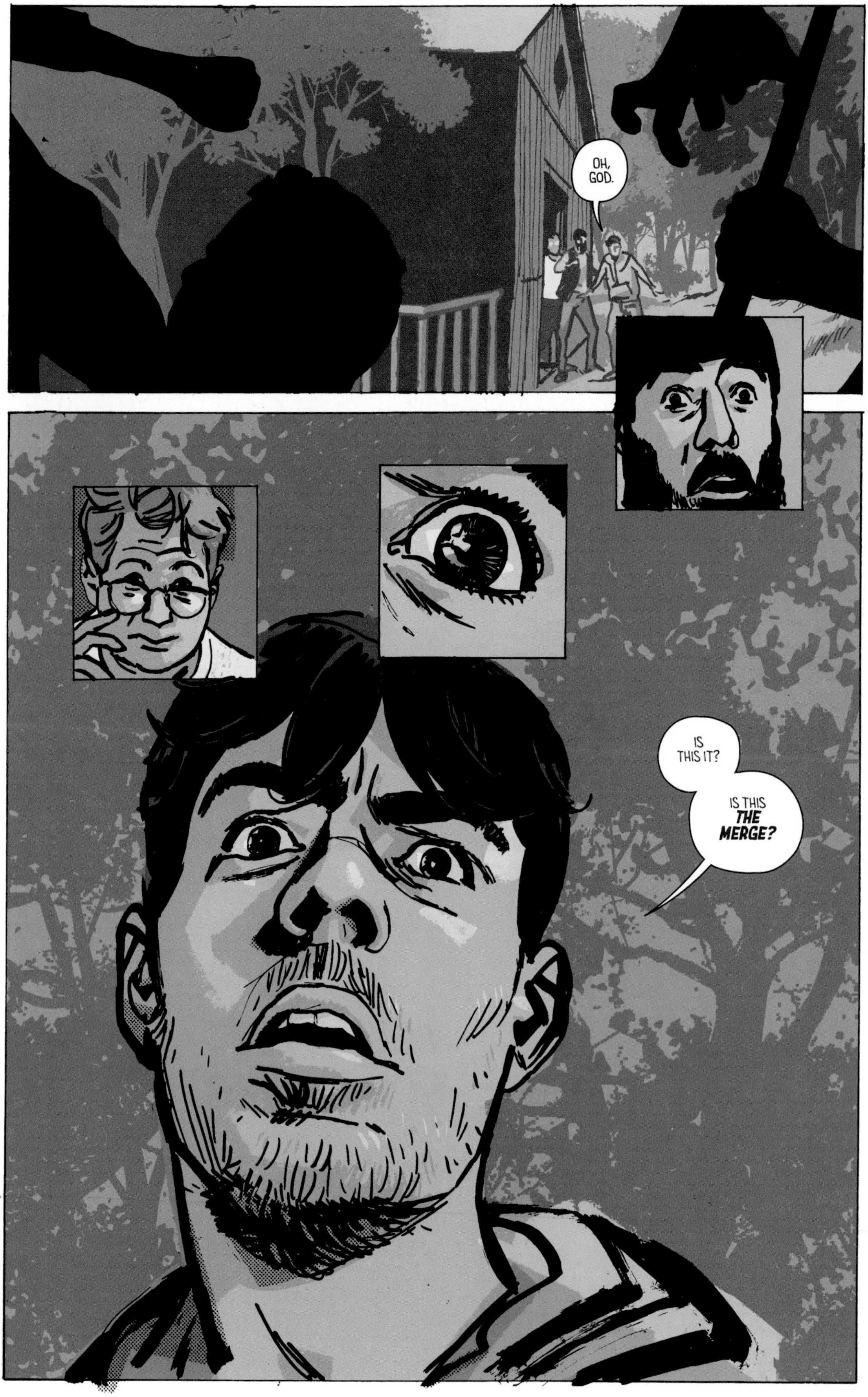
OH, GOD.
IS THIS IT?
IS THIS THE MERGE?

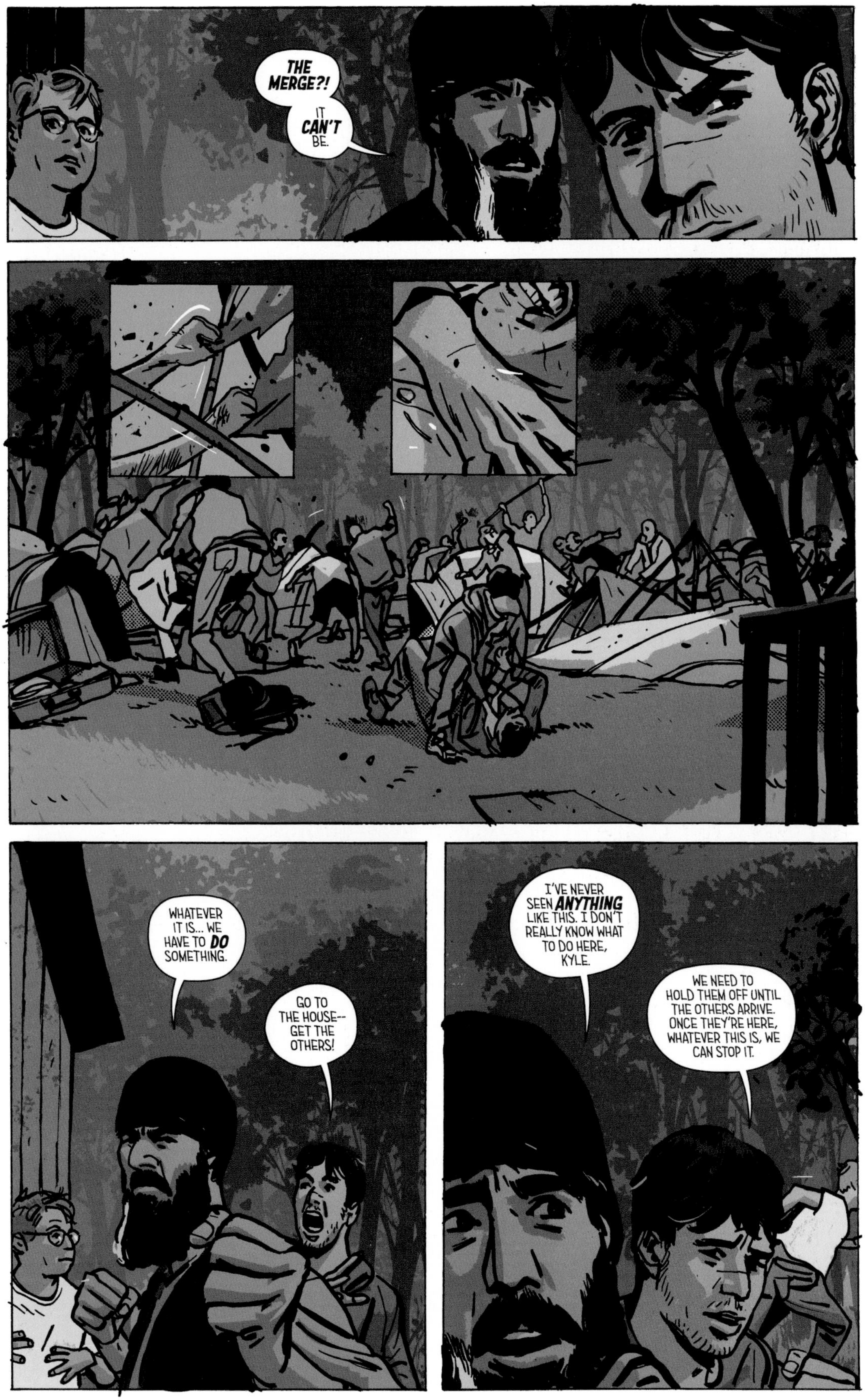
THE MERGE?!
IT CAN'T BE.
WHATEVER IT IS... WE HAVE TO DO SOMETHING.
GO TO THE HOUSE-- GET THE OTHERS!
I'VE NEVER SEEN ANYTHING LIKE THIS. I DON'T REALLY KNOW WHAT TO DO HERE, KYLE.
WE NEED TO HOLD THEM OFF UNTIL THE OTHERS ARRIVE. ONCE THEY'RE HERE, WHATEVER THIS IS, WE CAN STOP IT.

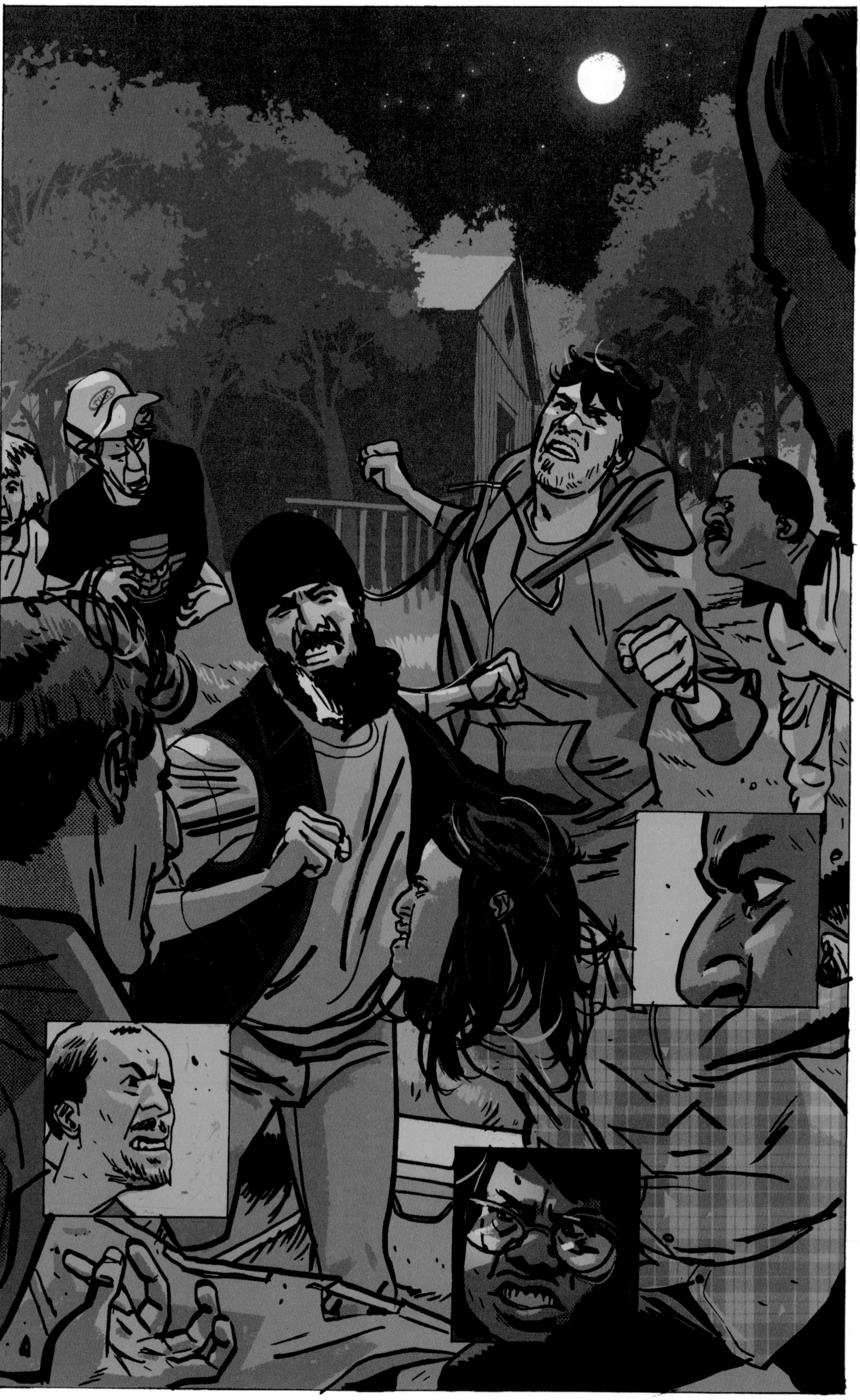

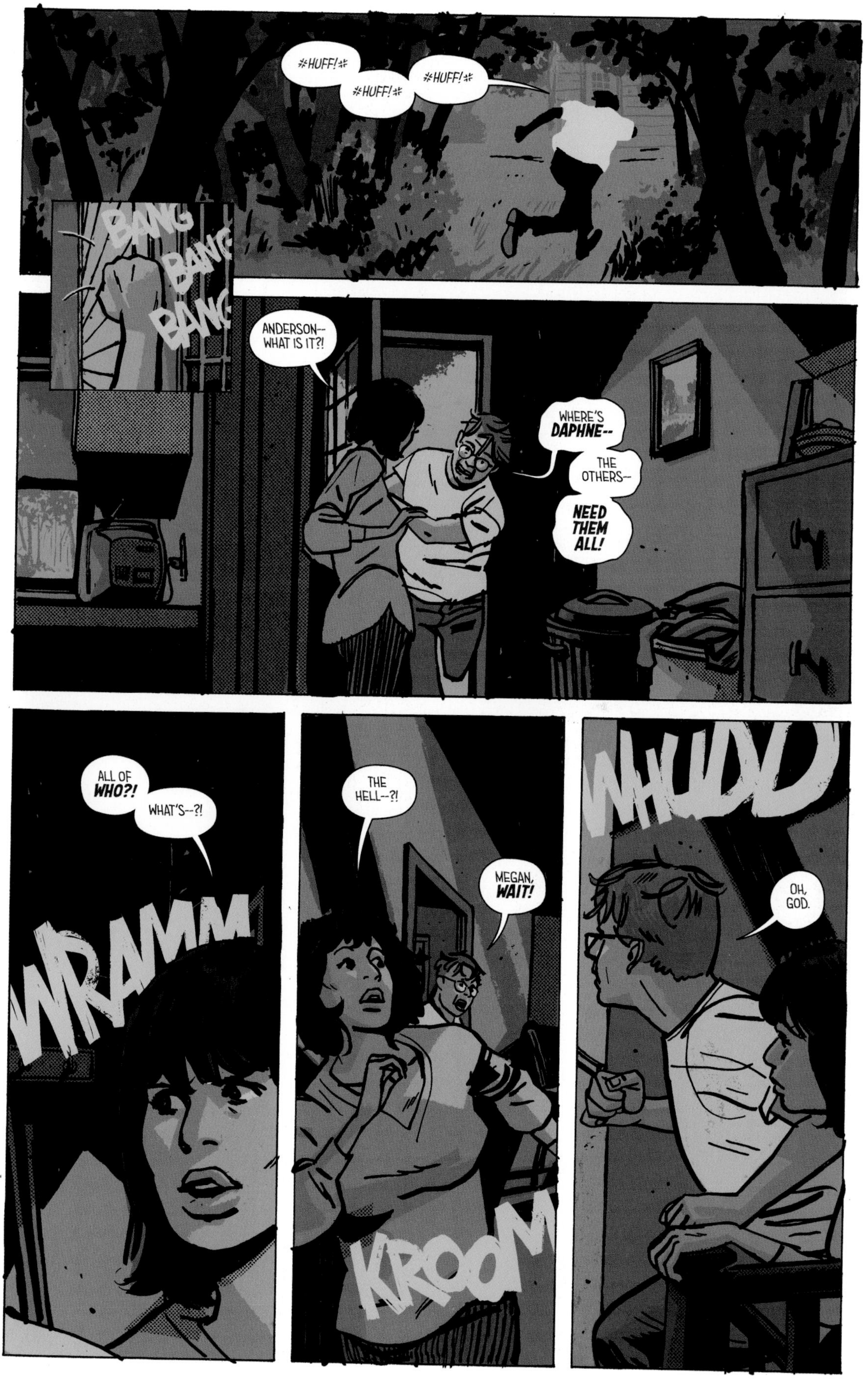
HUFF!
HUFF!
HUFF!
BANG
BANG
BANG
ANDERSON-- WHAT IS IT?!
WHERE'S **DAPHNE--**
THE OTHERS--
NEED THEM ALL!
ALL OF **WHO?!**
WHAT'S--?!
WRAMM
THE HELL--?!
MEGAN, **WAIT!**
KROOM
WHUDD
OH, GOD.

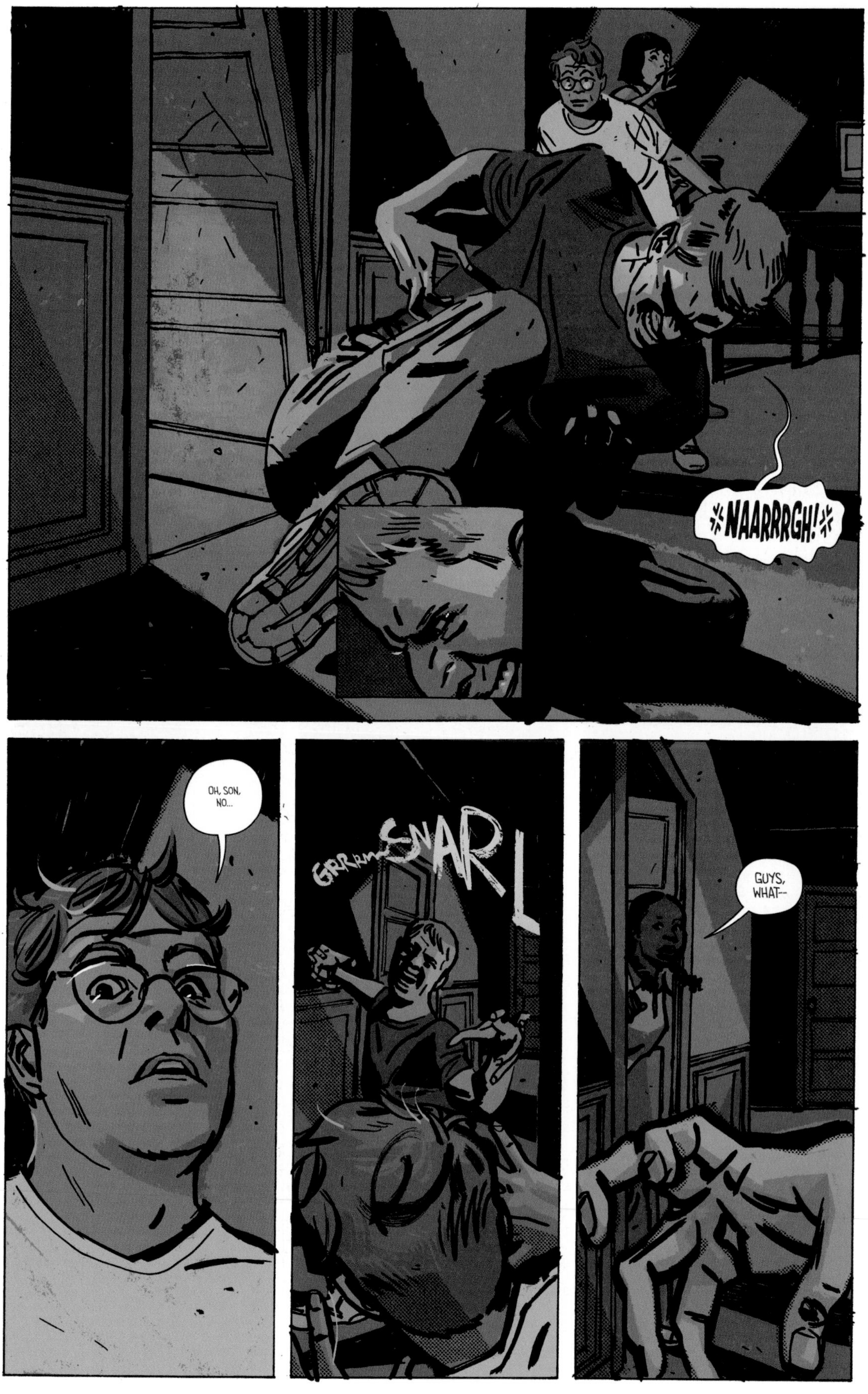
NAARRRGH!
OH, SON, NO...
GRRrrr SNARL
GUYS, WHAT--

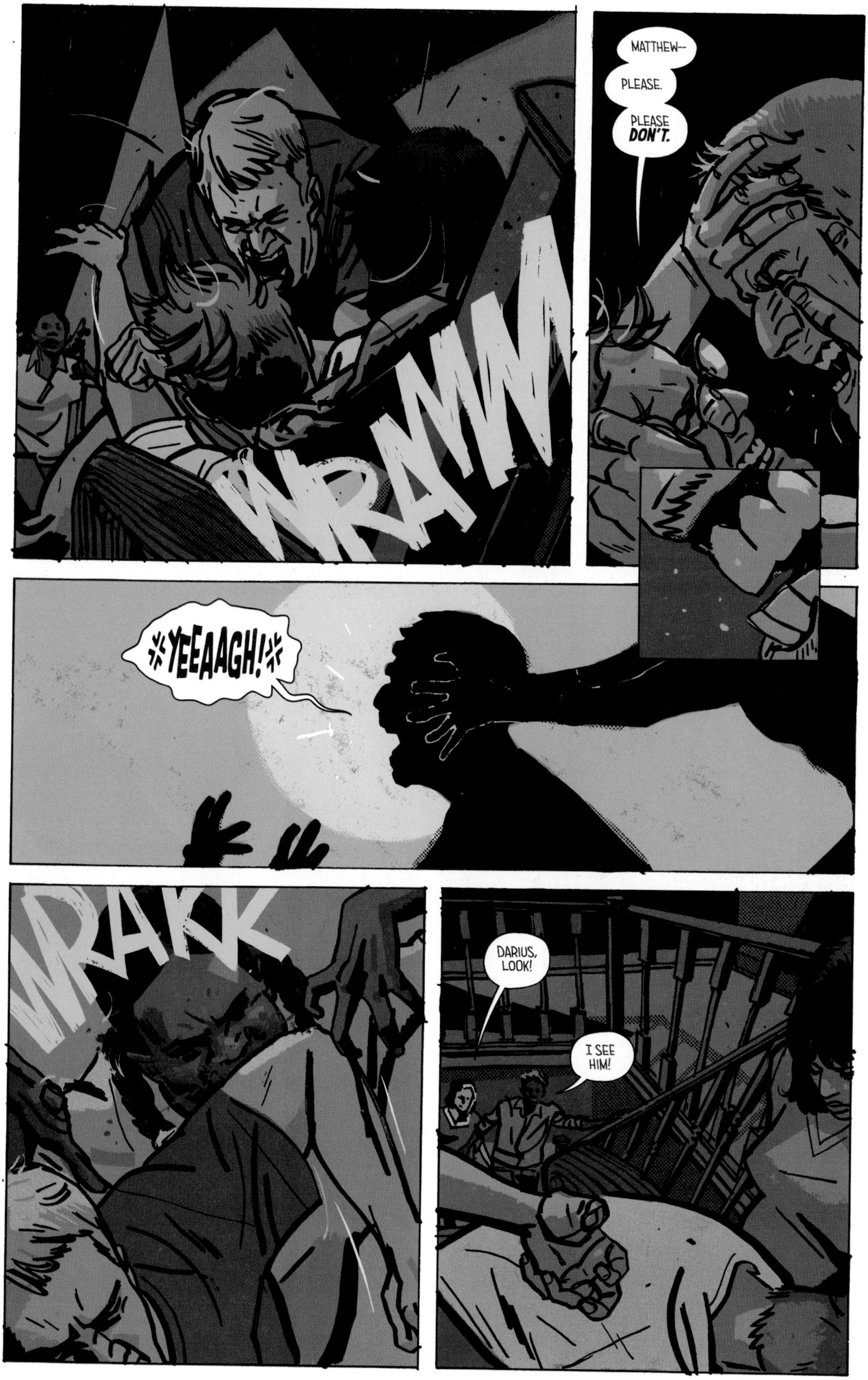
MATTHEW--
PLEASE.
PLEASE DON'T.
WRAMM
¤YEEAAGH!¤
WRAKK
DARIUS, LOOK!
I SEE HIM!

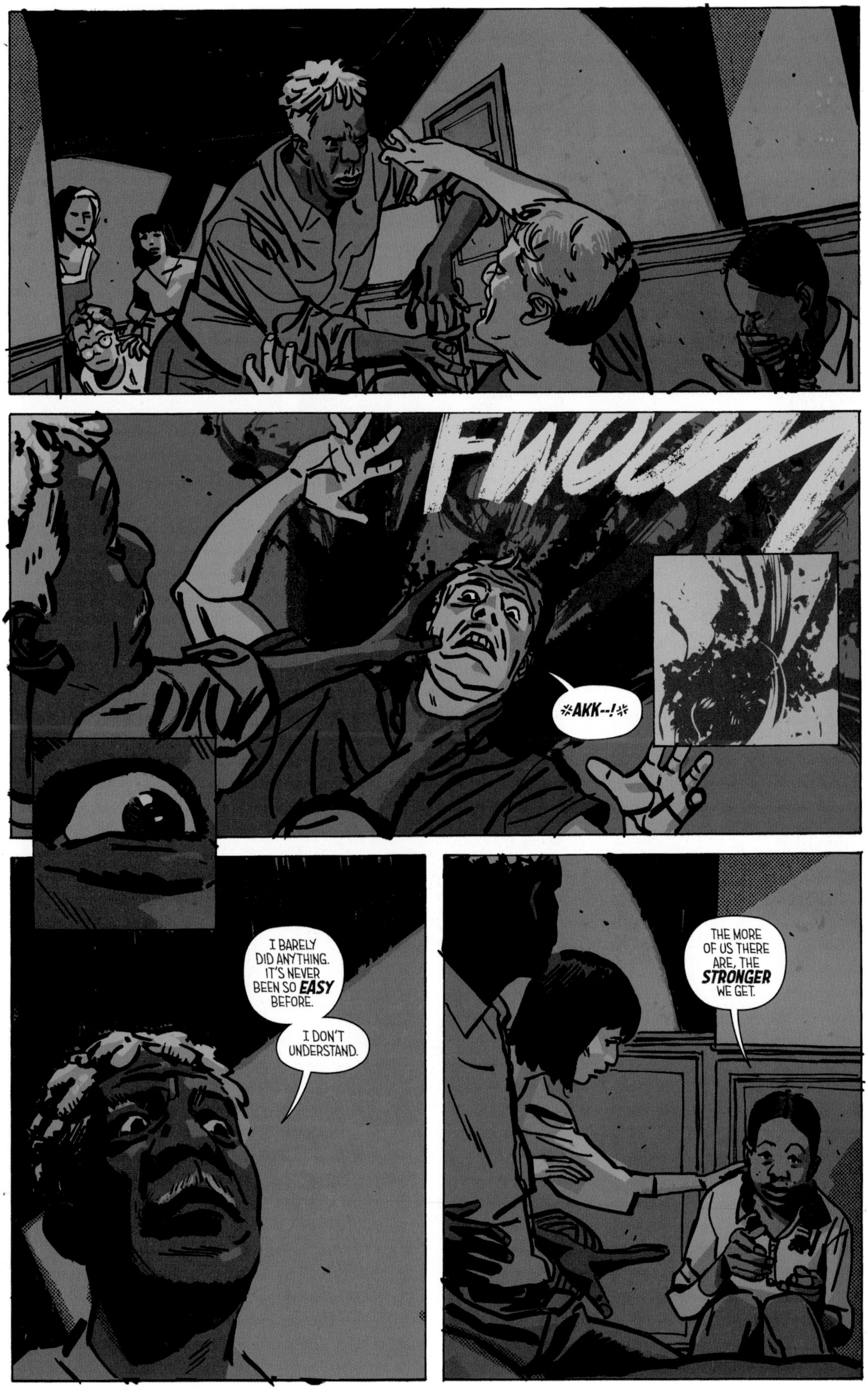

FWOOM
AKK--!
I BARELY DID ANYTHING. IT'S NEVER BEEN SO EASY BEFORE.
I DON'T UNDERSTAND.
THE MORE OF US THERE ARE, THE STRONGER WE GET.

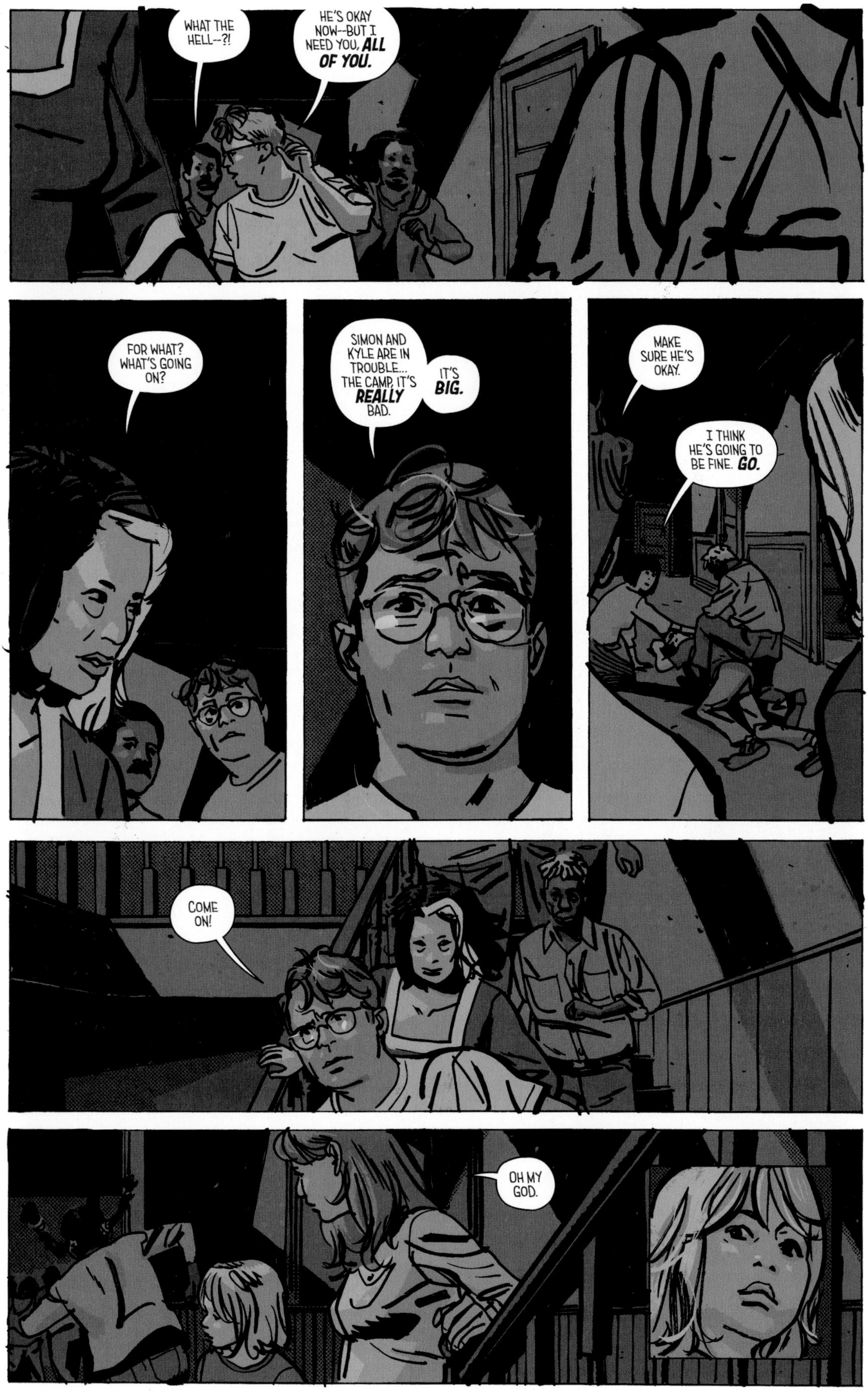
WHAT THE HELL--?!
HE'S OKAY NOW--BUT I NEED YOU, **ALL OF YOU.**
FOR WHAT? WHAT'S GOING ON?
SIMON AND KYLE ARE IN TROUBLE... THE CAMP, IT'S **REALLY** BAD.
IT'S **BIG.**
MAKE SURE HE'S OKAY.
I THINK HE'S GOING TO BE FINE. **GO.**
COME ON!
OH MY GOD.

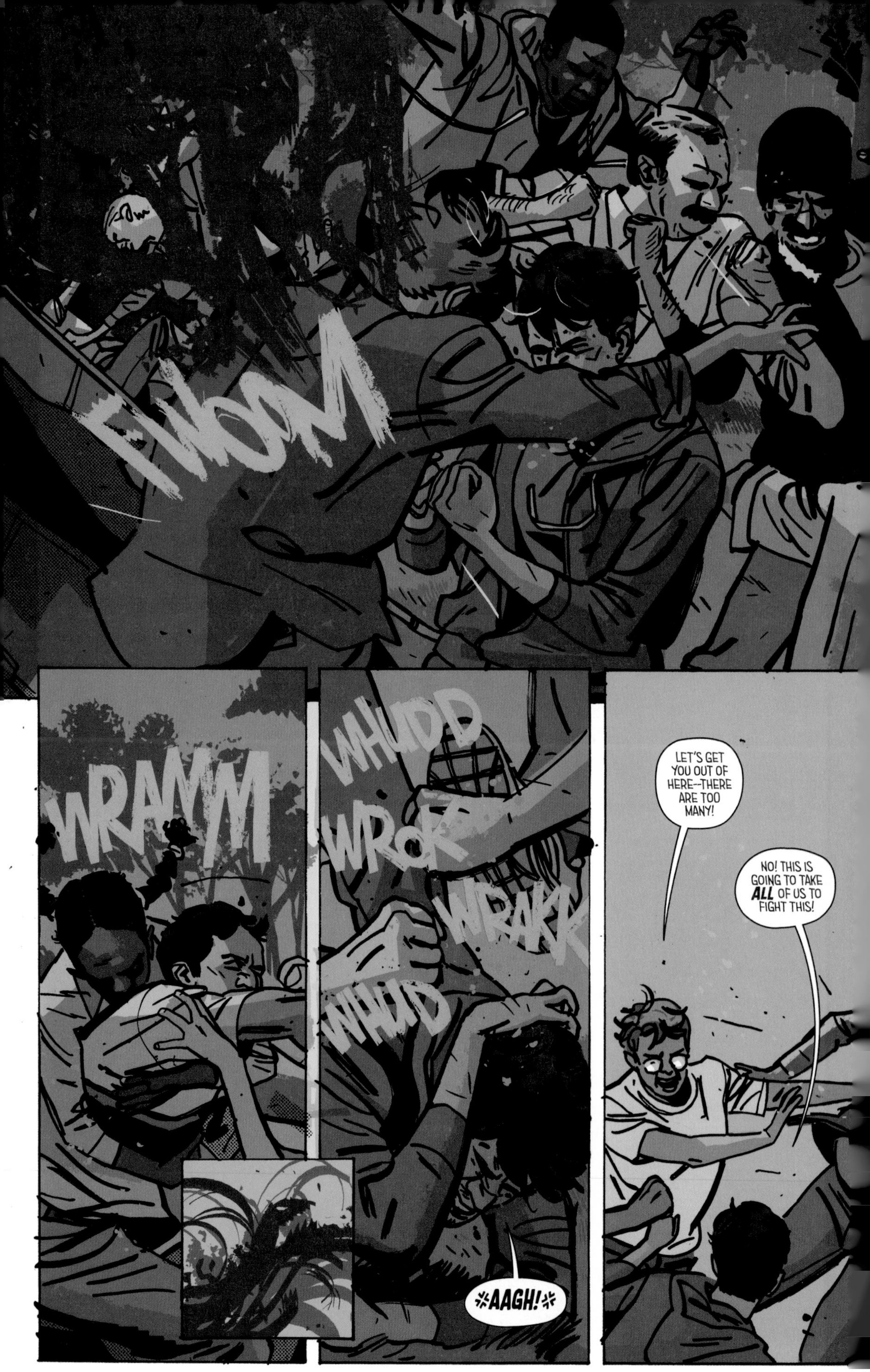
FWOOM
WRAMM
WHUDD
WROK
WRAKK
WHUD
AAGH!
LET'S GET YOU OUT OF HERE--THERE ARE TOO MANY!
NO! THIS IS GOING TO TAKE ALL OF US TO FIGHT THIS!

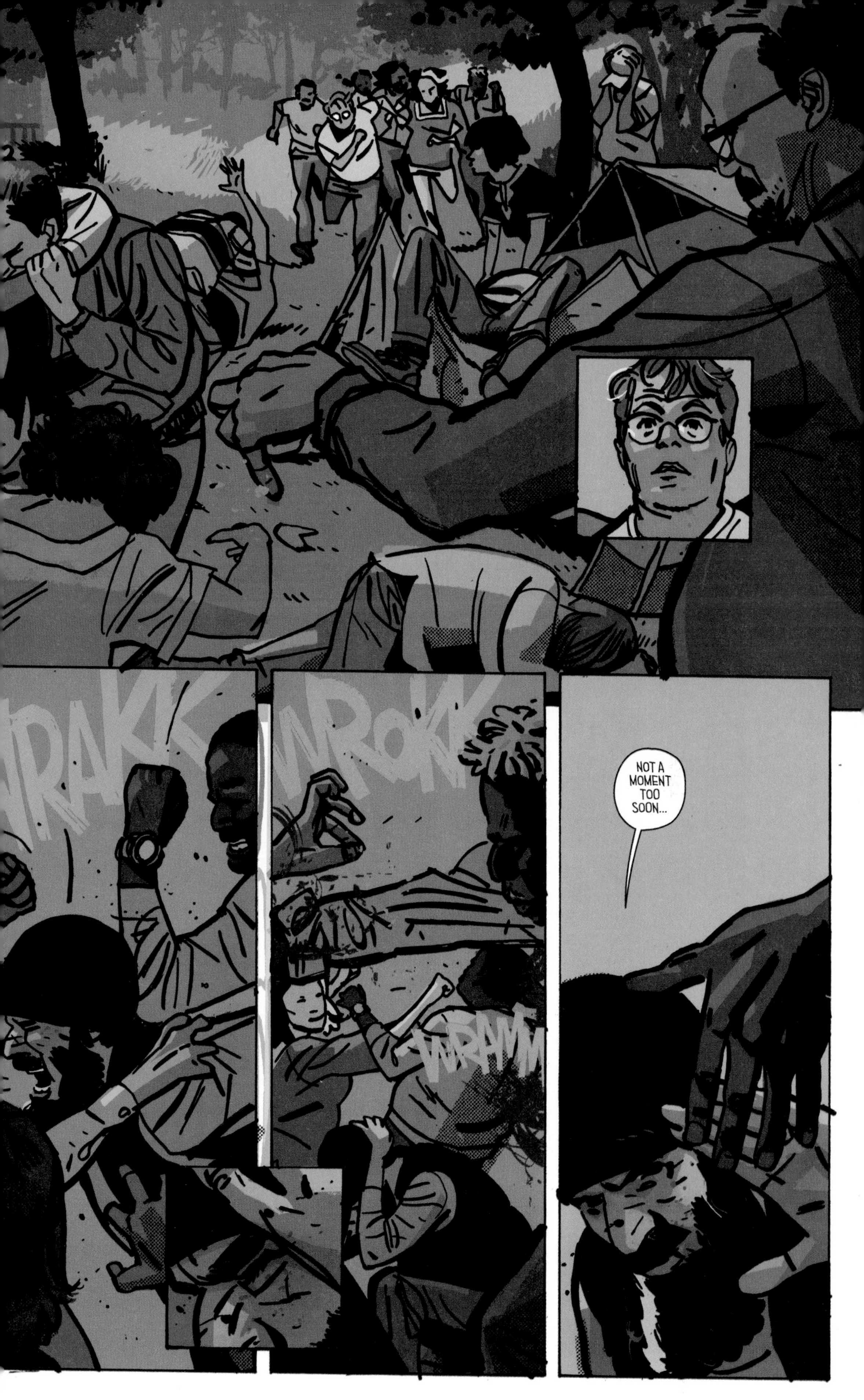
WRAKK
WROKK
WRAMM
NOT A MOMENT TOO SOON...

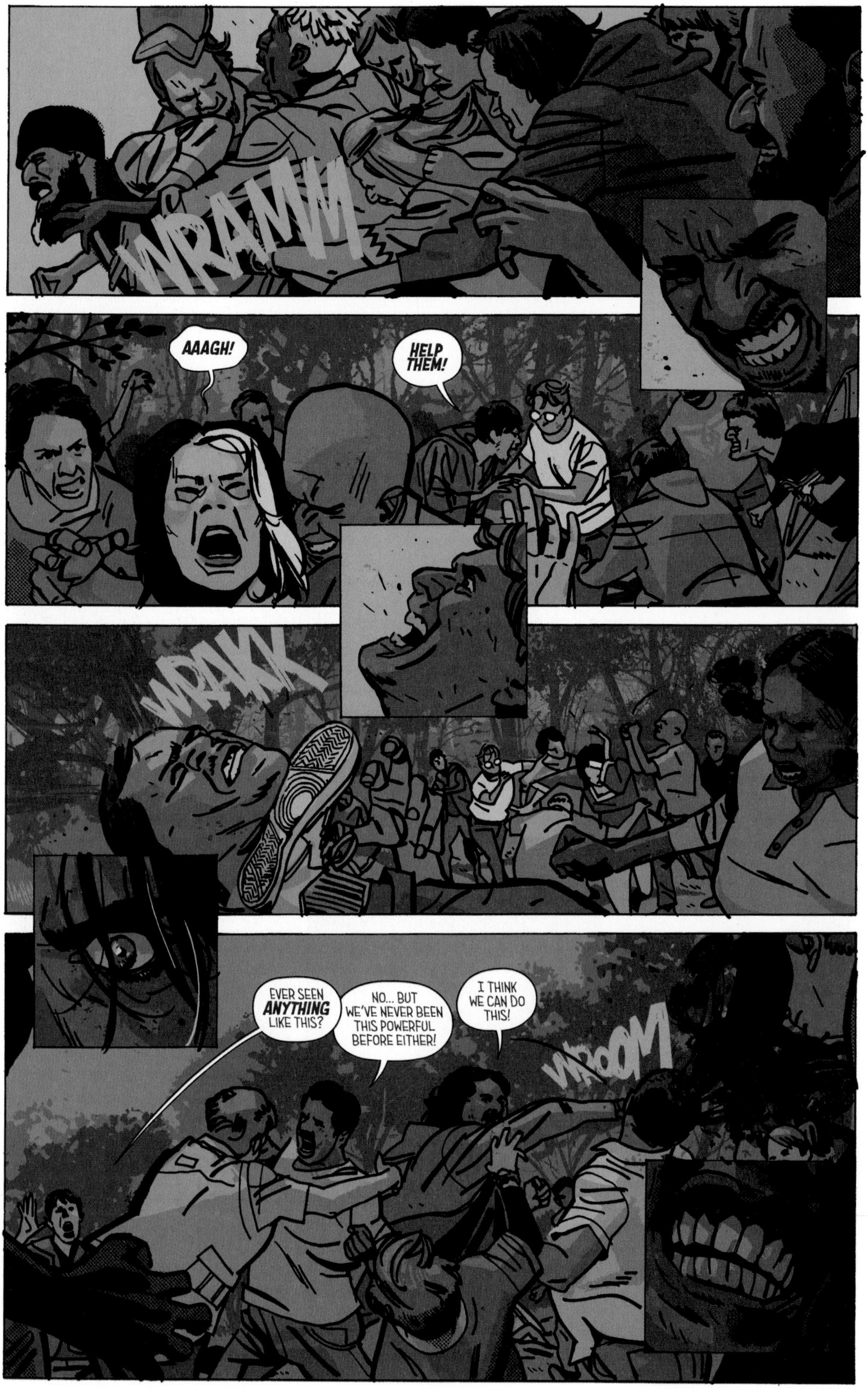
WRAMM
AAAGH!
HELP THEM!
WRAKK
EVER SEEN ANYTHING LIKE THIS?
NO... BUT WE'VE NEVER BEEN THIS POWERFUL BEFORE EITHER!
I THINK WE CAN DO THIS!
WROOM

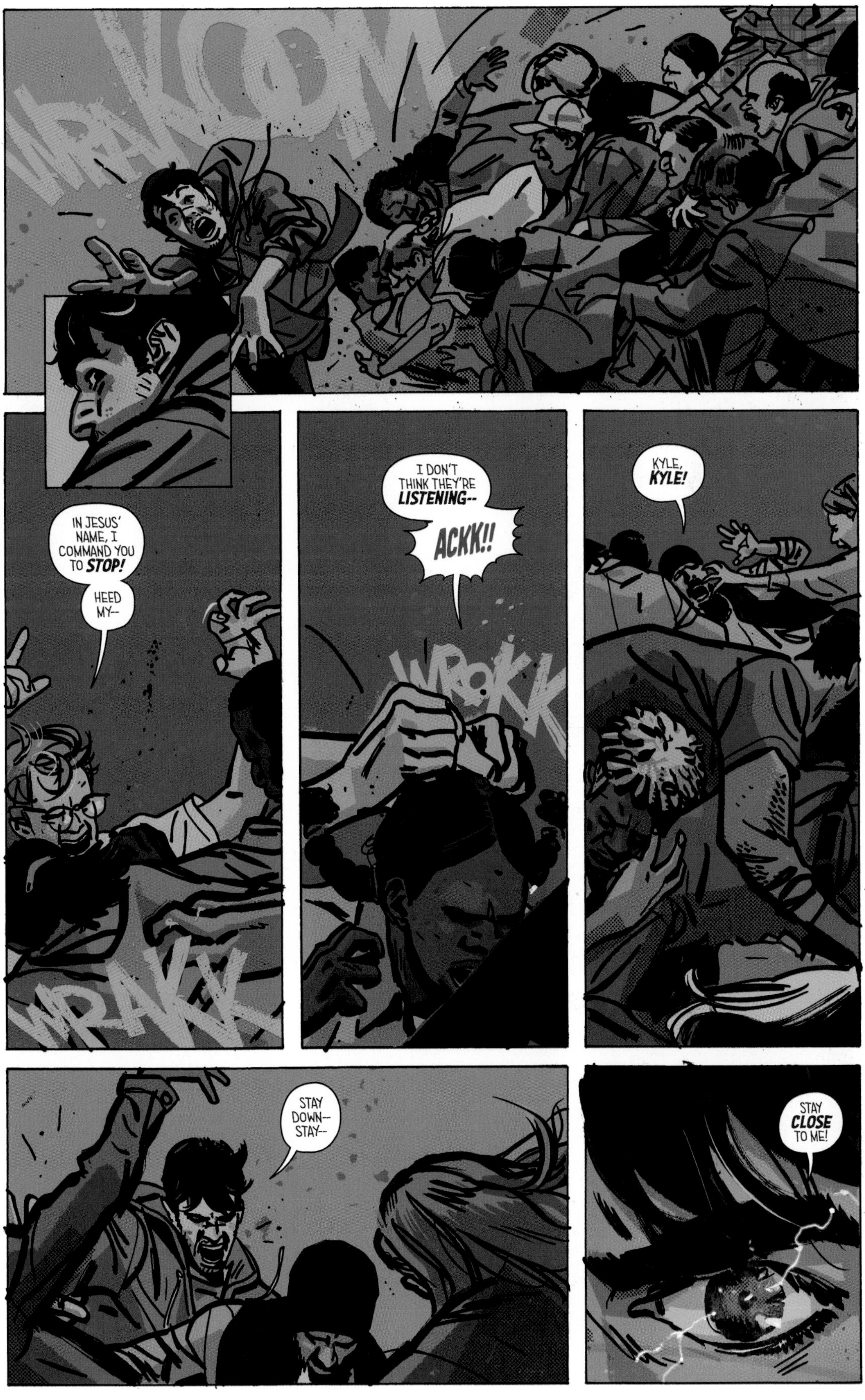

WRAKOOM
IN JESUS' NAME, I COMMAND YOU TO STOP!
HEED MY--
WRAKK
I DON'T THINK THEY'RE LISTENING--
ACKK!!
WROKK
KYLE, KYLE!
STAY DOWN-- STAY--
STAY CLOSE TO ME!

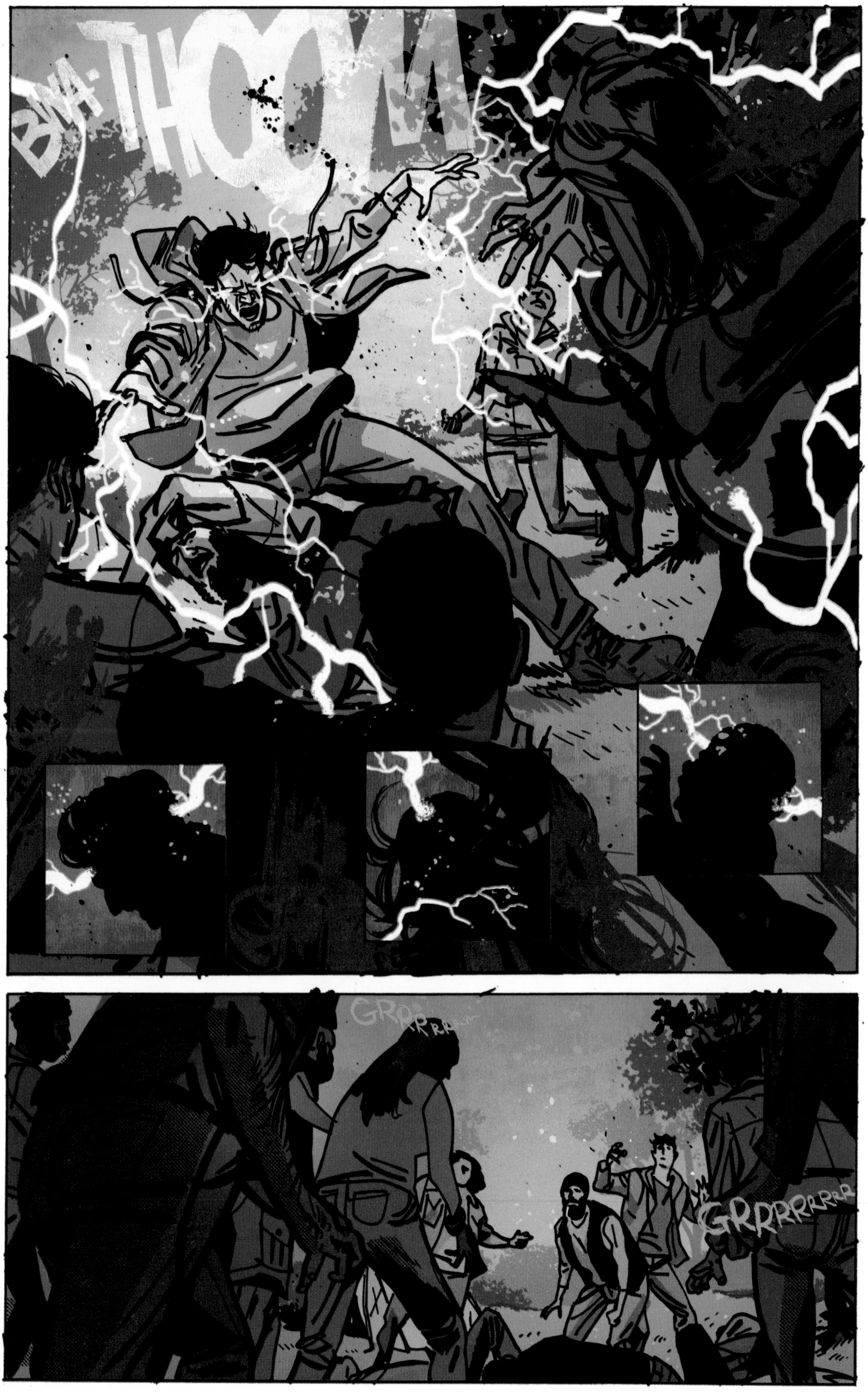
BWA-THOOM
GRRRRRR
GRRRRRRRR

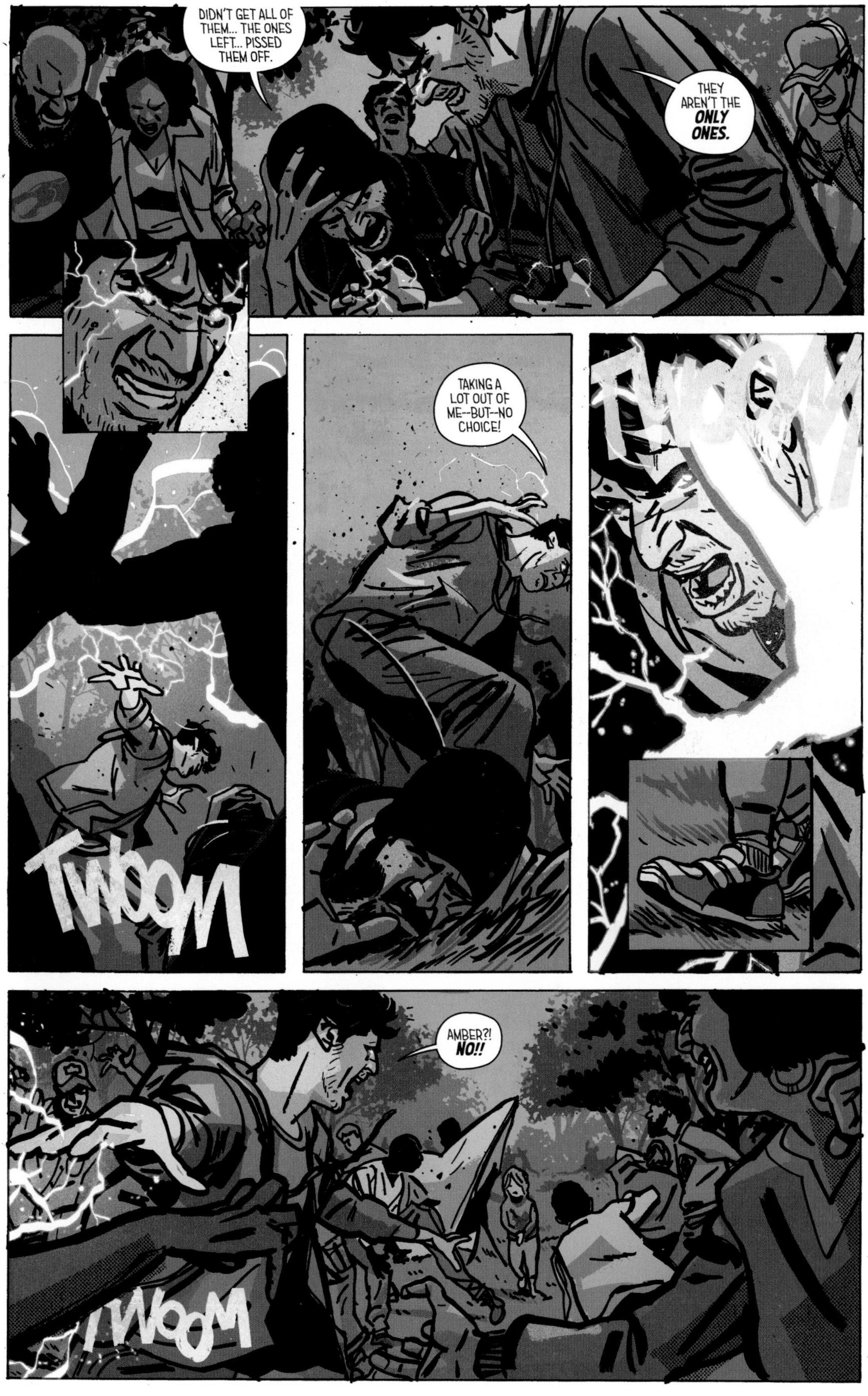
DIDN'T GET ALL OF THEM... THE ONES LEFT... PISSED THEM OFF.
THEY AREN'T THE ONLY ONES.
TWOOM
TAKING A LOT OUT OF ME--BUT--NO CHOICE!
TWOOM
AMBER?! NO!!
TWOOM

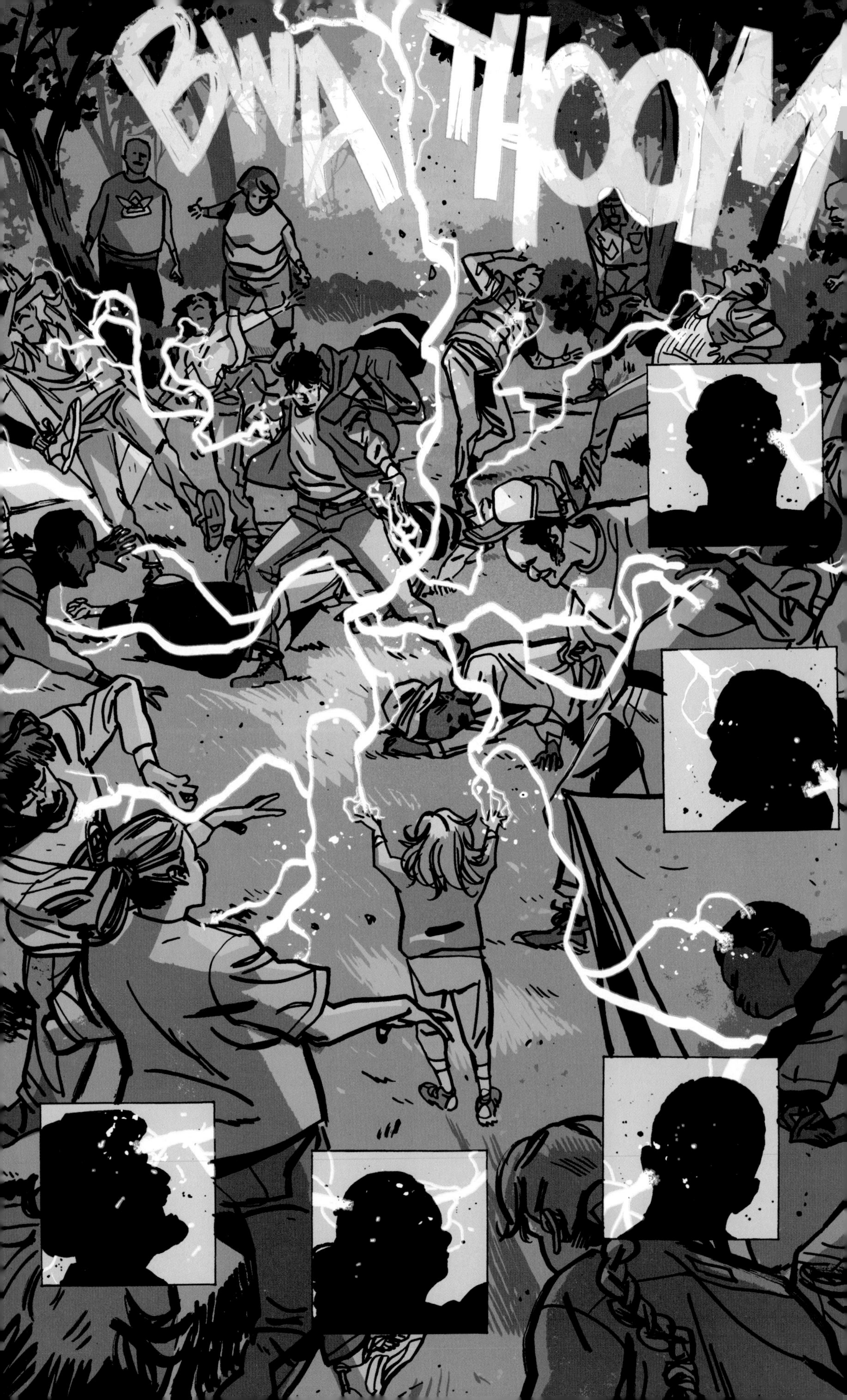
BWA THOOM

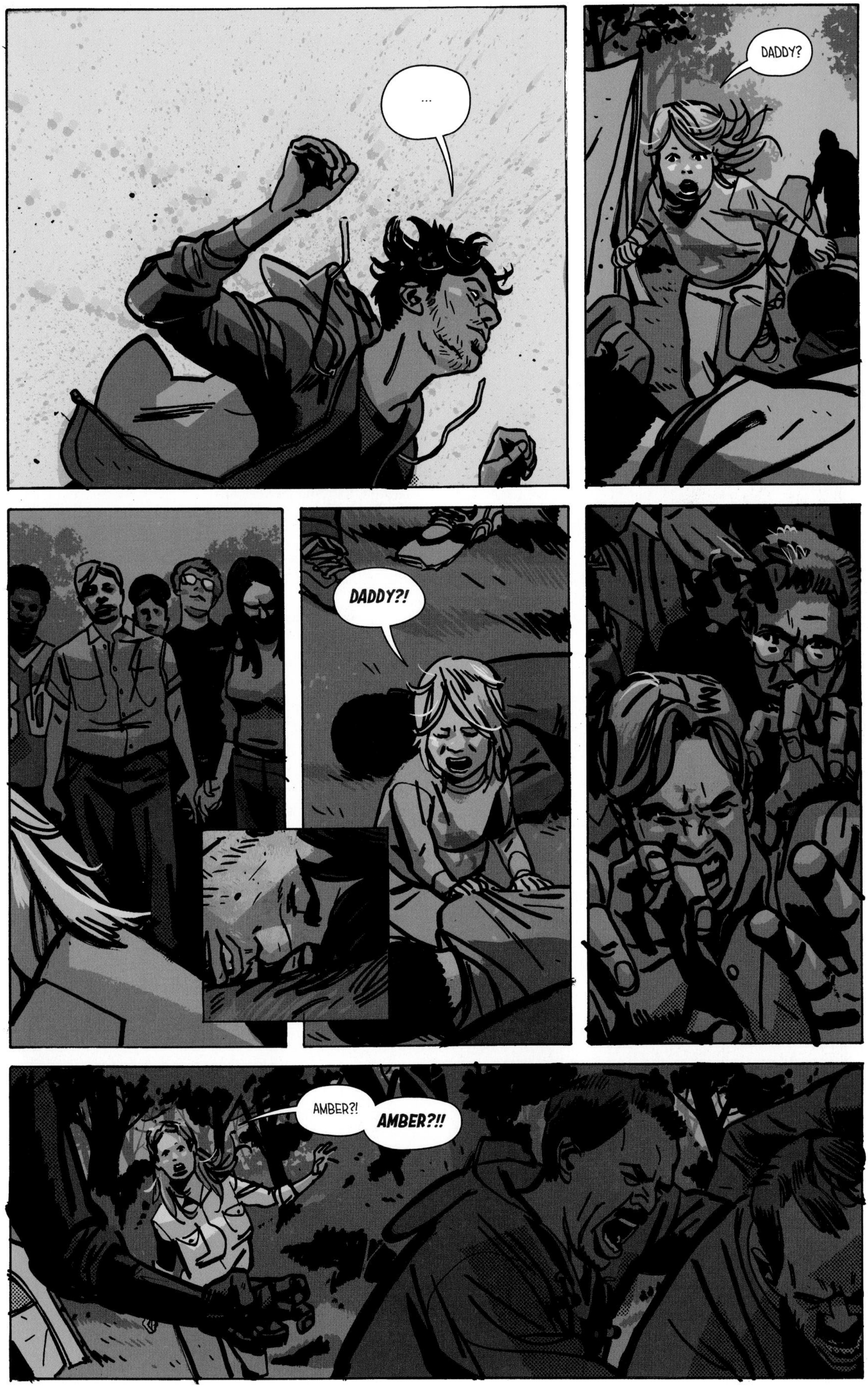
...
DADDY?
DADDY?!
AMBER?!
AMBER?!!

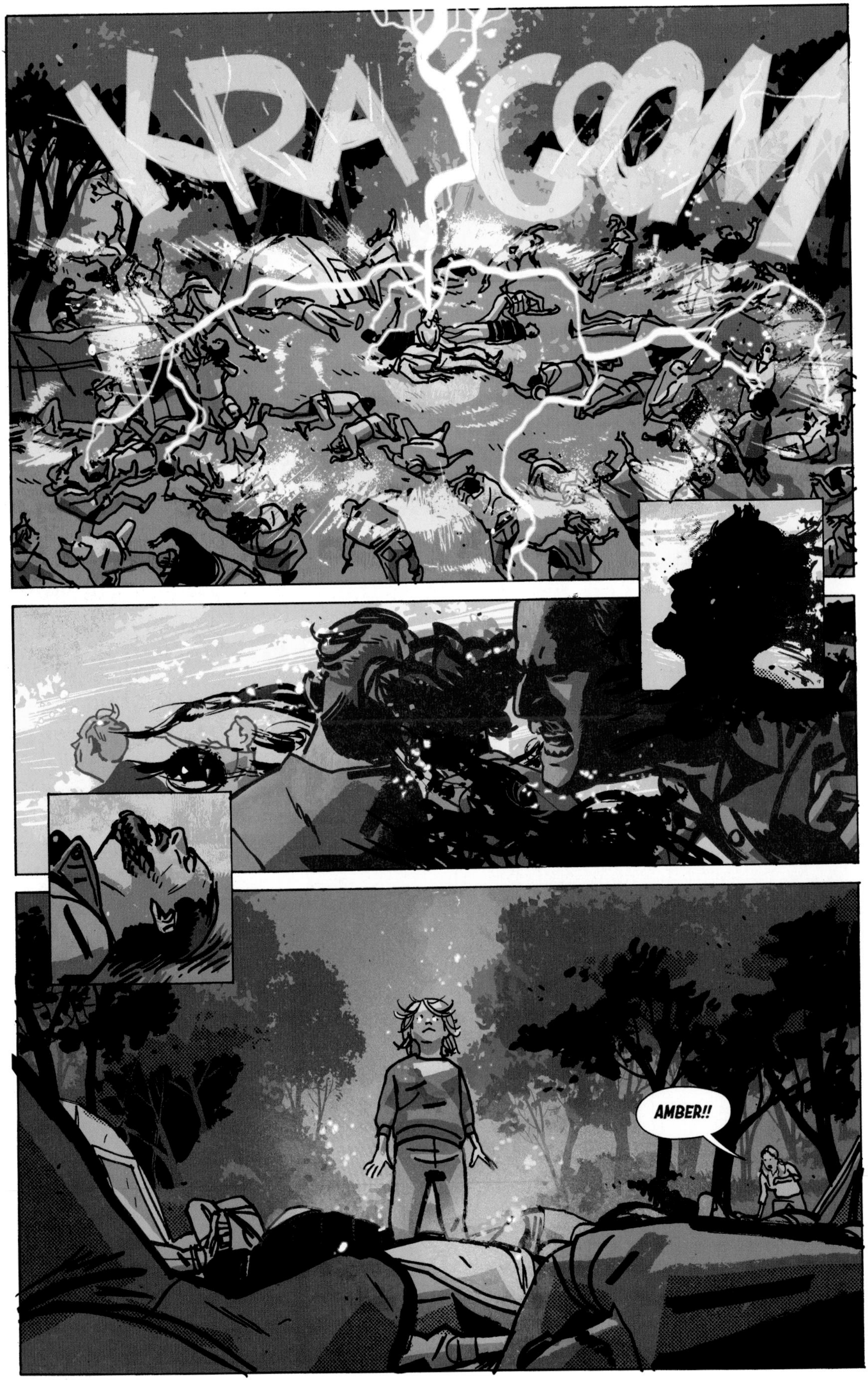
KRA-KOOM
AMBER!!

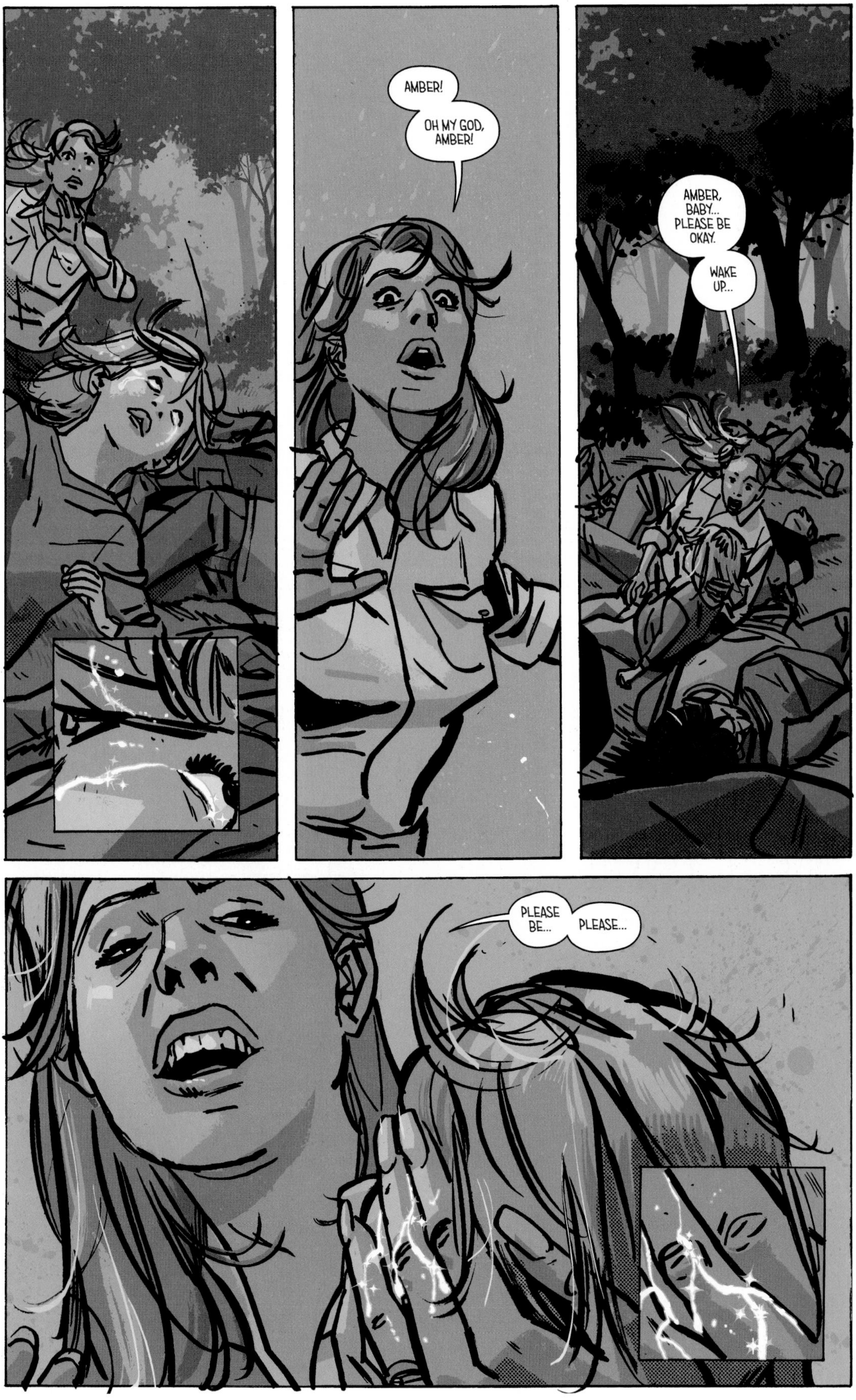
AMBER!
OH MY GOD, AMBER!
AMBER, BABY... PLEASE BE OKAY.
WAKE UP...
PLEASE BE...
PLEASE...

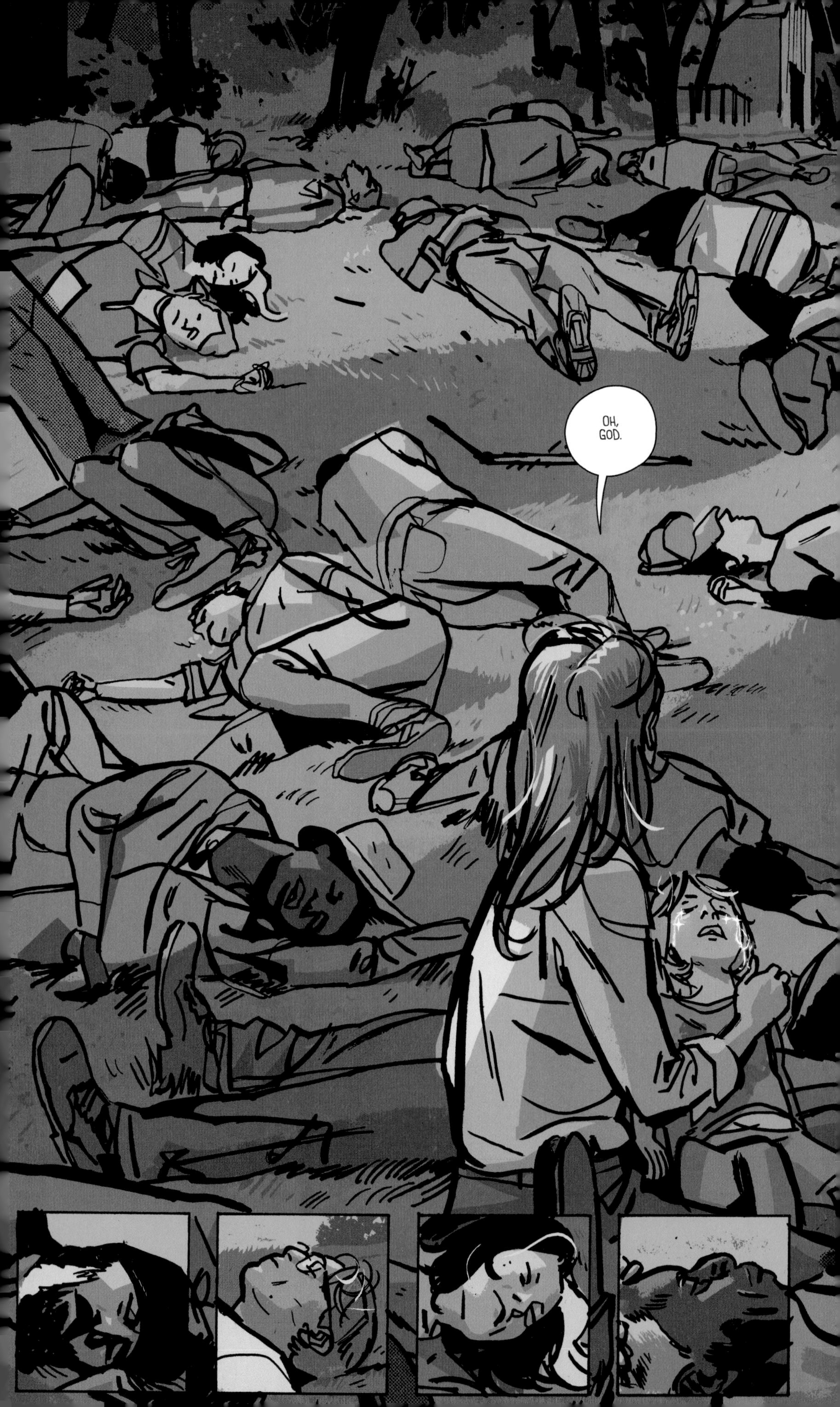
OH, GOD.

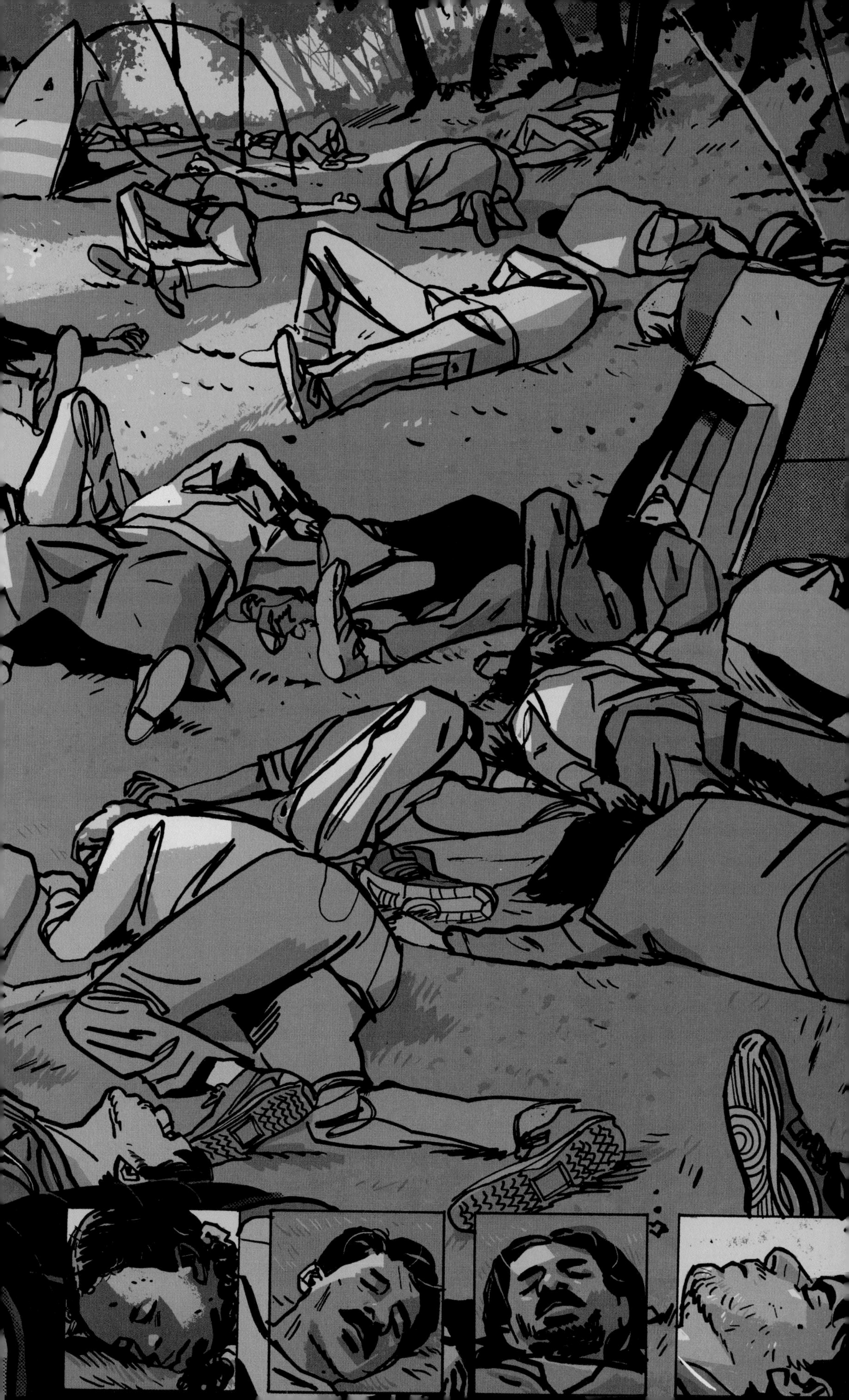

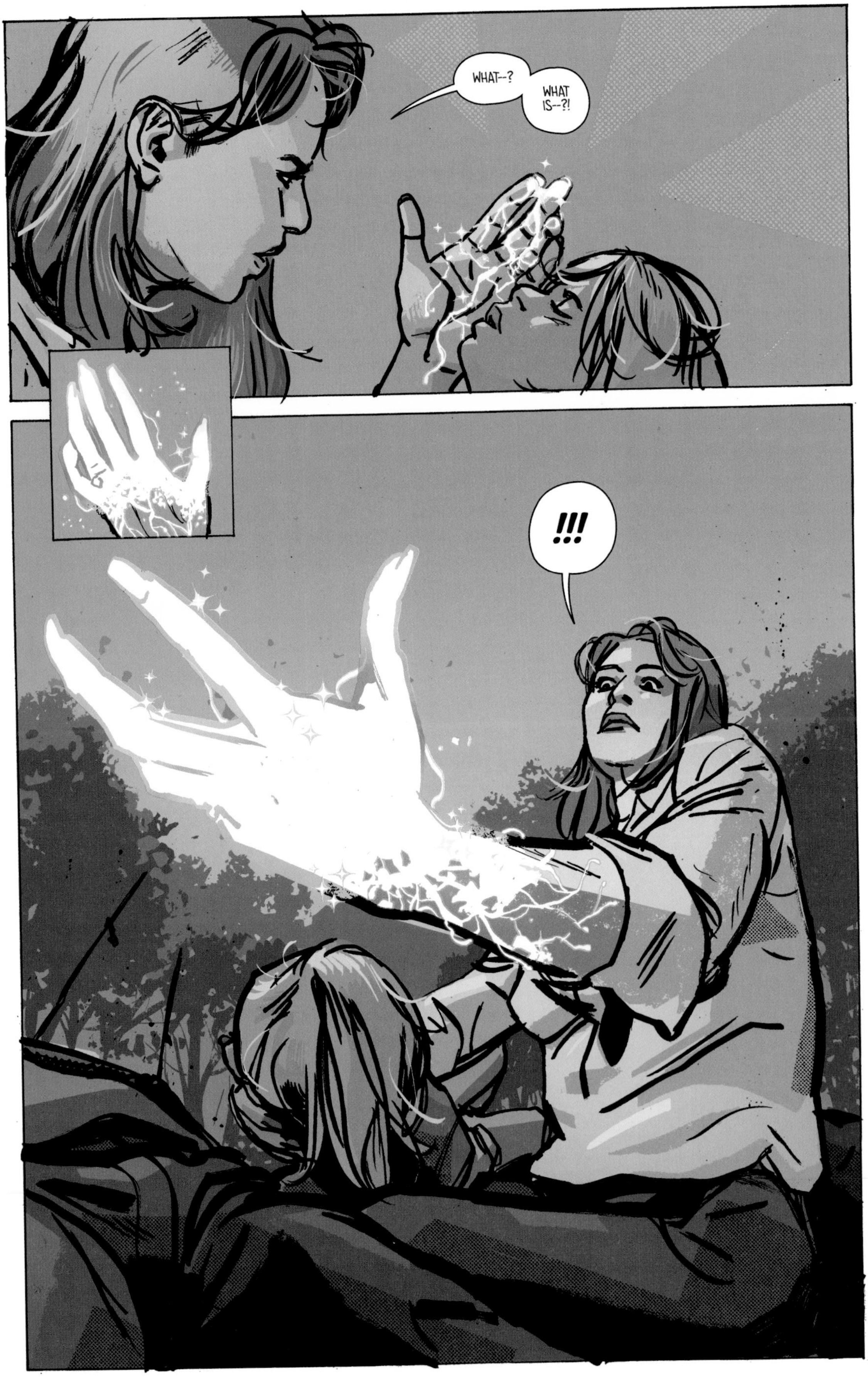
WHAT--?
WHAT IS--?!
!!!

TO BE CONTINUED

"Your light is so bright now

you can't hide it."

FOR MORE TALES FROM **ROBERT KIRKMAN** AND **SKYBOUND**

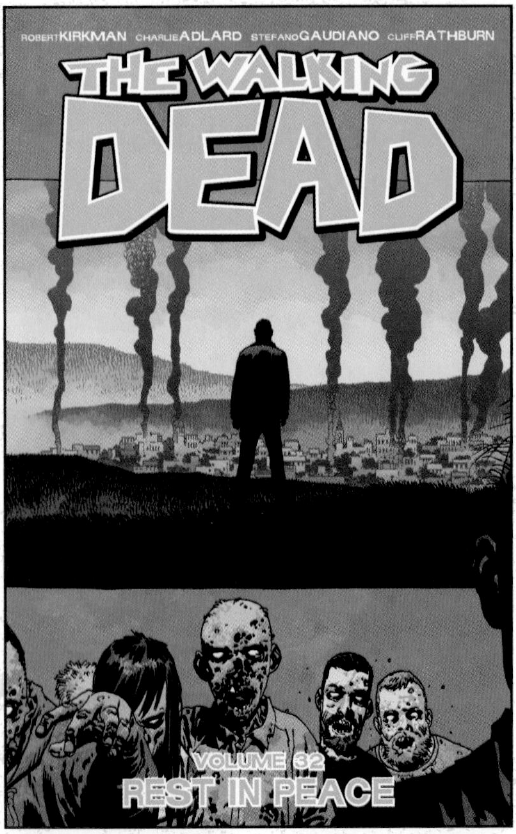

ROBERT KIRKMAN CHARLIE ADLARD STEFANO GAUDIANO CLIFF RATHBURN
THE WALKING DEAD
VOLUME 32
REST IN PEACE

VOL. 1: DAYS GONE BYE TP
ISBN: 978-1-58240-672-5
$14.99

VOL. 2: MILES BEHIND US TP
ISBN: 978-1-58240-775-3
$14.99

VOL. 3: SAFETY BEHIND BARS TP
ISBN: 978-1-58240-805-7
$14.99

VOL. 4: THE HEART'S DESIRE TP
ISBN: 978-1-58240-530-8
$14.99

VOL. 5: THE BEST DEFENSE TP
ISBN: 978-1-58240-612-1
$14.99

VOL. 6: THIS SORROWFUL LIFE TP
ISBN: 978-1-58240-684-8
$14.99

VOL. 7: THE CALM BEFORE TP
ISBN: 978-1-58240-828-6
$14.99

VOL. 8: MADE TO SUFFER TP
ISBN: 978-1-58240-883-5
$14.99

VOL. 9: HERE WE REMAIN TP
ISBN: 978-1-60706-022-2
$14.99

VOL. 10: WHAT WE BECOME TP
ISBN: 978-1-60706-075-8
$14.99

VOL. 11: FEAR THE HUNTERS TP
ISBN: 978-1-60706-181-6
$14.99

VOL. 12: LIFE AMONG THEM TP
ISBN: 978-1-60706-254-7
$14.99

VOL. 13: TOO FAR GONE TP
ISBN: 978-1-60706-329-2
$14.99

VOL. 14: NO WAY OUT TP
ISBN: 978-1-60706-392-6
$14.99

VOL. 15: WE FIND OURSELVES TP
ISBN: 978-1-60706-440-4
$14.99

VOL. 16: A LARGER WORLD TP
ISBN: 978-1-60706-559-3
$14.99

VOL. 17: SOMETHING TO FEAR TP
ISBN: 978-1-60706-615-6
$14.99

VOL. 18: WHAT COMES AFTER TP
ISBN: 978-1-60706-687-3
$14.99

VOL. 19: MARCH TO WAR TP
ISBN: 978-1-60706-818-1
$14.99

VOL. 20: ALL OUT WAR PART ONE TP
ISBN: 978-1-60706-882-2
$14.99

VOL. 21: ALL OUT WAR PART TWO TP
ISBN: 978-1-63215-030-1
$14.99

VOL. 22: A NEW BEGINNING TP
ISBN: 978-1-63215-041-7
$14.99

VOL. 23: WHISPERS INTO SCREAMS TP
ISBN: 978-1-63215-258-9
$14.99

VOL. 24: LIFE AND DEATH TP
ISBN: 978-1-63215-402-6
$14.99

VOL. 25: NO TURNING BACK TP
ISBN: 978-1-63215-659-4
$14.99

VOL. 26: CALL TO ARMS TP
ISBN: 978-1-63215-917-5
$14.99

VOL. 27: THE WHISPERER WAR TP
ISBN: 978-1-5343-0052-1
$14.99

VOL. 28: A CERTAIN DOOM TP
ISBN: 978-1-5343-0244-0
$14.99

VOL. 29: LINES WE CROSS TP
ISBN: 978-1-5343-0497-0
$16.99

VOL. 30: NEW WORLD ORDER TP
ISBN: 978-1-5343-0884-8
$16.99

VOL. 31: THE ROTTEN CORE TP
ISBN: 978-1-5343-1052-0
$16.99

VOL. 32: REST IN PEACE TP
ISBN: 978-1-5343-1241-8
$16.99

BOOK ONE HC
ISBN: 978-1-58240-619-0
$34.99

BOOK TWO HC
ISBN: 978-1-58240-698-5
$34.99

BOOK THREE HC
ISBN: 978-1-58240-825-5
$34.99

BOOK FOUR HC
ISBN: 978-1-60706-000-0
$34.99

BOOK FIVE HC
ISBN: 978-1-60706-171-7
$34.99

BOOK SIX HC
ISBN: 978-1-60706-327-8
$34.99

BOOK SEVEN HC
ISBN: 978-1-60706-439-8
$34.99

BOOK EIGHT HC
ISBN: 978-1-60706-593-7
$34.99

BOOK NINE HC
ISBN: 978-1-60706-798-6
$34.99

BOOK TEN HC
ISBN: 978-1-63215-034-9
$34.99

BOOK ELEVEN HC
ISBN: 978-1-63215-271-8
$34.99

BOOK TWELVE HC
ISBN: 978-1-63215-451-4
$34.99

BOOK THIRTEEN HC
ISBN: 978-1-63215-916-8
$34.99

BOOK FOURTEEN HC
ISBN: 978-1-5343-0329-4
$34.99

BOOK FIFTEEN HC
ISBN: 978-1-5343-0850-3
$34.99

BOOK SIXTEEN HC
ISBN: 978-1-5343-1325-5
$34.99

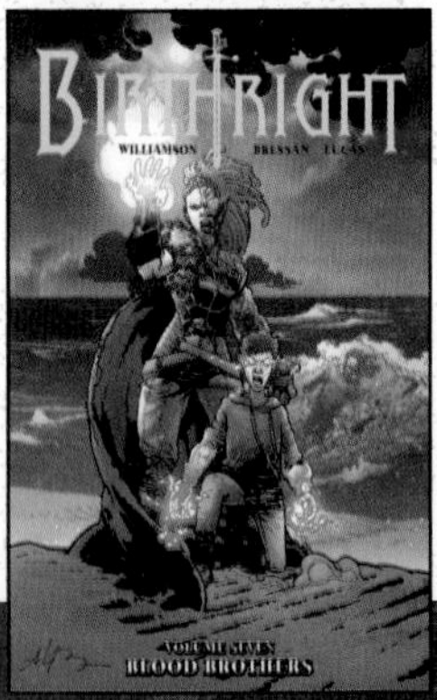

BIRTHRIGHT
WILLIAMSON BRESSAN LUCAS
VOLUME SEVEN
BLOOD BROTHERS

VOL. 1: HOMECOMING TP
ISBN: 978-1-63215-231-2
$9.99

VOL. 2: CALL TO ADVENTURE TP
ISBN: 978-1-63215-446-0
$12.99

VOL. 3: ALLIES AND ENEMIES TP
ISBN: 978-1-63215-683-9
$12.99

VOL. 4: FAMILY HISTORY TP
ISBN: 978-1-63215-871-0
$12.99

VOL. 5: BELLY OF THE BEAST TP
ISBN: 978-1-5343-0218-1
$12.99

VOL. 6: FATHERHOOD TP
ISBN: 978-1-53430-498-7
$14.99

VOL. 7: BLOOD BROTHERS TP
ISBN: 978-1-5343-1053-7
$14.99

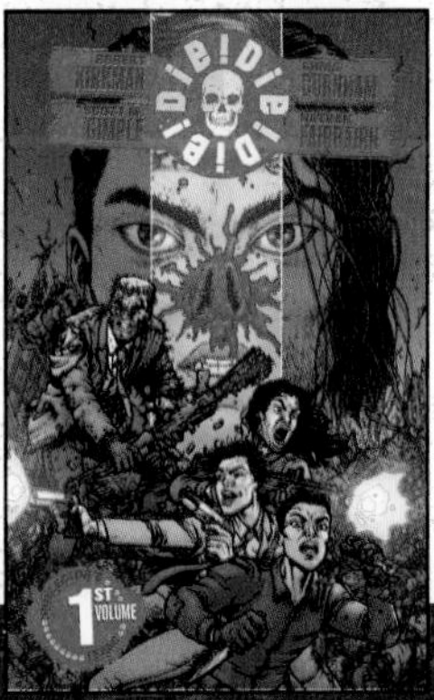

DIE!DIE!DIE!
1ST VOLUME

VOL. 1
ISBN: 978-1-5343-1214-2
$19.99

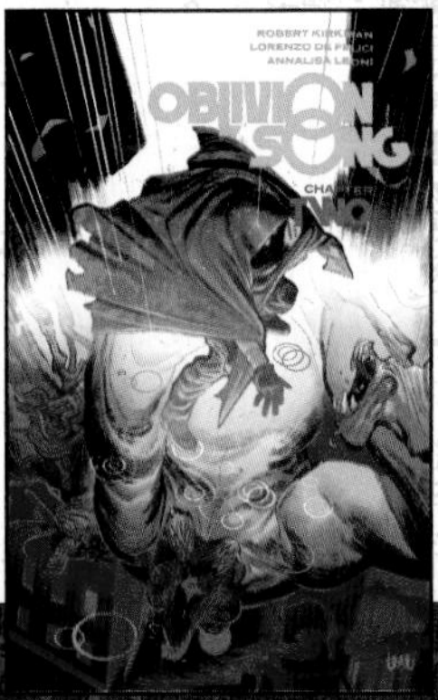

OBLIVION SONG

CHAPTER ONE
ISBN: 978-1-5343-0642-4
$9.99

CHAPTER TWO
ISBN: 978-1-5343-1057-5
$16.99

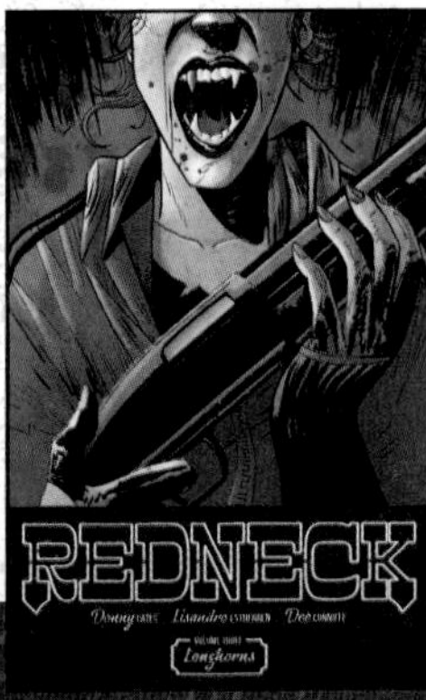

REDNECK
Longhorns

VOL. 1: DEEP IN THE HEART
ISBN: 978-1-5343-0331-7
$16.99

VOL. 2: THE EYES UPON YOU
ISBN: 978-1-5343-0665-3
$16.99

VOL. 3: LONGHORNS
ISBN: 978-1-5343-1050-6
$16.99